GREECE

*Four Inspirational Love Stories
with all the Romance and Mystery
of Today's Greece*

MELANIE PANAGIOTOPOULOS

BARBOUR
PUBLISHING, INC.
Uhrichsville, Ohio

Fortress of Love © MCMXCIX by Barbour Publishing, Inc.
Odyssey of Love © MCMXCVII by Barbour Publishing, Inc.
Race of Love © MCMXCVIII by Barbour Publishing, Inc.
Christmas Baby © MCMXCVII by Barbour Publishing, Inc.

ISBN 1-57748-642-0

Published by Barbour Publishing, Inc., P.O. Box 719, Uhrichsville, Ohio 44683 http://www.barbourbooks.com

 Member of the
Evangelical Christian
Publishers Association

Printed in the United States of America.

Melanie Panagiotopoulos
was born in Richmond, Virginia, and currently resides in Athens, Greece, with her husband of nineteen years; their two teenage children, Sara and Jay; a German shepherd dog; and a Siamese cat. Melanie has done extensive research into the early Christian and medieval period of history and has published numerous articles on both subjects, something which is reflected in her books. To be where the early Christians, and especially that great Apostle to the Gentiles, Paul, worked and lived has inspired her greatly. She has spent many weekends with her family exploring little-known sites and many a winter morning sifting through dusty but fantastic books at some of the wonderful old libraries Athens has to offer.

FORTRESS OF LOVE

With love to my mother and father, Sara and Sayre Karis.

Chapter 1

Light from the early winter afternoon filtered softly through the four windows of the bedroom, bringing the shimmering gold of the woman's metallic evening gown to glittering life.

Melissa Kincaid looked pensively at her image in the cheval glass. She regarded her amber eyes, full mouth, and tall, slim figure—but she knew that her physical form told nothing about who she was. Ever since she had called off her wedding to Brian Cartwright, who she was seemed unclear.

She shook her head, denying the self-deceiving notion that her breakup with the senator's son had somehow clouded her identity. The truth was, she hadn't been sure of herself for years.

Sighing, she ran her hands down the radiant sheen of the sparkling cloth. The dress made her look warm and at ease, a true testimony to the creative abilities of the designer. In her heart, Melissa felt cold and numb. She had bought the elegant gown as a part of her trousseau. And if she hadn't canceled the wedding—canceled her life with Brian—she might be wearing the gown this very evening on her Caribbean honeymoon, instead of dreading the Ridgedale Country Club's annual Christmas ball.

She hastily shifted her eyes away from the mirror and glanced out the nearest window. Through the diffusion of the sheers she gazed at the snow-covered grayness of the waning afternoon. Calling off the wedding was the one right and true thing she had done in a long time—and the only decision she felt certain of. Brian was cut from the same cloth as her aunt and uncle, a social machine who would have totally devoured a woman like Melissa, who wanted more out of life than one cocktail party after another. She wasn't sure exactly what she wanted, but she knew it wasn't the social whirl of Ridgedale society.

Melissa shook her head. Her nearly black hair glistened against the gold of her dress like a jeweled accessory. Walking over to her dressing table, she sat heavily on the velvet stool and slipped her silk-clad feet into the black kidskin pumps that had been fashioned to accompany the dress. The last thing she wanted to do was to attend the Christmas ball that evening. It was *the* event of the year, and she knew that everyone would be talking behind their hands—and behind her back—about her canceled engagement. She also knew that the prevailing sympathies were with Brian. She had dared to spurn a Cartwright, one of the oldest and most respected names in the state. In the eyes of the community, she was in disgrace.

Propping her elbows on the table, she rested her head in the palms of her hands and sighed. Practically no one, not even those she had considered her closest friends, understood that, at twenty-two, not only was she not ready to get married, but even if she had been, Brian Cartwright was all wrong for her.

When she had started dating the fair-haired, handsome attorney a little over a year ago, she had been flattered by all the attention. Already socially prominent through his law practice and family connections, it was obvious to all that Brian was going to follow in his father's political footsteps. And in Melissa, he had been delighted to discover the perfect woman to support his plans.

The daughter of a physician, Melissa had lived with her aunt and uncle in their antebellum home above the river since her parents' untimely deaths when she was a girl. She had learned the social graces from her aunt and was young enough to be molded. Best of all, in this permissive day and age, she was a girl of high morals.

Like a prince planning his future reign, Brian didn't want a girl whose past might embarrass him someday, or even worse, cost him votes. So, along with his political career, he had pursued Melissa diligently, and like a leaf caught in a flood, she had been swept along in the tide of his powerful personality.

Although she believed that Brian loved her, she couldn't help feeling that he wanted her as much for his résumé of qualifications for office as for herself. When she realized that her own identity was in danger of being overwhelmed, she knew that she had to get out of their engagement or risk sinking into a hollow existence—a place that she feared would be much worse than what she had experienced since coming to live with her aunt and uncle in their mausoleum of a mansion.

The staccato rap of hard knuckles against her bedroom door brought her thoughts to an abrupt halt. Melissa was well acquainted with the sound. Her aunt, the monarch of the house, was on the other side demanding entry into her domain.

A grimace crinkled the smooth features of Melissa's face. When she was a girl, the knock at the door meant that it was time to practice her diving and climbing skills. She would either dive under her bed or climb through the tiny opening to the attic in the ceiling of her closet. Anything to escape her aunt's hateful tongue. Melissa couldn't help but wish that there was a place of refuge for the grown woman she was now. But there hadn't been for years.

"Me–lis–sa." Her aunt's clipped, autocratic voice sounded through the oak of the door and Melissa wondered, not for the first time, how someone could take a melodious name like Melissa and make it sound so ugly.

"Me–lis–sa," her aunt called out again, chopping her name into three syllables like a novice cook chopping an onion.

Resigned to hearing whatever her aunt had to say and getting it over with, Melissa called out, "It's unlocked."

The door opened and Melissa was face-to-face with all the anger, disgust, and even a little envy, that glowered in Mrs. Kincaid's frosty eyes. With a sudden flash of insight, Melissa realized that her aunt had looked at her the same way ever since the first day Melissa had come to live with her ten years before. In fact, now that she thought about it, the only time her aunt's eyes had offered a degree of acceptance had been while she was engaged to Brian.

"Your uncle and I have been waiting for you." Her aunt spoke with an affected southern accent that grated on Melissa's ears like an untuned piano. A southern accent was beautiful when it was real. But her aunt's wasn't. She was from Oregon. "Do you suppose you could *grace us with your presence?*" The older woman placed a sickly sweet, sarcastic emphasis on the last few words—another habit to which Melissa was accustomed. "You know how your uncle likes to arrive first at gatherings."

Melissa knew. She also knew why. It was his way of keeping tabs on everyone, including her. The line of Melissa's mouth thinned with distaste at the thought of the evening that stretched out before her. As she reached for her evening bag, she answered, her voice as bland as her eyes, "I'll be right down."

Seemingly satisfied, her aunt swiveled to leave, her gown rustling like crinkling paper. A second too soon, Melissa let the breath she had been

9

holding escape through her teeth. Her aunt threw a stinging glance over her shoulder and said with venom in her voice, "But heaven knows, *you* shouldn't even be coming to this ball."

Melissa flinched at the attack. She knew that her aunt was implying that she should have been on her honeymoon right now. Melissa wasn't sure if it was anger, hurt, or something else that welled up inside of her, but she flung her purse down on the dressing table and fired back at her aunt, "Fine. If that's the way you feel, I won't go."

The older woman stalked back into the room and between pinched lips spat out, "You most certainly *will* go! It's enough that you should humiliate your uncle and me by canceling your wedding three weeks before the ceremony. But not to come tonight would be the same as admitting to the world that it was shameful."

Melissa's amber eyes became as foggy as sea glass. "Isn't that what you think?"

"It doesn't matter what *I* think. It matters only what we show to the good citizens of this city."

"Show." Melissa repeated the word as if it were the foulest word in the English language. She was totally disgusted by the superficiality it signified. Without thinking, she blurted out the one question she knew should have remained unasked. "Tell me, *dear* Aunt, are you more upset that I didn't marry Brian because of his social connections or because you lost your chance to get rid of me?"

Shock registered in the older woman's eyes. Her mouth moved for a moment before the words tumbled out weakly. "You shouldn't have canceled the wedding. You should have married Brian."

"Why?" Melissa taunted. "So that I'd be out of your house for good?"

Her aunt's face suffused with red. Like a malfunctioning pressure cooker, she finally exploded. "Yes!" she shouted. "So you would leave me alone with my husband. I never wanted you here! I never wanted to share my house with you! If you had been my own child, fine. But taking you in was pure charity as far as I'm concerned."

Melissa felt as though she had been kicked in the stomach. She had always suspected that her aunt hadn't wanted her—but hearing the words was a million times more hurtful than she ever would have imagined. Even though Melissa recognized that she was partly at fault for goading her aunt into such an admission, now—like a wounded beast—she only wanted to strike back. And she did, with some venom of her own.

"Well, don't worry, *dear* Aunt." The tone Melissa placed on the adjective was anything but an endearment. "We don't live in the Middle Ages." She grabbed her beaded evening bag off the table and as she stalked past her aunt toward the door, she flung a parting shot over her shoulder. "Maybe I'll find a man tonight and move in with him."

At the gasp that came from her aunt, Melissa knew that her arrow had found its hurtful mark.

Reaching out a clawlike hand, the older woman grabbed hold of Melissa's arm. "You wouldn't dare," she hissed. Melissa knew that, according to her aunt's strict code of etiquette, moving in with a man outside of marriage would be the ultimate in social horrors.

Melissa looked at the hand on her arm as if it were a reptile. But before she could say another cross word, the absurdity of her last statement washed over her mind. If she hadn't been so angry, she might have laughed. She knew that she was as old-fashioned as her aunt about courtship and marriage—only not for the same reason, not because of social norms. Melissa's parents had instilled a sense of morality in her years ago, and she clung to her values of right and wrong tenaciously. Besides that, she had no desire for another relationship anytime soon. After an awkward moment of silence, she finally whispered, "No, Aunt. You know I wouldn't."

≫

The tension in the plush Mercedes was as thick as the new snow that was quickly piling up along the side of the road. From her place in the backseat, Melissa peered out through the windshield and surveyed the whiteness.

In the light of the car's high beams the pristine snow glowed like something out of a fairy tale. Melissa wished that she could fall into it and make snow angels, or become an angel, a pure being without a worry in the world. She wanted nothing more than to escape into the luminosity of the night—maybe find a deserted cabin in the woods, a refuge—and leave all her thoughts, all her cares, far behind.

She sighed and pulled her expensive, faux fur coat tighter around her. She shivered in spite of the heat in the car—chilled in her spirit more than anything, because she knew that she wasn't free to escape; and that the cabin in the woods was a fantasy. And even if she could escape, her thoughts would come with her like unwelcome guests. Activity, keeping busy, was the only way to get any rest from the swirling confusion in her mind.

That was one good thing about the Christmas ball. All the small talk would provide a diversion from her thoughts. Despite her angry outburst at her aunt, she hadn't relished the idea of being left behind—alone—to rattle around the big house. Even the housekeeper and cook had been given the night off.

Looking out the window, she knew that if she could be granted one wish it would be for a friend, a real one, someone to talk to. Adding to the pain of the breakup was the discovery that her so-called friends were as false as the social graces that they hid behind. Not a single one had supported her decision. Only an acquaintance, the pediatrician at her uncle's medical clinic, had seemed to understand and had offered her a shoulder to lean on.

Melissa was confident that her university friend, Kristen King, would have been on her side, too, if she had known. But Melissa hadn't told Kristen, who lived in a distant town. She was newly engaged to Ted—a man Melissa didn't think much of—and Melissa hadn't wanted to mar her friend's romance with her own problems.

Smoke from her uncle's cigar drifted into the backseat, making Melissa cough. Annoyed, she swung her cashmere and leather glove in front of her nose. "Can't you do without that pacifier for even a few minutes?" she snapped. Her words broke the uneasy truce that she and her aunt had maintained in her uncle's presence.

"How dare you talk to your uncle in that fashion," her aunt snarled in a voice heavy with self-righteous affront.

With exhaustion in his voice, Uncle Bob cut in before Melissa could respond. "Do you two suppose we might enjoy ourselves tonight? This is a very important party." Ignoring Melissa's disgusted sigh, he continued, "And I will not have you showing us to be anything other than a loving, *united* family." Through the rearview mirror he pierced Melissa with his amber eyes. "You must understand, Melissa, your aunt is very upset that your engagement to Brian didn't work out—"

"Didn't work out?" Melissa repeated, rolling her eyes away from his. "Your ability to rewrite history is amazing, Uncle Bob. It wasn't that the engagement didn't 'work out,'" she challenged. "I called it off!"

Her uncle continued to speak, as if she hadn't said a word, something Melissa was used to. "And I will not have you cause her more worry."

Melissa didn't dare glance toward her aunt, knowing that she would be wearing a hurt, yet gloating, expression that Melissa despised the most. "But Brian is not the only man on the face of this earth," her uncle continued, and Melissa's eyes swiveled back to meet his in the mirror. She was appalled.

"How many times do I have to tell you, Uncle Bob? I—don't—want —to—be—involved—with—a—man—right—now." She spoke each word carefully and distinctly. "I have no desire to get married anytime in the near future. I'm not ready for it."

"You just haven't found Mr. Right," he stubbornly insisted.

"And I hope I don't for several more years," Melissa returned. Then, taking a deep, steadying breath, she tried once more to make him understand. "Uncle Bob, I don't want to 'find' Mr. Right until I can first 'find' myself."

Her uncle chuckled, a deep throaty sound, the by-product of too many years spent puffing on cigars. "I didn't know you were lost."

Uncle Bob was attempting to be funny, but his words went through Melissa like a knife.

That's exactly what I am, Melissa thought as she closed her eyes and sank back in her seat. *Lost.*

She had been lost for a very long time and didn't know which way to turn. The happy, secure girl she had been when her parents were alive had wandered off somewhere along the road to womanhood.

"Regardless," her uncle continued, breaking into her thoughts, "tonight, I will introduce you to the newest and brightest doctor at the medical clinic—"

"No!" Melissa's eyes flashed back to his. "I'm not interested in meeting another man." Everything she had heard about the new doctor was admirable. But even though he apparently was a very capable physician and a man of good character, she wasn't about to fall for another one of her uncle's misbegotten matchmaking schemes.

Her uncle chuckled knowingly, cigar smoke puffing out with each breath like a fire-breathing dragon. "You will this one. All women do. He's half Greek and I think I've heard more than a few of the ladies at the clinic describe him as a Greek god." He chuckled again, as if he personally had something to do with the man's good looks. "And I must say, it certainly doesn't hurt business having such a handsome—and available—doctor working with us."

"Then why would you want me to take him off the eligibility list?" Melissa asked with disdain. "Wouldn't that hurt *business?*" Practicing medicine had always been more of a business than a calling for her uncle. Unlike her father, who had exhibited a wonderful and caring bedside manner, healing and compassion were lower on the list of priorities for Uncle Bob—after business, socializing, and prestige.

How two brothers could be so different was a mystery to Melissa. Her father had given up a lucrative practice at the clinic he and Bob had founded, to go into the depths of the Appalachian Mountains to treat folks who would not have received medical care otherwise. Melissa's mother, a nurse, had worked alongside her husband until the day they were trapped and killed by a flash flood in a remote region of the mountains, where they had gone to perform an emergency appendectomy. They had saved a young man's life and lost their own.

"Well, I doubt I have to worry about that," her uncle was saying. Melissa frowned as she tried to remember what they had been talking about. "You're too negative concerning relationships," Uncle Bob continued. "I'm sure Dr. Luke Karalis will take one look at you and turn away. Why should he concern himself with an unwilling woman when there are so many who aren't?"

Just then, the sprawling Ridgedale Country Club came into view. The clubhouse building was elaborately decorated for the holidays. "There must be thousands of lights up there," Uncle Bob said with awed admiration in his voice.

"My, haven't they outdone themselves this year," his wife purred approvingly.

"Very nice," Uncle Bob agreed, nodding his head.

To Melissa, the decorations looked presumptuous and fake. Tilting her eyes toward the pristine forest to her left, she longed for a snow-covered cabin once again—something solid, safe, and real.

Chapter 2

The showy splendor of the annual Christmas ball was not a big attraction for Dr. Luke Karalis. As a child, he had studied the anatomy of such parties from a secret hiding place in the stairwell of his parents' mansion in Athens, Greece, and he had long since concluded that these social gatherings were only for those who feasted on idle chatter and superficial graces—both of which were demeaning to the human spirit as far as Luke was concerned.

More times than he cared to count, he had seen the twisted tangle that the so-called glamorous life produced. His parents moved easily in that world and he had lost them to it. Luke had no desire to be like them and he had even less desire to attend this ball. He would have much preferred to have driven the forty minutes to his cabin on the shores of Lake Breeze. Even if it meant going alone. But Dr. Robert Kincaid, the founding member of the community's largest medical clinic, where Luke was the newest physician, had made it clear that he was expected to attend—in tuxedo.

By the time Luke entered the country club, which was lit up so brightly that he was sure the orbiting space shuttle crew could see it from space, the party was in full swing. After checking his coat, Luke paused in the atrium and watched the merry parade of humans with detached interest.

Women wearing gowns expensive enough to feed an average American family for several months, fluttered and moved around the room like colorful insects. A florid-faced woman, with a red gown to match, was the ladybug; the faded blond in the iridescent green dress was the grasshopper; a middle-aged matron in a silvery sheath was like a white scorpion; and the queen bee of them all was garnered in gold.

His eyes casually followed the tall woman in the gown of shimmering golden light as she moved across the room. She was definitely a social bee. The Greek word for bee, *melissa,* came to mind as he watched her buzz from one circular clutter of brightly dressed people to another. But he had to concede that she was a stunning woman, graceful and fluid. When she glided out of his sight behind a group of people, he breathed out deeply.

She might be beautiful to look at, but she's probably just as superficial as the rest of them, he thought. Although Luke desired a lasting relationship, he'd met enough one-dimensional, shallow women to last a lifetime.

He turned his attention from the hum of the party and glanced at the antique, Early-American clock chiming beside him. He grimaced when he saw that it was only seven o'clock. The collar of his dress shirt was already irritating his skin, in much the same way that the party was chafing his mood. He rubbed his hand along the back of his neck and looked at the clock again. Seven-o-two.

The stench of a Cuban cigar alerted Luke to the proximity of Dr. Robert Kincaid. Luke lowered his arm and straightened his shoulders. He had hoped to avoid talking to the boss tonight. Dr. Kincaid reminded Luke too much of his own father, not a good point of comparison. Both men were self-serving and pretentious. And they both smoked cigars like babies sucking on a pacifier.

"So glad that you could make it, Doctor," the older man bellowed as he grabbed Luke's arm. Luke took a step back and turned his head away from the billow of smoke that accompanied the older physician.

"I didn't know I had a choice," he stated dryly.

"Now, now, my man." Dr. Kincaid spoke with a voice that evoked an image in Luke's mind of a frog with a mouth full of marbles. It grated on nerves that were already rubbed raw. "It's all part of the job, and not so difficult. There are a lot of beautiful women in that room, Son. . ." Dr. Kincaid motioned with his cigar toward the ballroom, "All polished and painted and decorated better than any Christmas tree you might see. Loosen up, Doctor; enjoy yourself. You cut a fine figure of a man." He winked, took a deep drag on his cigar, and continued conspiratorially. "All women like a handsome doctor, and business is even better when they're single."

Luke's jaw tightened. "I was under the impression, Doctor, that people came to us for our knowledge in medicine."

The portly man leaned closer to Luke. "Don't delude yourself, Doctor. You'll build your first home on hypochondriacal women alone," he said.

Nodding toward the humming mass of people that nearly drowned out the background music of the orchestra, he added, "And believe you me, there are plenty in here to cultivate."

Before Luke could reply, Dr. Kincaid turned and waddled off toward the ballroom, dingy gray smoke trailing in his self-satisfied wake. Luke rocked back on his heels and blew a stream of air through his teeth. *Just like Dad,* he thought with disgust. He stuffed his hands into his jacket pocket and pulled out his coat check ticket. Pivoting toward the cloakroom, he decided to go home. He'd done his civic duty and had been seen by "the man," which he knew was far more important to Dr. Kincaid than it was to him.

"Are you leaving already?" The voice behind him was very feminine, velvety, and soft-spoken.

Luke turned toward the voice, and his mouth went dry when he saw the woman in the golden gown, the social bee, standing next to him. She smelled delicious, with just the right touch of a subtle perfume, and she had the most startling amber eyes he had ever seen. They reminded him of a bee in springtime, and her choice of evening dress was the perfect complement. Black lines radiated through the deep-hued irises into even blacker pupils, a magnet that demanded a closer look. If the eyes are truly windows to the soul, what he saw was hauntingly at odds with the first impression of this woman that he had made from afar.

She glanced down at the ticket stub that he was self-consciously rubbing between his thumb and forefinger. "I was considering it," he said tentatively.

"Please don't let my uncle bother you," she softly advised, and Luke's eyes widened.

Her uncle? He restrained the impulse to look at the receding back of the older doctor, who had taken his glad-handing act to the far side of the ballroom. If she saw his surprise, she gave no indication but softly continued. "Uncle Bob. . .he doesn't know any better." She slightly shrugged her shoulders. "It's just his way," she explained with an unaffected Southern accent that soothed Luke's raw nerves like a balm. He smiled as he watched her glossy mouth move as if to continue. But her loyalties, something he couldn't help but admire, seemed to prevent her from saying any more.

Dr. Kincaid's niece, he said to himself. *Doesn't that just figure?*

17

The young, raven-haired beauty seemed to read his mind—that being a Kincaid was a strike against her—and she smiled, a sad, yet whimsical twisting of her lips, before gliding gracefully away into the crowd.

Luke watched her go. *Dr. Kincaid's niece?* This time the thought was a question. *That doesn't quite fit.* And yet, as he stretched to his full height in order to see over heads as she eased her way into the thicket of party-goers once again, he had to admit that she was definitely an accomplished social bee, totally at ease buzzing through the night's work of small talk and laughter, seemingly at ease in Bob Kincaid's world.

In spite of himself, Luke knew he was smitten, in that inexplicable way that a man is drawn to a particular woman. She was beautiful, she was graceful, and there was a depth of. . .of. . .something in those lovely, amber eyes. Luke shrugged his shoulders. He wasn't sure he wanted to tangle with Dr. Kincaid's niece. And hadn't his colleague, Jane, mentioned recently that the woman had broken her engagement to some big-shot lawyer, practically on the way to the altar? What did that say about her?

And yet, for just a few moments they had shared something, a deep, unspoken connection. She had been troubled by what her uncle might have said to him, and it was as if she had wanted to convey that he was not alone in his feelings.

Luke looked down at his coat check ticket and then hastily shoved the stub into his pocket. Kincaid's niece or not, he wanted to talk to the lovely *melissa* again.

The party grew louder and more jovial as more drinks were poured and alcohol began to rule the merrymakers. Luke never drank and he had never quite understood the abuse that people inflicted upon their bodies in search of pleasure or escape. Looking around the ballroom, he wondered whether Kincaid's niece drank. He wasn't sure he would have anything to do with her if she did. The sweet scent of her perfume flooded his mind once again as he saw her buzzing from clique to clique at the opposite end of the ballroom. She certainly hadn't smelled of alcohol. And from his vantage point near the doorway, he noticed that, as before, she wasn't holding a glass.

Luke walked over to the large picture window and looked out at the serene beauty of the winter scene. Once again, he considered driving up to his cabin, his Shangrila, on Lake Breeze. Only medical journals awaited him in his small apartment near the hospital. But the prospect of going to the cabin alone didn't appeal to him. Instead his eyes narrowed as he thought about all the women he'd dated since coming to Ridgedale. Although most were very nice, something had been missing in each instance; a spark, something that would make him want to know more.

He blew out a deep unsettling breath. He wished there were someone special to share the beauty of the cabin on this crisp winter night. A picture of the woman in the golden gown flashed into his mind, but he quickly dismissed the thought. *Unrealistic and undesired,* he said silently to himself. *We haven't even officially met each other yet, and she's Kincaid's niece. There's two strikes already.*

Even as he was shaking her image from his mind, Luke turned instinctively and scanned the room to see where the *melissa*—the social bee —had landed. He didn't see her immediately and his attention was once again drawn to the intricate ballet of partygoers laughing, talking, and moving around in their elaborate costumes and evening finery. With a cynical snort, he decided that the social columnist for the city newspaper would probably describe the room as "vibrantly alive." But Luke could only see a space filled to capacity with people all intent on impressing one another at any cost. Actors and actresses. He shook his head and glanced at his watch. Another ten minutes or so and he would head for the cloakroom again—and this time keep on going.

"Doctor. . ." Robert Kincaid's drawl reached Luke just as he plopped a handful of cashews into his mouth. Luke noticed that he had lit a new cigar. "I want you to meet some wonderful people. Ted and Betty Jones, this is Dr. Luke Karalis—the newest and brightest star at the Medical Clinic of Ridgedale," he said, repeating the same phrase he used every time he presented Luke to others. Luke's lips thinned in disgust. He had grown to hate Kincaid's pat introduction.

He managed to swallow the nuts and brush the salt off his hand before shaking Mrs. Jones's soft, well-manicured hand. Her nails were unnaturally long and painted a fiery red. Mr. Jones, balding and red in the face, looked old enough to be her father.

"How do you do?" Luke nodded.

"Ted is the CEO of Health Pharmaceutical," Kincaid proclaimed loudly, and Luke could tell that he was endeavoring to impress.

But Luke wasn't impressed. He'd been meeting corporate bigwigs his entire life. His father was CEO of one of the world's largest chemical companies. Of course, Dr. Kincaid didn't know that, and Luke would make sure it remained that way.

"I see," was all Luke said. After a moment, it became apparent that they were waiting for him to say something flattering about Jones's position, but Luke purposefully changed the subject. "Do you have children?"

The man blinked at the non sequitur. "Yes. We have a boy and a girl." The way he said it made Luke think that he was referring to his latest acquisition of stocks or fancy cars.

"And a full time baby-sitter," his wife purred.

Luke's eyes flicked over to the woman. She reminded him of his mother, who had no doubt uttered the same words many times. "Don't you think that children are a blessing?" he asked.

Nonplused, Mrs. Jones responded breathlessly, a puff of expensive perfume coming from her as she waved her diamond-studded arm elegantly before him. "Yes. But. . .so are nannies. Do you have children, Doctor?" Her eyes had a blank, disinterested look; the question was a formality.

"I'm not married," he said.

"Oh." Her eyes widened ever so slightly. She was interested now. He had seen that look numerous times before. It was an invitation.

"And my wife, Mrs. Kincaid," Dr. Kincaid interrupted, as if no other conversation had occurred.

"Mrs. Kincaid," Luke took her hand in greeting and nodded. She was the silver-gowned matron he had earlier dubbed "the scorpion," but right now she was behaving like a queen bestowing the favor of talking to one whom she considered beneath her.

"Dr. Karalis, we will have you to dinner soon." Her perpetual smile, a by-product of one too many face-lifts, didn't quite reach her eyes. Luke wondered why, after so many months, it was suddenly important to invite him to dinner. "You must meet our niece."

He had his answer. Maybe a young doctor wasn't so low in her opinion after all. "I've already met her," he answered honestly. He was rescued from further discussion when Robert Kincaid pulled her away to introduce her elsewhere.

Luke grabbed another handful of cashews and wandered over to the window again. As he gazed out at the snowy landscape, he thought about having children. He realized that he had experienced enough of the casual dating scene. In exchange for noninvolvement of the heart and sexual freedom, people paid with a loss of dignity. As his wise godfather, *Nono*, had reminded him many times, the old ways—courtship and marriage—had worked for centuries. Luke knew that he was ready for marriage. He wanted to love and care for a woman and to have her want to spend her life with him. And, he wanted children. Perhaps having a family of his own would replace the loneliness that tugged at the far corners of his heart.

He absentmindedly wandered over to the Christmas tree. It was silvery. It was glittery. It was even pretty. But it wasn't real. Luke shook his head in amazement. "Surrounded by forests and they put up a fake tree," he muttered under his breath. He bent down and lifted one of the exquisitely wrapped boxes that sat enticingly under the tree.

He shook it.

Empty.

In disgust, he tossed it back under the tree. An artificial tree with empty presents under it. What else did he expect?

"No fair opening the gifts until the big day, Doctor." The woman with the honey-smooth southern voice and the golden evening gown spoke from over his shoulder.

With a sense of excitement that Luke couldn't remember feeling in a very long time, he turned to her and smiled.

Chapter 3

The woman's amber eyes twinkled as Luke quickly stood up and turned to face her. He tried to formulate a quick-witted response to match her teasing remark, but nothing came to mind. After what seemed an eternity, but was probably only a few seconds, the woman raised an eyebrow and tweaked him with another barb. "I guess there's not much you can say when you're caught red-handed."

"You got me there," Luke managed to say, and he could feel his ears begin to grow warm.

"I just realized that we were never properly introduced," the woman said. "I'm Melissa Kincaid."

Luke's eyes went wide with amazement. "Melissa?" he said, wondering if he had heard correctly.

Melissa looked puzzled. *Is my name so unusual?* she thought to herself. Narrowing her eyes and tilting her head, she said, "Yes, Melissa."

"Bee," he said, and now Melissa was the one to look surprised. "Your name means 'bee' in Greek. I'm half Greek," he stated by way of explanation.

"Of course," she murmured. She remembered that Uncle Bob had mentioned something about that in the car. And now that she noticed the thick, brown hair combed off to the side, the deep-set eyes and light olive skin, his Mediterranean ancestry was obvious.

"In Greek, your name is pronounced with the accent on the first syllable," he continued. "*Mel*issa," he said smoothly as his eyes locked with hers. Deep green met glowing amber and in that moment the dull, frozen reaches of her heart melted like an ice sculpture in the summer sun. Feelings—sensations—she didn't even try to understand, didn't want to understand, scattered throughout her body and brain, replacing the numbness with a sense of lightness, of freedom.

"Your parents did well to call you Melissa," Luke murmured. His gaze held steady on her eyes. "Your irises hold all the colors of a bee's body."

Melissa blinked. "My father used to tell me that." She frowned slightly as the thought occurred to her that during the entire year she had been with Brian almost daily, he had never said a word about her eyes. Probably because he had never really looked at her. By contrast, the man she was looking at now seemed to be trying to peer into her soul. Small shivers of pleasure ran down her spine. She quickly squared her shoulders and broke eye contact with the young doctor.

"Your father was right," he agreed. "There is amber and black, yellow, brown, and even a touch of orange floating around in them. Very unusual." His deep voice sounded almost like a caress and Melissa laughed, a too-bright sound that didn't fit the moment.

But that's what she wanted—to change the mood, to keep the electricity that was humming between them from becoming anything more than a platonic connection. Turning to the tree, she brushed her fingers across the artificial branches. "You know what's kind of funny, though," she said as she risked a glance at him before looking back at the tree. "I'm terrified of bees."

"I'm not." Luke responded as quick as a pulse beat, and the sudden look she threw over her shoulder told him that she had caught his double meaning. But from the way her pupils dilated, eating up their amber light, he also suspected that she didn't like it.

In Luke's thirty-one years of life, he had learned a few things. And one of them was when to push a person and when to back off, especially when the person was important to him. And somehow, Melissa Kincaid was important. He decided then and there that if friendship was all she wanted, then that was what he would accept.

She just broke up with her fiancé. No need to rush, he thought. Besides, friendship was a good place to start anyway. "By the way," he said cordially, "I'm Luke Karalis."

From the pucker in her bottom lip, he could tell she was trying to decide whether to trust the sudden change in his tone. He made his smile as bland as possible, kept his eyes as bright as a playful puppy's, and waited.

When her wary look was replaced by a mischievous gleam, he knew that he had succeeded. "Yes, I know. Dr. Luke Karalis. . .'the newest, and brightest star at the Medical Clinic of Ridgedale,' " she repeated her uncle's pat introduction, and saw Luke cringe.

"Ah. . .yes. . .well," he shrugged his shoulders and his lips twisted wryly. "What can I say?" He was taken aback by the mocking tone of her voice. Evidently, she was not impressed.

"Nothing really," she replied, taking pity on him. "My uncle is a man who says and does exactly what he wants. It's best just to roll with the punches and wait for it to pass."

He shot her a questioning look. "Are you speaking from experience?"

She almost returned with a flippant answer. But something in his face, something sincere and benevolent and kind—something she hadn't seen in anyone for a long time—stopped her. And with sudden insight, she realized that he was asking out of genuine interest. She swallowed the glib words that almost passed her lips and whispered the truth. "Yes."

When his eyes darkened, not with passion, but with concern and respect, she was glad that she'd trusted her instincts. For the first time in a long time, Melissa felt as though she was free to say what she really believed, rather than glossing over her feelings as she had become accustomed. It was a heady feeling, and she looked for a diversion to regain her balance. Spying the packages beneath the tree, she knelt down and reached for one.

"They're all empty," Luke warned as she rose with a box. She shrugged an elegant shoulder and in the lighting of the tree Luke thought that her gown shimmered like wishes from a dream.

"They've been empty ever since I was twelve," she murmured, fingering the exquisitely wrapped gift.

Luke sensed that her response was something more than an idle comment, and his curiosity got the better of him. "What happened when you were twelve?"

Melissa fidgeted with the velvet ribbon before lifting her face to look at him. "My parents died," she responded simply.

Clicking his tongue he answered, "That's a tough thing for a twelve-year-old to deal with."

"It's a tough thing for a twenty-two-year-old to deal with too," she said. It was something she hadn't confessed to anyone, not even to Brian.

Luke glanced at the present in her hand before training his deep-set eyes back on her. "And it hurts more at Christmas than at any other time of the year." It was a statement, not a question.

"You know?" she whispered, her brows coming together as she wondered how he understood so well.

"Holidays are not only the 'most wonderful' time of the year, but for many. . .the hardest."

Tilting her head to the side in a way that was becoming familiar to Luke, she asked, "Are you speaking from medical knowledge or personal experience?"

Shrugging his shoulders and ignoring the chafing of his shirt collar against his neck, he admitted, "Both, I guess. I've never been close to my parents. They've always spent the holidays with friends skiing in Switzerland or sailing in the Caribbean, so I don't really have any of those warm, Christmasy memories that everyone talks about. But I've also seen it in my medical practice." He paused and his lips pressed together in a grim line, which turned them a shade lighter in color. "Working in the emergency room of a big city hospital, you see the attempted suicides during the holidays."

Melissa was amazed. He really did seem to understand. Something inside of her responded and without giving it more thought, she shared her feelings with him. It seemed the natural thing to do, but for Melissa Kincaid, it wasn't natural at all. "My parents are only a hazy memory to me now, but I sometimes wonder how different my life might have been if they hadn't died. You see," her eyes were animated with the need to explain, "my father was my uncle's younger brother. He was a doctor too, but he was a real man of healing, a man with a calling, not just—"

She stopped herself, suddenly remembering that she was talking to a colleague of her uncle's. Feeling at once disloyal and uncomfortable, she tossed the empty package back under the tree. But when the golden strap of her vintage evening bag snagged on a branch, jarring loose a glass ball, she cringed in helplessness as the ornament tumbled down the branches toward the parquet floor.

With reflexes quick as a sword flash, Luke reached out and caught the ball. Gently cupping the delicate Christmas decoration in his hands, he softly replied, "I understand."

"You do?" The words were out before she could catch them. She blushed, which only deepened her embarrassment.

Luke's eyes narrowed as he considered how much to say. He could tell by her pink-tinged cheeks that she had become uneasy with the conversation. "I only have to work with your uncle. Not live with him," he replied cautiously. He reached over and carefully reattached the blue ornament to the tree.

Luke saw the glaze settle over her eyes as she quickly reverted to the role he had watched her perform so artfully all evening. As if the curtain had suddenly gone up on Act Three, she switched from being a friend to being the accomplished social bee.

"Melissa?" He jumped over the rules of propriety by using her first name, but she didn't seem to hear him. Her eyes flitted over his shoulder to scan the room as she said softly, "Yes, well, that's the way it is sometimes." Her veiled eyes rested on him only long enough for half of the sentence to be spoken. "It was nice to finally meet you, Dr. Karalis." She held out her hand to shake his. "I hope that we see each other again."

But Luke wasn't about to let her get off that easily. Instead of gently clasping and releasing her hand as she intended, he held on to it. "I'm certain we will, Miss Kincaid," he said firmly. "Your aunt has already invited me to dinner."

Her eyes darted up to his. He had her attention again. He nodded and shot her a quick, ironic smile. "It seems she wants me to meet her niece," he explained. Melissa cringed, and to Luke's relief she dropped the social pretense.

"I think it's only fair that I warn you," she gave a little laugh that was flavored with both embarrassment and chagrin, "my aunt and uncle are probably playing matchmaker. They won't rest until I'm. . .well. . .er. . . married." She slanted her head self-consciously at him. Something in his look gave her the impression that the possibility of a lasting relationship didn't bother him in the least. She hurriedly explained her position. "But that's the furthest thing from my mind. I still have university to complete and I'm not ready for such a commitment." She stopped and shook her head in bewilderment. "I don't remember ever talking so freely with anyone before."

"Not even to the man you were to marry?" he said. She dropped his hand like a red-hot coal.

"My, doesn't good news travels fast around here." Her eyes narrowed and began to study the crowd over his right shoulder. "Or is that a bit of juicy gossip that my aunt fed you?"

Luke held his hands up, palms facing forward, and quickly said, "I'm sorry, Melissa. I was out of line. I'm truly sorry."

Her eyes fluttered shut momentarily and she let out a long, weary breath. "I've heard enough 'I'm sorrys' tonight to last me a lifetime."

Luke couldn't help himself. With a hint of a laugh in his voice, he said, "Well, I feel as though I should say 'I'm sorry' again, but that would only add to your misery."

Her eyes flew open and she looked at him with amazement. *How can he make light of this?* Melissa was incredulous, but before she could formulate her next thought, Luke rambled on, trying to repair the damage.

"Maybe this will help," he said quickly. "I wasn't told about your engagement as gossip. In fact, it was said in passing by someone at the clinic who thinks you did the right thing."

Melissa's dark brows drew so close together that they almost formed a straight line across her forehead. "At the clinic? Who?" As far as she knew, hardly anyone sided with her, especially not at the clinic.

"Bond," Luke said in a mock-British accent. "Jane Bond."

"Jane!" she exclaimed, and like a sentry lowering her guard, her facial muscles relaxed. "Dear Jane. She's my only ally at the clinic. And, by the way, that is the worst British accent I have ever heard." Melissa wrinkled her nose and laughed merrily. To Luke it sounded like chimes touched by the wind.

"Well, Melissa—do you mind if I call you Melissa?—if you will accept my apology, you can count me as another ally at the clinic. And please call me Luke."

"Thank you, Luke. I will. To both," she replied. Using his name for the first time made her feel suddenly warm. To hide her embarrassment, she scanned the room looking for her friend. "Do you know if Jane and her husband are here tonight?"

"Jane and Dale?" He had spoken to them for a few minutes when he first arrived, but hadn't seen them since. "You know, they're still newlyweds, and I kind of got the impression they had better things in mind for the evening," he said.

The soft blush that touched Melissa's cheeks made him feel weak in the knees. In that moment, he knew that he wanted more than anything in the world to be alone with this woman—away from the social charade and endless chatter of the Christmas party. He glanced at his watch.

Eight-o-three. If they left right now they could get to the cabin by nine-thirty at the latest. It was a crazy idea, but he blurted it out before he could change his mind.

"Hey, Melissa, let's you and me get out of here too."

She looked at him sharply, and her amber eyes darkened to a rich brown. "What?"

"Let's leave," he repeated. "I know the perfect spot and. . ."

Melissa shook her head and began to walk away. Luke placed his hand lightly on her shoulder to stop her. The effect of his touch on Melissa was electric. She turned to face him again, her eyes searching his for something sensible she could hold on to.

"Look, before you say another word, just hear me out, okay?" Luke said.

Melissa bit her lip and nodded. "Go ahead. I'm listening."

"I know we've only just met," Luke said gently, "and I know there are some complications with your aunt and uncle and all that. But one thing's for certain: I want to get to know you and it isn't going to happen here amidst all this bedlam. I have a cabin up at Lake Breeze, and we could be there in about an hour. I promise to be a complete gentleman, and I will have you home safe and sound before the sun comes up. Guaranteed."

Melissa's head was spinning. "You have a cabin. . . ?" she asked in disbelief. *This is not happening, Melissa. You must be dreaming. Pinch yourself and wake up.* She shook her head and looked down at the floor. "Yes, but—" She surfed around for words. "I can't just leave with you, I'd be the talk of the town."

"Don't take this wrong," Luke said tentatively, "but from what you said earlier, everyone is already talking. I don't want that to keep us from seeing each other."

Unsure of how to respond, Melissa turned away from him and glided over to the picture window.

Luke followed.

And as she stood and watched the big, fat, feathery flakes of snow falling outside, she admitted to herself that he was right. She was already the talk of the town. What difference would it make if she left the party with him? It came as a surprise to her to realize that she really wanted to go. In her mind, she pictured a cozy cabin in the woods, with a cheery fire burning and a cup of hot chocolate in her hands.

Just then she became aware that Luke was speaking to her again. His voice was soft in her left ear, "There's pleanty of dry wood waiting to be burned, a huge picture window looking out over the lake and the surrounding hills, and snow tires on my Jeep to get us there."

"What about hot chocolate?" she asked.

"I make mine with whole milk, so it's good and rich," he replied. "None of that watery instant stuff." He looked at her and smiled. "So whatta ya say? Are you ready to ditch your social connections?"

Luke waited, hardly daring to take a breath. He didn't analyze why it was so important for her to come with him, but somehow it was. He'd felt this way only once before—years earlier when he'd been waiting to see if he'd made it into medical school.

He watched Melissa's face as a small quiver at the corner of her mouth turned into a wide grin. "This is absolutely crazy," she said, "and I have no idea what to tell my aunt and uncle—but yes, I'd love to go with you."

Luke exhaled and Melissa laughed at his obvious relief. "I'll tell you what," he said. "If you don't mind getting our coats, I'll take care of Uncle Bob for you and meet you at the cloakroom." He handed her his claim check and strode purposefully across the ballroom. Melissa watched him go and shook her head in amazement. She had been accustomed to having Brian take control of situations, but it had always been for his own benefit, never for hers.

A few moments later, Luke reappeared, smiling. He gave her the thumbs-up sign, helped her on with her coat, and without another word guided her toward the door.

When they were settled in the car, a sudden, worried thought popped into Melissa's mind. She turned toward Luke with an anxious expression on her face. "Luke, I don't want you to get the wrong impression. I don't normally become close to people so quickly and I don't. . ." She faltered. "I mean, I just want us to be friends. Nothing more. I need a friend. I—"

"Melissa. . ." He placed his finger against her lips, stopping her. He felt the softness and warmth of her breath but immediately pushed the thought aside. She trusted him and that was more important than anything else at the moment. "I don't have the wrong impression, and I meant what I said before. We can go to the cabin and we can talk. We can get to know each other and then we can see what happens." He immediately regretted his last words when he saw Melissa's face darken.

"It will be a long time before I want anything more," she warned. "I just want to be honest about that—from the start."

Luke nodded. He understood that the wounds from her broken engagement were still fresh. She needed some time to heal. But he doubted that she would feel that way for long. He hoped not, anyway, because he was beginning to realize that he wanted more of a relationship with her.

A whole lot more.

Chapter 4

Luke and Melissa made three stops on their way to the cabin. The first was at the Kincaids' house, where Melissa changed into warm wool slacks; a soft, holiday-red cashmere sweater; and a down-filled parka. At their second stop—Luke's apartment—he gladly exchanged his itchy tuxedo for a vivid green plaid flannel shirt, thick cords, a down vest, and his ancient sheepskin jacket.

When the two of them were back in the car and headed toward the highway out of town, Melissa's curiosity got the better of her. "So what did you say to Uncle Bob, anyway?" she asked. "I assume everything was okay?"

"I just told him I was taking you out for hot chocolate and we'd be home later," Luke said with a mischievous grin. "Judging by the way he looked, I'd say he'll probably be sleeping in tomorrow morning. I'll have you home in plenty of time."

Melissa was looking at Luke and she startled when he suddenly turned the Jeep in at a Christmas tree lot. "I hope you know how to put up a tree," he said, his cypress green eyes shining with a youthful happiness that Melissa hadn't seen before. "I've never done it before."

Melissa's chin dropped. "You've never had a Christmas tree!"

Luke laughed, and qualified his statement. "Of course I have." He paused, remembering the elaborately trimmed trees in his parents' home, decked in crystal and gold, satin and silver, designed and assembled by professional home decorators every December 15. "What I mean is, I've never helped to trim one."

She searched his face with her eyes. He had told her that he didn't have any warm holiday memories, but never to have decorated a Christmas tree sounded almost criminal. "But. . .that's one of the best parts of Christmas!" she exclaimed.

He looked around the tree lot and laughed. "I'm beginning to think so!"

31

With the kind of excitement normally reserved for children, they selected a Scotch pine—a little bit taller than Luke's six feet, two inches —and three boxes of shiny glass balls that the tree lot proprietor had for sale.

"Not much variety on the ornaments," Luke said, "but not bad for short notice."

When Luke had secured the tree to the luggage rack, he and Melissa climbed back in the jeep and headed for Lake Breeze. Along the way, Luke talked about his childhood and how he'd wanted to grow up to be a doctor.

Before Melissa knew it, Luke turned into a narrow gravel driveway that ran for a quarter mile through the woods before opening up to a turn-around in front of a rustic cabin. Its wooden walls were shrouded in a pure white blanket of snow, making it look like an enchanting holiday house made of gingerbread. Melissa took one look and was breathless. The moon peeking down through a break in the clouds sparkled on the snow-covered roof. Behind the cabin, Lake Breeze was a dark, shimmering jewel. "Oh, this is even better than I imagined," she said with delight.

Inside, the wood-paneled walls smelled of cedar and the stone fireplace was already set with kindling and a dry oak log. In minutes, the crackling warmth of the flames began to chase the chill from the room. The Christmas tree turned out to be crooked, but Melissa and Luke didn't care. They agreed it was the most beautiful one they had ever seen.

When Luke had prepared two steaming mugs of his "world famous" hot chocolate, he and Melissa settled onto the leather sofa and talked until their eyelids began to droop. When Melissa looked at her watch, she was amazed to see that it was 2:35 in the morning. "Luke, do you think you can stay awake long enough to drive me home? I don't want this night to end, but I do have a reputation to consider."

Luke yawned and stretched his arms above his head. "Your reputation is set as far as I'm concerned. You're an angel. But you're right," he said as he reached into his pocket for his keys, "it's time to go home."

The seeds of friendship sown in the coziness of the winter cabin blossomed with the flowering of spring into something as special and precious as the magnolias that decorated the trees around town.

Luke had remained true to his word. He was the perfect gentleman.

But even though their friendship was perfect in every way, Melissa knew, as time went on, that Luke wanted more from their relationship than the boundaries she had set would allow.

In deference to her wishes, he'd tried to hide it, but the set of his jaw, the sparkle in his eyes, and the way his hand often reached for hers but stopped a hair's breadth away told Melissa how much more he desired.

If she were completely honest, she knew that she would have liked more too—but she didn't know whether she could handle it. Like fireworks set to explode on the Fourth of July, the chemistry between them was a volatile mixture waiting for the proper spark to ignite it. But Melissa knew that once the fuse was lit, there was no turning back—and that was what scared her.

On the other hand, if their friendship fizzled out because they never lit the fuse, she didn't know if she could handle not having Luke Karalis in her life. Somewhere along the trail of months, he had become much more to her than a friend. Though he rarely touched her physically—his self-control was nothing short of amazing—his care and concern touched a deep inner part of her that she didn't even understand. With him, her soul was happy and she felt safe and protected and. . .loved. In fact, the emotions that floated around inside reminded her of the security she had taken for granted when her parents were still alive.

And that was what frightened her the most. Her parents had been everything to her. And they'd been taken away from her. When they died, she had lost the center of her life, and she had floundered around for years, until Luke had come into her life.

He had saved her.

She knew with a certainty that he had saved her.

He had become her fortress, her place of refuge in a world that had been overwhelming her. She knew that she shouldn't depend on him so completely, but she reasoned that as long as they remained friends, without the complication of a closer relationship, everything was okay.

⊷

Luke wasn't sure exactly what was preventing Melissa—or *Meli*, his "honey," as he had started calling her—from letting him win her heart. He understood that her reticence had something to do with her disastrous engagement, but the doctor in him suspected a secondary cause to a very complicated condition. For his part, Luke was certain that he loved her in a way he hadn't believed possible. He loved her eyes, her smile, her voice, the way her toes curled when they were cold. But more than anything, he loved knowing that she needed him. He had felt needed professionally many times, but never before on a personal level. He liked the way it made him feel. He had offered her friendship because he knew at the time it was all she was willing to give. But now he wanted more—needed more. At least the promise of more. He loved her as a friend, but he wanted her for his wife.

Love and marriage. His godfather had been right; love and marriage went together—especially when a man found a woman who meant everything to him.

Early one spring day, as they sat on a carpet of pale pink almond blossoms outside the cabin, Luke realized he could no longer be the friend Melissa wanted him to be.

Slowly, he leaned toward her.

He kissed her gently, but with a passion that could not be mistaken. When her lips stirred beneath his, matching the warmth and intensity of his passion, he knew they had stepped over the line and could never go back to "just friends" again. Luke thought that that was good. Very good.

Drawing back, he smiled and looked deep into her beautiful amber eyes. With a confidence bolstered by the memory of her sweet lips, he whispered, "Meli, be the half that makes me whole? Marry me?"

Her countenance darkened, and for a split second, Luke saw love and indecision mingled in her eyes. But before the flicker of a "yes" could become a flame, she blinked and the fire went out. She began shaking her head back and forth and with a growing resolve she nudged him away from her.

"No, Luke. I don't want us to do this." Her voice held a frantic edge.

Luke drew his eyebrows together—a picture of innocence. "To do what?" he asked casually.

"This!" she said a little louder and with more venom than she intended. She waved her hand between them, not looking at him but at some indistinct point in the middle. "I don't want to do *this.*"

A low rumble built in Luke's chest. "Meli, I love you." He touched her face with a gentle caress. "And I think you love me too."

Her eyes opened wide and she scrambled to her feet. "Luke, I told you the very first night we met that all I wanted was a friendship."

Throwing his hands up in an open, beseeching gesture, Luke used every ounce of willpower he possessed to speak softly, persuasively. "And I've given it to you, Meli. You're my best friend." He paused before whispering his wish, "And I think that I'm your best friend too."

Tears burned the back of Melissa's eyes. "Oh, Luke," her voice caught, and she exhaled sharply, a husky, wavering sigh. "You're the very best friend I've ever had."

"Don't you think," Luke said gently, his voice as comforting as a down-filled quilt on a snow-covered day, "that a love based on something as solid as our friendship is the best kind of love there could be?" Luke stood slowly to his feet and offered his arms to Melissa.

Suddenly exhausted, she let him draw her into his embrace and rested her head against his chest. She closed her eyes and savored the strength of his arms, the sound of his heart beating against her ear, his masculine scent. He was solid and safe and warm, and she wished that she could stay in his arms forever.

"Marry me, Meli. Marry me," he whispered into her ear. It was the hardest thing she ever had to do to deny him.

"I can't, Luke," she whispered back, forcing the words through her lips.

"But why?" he said. "Is there something wrong with me? Something you haven't told me?" He was reaching for straws and he knew it.

Melissa stepped back from his embrace and brought her hands up to her chest, over her heart, and tried to explain. "Something's not right with *me*," she said. "Right here." She patted her chest for emphasis.

"With your heart?" Luke said with confusion in his voice.

She nodded. "With my heart."

Luke smiled, a grin that would have been condescending if it hadn't been so honest. Gently, he placed his hand over hers. "I'm a 'heart' doctor, remember? Let me heal it." His voice carried all the love and concern that he wished she could accept from him.

Steeling herself against the pain she knew her words would cause, she pushed his hand away and replied, "You can't. The kind of heart disease I have isn't found in your medical books. It isn't my flesh-and-blood heart that needs healing."

"Meli, we only have one heart," the scientist in Luke was a bit too quick to respond.

She nodded in agreement. "Yes, but it has many parts. It has the part you can hear and the part you can feel." She touched her ear and rubbed her fingertips to her thumb. "But I believe there's also a part that can't be heard or felt, a part that can only be perceived through our souls." She paused as she realized she was explaining to herself as much as to Luke. "And I think," she said quietly, carefully wending her way through unfamiliar territory, "that it is the center of our being."

"Meli," Luke reached for her arms and gently drew her close to him again. "Let me be the center of your being," he whispered.

"You already are, Luke," she admitted, and Luke didn't think that he had ever felt richer in his life. Not even what she said next could dim that feeling. "But, that's just it. I don't think it's healthy. You should be a part of my being, yes. But not the center."

"What do you want me to do, Melissa?" he asked.

She licked her lips. She knew there was no way for them to return to a platonic friendship. It would be asking too much from him—and too much from her. "Just. . .slow down a bit."

"Meli," his chest heaved a sigh. "I've been about as slow as a snail."

Her eyes flashed. "And suddenly you're a grasshopper—jumping all the way to marriage?"

"Maybe." His eyes turned down at the outer corners, reminding Melissa of a doleful puppy. "But only because I love you."

"Oh, Luke," she cried out. "I love you too, but—"

"You do?" he cut her off. This was news—very good news, as far as he was concerned.

"Of course I do. *But*—" She put her hands up to prevent him from embracing her again. She wouldn't be able to think if he was holding her. "But marriage is not something I can consider. Not yet, at least."

"Then what *would* you consider?"

She shrugged her shoulders, uncertain of how to respond. Then a sudden thought jumped into her brain, and she decided to run with it. She slanted her head to the side, squinted her eyes, and asked, "How about if we try. . .'courting?' "

Luke blinked. *Courting?* That was the last thing he had expected her to suggest; yet he had to admit that he found the idea very appealing. Granted, it was old-fashioned, but somehow, it sounded nice.

Reaching for her left hand, he brought it up to his lips and planted a light kiss on her knuckles. "Does that mean. . .will you be Lizzy to my Darcy?"

Melissa giggled before she could stop herself. "You've read *Pride and Prejudice?*"

"Required reading, English Literature 101." He smiled, and ran his thumb across her jaw. "But I think, dear Meli, upon further consideration, I would prefer you in the roll of Emma—from the book by the same author. She's a lady with some spunk," he chuckled. "A lot like you."

Melissa gasped. "You've read *Emma* as well?"

"Well. . .I saw the movie."

She laughed, a lighthearted trill. "That's cheating."

"So how about it?" he plowed ahead, unperturbed. "Will you play Emma to my Knightly?"

Melissa tilted her head to the side, as though she were giving his proposal careful consideration. "Does that mean that you will be as courteous —and patient—as dear Mr. Knightly?"

"As long as you remember, my dear," he tried his lame English accent again, "that at the end of the story. . ." He paused for maximum effect. "They marry."

"I'll tell you what," she tossed back at him with an impish grin, "I'll remember how the story ends, if you'll forget that English accent."

"My dear lady, you have yourself a deal."

Chapter 5

As springtime blossomed into summer, Luke courted Melissa like a hero right out of Jane Austen. It wasn't exactly the relationship he wanted, but at least it appeared they were moving toward his goal.

Marriage.

Melissa bloomed along with the flowers. She became happy and carefree, and for the first time in a long time, she was at peace. Luke had the satisfaction of knowing that he had helped her find that essential ingredient to a happy life.

With summer came warm, lazy Saturdays at the cabin, eating salad and fresh lake trout and rowing and swimming in the lake's serene waters.

But one soft, late summer, cricket-singing day, while they were lazing around on the dock after a swim, courting was suddenly no longer enough for Luke. With the same familiar surge of passion he had felt for her many times before, he knew he needed more of a commitment from Melissa. He needed at least the promise of something more.

He watched as Melissa stretched herself out on a chaise lounge she had dragged out onto the deck. He stood up from where he had been sitting on his beach towel and shook droplets of water out of his hair. Melissa leaned back and closed her eyes to the warm rays of the sun. The glow of the sun on her face was more than Luke could stand.

Taking care not to cast a shadow on her face until the last possible moment, he bent over and touched his lips to hers, reveling in the refreshing, delicious way they tasted.

Her eyes opened and he stepped back with a sheepish grin on his face. Before she could protest, he whispered the words he had spoken once before, "Be the half that makes me whole, Melissa. Marry me."

He smiled, but the look on Melissa's face erased his joyful hope in an instant. Months had passed since his last proposal, and his love for her had grown more deep and intense. Still, he wasn't sure he could take another negative answer from her. He needed her. He needed her to say yes.

His eyes narrowed and a muscle tensed in his jaw as he waited for her response.

"I want to, Luke," she finally admitted on a whisper. Sitting up, she looked out over the placid water and tried to make sense of the jumble of emotions that were careening through her mind.

Luke waited.

"Melissa?" He finally broke the uneasy silence, and she turned back to face him.

"I want to, Luke," she repeated. It was the truth and she had to make sure he believed that. "But, don't you see. . .I'm not a complete half."

"No, Melissa," his voice was deep and definite. "I don't *see* that at all." He started to reach out to trail his fingertips down her face, but he caught himself and rubbed his jaw instead. "What I see, what our months of courtship have shown me, is a woman who is perfect and whole in every way."

"No," she groaned. "I'm not, and I don't want you putting me on some imaginary pedestal. I still have so much to work out," she said, tapping her head, "in here."

"Then let me help you," he encouraged, his eyes so bright with love that she had to look away. She felt horrible for not accepting his genuine offer of support, but she couldn't. To move any deeper into their relationship would kill it. She was sure of it. Shaking her head, she was about to appeal to his sense of logic—which he possessed in abundance—when a bee buzzed behind her left shoulder, sending terror through her system.

"Aieee!" she screamed, with all the fear of a true phobic in her voice.

"It's okay," Luke said. He caught her with one arm while gently pushing his free hand through the air, directing the insect away from her. "It's okay." He soothed her like she was a small child. Though Luke had never treated her phobia lightly, at the moment he didn't mind using it to advance his cause. Long after the bee had disappeared over the calm water of the lake, he continued to hold her and speak softly in her ear. "See, with me around all the time, you'd never have to fear bees—or anything," he laughed, a deep, masculine sound that Melissa had grown to love. "I'd always take care of you, Meli," he whispered.

Swiveling in his arms to face him she replied, "But, don't you see,

Luke? I don't want to have to depend on you."

"Melissa," he shook his head impatiently, refuting the connotation she had placed on his words. "I don't mean to imply that you are some sort of weak little woman, who needs a 'big man' to hold onto. No, I'd be holding onto you every bit as much." He gripped her hand with the urgency of a drowning man. "And wouldn't life be so much better, so much sweeter, if we could hold onto each other?" He lifted their inter-twined hands and kissed the back of hers.

With her free hand, Melissa reached up and ran her fingers across the side of Luke's face. His skin was soft beneath the texture of his beard. "Luke," she murmured, "that sounds so nice, but. . ." She sighed, and lowered her arm in a gesture of defeat, "but something else is missing in my life and until I find out what it is. . ." Her voice trailed off.

Luke wasn't buying it. "Meli," his voice was coaxing, yet firm. "Hasn't it ever occurred to you that I could be that missing something?" Her eyes darted up to his, but Luke could tell by the way her pupils dilated that she wasn't looking at him. It seemed she was lost within herself.

For the first time, Melissa wondered if he could be right. Could the love of a good man, could Luke's love—a love based on both physical attraction and a deep abiding friendship—be what was missing? Was she fighting the very thing that could take all the questions away? Could he be a refuge from her confusion and doubt? She shook her head. If any-thing, she was even more perplexed.

"Let me fill the empty places in your soul," he prompted, almost echo-ing her thoughts. "Meli. . ." He smiled a lopsided sort of smile that always made her insides tickle. "I love you. Marry me."

"Luke. . ." She moaned his name and dipped her head down. "Don't you understand? I want to, but—"

He put his finger to her lips and shushed her. "I know you do. . .and everything else, we can work out later, okay? I want your life to be mine, and my life to be yours. Together," he let out his breath, "our lives become one."

She closed her eyes. It sounded so perfect. "Me too," she admitted. "But. . .is our wanting it. . .enough?"

"Yes," his answer was adamant. "It is." With his voice suddenly husky with emotion, he continued. "Meli, I want to make my home, *our* home; my bed, *our* bed. And I want us to have children together—to see if we can replicate those gorgeous eyes of yours in another, little human being."

Her eyes widened in wonder. "That's just it, Luke. You're talking about a love that lasts forever and passes on to another generation. And I'm just afraid I don't have *forever* in me."

Luke watched her as she sat looking out over the lake. A split second before, his dream had been almost within his grasp. But suddenly, the love of his life seemed remote, untouchable. Ignoring the knot that was beginning to tighten in the pit of his stomach, he said, "Forever plays out one day at a time, Meli. You can't eat the whole enchilada in one bite. But you also don't have to."

She shrugged her shoulders and looked back at him. Her voice sounded weary and flat. "I can't help it, Luke. Here we are, talking about starting our lives together. . ." Her voice trailed off. She sat with her arms clasped protectively around her knees and rested her head on her shoulder, once again staring out across the lake at nothing in particular.

After what seemed to Luke like an eternity, Melissa stood up and turned around to face him. "Luke, I'm missing something that I had as a child. It's like a part of me got left behind. And I feel like I want to go back for it, but I can't."

Luke heard defeat in her tone and it made him feel raw and tense. She didn't have to feel that way. He knew the answer, if only she would listen to him. "It was love, Meli," he said quietly. "It was love from your mother and father. And you feel like it was left behind because they were taken away from you too soon. But you're right; you can't go back, and I can't replace the love of your parents—nor do I want to. But I can offer you a love that is just as genuine, just as pure, and just as strong—if you'll let me."

Melissa blew a long stream of air between her lips. Luke couldn't tell if it was a sigh of resignation or relief. He looked anxiously at Melissa and waited for her to speak.

"Maybe you're right," she conceded. "Maybe love is what I've been missing all these years." She paused and looked nervously at Luke. "But I'm afraid of losing it again."

Luke took Melissa's face gently in his hands and looked her straight in the eye. "Meli, the only thing we're losing is the opportunity to be together and to make each other happy." He looked at her tenderly and caressed the side of her face with his thumb. "Marry me, Meli. Marry me—before Christmas. Let's not lose another day."

Her smile was tentative at first, but soon it spread to light her entire face. For the first time, she saw a world filled with hope, a world filled with love—and Luke. Tears came to her eyes and she nodded her head with determination. "Yes, Luke. I will marry you!" She threw her arms around his shoulders, knocking him off balance. He took a step backward and the two of them toppled off the pier together. They surfaced, splashing and laughing, hugging and kissing. "If you're willing to have me, confusion and all, then I'm the luckiest woman in the world!" Melissa spluttered.

Luke shook his head and said joyfully, "No, Meli, I'm the luckiest *man* in the world," he corrected. When they were safely back on the dock, he swept the wet hair away from her face, pulled her into his arms, and kissed her boldly.

❧

For one blissful month, they were extremely happy, reveling in their professed love for each other and making excited plans. They set the wedding date for exactly one year to the day after their first meeting. Congratulations and good wishes came from their friends, and bridal showers were given for Melissa. After struggling to trim their guest list down to a somewhat manageable number, they sent out the invitations. Luke's family in Greece, including his godfather, his sister Anastasia, and her husband and young daughter, and of course his parents, made plans to attend.

Luke continued to encourage and reassure Melissa of his love for her, but from the moment he placed a diamond solitaire engagement ring on her finger, he noticed a subtle metamorphosis take place. Though he didn't want to acknowledge that she was changing, he sensed her gradually growing more distant, detached almost, from the wedding plans, and from him.

Melissa tried to hide her anxiety, but the uncertainty she felt about their future gnawed at her, bit by bit, a little more each day. As the leaves of autumn gave their final colorful dance to the earth, and later, as the trees' bare branches lay bravely silhouetted against the steely sky, nagging doubts hounded her, a growing fear that became more paralyzing with each passing day.

She didn't want to hurt Luke, but as their wedding day loomed closer, her thoughts were consumed by a temptation to run away to a safe place, a refuge from the torment of her mind. The cabin, which had once been such a wonderful haven, no longer soothed her. When she wasn't with Luke, she spent more time in her room than ever before—the one place that seemed reassuringly familiar.

Two weeks before the wedding, while Melissa was out shopping with her aunt for bridesmaids' gifts, someone broke into the Kincaids' mansion and ransacked the house. In addition to countless valuables stolen from almost every room in the house, Melissa's aunt lost irreplaceable jewelry, and Uncle Bob's collection of Civil War memorabilia, which he had painstakingly assembled over the years, was completely gone.

When the thieves had finished downstairs, they had entered Melissa's sanctuary and taken everything of monetary value—and then had the audacity to steal her wedding dress.

After the police finished cataloging what had been stolen, Melissa was relieved to close the door to her room and block out the sound of her aunt's angry tirade down the hall. Slowly, she picked her way through the debris in the middle of her floor. Casting her eyes around, she didn't know which way to turn. The room didn't feel as though it was her space—her refuge—any longer. Clothing was scattered all over the floor and books lay tumbled and torn from her shelves. Even her bed had been rudely pulled apart when the thieves looked for valuables under the mattress. Her dressing table, with its array of expensive perfumes, had been wiped clean. Nothing remained on the marble surface except a few coins the intruders hadn't bothered to grab.

Melissa felt as though the room had been contaminated, fouled by an unknown enemy, and she shuddered. She didn't want to touch a thing. But she knew she had to. The rest of the house was such a wreck that no one would be available to help her sort out the mess in her room.

Rubbing her hands down the length of her jeans, Melissa decided she had better start somewhere. She stepped over a smashed ceramic bunny, bent down, and picked up a large, black book that had been flung into the middle of the room. When she turned it over in her hands, an involuntary gasp escaped her throat. It was her father's Bible.

In their frenzied search through Melissa's room, the burglars had dislodged the Bible from the back of the bookshelf where it had been stuffed and forgotten years earlier. Melissa felt the texture of the leather cover and smoothed the corners of the pages that had bent when the Book was tossed across the room. She had a sense that what the thieves had cast aside as worthless was the only thing of lasting value that she owned.

Clutching the Book close to her heart, Melissa sank to the littered floor. A tear slipped out of the corner of her eye as she remembered the wonderful and special moments when her father had read to her mother and her from this same Bible. How could she have forgotten those times for all these years? And like a veil had been lifted from her mind, she remembered how her father had lived by the precepts and commands written on these pages. In that instant, a flicker of understanding ignited in her heart. Like a tottering child taking its first wobbly steps, she began to understand why she had felt lost and vulnerable for so long.

Slowly, reverently, she opened the pages of the Book, and began to read.

Chapter 6

L uke paced the floor of his apartment like a lion in a cage. Melissa had just called to tell him about the burglary, and he was seething.

He was angry that someone had dared to invade her home—and angrier still for the impotent way it made him feel. He wanted to take care of her, to protect her from everything bad—and now this! He slammed the palm of his hand against his thigh. The burglars had proven the futility of his efforts.

He had wanted to go over immediately, to comfort Melissa, support her, help her clean up. But she had assured him that she was fine—actually better than fine, under the circumstances—and she didn't need his help. Her gentle and unintended put-down was like a punch in the stomach to Luke. He had become so accustomed to hearing doubt and vulnerability in her voice that her calm refusal of help took him off guard. And when she had told him, with a new and bewildering serenity, that she needed to discuss some important matters with him the next day, a shiver of apprehension had sliced through him like a scalpel.

She seemed strangely unaffected by the burglary. Something more was on her mind and he knew that he wouldn't rest until he found out what it was. He wished that it was two weeks down the line. He wanted Melissa as his wife more than ever. He needed her. And he needed her to need him. And at this point, he would do anything—anything—to ensure that she would walk down the aisle on the appointed day.

Flopping his large frame down on the sofa, he picked up a medical journal and absently started to read. Studying would hold him over until he saw Melissa. Studying had always helped him get through his problems.

❧

The next day, Luke thought his appointments with patients would never end, but by midafternoon he was driving across town toward the Kincaid estate. When he arrived, he was surprised to see Melissa standing outside the gate at the end of the long driveway. Before he had a chance to unbuckle his seat belt and come around to open the door, she yanked the door open and slid into the seat.

"This is a surprise," he said, leaning over to kiss her. But before his lips could find hers, he noticed that she wasn't wearing any makeup and dark circles underlined her eyes. He reached out and touched the half-moon shadows. "If the robbers stole all your makeup, that's okay with me, but these circles are a concern. They're your body's way of telling you that you need more rest, more sleep."

"I know. . . ," she said softly.

"But Meli, if you couldn't sleep, why didn't you call me? I know you wouldn't have wanted a sedative, but I could have prescribed some warm milk and boring conversation with me to help you get to sleep."

Without a word, she slid her hands around his neck and pulled him closer, nuzzling her nose just below his right ear. He knew she loved to do that—and he definitely liked it—but she hadn't been quite this friendly for several weeks. "How about some of that 'world famous' hot chocolate, Doctor?" she murmured.

"Sounds good to me," he said. "Let's grab some milk and head over to my place." He reached for the handle to put the car in gear, but Melissa placed her hand on his arm to stop him. "Luke, the cocoa sounds wonderful, but there's something we need to talk about, too."

Luke glanced at Melissa and from the somber seriousness of her lips, which were drawn into a tight line, he knew there was nothing simple about what she wanted to say. His stomach muscles tightened.

"Does this have anything to do with the robbery?" he asked weakly.

She looked down at her diamond engagement ring, the only piece of jewelry she had left, and twisted it. *Does it have to do with the robbery?* she wondered. *I suppose in a roundabout way it does.* If the thieves hadn't thrown her father's Bible into the middle of her room, she wouldn't have found it and read it—and the life-changing stirrings in her heart would still be dormant. But she knew that Luke didn't know about any of that. "No, it has to do with us," she said simply.

The knot in his stomach pulled tighter. Facing forward, he put the Jeep into gear. "We'll talk at the cabin."

They drove in silence, and hot chocolate was the furthest thing from their minds.

❧

The cabin was freezing. Luke quickly set to work lighting a fire in the huge stone fireplace and Melissa went from window to window opening the shutters. Then, while Luke fussed with the kindling, she went into the kitchen to prepare two mugs of coffee. "We forgot to stop for milk, so I guess it's coffee time."

They both liked instant coffee. Melissa drank hers black, but Luke preferred his Greek style. Melissa knew the recipe and he could hear her making the necessary preparations. She measured two spoons of sugar, one heaping spoonful of coffee, and one teaspoon of water. He didn't have to turn around to know that she was sitting on her favorite stool at the kitchen bar as she stirred the concoction.

He also knew that her eyes were on him. They burned into his back as hotly as the leaping flames in the fireplace were warming his face.

The new fire popped and sizzled, the metal spoon stirred and stirred, a hollow sound against the inside of his favorite ceramic mug. The outside world was hushed, as if waiting breathlessly for the big news.

The stirring stopped and he could hear Melissa adding boiling water to the whipped sugar and coffee, the finishing touches on a steaming cup of coffee with a frothy, golden top. The moment of truth had arrived.

He glanced up at the Christmas tree they had decorated the previous weekend. He was almost envious of the little man-and-woman ornament he had found for the top of the tree. Their world never changed. They were perpetually happy.

He felt Melissa come up behind him and smelled the aroma of the coffee. "Here you go, sweetie," she said.

He didn't respond for a moment. He didn't want the moment to change. He wanted the warm feeling of the fire and the quiet calm of the cabin to last forever. He was afraid that what Melissa wanted to talk about would change everything forever. Finally, he shifted his eyes away from the wooden couple on the tree, stood up and turned to face Melissa.

She held out the mug to him. Its tranquil woodland scene mocked him. "It's nice and hot," she coaxed.

Taking it from her hands, he put it to his lips and took a swallow.

The steaming beverage slightly burned his throat, but it felt good. "Thanks. It's perfect. Just the way I like it."

She smiled, and her smile held wisdom, sadness, and love all wrapped up together. It only served to deepen Luke's confusion.

Melissa turned to walk over to the armchair. Luke caught her hand in his before she moved out of reach and motioned toward the *flocati,* the sheepskin rug that his sister had sent from Greece the previous Christmas. "Let's sit together. You can lean on me."

He started to sink himself down onto the thick, woolly rug, but paused when he felt Melissa hesitate. It was an almost imperceptible hesitation, a tenth-of-a-second stutter, but like an electrical current, it ran all the way down her arm to the tips of her fingers.

The tiny pause spoke volumes. Melissa's eyes met Luke's, and he knew, with 100 percent certainty, what was flashing through her mind.

She was going to break the engagement.

A muscle twitched in his jaw, but his resolve was set. He wasn't going to let her off the hook.

Releasing her fingers, he settled his long body onto the rug and with his eyes implored her to join him. He thought for a moment that she was going to refuse, but she didn't. When she sat down, he pulled her into the crook of his arm—she fit so perfectly—and rested his cheek against the freshness of her hair. As always, it reminded him of the bluff above his sister's home on the shore of the Ionian Sea, smelling faintly of rosemary and honey.

They sat close together, quiet, still, and watched the flames dancing in the fire. They sat for so long that Luke began to consider that he might have misjudged her intentions. But when she turned her eyes up to meet his, his hope plummeted into the pit of his stomach again.

"Luke, I—"

He kissed her, cutting off her words. Her lips were warm, but dry and offered no response. She pulled away, but Luke could feel her reluctance. "Luke, I don't want to hurt you, but—" She rushed on, wanting to get the words out, "I've been so unfair to you. I—"

"Meli," he cut her off and begged her, with eyes that were both sad and knowing, to be silent for just awhile longer.

She looked at him the same way she had the night they met, gazing deeply and fully into his eyes, and nodded. She knew that he suspected what was coming, and she settled back in his arms. Luke sensed that she needed the time as much as he did.

Taking his right hand in her left, she squeezed it, intending to comfort him. But the cold-to-the-bone feel of her skin didn't soothe Luke at all. Instead, it shocked him. If he had needed any concrete evidence that her decision was wrong, he had it now. If breaking up made her cold, then Luke was certain that he must stop her before the chill reached her heart.

He reached across her to grasp her other hand. Freezing too. Raising both of her hands to his lips he blew his warm breath on them.

"Oh, Luke," she murmured, nuzzling her icy nose against his warm neck. "What are we going to do?"

Luke knew the only thing he *could* do. Wrapping his arms tightly around her again, he held her, rocked her, kissed her. They clung to each other as if they both sensed that this might be the last time. Their silent embrace spoke far more eloquently than words.

Luke felt her shiver and shifted his chest to cover more of her back. He couldn't hold her any closer, but he flexed his arms to tighten his grip.

With an apologetic "Oh!" Melissa pulled away from Luke and swiveled around to face him. "That hurt," she said.

He looked at her with a tortured expression on his face. "Sorry, Meli. You know I would never try to hurt you."

She started to reach for him and he thought she was going to touch his face; but instead her hand went to the heavy gold chain around his neck. She pulled gently on the chain and drew a gold pendant out from beneath his sweater. Luke watched as she cradled the piece of jewelry in her hands almost reverently. He looked down at the heirloom gold cross that his godfather, his *nono*, had given him the day he had graduated from medical school. The words "May God bless you always, Son" were inscribed on the back.

"Your cross," Melissa said, as if the two words explained everything. "I know I've seen it before, but I never really noticed it."

"Why the sudden interest now?" he asked guardedly. His voice sounded sharper than he had intended, but he was wound up tighter than a new coil and couldn't help it.

"Luke. . ." She licked her lips and spoke tentatively. "Something happened to me last night. Something amazing, actually."

An involuntary shiver ran down Luke's neck.

"Your cross reminds me of what was so special about my parents."

Something inside of Luke wanted to interrupt her, to stop the words; but he felt like the barren trees outside trying to stop the icy north wind from whipping through their branches, and he knew there was nothing he could do but listen.

Melissa rubbed the cross again, oblivious to the chill that had settled in Luke's heart, and continued her explanation. "My parents loved each other, but even more, they loved God. Their great love was possible, Luke, because they loved God first." Her eyes searched his, imploring him to understand. "Honey, God is what—" She shook her head, correcting herself. "No, God is *who* is missing in our lives." There was awe in her voice, as if she had just made the greatest discovery of all time. "God," she repeated softly.

With a crashing finality, Luke felt as though his world was collapsing around him.

Chapter 7

Luke stood up abruptly, and Melissa had no choice but to release her hold on the gold cross.

"What are you talking about?" he asked. But he already knew the answer, and he couldn't—wouldn't—deal with it. His parents were "good Christians." They hardly ever missed a Sunday service, but they had missed—by a wide mile—how to treat their fellow human beings, and especially their children.

"I'm sorry, Luke." She stood up, and taking a step toward him continued, "but until we get ourselves straightened out with God, I can't marry you."

"*God?*" he exploded. He turned his back to her and stared out into the darkness beyond the picture window. "You're confused, Melissa," he said sharply.

She nodded her head. "You're right, I am," she agreed. "Which is precisely my point."

"You don't *have* a point," he said acidly, and for the first time he didn't care if his words stung her. "You're afraid of bees, you're afraid of commitment, you're afraid of yourself. And now you want to hang all the blame for your problems on God." He swiveled around to glare at her and was amazed to see that she was smiling.

"I think you're exactly right, Luke. I am afraid of myself. My life is tumbling forward, slip-sliding out of control and—" She paused before dropping her voice to an imploring whisper. "Don't you see? I have to put everything—everything—on hold until I learn—"

"About God?" Luke finished her sentence with a derisive laugh.

Melissa nodded. "Yes, about God," she said firmly. Luke rolled his eyes. Ignoring his rude response, Melissa continued. "Last night, Luke, in the middle of the mess the robbers made of my room, I found my father's Bible." She shook her head. She was still amazed by the unusual

51

turn of events. "Anyway, I think it's the place for me to start finding out about God. . .and the cross. . .you know, exactly what it stands for." She reached out and took the gold cross in her hand again.

This time, something exploded inside of Luke with the force of an atomic bomb. He had never raised his voice to Melissa before, but he was shouting now. "Here, take it!" He yanked the necklace from around his neck and rudely slipped the chain over her head. "You seem to think it's some sort of talisman, a good-luck charm, that holds all your answers—"

"No, Luke," she said, shaking her head and cutting off his verbal rampage. He turned his back on her and walked angrily across the room. Melissa watched as his breath heaved his shoulders up and down. She felt wretched, helpless, and totally confused by his explosive response. She was accustomed to hearing venomous remarks from her aunt, but this was a side of Luke Karalis she had never anticipated. But she also knew that there was no going back, only forward. She had to make him understand how she felt. Speaking to his back, she tried again. "I don't think a cross is a good-luck charm, Luke. It's a reminder, a symbol of God—somehow." She laughed sadly. "I've seen it as a piece of jewelry for so long that I don't know exactly," she admitted. She quietly turned toward the fire.

When she started to speak again, Luke somehow had the feeling she was talking more to herself than to him.

"Strange, isn't it? I've read thousands of books, but never once have I read the Bible." She took a deep breath. "But thanks to the break-in, I've found the Book—the actual Book—that was the center of my father's faith. I've discovered the same Bible that he used to read to my mother and me." Luke was intrigued by the faraway quality of her voice. He turned to look, but when he saw that she was lost in her own little world, his curiosity turned back to anger. He felt as though he were suddenly of secondary importance to her—if she even still cared about him at all.

"But I'm going to read it now," she was saying. "I'm going to read every word."

He looked at the gentle curve of her hips and how her ebony hair cascaded over her shoulders, and he was reminded of the first time he had seen her and called her *melissa*—the social bee flitting from one group to the next at the Christmas ball. But now, in his anger, he thought *sersegia* was a more apt description. The *sersegia* were killer bees that buzzed during the summer months in Greece. That's what she was doing, killing a part of him that he doubted would ever find life again.

Melissa had stopped talking and she was looking at him as if she expected an answer to a question he hadn't heard. Instead of responding to her, he launched into his own little diatribe. "Who are you, Melissa?" There was a steely quiet to his voice. "A little girl who is frightened of the unknown? Or a woman who likes to break engagements, to sting the men of your life with a stinger you keep well hidden until it suits you to use it?"

His sudden reference to her previous broken engagement hit her like a solid punch to the stomach. Closing her eyes and whispering a prayer for strength—the first real prayer of her adult life—she responded with a gentleness that surprised her and completely disarmed Luke.

"I don't think I'm either of those, Luke. I'm just a woman who's confused and has been for a long time. But I think I've finally figured out where to find answers." She paused for a moment and then said, "And I just want you to know about it too, and to explore it with me—together."

She looked at Luke and smiled sweetly. He realized with a helpless feeling that there was nothing he could say.

"I don't want to break our engagement, Luke," Melissa continued. "I just want us to wait a while to get married. A few more months, maybe," she suggested.

"A few months?" he mocked.

"Luke, I love you. But I've been filling my days with senseless activities for so long that I've never learned who Melissa Kincaid is, or what she believes. You've been pushing me to get married, and I finally said 'yes,' but before I can think about building a marriage, a home, and a family with you. . .I have to learn who I am. Please. . .give me some time so I can be the wife you need."

In a deep, far-off corner of his brain, Luke knew that what she said made sense. It was even logical. But even more logical was the thought that invitations had been sent and guests were planning to attend their wedding—in less than two weeks!

Casting aside her argument without comment, Luke tried a different tack. "Melissa. You do realize that my sister, Anastasia, her husband and daughter, my godfather, some close friends, and my *parents* have all made arrangements to come from Greece for our wedding?"

"Luke!" For the first time, exasperation sounded in her voice. "We can't get married just because it would upset our guests' plans if we don't. I'm not ready to walk down the aisle. I have to—"

"Sorry, Melissa," he cut her off, speaking her name as if it were an unpleasant word. "You can't have it both ways."

"Both ways?" She was surprised at his stubbornness. She had expected him to be upset, but not like this. She didn't want to break up, just postpone things awhile. "Luke! All I want is a little more time!"

"No." He was adamant. She had taken all the patience he had to give. There was nothing left.

"Why?" she asked.

He remained silent.

"Luke, just a little time," she pleaded again. A quivering fear began to creep in at the corners of her mind—and she was terrified at the thought of losing him. For months he had been her only security in this very scary business called life, and it had never occurred to her that he wouldn't give her the time she needed. He had given her everything else she'd asked for.

"No." The answer was flat, final.

She looked at him with an expression that he couldn't quite read. He saw unshed tears begin to pool in the corners of her eyes, but even when her shoulders slumped and she reached down to pull her engagement ring from her finger, he saw a strength in her that he had never seen before. And it was a strength that had nothing to do with him.

She gave him the ring, but when her hands reached up to remove the cross, he encircled her wrists with his fingers, stopping her.

"It's yours."

She looked up, confused. "I can't keep your cross. It's part of your heritage, part of your family."

"My family," he said with a sarcastic snort. "Funny, but I thought you were going to be my family in another two weeks."

She tried to remove the necklace again, but his hands tightened around her wrists. "Don't you see? The ring would bind me to you, but the cross frees me from you. I would never wear it again after today, anyway. You seem to love it—so you might as well have it." He dropped his hands and walked across the room to the Christmas tree.

"You're wrong, Luke," Melissa said as she followed him across the room. "The cross binds me to you much more than the ring ever could."

She clutched the shiny pendant tightly in her hand, and said, "I don't know why, but the symbolism behind the cross seems a whole lot stronger than the significance of the ring. And when I can explain why that is, I'll give it back to you."

"You do that." Reaching up to the top of the tree, he angrily grabbed the little man-and-woman ornament and tossed it into the woodpile.

"Luke, I understand how you might be frustrated, but your anger is really disturbing after all the times you've told me you loved me."

He turned abruptly on his heel and walked into the kitchen, where he filled a container with water. Striding purposefully back into the living room, he poured the water on the fire. "This is what our love has become, Melissa." The fire went out, leaving only a sizzling pile of soggy ashes. "Black ash and smoke."

"Luke, please," she implored again. "Even after all the hurtful things you've done and said today, I still love you—and not like ashes and smoke." Luke glanced over his shoulder at her. "Let's not break up," she continued. "We can postpone our wedding and do it right—when *we're* right."

Luke didn't say a word. He finished putting out the fire, and when he had dumped the last of the ashes into the can outside, he slid behind the wheel of the Jeep and waited for Melissa to lock up the cabin. The drive back to town was as quiet and as lonely as anytime he could remember.

❧

For the next two weeks, Melissa spent every spare moment with her nose in her father's Bible. When Jane Bond heard about the broken engagement—and why—she called Melissa and invited her to church the next Sunday. The pastor's sermon on the love of God touched Melissa deep in her heart, and when she met with the pastor the next Monday, he explained the good news in a way that made a lot of sense to her. As Melissa studied and prayed, the significance of the cross—and her understanding of the Christian faith—grew and grew.

On the day that should have been her wedding day, Melissa gave her life to Christ, and by the following week she was ready to face Luke and tell him about the cross—the one and only foundation on which to build their love.

But by then it was too late.

Luke was gone. He had disappeared without a word to anyone.

Dr. Robert Kincaid was livid when it became apparent that the young surgeon was not going to return, and he blamed Melissa for causing the situation. Their relationship, which had always been distant, became even more strained. Melissa's aunt could barely look at Melissa without becoming angry, and she spoke to her niece only when absolutely necessary.

When loneliness and regret washed over Melissa over the next several months, she visited the shuttered cabin at Lake Breeze to think and dream and pray about Luke.

Her love for him had never been stronger.

Chapter 8

Greece
Eighteen months later

The picturesque ruins of the Byzantine castle of Beauvoir sat atop a jutting peninsula overlooking a vibrant blue bay, where a public swimming beach belied the area's bustling ancient and medieval past. Olympia, about twenty miles to the east, once had its seaport here and artifacts of those early days still could be found deep beneath the waves, where only divers can read the archaic story.

Luke's history—on his father's side—was here too. But he wasn't thinking about the past as he gazed across the undefined horizon from the verandah of a modern fortress of stucco and marble.

He was thinking about the future.

He fingered the letter in his hand before glancing down at Melissa's neatly penned words. He didn't need to read them. After nearly a month, he knew every word on the scented pages.

I'm going to be in Greece researching the country's castles. I'd like to see you. I want to give you back your cross... Luke reached up and rubbed his fingertips against the back of his neck, where the clasp of the chain would have been if he still had it. *I know the meaning behind it now...*

But after more than a year of missing her, Luke knew the meaning behind the cross, too. It meant death. It had taken her from him and destroyed their love. Melissa had loved it—and whatever she thought it stood for—more than she had loved him.

He balled up his fist, inadvertently crushing the letter in his hand. Sweet Melissa. Lovely Melissa. Confused, hurtful Melissa. The only woman Luke had ever loved.

He'd wanted to be everything to her. Instead, he'd become nothing.

He tilted his head upward as military planes from the nearby air force

57

base blasted out from behind the extinct volcano to buzz over the sprawling villa, shaking its windows. Luke laughed, but it was a mirthless sound. Melissa was about to invade his home, and he could only hope she wouldn't drop any bombs.

As the subsonic vibrations of the jet engines faded out over the Ionian Sea, they were immediately replaced by the insistent buzz of a giant bee, a *sersegia*. The segue in the sound fascinated Luke.

With narrowed eyes, he watched the bee as it moved to and fro above his head. He remembered how scared Melissa had been of the smaller bees up at Lake Breeze, but he had never been afraid, even of *sersegia*.

As he watched in amazement, the bee suddenly alighted on the square nail of his left ring finger. A frown flicked across his face. His first impulse was to shake it off, but his scientific mind restrained his reflexes. As he sat in the cool, symmetrical shade of a stoic cypress tree, he scrutinized the insect as it crawled up his finger and settled just below the third knuckle.

Five times bigger than most bees, the *sersegia* was like seeing a normal bee through a magnifying glass. The difference was that this specimen was very much alive—and very, very dangerous.

"You're playing a deadly game," Luke's friend, Gabriel Crown, warned as he walked up beside him. "Remember what it did to me last summer."

The chief of security at the American embassy in Athens, Gabriel had almost lost his life to a *sersegia* sting the previous summer. Except for cortisone, adrenaline, and Luke's skill as a physician, the bee would have accomplished in peaceful, rural Greece what years spent in war-torn countries hadn't managed to achieve. Luke's lips thinned as he remembered gravely that Gabriel had almost been done in by a bee.

"How delicate, beautiful—vulnerable even," Luke observed. But when the bee turned and he could see the barbed stinger, it took every bit of his self-control, and the steady hand of a surgeon, to avoid a quick movement. Long, sharp, and threatening, the stinger was not something to treat lightly. "And how menacing—just like Melissa," he muttered.

"Get rid of it," Gabriel ordered, taking command of the dangerous situation. "And get over it," he said with a wry lilt in his voice.

Luke ignored Gabriel's comment. He was engrossed in his analytical case study of the bee—in all its connotations. "Melissa's 'stinger' wasn't as openly apparent," he muttered sardonically to himself. "In fact, until the day of the 'sting,' I didn't believe she had one. One that she would use, anyway."

The bee on his finger began to buzz—a warning. For an instant, as it lifted off and hovered above his hand, something primitive, a primeval force deep inside him, demanded that he flick the insect to the ground and crush it with the heel of his shoe. But again, Luke didn't move. Instead, he watched as the *sersegia* charted its course down over the sweet-smelling bluff to the deep, blue sea below.

Luke was about to heave a sigh of relief, when Gabriel knocked the wind out of his sails with a sharply spoken question. "If Melissa upsets you so much, then why did you invite her to come?"

With narrowed eyes, Luke turned to look at his friend. Gabriel's tall, slender build and professorial goatee belied the iron that lay beneath his fair skin. Luke knew that Gabriel was a professional security man, who calculated risks and took protective action.

"I don't want Anastasia hurt by Melissa being here," Gabriel continued, and Luke understood what Gabriel's concern was all about.

"It's my business," Luke said defensively and flicked an accusing glance over his left shoulder toward the crumbling fortress, as if it were somehow responsible for his problems.

"If it were just your business, I would honor your decision," Gabriel persisted. "But it doesn't concern only you. Anastasia's well-being is at stake and I don't think it's wise for you to invite 'trouble' to come for a visit."

"I would hardly describe Melissa as 'trouble,' " Luke shot back.

Gabriel's voice was even and low. "I look in your eyes, my friend, and I see trouble."

Luke's hard, green eyes met the steely, unflinching gaze of his friend.

"It's still my business," Luke reiterated, but the nervous coil in his stomach, which had never quite relaxed since the letter from Melissa arrived, tightened a few more notches.

Gabriel shook his head and spoke deliberately. "Anastasia—she's both of our concern."

A sarcastic smile twisted Luke's mouth. "Tell me, friend. How can you love a woman who barely greets you, even after weeks of separation?"

Luke watched as Gabriel looked out across the water toward the blurry line where the sea gave way to the sky. He thought the fuzziness of the horizon somehow matched Gabriel's love for Anastasia. Hazy. Unclear.

A love Luke couldn't fathom.

When at last Gabriel spoke, it was as if he were speaking to some far-off place that his eyes couldn't see, but which he knew existed. "I remember her before the accident when she was. . .whole. . . ." His voice trailed off for a moment. "And I remind myself that God can restore the woman inside, even if He chooses not to give her back her legs."

Gabriel looked at Luke with eyes that were sad, yet caring. But what struck Luke the most was that Gabriel hadn't returned anger for anger. Luke had intended to skewer his friend, but he came away knowing that he was a lesser man for attacking the love his sister was so fortunate to have. He flexed his shoulders as if to shrug off imaginary talons that were digging into him. He didn't like people questioning his judgment, but Gabriel wasn't just anybody.

"I'm sorry," Luke said. "I don't know what made me say that."

Reaching out, Gabriel patted Luke's upper arm. "I do, and even if you don't want to hear it, I'm going to tell you." Gabriel spoke without malice, and Luke turned his head to look at his friend. "You're jealous of the love that I have for your sister, broken and depressed as she might be, because you wanted to love Melissa in the same way—unconditionally, with all her foibles—but you ran away when your love was tested."

Luke looked away and shook his head. He knew that part of what Gabriel said was true. But only a small part. "I did love Melissa," he declared. "But she wouldn't have me."

Gabriel exhaled loudly and Luke had to admit that, even to his own ears, his assertion sounded shallow and childish. "Are you sure that's how it was?" Gabriel finally asked. Before Luke could answer, his friend stood up and said, "Well, I've already said good-bye to Anastasia and little Emilia. I've got to get back to Athens. I promised my pastor that I'd be on hand to help welcome in refugees from the east that are due to arrive tonight."

Luke nodded. "I'll see you in a few weeks."

Gabriel smiled, a strong sure curve of his lips between his mustache and his goatee, and Luke knew that their friendship was intact. Maybe even a bit stronger. The coil in his gut loosened a turn.

"Right. I'll see you then," Gabriel said. He turned and walked to the stairs, but before he started down, he paused and turned back to look at Luke. "You know, Melissa's probably changed. Give her—you—a chance."

Luke returned Gabriel's smile, but he knew, deep within himself, it was the change in her that he feared the most.

The church bell clanged from the little whitewashed chapel at the far end of the bay, and Luke tilted his head toward the sound. Despite his reservations about Gabriel's religion, he admired Gabriel's devotion. But what most impressed Luke about his friend was that, except for a worn Bible that he carried around with him, Gabriel didn't wear his religion like a mantle of righteousness. He didn't even make a big deal over missing the Sunday morning service to spend the time with Anastasia.

Luke remembered that his parents had never missed a service. But church had always been, and still was, nothing more than a big social event for them. He frowned. *Everything* was a social event for them. But for Gabriel Crown, religion was something more. Luke didn't understand it—and didn't want to—but he knew it was something more.

His frown deepened as he considered how it didn't bother him that his best friend was religious, but when Melissa had started talking to him about God that day at the cabin, he had become livid. He remembered feeling as though his place in her heart had been usurped by some far-off God. The difference between Gabriel and Melissa was that Luke didn't mind if Gabriel's heart was filled by God. But with Melissa, he felt threatened.

He glanced at his watch. She wasn't due to arrive for another two hours.

His head pounded. He wanted to blame it on the heat, but he knew the sultry afternoon was only part of his problem. Undoing a shirt button, he looked out over the bay. A bee—a *melissa*—buzzed in front of him. The amber and black insect brought his mind back to the amber and black beauty of Melissa Kincaid's eyes. He didn't want to think about that. He couldn't. He willed himself to focus instead on the sound of children laughing and frolicking in the warm waters off the beach below the villa. He knew that his little niece, Emilia, was probably right in the middle of the action. He smiled at the thought of his olive-skinned niece, the joy of his life. He only wished that Anastasia was still able to care for her daughter.

For a long time now, Luke had felt that Anastasia just needed something, some sort of catalyst, to get her back into the act of living again. He could sense that his sister wanted to change her life. She just needed a reason to do so. All the old reasons, including Gabriel's love, had become stale.

He expelled a deep breath and rubbed his hand against the side of his neck, where the chain he had worn for years would have been if he hadn't given it to Melissa. He missed the cross. As it turned out, its absence had reminded him of Melissa much more than if he had worn it. As if he had needed a reminder.

For the first time since he fled from Ridgedale, Luke considered the possibility that he had acted too quickly in breaking up with Melissa. "Just a little more time," she had pleaded. But he had refused her. *Dumb.*

Luke finally admitted that he was willing to give their relationship another chance. If only he hadn't been so reactive, so headstrong, they might have been married by now. Maybe there was still hope. But no sooner had he felt his spirits begin to rise, than the memory of the issue that had divided them came crashing in and set his mind spinning again. The whole matter was exhausting, and Luke suddenly realized how tired he was. He needed to sleep before he would be able to face Melissa.

Glancing down at his watch, he decided to follow the custom of the country for once and escape the oppressive heat of the afternoon by sleeping it away. Standing and stretching, he turned and walked into the welcome coolness of the house. Upstairs in his room, he shrugged out of his damp shirt and flopped onto the bed.

Just before he drifted off to sleep, he thought he heard the sound of a buzzing bee caught in the folds of his curtains. His last thought before he began to snore was that he wanted to set it free.

Chapter 9

Melissa rubbed her hand across the outline of the cross that lay hidden beneath her dress. Except to bathe and swim, she hadn't taken it off since the day Luke had angrily given it to her. She never would have agreed to keep it if she had known that he would disappear before she could give it back. She had intended to return it to him within a few days—weeks at the most. It had never occurred to her that eighteen months would pass and that she would have to travel halfway around the world to find Luke.

But at least now she had a pretty good idea of what she wanted to say—*if* she could get the words out while looking into Luke's beautiful green eyes. With the help of her pastor and her friends at the church who had invited her to join their weekly Bible study, she now understood the meaning of the cross. But that was the easy part. The other half of her dilemma was to repair the breach in her relationship with Luke, which had resulted from their argument at Lake Breeze. She wasn't quite so confident about that. She'd thought and prayed many times during the past year and a half about what had happened to them. After much soul-searching she had decided that even though she had made a mess of trying to explain why she couldn't marry him as planned, Luke needed to be held accountable for running away without so much as a word to anyone. If he hadn't finally written to Uncle Bob to settle his contractual obligations with the clinic, she might never have known for sure where he had gone.

As she maneuvered the small sedan along the highway out from Athens, she let her mind drift back to that eventful day at the cabin. She hadn't wanted to break up with Luke; she had simply needed more time. And after the blowup, she had at least hoped for an opportunity to return the cross and explain to him what she had learned.

She rounded a bend in the road and Chlemoutsi Castle suddenly

63

loomed on the horizon. She looked at the grand Frankish castle and was reminded of the steps that had led her on this journey.

She had never been especially interested in ancient history before Luke left Ridgedale, but his disappearance had started her on an interesting path that eventually culminated in an in-depth study of famous fortresses.

By studying her father's Bible, she had learned that God was the only real source of security in the world. But when she was honest with herself, she knew that she still looked to Luke to fill that role. She had expressed her conflicting emotions to her new pastor and he had responded by giving her a study Bible with a concordance and telling her to look up all the verses in the Bible that had the words "security," "refuge," "fortress," "rock," and "stronghold" in them.

At first, she had thought it was a strange combination of words, but it didn't take her long to see how beautifully those words were intertwined in Scripture and to learn that they all pointed to the Lord as the only source of true security.

Tightening her grip on the steering wheel, she marveled at Chlemoutsi's gigantic walls as she recited some of the wonderful verses she had found in Psalm 18: " 'I love you, O Lord, my strength,' " she said with renewed understanding. " 'The Lord is *my* rock, *my* fortress and *my* deliverer; *my* God is *my* rock, in whom *I* take refuge.' "

She paused thoughtfully as the castle receded in the rear-view mirror. *"My* rock. *Mine,"* she repeated with feeling. " 'He is *my* shield and the horn of *my* salvation, *my* stronghold.' " She touched her hand to her heart and patted it. "Mine." And it was as personal a prayer to her as it had been to David, the shepherd, the king, who had first penned it three thousand years ago.

A few minutes later, as she turned off the main highway onto the country road leading to the little seaside village of St. Andreas, where Luke now lived, she prayed Psalm 18 again as a reminder that God was with her on this most important journey.

She repeated the psalm until she rounded a curve and she saw the ruins of the little fortress of Beauvoir, which she knew sat above Luke's home. She saw the sign, *Villa Beauvoir,* Luke's home, and drew in her breath. She felt her pulse quicken as she turned onto the long, cypress-lined drive.

Luke stood on the verandah, a glass of iced coffee in his hand, and looked out over the driveway. He felt refreshed by his deep afternoon sleep and decided he was as ready as he could be for Melissa to arrive.

He hooked his shoe around the banister as his eyes scanned the long ribbon of asphalt leading up to the house. An angry cloud of dust billowed above the tall cypresses, and he knew that Melissa had turned in from the road. When a small orange sedan came bursting through the trees—like a ray of sunshine on a dreary day—Luke's heart pounded with an emotion he hadn't felt in a long time. Was it happiness, uncertainty, or fear? He couldn't tell. The only thing he knew for sure was that the one woman he had ever loved was coming toward him.

"Melissa." He whispered her name. Behind his dark glasses, his eyes softened into a smile.

Chapter 10

A golden arm reached out the open window of the car and waved. That was it. A simple wave, natural and sure—and hauntingly familiar.

A few seconds later, the car came to a rolling stop and Melissa turned her face toward him with a look of bright openness and a huge smile. Something inside of Luke—something good that wouldn't allow past anger and bitterness to ruin the magic of the present moment—sent all his negative emotions shuffling off to a far closet of his soul.

The pounding of his pulse drove him forward. Removing his sunglasses, he bounded down the stairs and walked briskly across the driveway. When he reached the small sedan, he was surprised to see that he still had his iced coffee in his hand. Setting the glass gingerly on top of the car, he braced his hands against the metal rim of the driver's side window and leaned down to eye level with Melissa. She looked up from gathering her purse and folding the map and looked at him with her sparkling amber eyes.

Luke felt suddenly alive. It was a familiar yet long forgotten sensation. A small smile creased the corners of his mouth. "Welcome to St. Andreas, Melissa."

Her smile widened. When Luke swung the car door open, she didn't hesitate. Stretching out her legs, she stood up, and for the first time in more than eighteen months, they stood face-to-face, with less than a hand's length between them.

They looked deeply into each other's eyes.

She wanted to touch him, hold him.

He wanted to touch her, hold her.

Neither one moved, but the air around them seemed to vibrate with electricity. Then, as naturally as a wave rolling to the shore, their arms went around each other and they eagerly embraced. Melissa's nose found its favorite place just under Luke's right ear and his chin rested against the top of her head, just as it always had.

Heart to heart, they beat to the same rhythm.

Luke felt it.

Melissa felt it.

They clung to each other and savored the moment as the heat of the day wrapped itself around them like a blanket of warmth, of comfort, of protection.

Luke breathed in the soft scent of her hair. She smelled like spring-time on the Ionian Sea. Every time he'd opened a window or stepped outside and caught a fragrant breeze from the bluff below the house, he had dreamed that she was about to appear.

He squeezed her gently closer. He could hardly believe she was there and he was holding her. The anger and bitterness of their last conversation was as far from his mind as it could be. It was almost as if that day at the lake had never occurred.

Easing her back to arm's length, he took in the full measure of her beauty. "You look great. Just the same as ever," he said with a hint of wonder in his voice.

She looked at him with a twinkle in her eye and said, "Yep, the packaging is the same, but the insides are brand-new!"

His face immediately clouded and he took a step back. Things were not the same as ever—or maybe they were. He was remembering the days of their courtship, when even the thought of her made his pulse quicken, but maybe the gulf that had sprung up between them eighteen months before was too wide to bridge, and the water too deep to cross.

Cross. The cross. With a nervous shake of his head he glanced down at the front of her dress. At the neckline, he could see where the heavy gold chain disappeared beneath the light cotton fabric.

Following the path of his eyes, Melissa knew immediately what he was thinking. Unconsciously, her hand moved up to her chest and she felt the gold cross. It was a gesture she had repeated countless times in the past year and a half.

"I still have it," she said shyly. But when she saw the ambiguous haze in his eyes, she moved quickly to lighten the mood. Her eyes darted quickly around the area and she spied the iced coffee on the roof of the car. "Hey, you're still drinking iced coffees, I see. Mind if I have a sip?"

She reached for the half-empty glass.

"I'd be happy to make you a fresh one," Luke offered, shifting smoothly into his role as host.

Melissa shook her head. "Just a sip of yours will be fine." She suddenly longed to drink from his cup. Wrapping her fingers around the frosted glass she brought it to her lips. The cool liquid filled her mouth, refreshing and sweet. It was so totally Luke. He had introduced her to iced coffee their first summer together, and there was something familiar, something intimate about drinking it from his glass again. It was a link with their past—a happy link.

She brought the glass to her lips again and took a long, slow swallow. With an embarrassed giggle, she handed the nearly empty glass back to him. "Oops. I didn't realize I was so thirsty."

"Neither did I," he said, and his voice was deep and husky. Melissa had been a woman long enough to know that he was referring to a different kind of thirst. And from the way his lips drew together, she knew that he was about to kiss her.

With timing so perfect that it couldn't be coy or teasing, she stepped away from him and waved her hand at the surrounding beauty. "What a gorgeous home," she said with genuine appreciation. "And just look at Beauvoir." She turned to gaze up at the crumbling tower. "It's enchanting."

"Pondicokastro." Luke automatically breathed out the name that the locals called the fortress, and Melissa was buoyed by the hope that the difficult moment had passed.

"Mouse castle," she quickly offered the translation. "But the question is, was it called that because it was overrun by mice or because this peninsula looks like a scurrying mouse when viewed from the sea?" She tilted her head back to look at him.

Luke chuckled. It was as if they were back in time, discussing the hills and forests around Lake Breeze, with Melissa speculating in her soft southern accent about the early history of the colonial United States. Luke suddenly realized that her voice was a soothing balm—something else that hadn't changed. "Probably a combination of the two," he offered, bringing his thoughts back to the present question.

"Probably so," she agreed.

"How did you get involved with studying Greek castles, anyway?" he asked with genuine interest. After all, they were the reason she had come to Greece.

"Because of you."

Such a simple answer, and exactly what Luke would have hoped to hear if he had given it any thought. He didn't know what to say next, so he didn't say anything.

Melissa was quiet, too, but it wasn't an awkward silence. Instead, it was a silence wiser than a million words and more healing than a thousand apologies. In the absence of conversation, the earth played a loving tune around them. The scratching of the cicadas, the children romping on the beach, the sheep bells clanging in the distance, combined into a lullaby, a sweet symphony of sound that was simple and basic and exactly what they needed.

With a casual sweep of his hand, Luke reached out and caressed Melissa's cheek with the back of his hand. "Look, Melissa, there's a lot that we need to talk about, but I think—" He paused. "I think this time —we have the time." Her eyes widened at his choice of words, but she remained silent.

For a moment longer, Luke stared at the horizon—still hazy and undefined in the summer heat. "I don't know, Melissa. I was probably wrong. I should have given you the time you asked for that night."

Joy as bright as an exploding star filled Melissa's heart. She had not expected him to admit he was wrong—at least not right away. Maybe reconciliation would be easier than she thought. She smiled at the thought that they could be back together and discussing their future—together—maybe as soon as this afternoon! She squeezed her eyes shut in thankfulness, not realizing that he was watching her—and was totally misreading her reaction.

To Luke, it looked like she was reveling in self-righteousness, perhaps even gloating over his admission. Something burst inside of him, a deep and ugly wound that had been festering a long time. Slamming his fist down on the railing, he snarled, "Why, Melissa? Why?"

Her eyes popped open.

"Why?" he repeated. In a voice that was low and ominous, like a growling German shepherd, he continued, "I went to your house on the day we were supposed to get married to tell you that I would give you your precious time."

"You came. . .to see me?" Melissa shook her head, bewildered. The thought flashed through her mind that her aunt might have contrived to keep them apart. But nothing had ever been mentioned at the Kincaid mansion about Luke stopping by.

"Oh, yes, fool that I was, I came. But you. . . ," his lips thinned, "you had already moved on."

"Huh?" She took a startled step back. She hadn't moved out until six months after Luke's disappearance. The gnawing suspicion that her aunt was somehow involved became more intense. Her throat went dry as she tried to respond. "Luke," she rasped. "What are you talking about?"

A muscle twitched in his jaw. "On the day of our wedding, I came back to you—"

She shook her head vigorously, denying that he had.

"Don't tell me I didn't!" he snapped angrily. "I drove up and saw you at the gate of your uncle's home hugging another man. You didn't even look up when I pulled the Jeep up to the curb. That was all I needed to see. I left."

"I. . .was hugging. . .a man?" she repeated, totally baffled. There had not been another man in her life since Luke. And if she had her way about it, there never would be another. She searched her brain for what he could have seen, and when she remembered, she felt herself go cold all over. Rubbing her hands up and down her arms, she asked, "Luke. . . do you mean, we've been apart all this time because. . .of what you think you saw that day?" Her voice was high and tight.

"I didn't *think* I saw anything. You were standing there with this *guy* in broad daylight—and I don't need glasses."

"Luke. . . ," she fairly wailed. "He was the pastor from my new church. The *pastor*," she repeated the title. "He and his wife had just driven me home. She was sitting in their car with their two children. Luke, it was a comforting hug."

It didn't surprise Luke to hear that there was a reasonable explanation. Still, it had made his blood boil to see her in the arms of another man— whatever the reason—and he had used his anger at that moment as an excuse to leave her behind. But he wasn't going to apologize. She had called off their wedding and changed their lives, and that is what he had focused on for the past eighteen months—her fault, not his own. "I see," was all he said, his jaw hard and unyielding.

70

"Maybe *you* see," she fired back. "But I don't 'see.' Why did you leave Ridgedale without at least saying good-bye? And why didn't you ever write to me?" She hadn't wanted to land her two main punches, like a cornered prize fighter, quick and hard, but she couldn't stop herself. Those questions had plagued her far too long, and his stubbornness made an inviting target.

"Like I said," a mask seemed to slip over his features, "I think we have time to talk about the past. . .and the present—later. Let's get you unpacked." He slammed the car door shut to emphasize the end of the conversation.

Melissa shrugged and opened the car door to retrieve her purse. She would wait for the right moment before opening the discussion again. Patience was something she had learned while waiting to hear from Luke for all those months.

Luke was surprised when she calmly dropped the subject. He had thought that she would fight him, but when she turned from gathering her purse, all she did was push a few stray hairs behind her left ear and stand up straighter, as if on the alert. It was a familiar gesture that reminded him of before.

Almost, but not quite.

When he'd known her before, an insecure look would always accompany the straightening of her spine, as if she weren't quite sure that she could stand up to him. But now, even with their disagreement fresh in the air, there was openness and light in her eyes. She wasn't fazed by his outburst. Luke suddenly realized that she was a mature woman, who knew who she was and what she wanted out of life. He knew that he should feel glad, but her new confidence only made him feel uneasy.

He took the keys from her hand and went around to the trunk of the car to remove her luggage. He'd spent the past year and a half immersed in bitterness, while she had been doing exactly what she had asked for time to do: figuring out who she was and what she wanted. He realized that he was completely unprepared to face the woman Melissa had become.

He slammed the trunk lid much harder than he had the door.

"Hey," she laughed, trying to make light of the situation. "I have to give this car back in one piece!"

"Sorry," he murmured. She reached into the backseat and pulled out a pink guitar case. He raised an inquisitive eyebrow and asked, "When did you start playing?"

"Shortly after you left."

His sharp look made her wish she had been more diplomatic. She knew what he was thinking: *Another change.*

"Do you play well?" he asked and covered his eyes with his sunglasses.

"I'll play for you later and let you decide," she bantered, but he didn't pick up on it. His face was grim and strained. He wasn't in the mood for chitchat. Lifting her two suitcases, he motioned for her to follow him up to the verandah.

As they climbed the steps, Luke was lost in his own thoughts. He was amazed by what Melissa had done. All the changes made him very uncomfortable, but he had to admit they were good changes, healthy changes. The Melissa he had known before would never have volunteered to play for him. She would have coyly dismissed her abilities and gone on to another subject. He couldn't help but wonder if she realized how much she had changed.

Melissa knew. And she knew that the cynical change she saw in Luke was because of her. She had hurt him. He thought that she had rejected him that day in the cabin, and then again when he had come to see her at the house, even though she hadn't seen him. But she hadn't rejected him. She had only begun to accept God and she hadn't known enough then to explain it to Luke. And he'd left before she could.

But she had the opportunity now and she was confident that her Lord—her Rock—had directed her steps to this man for just that reason. Looking up at the little fortress of rock and stone on the hill above her, she thought about what the prophet Isaiah had written: "Trust in the Lord forever, for the Lord, the Lord, is the Rock eternal." Melissa nodded. She would always remember to trust. The reminder brought a peaceful smile to her face.

Luke chose that moment to turn around to look at her. Her serene expression nearly knocked the breath out of him. She seemed to glow from emotions that were light and clean and good, and the contrast with his sour disposition was not lost on Luke. He wanted to be happy, and to feel good about seeing her, but an overwhelming sense of failure, of deficiency, swooped in on him. He wanted to be the one to bring her such joy. But she had done it without him—perhaps even in spite of him.

He considered the possibility of another man in her life. She had the look of a woman in love and jealousy hit him like a boulder. All the pain, bitterness, and anger that he thought he had put away, now slithered out of the distant closet of his soul as he wondered who had given her what he hadn't been able to give.

Melissa saw his shoulders tense and she knew that something was tormenting him. She was about to ask him a question, when the distant ringing of a phone interrupted her sentence before it even started.

Over his shoulder Luke called out, "Soula, I'll get it," and when he turned back to her, Melissa was certain that he was glad for the excuse to get away from her.

"My housekeeper will show you to your room, where you can bathe and rest," he said. His tone was clipped and hard, the voice of an adversary, not a friend. Not waiting for her reply, he dropped her suitcases and turned and walked away.

She watched until the darkness of the house's interior swallowed him, and then, sighing, she placed her guitar next to her suitcases. Wearily, she reached for the wrought-iron lounge chair in front of her and sank her tired body into the soft, floral printed cushions.

She was spent. It had been thirty-five hours since she had seen a bed, and she suddenly felt fatigue in every moving part of her body. The emotions she had sensed in Luke just now had tipped the balance. The long air trip and the long drive were nothing compared to the dosage of raw anger he had just measured out.

It was as if his soul were tormented, which she had never seen before, and a shudder passed through her as she realized that she had most likely caused him to become like that. Guilt, like a sudden storm, swept through her. But she knew it was guilt that she had to get rid of.

Dear God, she prayed. *Dear God, what did I do to that man?* Instinctively, she reached inside the neck of her dress for the cross. *What did I do to him?* Her feelings of guilt made her heart beat too fast and her skin flush in panic. The last thing she had ever said to Luke was to ask him for more time. Granted, two weeks before their wedding date was poor timing. But she hadn't wanted to break up. She'd just wanted more time. And she hadn't left town. He had.

But still, reason didn't add up to what she had just witnessed in him. He was tormented by something. But what?

Dear God, she breathed out a plea for help. Twisting her head to the side, she spied the little castle on the hill and the words from Psalm 46 ran through her head.

"The Lord Almighty is with us; the God of Jacob is our fortress."

God was her fortress. He had been with her in the United States and He was with her here, an ocean and a continent away. She didn't understand what she had done to Luke to fill him with such anger—but God did. And that was good enough for Melissa.

She would give the feelings of guilt—which were about ready to consume her—over to God. And she would run to His arms, to her Fortress in times of trouble. She would take refuge in Him just as the people of this land had once sought safety from the enemy in the little fort on the hill.

Melissa knew that Luke wasn't her enemy, but guilt was. If guilt had its way, her life with Luke would never become what she wanted it to be. And only God could protect her from guilt.

She closed her eyes and with the lulling sound of the cicadas soothing her, and the words of the psalm running through her head, she fell into the deep, undisturbed sleep of a child who knows that her loving Father is close by.

Chapter 11

Soula completed snapping the beans she was preparing for supper and hurried onto the verandah as fast as her arthritic legs would carry her. She was prepared to meet a sophisticated woman with high heels and pearls, stylishly sitting in wait and coolly surveying the sea, like the few friends who still came to visit Anastasia.

What Soula found instead was a sleeping girl so innocently beautiful that the maternal instincts in her blossomed. Lowering her large body onto the stool beside the lounge chair, she sat and stared at Melissa.

She finally understood some of Luke's pain. To have been engaged to this exquisite creature and then have it called off would have been torture for any man—even one who had a loving family to fall back on. But Luke had only Anastasia, and after the accident, she needed more understanding and support than he did. His parents had given him money—plenty of it—but that was no substitute for their love and concern, which had always been lacking.

Melissa stirred and Soula hastily stood, not wanting to be caught staring. But when Melissa's hand relaxed its grip on the object that hung around her neck, the housekeeper gasped, a loud sound that echoed across the marble verandah.

"Soula? What is it?" Luke asked, as he walked up behind her.

"Shhh. . ." Soula put a warning finger to her lips. *"Kemate."*

"She's sleeping?" He stood next to Soula and looked down at Melissa. He liked having the opportunity to look at her with her eyes closed; he liked not having to confront the shining radiance that spoke so plainly of another love. But as he searched the soft contours of her face, the peacefulness became almost more than he could bear. It sent his blood pounding and he wanted to gather her in his arms, wrap her close, and awaken her with a million kisses.

He shook his head and glanced at Soula.

He was startled to see her looking him right in the eye. Her hands were planted on her ample hips and her blue eyes bored into him like they had when he was ten years old and she had caught him and her son Kostas lying about where they had gone to swim. She had been almost like a mother to him and right now he felt like he was ten years old all over again.

"Soula?" His brows drew together. "What's wrong?"

"You told me that you lost it," she accused in a loud whisper.

Not understanding, Luke's frown deepened. "Lost what?"

With a jut of her chin and fire in her eyes, Soula indicated the gold cross that Melissa still clutched.

Luke's eyes widened when he saw the heirloom that his godfather had given to him. It lay nestled in Melissa's hand, mocking him, haunting him with memories of Lake Breeze. *'I'll give it back to you when I can tell you the meaning behind it,"* she had said. The pain of that day was suddenly as fresh as if it had just happened.

"Did she steal it from you?" Soula demanded from his side.

Luke quickly clicked his tongue and tilted his head and eyebrows upward—the Greek sign for "no." "No, Soula. She didn't steal it."

"No?" Luke heard doubt in Soula's voice and he sighed, knowing that he owed her an explanation.

"No. . ." He paused to choose the right words. "But I did tell you the truth. The symbolic truth," he qualified.

Soula shook her head. "I don't understand."

"I *did* lose the cross," he turned back to Melissa, and he felt his chest tighten. He could almost believe that she was still his *Meli*. His eyes flicked to the cross. Except for that cross, she would been his wife. But how could he explain the situation to Soula? He didn't want to tell her that Melissa had been much more in love with his cross than with him. Somehow he knew that wouldn't sound right to the older woman's ears. In fact, Soula would probably think that Melissa had been right to choose the cross and what it stands for over him. And that thought wasn't something Luke wanted to consider. He had always valued Soula's simple wisdom, but this time, he didn't want to hear it.

"What do you mean?"

"I lost it at the same time I lost her." He wondered what else he could say. But he didn't have to say another word. True to her trusting personality, Soula was satisfied with his explanation.

"Well, I have some beans to attend to," she said. Gently squeezing his upper arm in the comforting way she had done since he was a boy, she turned and waddled on her arthritic legs back into the house.

Luke watched her go and then turned his attention back to Melissa. In the lingering heat of the early evening, her cheeks had grown rosy and a tiny rivulet of perspiration tickled the lobe of her ear. She began to stir and Luke took a step backward to avoid the impression he had been hovering over her.

He watched as her hand—the same hand that had once worn his ring—moved over the cross, hiding it, a split second before her eyes opened. When she awoke, she had the foggy look of one who isn't quite sure where she is. Luke wanted nothing more than to lean over her, to kiss her, to remind her. But he didn't.

"Luke?" There was question in her voice, as if she didn't quite believe her eyes.

He swallowed the lump that had formed in his throat. "You fell asleep." His voice was raspy. He tried to clear it.

Smiling, Melissa extended her arms and stretched. Luke wished that they were reaching for him. "I'm sorry. I guess traveling straight through finally caught up with me." She breathed out as she finished, and Luke forgot about the lump in his throat as fear sent a shot of adrenaline coursing through his system.

"Didn't you stay the night in Athens?" He'd assumed that she had flown into the city the previous day.

She shook her head. "I arrived from the States this morning." She paused and looked at her watch. She still hadn't set it to local time and it showed nine A.M. "At least," she smiled sheepishly, "I think it was this morning. I picked up the car at the airport and drove straight here."

"Straight—?" The thought of her being in a car accident scared him to his core. "Don't you know that you shouldn't drive when you're tired?"

"I slept on the plane, Luke. I wasn't tired while driving," she pointed out logically, calmly.

But Luke wasn't listening. His attention was taken up with trying to get a handle on his wildly churning emotions. At one moment he wanted nothing more than to take her in his arms and be fully reconciled, but in the next instant he was so angry with her he could spit.

Right now he was at the spitting end of the swinging pendulum. With a wide, dismissive wave in the direction of the pendant around her neck, he fired out, "Is this the reason you risked life and limb to get here?"

She glanced down and cringed when she saw the cross on the outside of her dress. She hadn't wanted him to see it yet. She'd envisioned giving it back to him so many times. But not like this. Never like this. Not with anger ruling the moment. She wasn't about to return it the same way she had received it.

"I wasn't risking my life," she responded with a self-controlled calm that took all of her concentration to accomplish. Sitting up, she pushed her hair to the side in order to slide the chain over her head.

Luke stopped her. "No. I don't want it."

She paused in midmotion, leaving the chain dangling halfway over her head. "Luke, it's your cross. I told you that I would give it back to you when I could explain—"

"I don't want the cross and I don't want to hear about it," he cut in. Reaching abruptly for her suitcases, he changed the subject. "Let me show you to your room."

With a sigh, she let the chain fall back into place and stood up to follow him into the house. Picking up her guitar case, she trailed behind him as he went through the French doors and into the house's cool interior.

The living room was long and wide, white and cold. Meticulously decorated in a contemporary Mediterranean style; it looked like it should enhance the pages of *Beautiful Homes* magazine. But somehow, like her aunt's house, it lacked the feeling of a true home. Melissa ran her hand across the white fabric of one of the three sofas and wondered if it had ever felt the warmth of a human body. She found herself daydreaming about how she would add some warmth, some life—if she ever got the chance.

When she snapped out of her reverie, she found Luke waiting for her at the south end of the long hall.

"What a lovely home," she said automatically, but her sweet southern accent made it sound like a genuine compliment.

"Thank you." His reply was formal and distant.

She walked into the room he indicated. It was dark, but when Luke brushed past her and opened the shutters a few inches, she was happy to discover that it was a friendly room with a lived-in feeling. Decorated in

78

soft blue and ecru with a patterned parquet floor, the room was regal, but comfortable.

"We keep the shutters closed against the heat of the day," Luke said. "This room gets the afternoon sun." He pointed to the ceiling fan and then toward the switchplate on the wall near the door to the adjoining bathroom. "There's the switch should you need it."

She nodded and crossed to the shutters. "Is it still too early to open them completely? I don't want to miss the show."

"What show?"

"The sunset."

"As I said, this room gets the afternoon sun. But if you want to swelter, be my guest." He shook his head in annoyance. "Dinner is at eight-thirty," he tossed back over his shoulder as he walked back into the hall.

"Eight-thirty!"

He poked his head back into the room. "This is Greece, Melissa. People eat much later here." His mouth quirked in a dry line. "But in deference to your eating habits, I will ask Soula to set out a plate for you at six on the verandah."

It sounded to Melissa like he was offering to leave a bowl out for the dog. From the way his mouth moved, she knew he was trying to annoy her. She didn't rise to the bait, but answered sweetly and honestly, "Thanks. I'll wait. My tummy is completely confused as it is. I may as well get on the Greek schedule immediately." Peering out through the partially opened shutters she said, "Besides, I think I'd like to take a swim in your famous Ionian Sea." Turning to face him, she asked silently with her eyes—as she had so many times before at Lake Breeze—for him to accompany her.

Luke ignored the invitation. "Fine. But the bay is deep, so be careful," he warned, just before clicking the door shut.

"As if you care?" she said under her breath, unable to stop her self-pitying thought. She was relieved that the thick door stood between her words and him.

But Luke had heard her and as his hand left the door handle, he flinched. *My problem is I care too much,* he thought angrily as he walked down the hall. He stopped to listen at a door ten feet from Melissa's. There was no sound from within. There never was. Not even a radio or television left running for company. He glanced down at the crack under

the door. Dark as expected. It was obvious that Anastasia wasn't anticipating a sunset "show."

As always, the silence bothered him and he was tempted to peek inside
to make sure his sister was okay. But seeing her sitting listlessly in her
chair or sprawled inelegantly on the bed was worse than wondering, so
he kept on moving.

Taking the steps two at a time, he headed for his home office and the
blessed relief—blessed oblivion—of his medical texts.

Chapter 12

Melissa didn't go swimming. As wonderful as the sea looked, the bed looked even better. She set the blue alarm clock on the Swedish pine night table for seven o'clock, switched on the ceiling fan, and fell asleep as soon as her head touched the pillow. She didn't awaken until the ringing of the clock forced her eyelids apart.

She awoke refreshed and remembered immediately where she was. She smiled, and swinging her legs to the side of the bed, she raked her hair back from her face and padded on bare feet over to the cracked shutters. Placing one hand on each leaf she pushed the wooden panels wide and a breath of wonder escaped her as her eyes took in the magic of the summertime evening that was laid out before her like a set from a play.

The bay of Saint Andreas was washed by a rainbow of muted colors. The cobalt blue water shimmered with the light of a million little diamonds that seemed to have been tossed upon its surface, and the sky glowed all red and pink and orange. An island of volcanic stone caught Melissa's eye. Long and skinny, a natural breakwater, it lay on the seaward side of the bay.

Feeling rested but lazy, she turned back to her room, which was painted in violet and pink by the light of the setting sun. She plunked herself back down on the bed. After a moment of stretching and yawning, she rolled over to the foot of the bed, reaching for her luggage, where Luke had abandoned it on a bench. She rummaged around in her large suitcase for her blue silk dress. Pulling it out, she was relieved to see that the steam from a shower would easily remove the few creases in it.

The water coursing down her body refreshed her in a way that only a shower can after a long journey. She stood directly under the spray for a few moments before lathering herself and washing away the grime from her dusty trip. While she bathed, she prayed that the Lord would wash away the hardness of heart that was so evident in Luke and give her the grace and the courage to speak honestly with him about the new joy in her life.

Wrapping herself in a thick bath towel, she unpacked her luggage while her hair dried in soft curls around her shoulders. When her clothes were all put away in the stately armoire along the side wall, she slipped into her dress, applied a tinge of blush and a streak of peach lip gloss and brushed out her hair. Then, stopping just long enough to retrieve her guitar from its pink carrying case, she answered the call of the setting sun and stepped out onto the verandah outside her room.

Balancing her guitar against a chair, she stood at the railing and inhaled the beauty of the sea and the sky and the land. Glancing up toward the little castle of Beauvoir, she reminded herself that she had to visit the ruins. After all, it was her excuse for traveling to see Luke. The western wall was bathed by the red light of the sun, a timeless spotlight on the scene, and Melissa heard herself whisper the words of Psalm 91: " 'He who dwells in the shelter of the Most High will rest in the shadow of the Almighty. I will say of the Lord, "He is my refuge and my fortress, my God, in whom I trust." ' " She smiled again at the fortress, picked up her guitar, and seated herself on a patio chair. Lovingly, her fingers moved over the guitar's sound hole and neck as she started softly finger-picking the tune to Martin Luther's ageless hymn, "A Mighty Fortress Is Our God." After a moment, her deep, feminine voice added the lyrics to mingle with the melody of the strings.

Her voice was peaceful and sure, a natural sound of praise every bit as much a part of the land as the swallows who sang as they found their homes for the night. One hymn led to another until only an orange glow remained in the sky. Melissa finished off with the song she had started and then sat cradling the guitar in her arms as she marveled over her first sunset in Greece. Peace washed over her like a gentle wave. Singing the ageless hymns had readied her to face whatever might come her way.

"Bravo!" A woman's sarcastic voice sounded from behind Melissa's right shoulder, followed by staccato clapping a split second later. Melissa swiveled around to see who it was and slammed the neck of her guitar against the rattan table. The instrument moaned in protest and Melissa found herself face-to-face with a faded young woman in a drab, institutional gray robe sitting in an equally drab gray wheelchair. Melissa quieted her guitar by placing her palm over the vibrating strings and waited.

"You sing very nicely," the woman said, but behind the flattery of her words, Melissa saw pain and envy in her eyes. In an instant, those raw emotions were concealed by haughty indifference.

"Thank you," Melissa murmured. When she turned, she noticed another door opening up onto the verandah further down. "I'm sorry. I didn't realize that we shared the same verandah. I hope I didn't disturb you," she offered.

"Disturb me?" The woman tilted her uncombed head upward in the Greek mannerism for "no" and answered her own question. "How can someone who doesn't do anything be disturbed?"

Melissa knew that the question didn't require an answer so she didn't even try. "Are you visiting here?" she ventured to ask, and watched as something close to amusement flickered in the woman's face.

"You might say that." She paused and with the timing of a born thespian, added, "I own the place."

Melissa's brows drew together. Luke had told her, back when they had been together, that he owned an apartment in Athens. She had assumed that he'd sold it when he moved here. Her frown deepened. Surely this haggard young woman wasn't—

"I'm Anastasia Petros," the woman stated, answering Melissa's unspoken question. "Better known as the house invalid," she explained with a sour twist of her lips.

Melissa's mouth dropped open. "*You're* Anastasia? Luke's sister?" she gasped, but she could have shot herself the moment the insensitive words left her mouth. It was just that this woman was so different from how Luke had described his fun-loving, vivacious sister.

"Amazing, isn't it? For such a handsome man to have such an ugly sister?"

"You're not ugly," Melissa rejoined and knew it was true. Even behind Anastasia's unkempt appearance Melissa could easily see the beauty of her classic features, which were much like Luke's, only finer and softer. To Melissa she looked like a person who just didn't care enough to make the effort.

"I don't like people patronizing me." There was a sharp edge to her voice, and Melissa knew that Anastasia was a woman who would brook no sympathy or lies.

"Neither do I," Melissa returned. "But I *am* sorry. I had no idea that this was your home. And neither did I know about—" She glanced down at the wheelchair.

"My useless legs?" Anastasia finished sarcastically. "Why should *you* know?" The emphasis on the "you" was almost unkind, and Melissa shrugged her shoulders helplessly.

"Well, your brother and I did almost get married once."

Now it was Anastasia's turn to be surprised. Shock animated her features as she exclaimed, "You're Melissa!"

Melissa nodded, but in a confused sort of way. It was Anastasia's home. Didn't she know who the guest was in her own home?

"Well, well, well. Things are getting very interesting around here," Anastasia smirked. Pushing her wheelchair closer in order to get a better look she said, "My brother tells me that an American lady is coming to write about our castles—which I think is pretty strange in itself—and now I learn that you're Melissa. *Luke's* Melissa." Like a dog anticipating a tasty morsel, Anastasia practically smacked her lips together. "A drama is about to unfold before my very eyes. How exciting."

Melissa didn't find it at all exciting. But quickly grasping from both Anastasia's appearance and attitude, that Luke's sister was probably suffering from depression and was most likely displaying more emotion than she had in a very long time, Melissa let it pass.

"Oh, don't look so grim, Melissa. You have to forgive me, but since," she motioned with her hands to her legs, "*this,* I don't follow social conventions. Truly, I'm happy that you're here. I'm happy for you, for Luke, and, believe it or not," she gave a short, but powerful laugh, "for me. I need a diversion in life and a good live drama fits the bill nicely," she finished honestly.

"Well," Melissa gave a small smile. "Hopefully there won't be a drama."

"Ha!" Anastasia fired back and slapped her hand against her knee. "Do you love my brother?"

Melissa's jaw dropped. It wasn't a question she had expected, particularly not from Luke's sister. But something inside prompted her to answer Anastasia openly, without minced words. "Yes, Anastasia. I love Luke very much."

The other woman fairly beamed. "Well, there you are. He loves you too. Now all that has to happen are a few arguments, a few love scenes, and a subplot of some sort." She motioned to the paperback book tucked by her side. "I read a lot of romances."

Melissa smiled and nodded her head wisely. "I seem to remember Luke telling me. . .when we were together. . .that you aspired to be a writer."

A distant look, as if she were trying to see something that she had almost forgotten, came into Anastasia's face. "I have a few unfinished manuscripts lying around here somewhere. But that was before—" She stopped speaking and glanced down at her legs.

Melissa took it as an invitation to ask. "How did it happen?" The last time she had talked to Luke about his sister, Anastasia and her family had made reservations to attend their wedding. Melissa remembered that Luke had argued against upsetting their guests' plans by putting the wedding date back a few months.

"An automobile accident," Anastasia whispered, and her face settled into the sad lines that had become a permanent part of the geography of her young skin.

Melissa grimaced. "I'm sorry."

"My husband and my unborn baby boy were killed, and I got a permanent front-row seat on life," she offered quietly.

"I'm so sorry," Melissa repeated, as the horror of the tragedy swept through her mind. She suddenly felt weak. From her personal experience she knew that no words were adequate to express such remorse. "I had no idea."

"How could you?" Anastasia's bitterness was as sharp as a two-edged blade. "It happened—" She clamped down on her words, prematurely ending her sentence.

Melissa quietly finished for her. "After Luke and I split up?"

Slowly, thoughtfully, as if weighing her response, Anastasia nodded. "Yes, that's right. After you split up."

"And your daughter?" Melissa remembered that the little girl, Emilia, had been the apple of Luke's eye even when he had been in the United States.

"She wasn't in the car."

"Thank God," Melissa breathed out.

"I don't think He was in the car either." Acid laced Anastasia's words and Melissa raised her eyebrows. They looked intently at one another for a moment before Anastasia turned her wheelchair away, closing the subject. Melissa let it pass.

This time.

At least now she knew how Anastasia felt.

She blamed God for the injury to her legs and for not saving her husband and unborn child.

Melissa understood. Hadn't she done a similar sort of thing when she had forgotten God as a child after losing her parents?

Better than most she knew that prayer, patience, honesty, and love were needed to break through the wall of anger and pain that encircled Anastasia's soul. In the days to come, Melissa resolved to try to give all that to Luke's sister. Besides, there was something about Anastasia that Melissa really liked. In spite of their differences, they had established a rare and beautiful quick rapport that could lead to a long and lasting friendship. Melissa needed a friend in Greece.

Glancing at her watch she asked, "Shall we go down to dinner together?" It seemed a good place to start.

Anastasia looked up sharply as if she suspected some sort of trickery in Melissa's question. Detecting none, she carefully replied, "I normally eat in my room."

"But then," Melissa wiggled her eyebrows up and down in an attempt to impersonate Groucho Marx, "how do you expect to see the 'drama' between your brother and me if you're closeted away up here?"

"You've got a point there," Anastasia grudgingly admitted. She unconsciously reached up and touched her hair—the universal female gesture that says, *I don't think I look up to par.*

"I'll help you get ready," Melissa was quick to offer.

Anastasia's eyes blazed. "I'm fine the way I am," she snapped, surprising Melissa with her sudden anger. Her emerald green eyes, a shade lighter than Luke's, seem to offer a challenge.

Undaunted, Melissa took it. Looking down at her own silk dress and delicate sandals, with the rhinestones glittering across the front strap, she said, "Oh, then, I must be overdressed." She looked straight back at Anastasia. "Should I put on my bathrobe?"

Anastasia's eyes darkened and Melissa thought that she might have gone too far. But suddenly, as if she finally understood the punch line to a joke, Anastasia laughed. In that moment, Melissa caught a glimpse of the woman she had been before the accident took so much from her life.

"All right. Let's shock my brother. I'll dress," she declared. "But I have one condition."

Melissa tilted her head and held her breath—a lifelong habit. She was already learning not to underestimate Luke's sister.

Motioning toward the guitar, Anastasia softly said, "You have to promise to play your guitar for me after dinner. It's so soothing."

Melissa let her breath out and caressed the smooth wood finish like a dear and true friend. "That's why I was playing," she admitted. "It fills my mind with peaceful images and the hymns calm and edify me."

Anastasia rolled her eyes in amazement. "Now there's a word I haven't heard in a long time—and I have both Greek and English to choose from. Why do *you*," she ran her eyes over Melissa, "need to be edified? You look pretty perfect to me."

Looking out over the now dark sea, Melissa lightly touched the outline of the cross beneath her dress before answering the question. "Everyone needs edification, Anastasia. Sometimes, those who look the most perfect need it most of all."

"And how does playing the guitar *edify* you?" she asked. Mixed with the skepticism in Anastasia's voice, Melissa detected a desire to know.

"It's the words of the hymns," Melissa explained. "They remind me that God is close by, that I've always got my Best Friend with me wherever I go."

Melissa read a mixture of amazement, unbelief, and sympathy in Anastasia's eyes. Yet when she spoke, it was with a gentleness to her words that hadn't been there before. "I have a friend who thinks that way. Gabriel Crown. He's very religious—a great man, though," she added as though being religious would make someone unpleasant. But Melissa knew what she meant. She'd met enough "religious" people in her day.

When Anastasia turned back to her it wasn't with anger but with confusion that she hurled out her words. "But I just don't understand why a God who loves as Gabriel says He does, would allow that accident to have happened. I think of my husband and little baby so often." She shook her head, a defeated gesture. "I can't do anything else because of it," she admitted. "I'm a horrible mother to my daughter—she hardly knows that I'm her mother—and I can't sleep for thinking about them all. To be honest, this," she admitted, motioning to her legs, "is nothing compared to the broken way I am inside. My useless legs don't really bother me. But my husband, my child, my little daughter who has a mother but doesn't. . ." Her voice trailed off into the dark, debilitating place of pain that too many people in the world have visited.

Melissa's heart cried with her. Leaning her guitar against the chair, she went over to Anastasia, knelt down, and wrapped her arms around her slight form. Anastasia immediately dropped her head against Melissa's shoulder, as if her head full of grief had suddenly become to heavy for her neck to support.

"I won't pretend to say I understand how *you* feel having lost so much," Melissa finally whispered, "but I know the anger and pain that *I* felt after losing loved ones of my own."

"You?" Anastasia lifted her head and looked at Melissa through a film of tears. "What happened to you?"

"My parents were killed in an accident when I was twelve."

Anastasia gazed across the verandah, as if she were trying to remember something from the deep, dark past. Slowly, she nodded her head. "Yes. I'm sorry. I had forgotten. Luke told me. Long ago." And then returning her attention to the present moment, she asked, "But how did you cope? You were just a little girl."

Melissa shrugged her shoulders and took a deep breath. "On the surface, I was fine. My uncle and aunt took me in and gave me everything money could buy. But mentally, well, quite simply, I didn't cope. I was confused, angry, superficial, hurt for years, until one night—many years after I lost my parents—burglars ransacked my uncle's house and tore up my room. They uncovered a book that I had stuffed on the bookshelf behind all the latest best-sellers." She paused and looked Anastasia in the eye as the wonder of that day again filled her. "Anastasia, it was my father's Bible. The thieves didn't want it any more than I had. They threw it into the middle of my room. I found it. I read it. And, I found the faith of my father. I cried out to God and I learned that I'm not made—not constructed—to carry all the hurt, confusion, and anger that living can bring to us. I learned after that how to give those feelings to God."

"Fine," Anastasia replied tersely. "But why didn't He save your parents?"

"He did."

"What?" Anastasia shook her head confused. "But you said. . ."

Melissa nodded and explained. "My parents were saved by God by believing that it was the Son of God who hung on that Roman cross for our sins."

"Riddles." Anastasia snorted.

"No. Not riddles. Truths." Melissa licked her lips and while sending up a silent prayer for guidance, she continued. "Look, Anastasia, what most people forget is that this earth of ours is ruled by evil. It was given over to Satan in the Garden of Eden and it has been that way ever since. This isn't home to God's people."

"Fiction," Anastasia snapped, dismissing Melissa's words. But her verbal response couldn't wipe out the question that remained in her eyes.

Melissa saw it. She pressed on. "No, Anastasia. Nonfiction. The truth."

From the way Anastasia's brows moved back and forth, Melissa could tell that she was amazed, maybe even a little envious of what she thought of as Melissa's blind faith. But Melissa knew that faith isn't blind.

"You really believe it?" she finally asked, and Melissa heard awe in her voice.

"I really do," Melissa confirmed. "I also believe that Satan laughed when my parents and your husband and your child were killed. But even more, I believe that God cried. He cried great big tears that were even bigger than my own and even bigger than yours, and then He took our loved ones, wrapped His big arms around them, and put them in a safe place free of pain."

Anastasia shook her head. "I don't know. You talk so much like Gabriel." And then suddenly, as the thought occurred to her, Anastasia asked, "Does Luke know how you believe?"

"Not really," Melissa grimaced. "I tried to tell him once. It's one of the reasons we broke up." She looked directly at Anastasia and was truthful. "It's one of the reasons I've come to see him."

Holding her hands out in front of herself as though reading a juicy novel, and smiling in a teasing way, Anastasia said slyly, "Hmmm. . .the plot thickens."

"Anastasia?" Melissa warned with a laugh, but when Anastasia sighed a heavy sound of yearning, Melissa asked, "What is it?"

Touching first her uncombed hair and then her faded dress, she murmured, "I never used to keep myself like this. I used to be quite into fashion and I was a fun, happy person."

"I know. Luke told me all about you. He adores you."

"Luke," Anastasia said his name and smiled. "I would never have made it even this far without him. He's been everything to me and like a father to my little girl. Emilia has come through all this okay because of him."

Melissa reached out and squeezed Anastasia's hand.

Anastasia squared her shoulders and sat up straight. "You were almost my sister through marriage, and I think," her eyes twinkled in a suddenly playful way, "that someday you might get another chance."

"I hope you're right," Melissa said.

Anastasia reached forward and touched Melissa's arm. "That's something I really like about you. You're real. Truthful. You say what you believe."

"I haven't always been like this," Melissa warned.

"Maybe not, but you are now. And I need that. I need. . ." She paused, and her hand wrapped around Melissa's arm like a vise. "I need someone who hasn't seen me like I've been since the accident. Except for tonight, you haven't, and I don't ever want you to again. My family needs me, but I need a push. I need a friend who hasn't been a part of my grief—one who is only a part of my recovery."

Tears sprang to Melissa's eyes. "Anastasia," she began, "I think many prayers are being answered tonight. I'm honored that you would ask me, but believe me, I need your friendship every bit as much."

"Bah." Anastasia shrugged her shoulders. She hadn't felt needed in so long that she had almost forgotten what a nice feeling it was. "It isn't possible."

"Anastasia, except for Luke, I don't know a soul in Greece. . .in all of Europe for that matter," Melissa reminded her.

Anastasia shook her head, and admiration for Melissa shone in her eyes. "How my brother ever let you get away, I'll never understand. Come on." She pushed on her right wheel to direct her chair toward her room. "I'll take you up on your offer to help me dress. Let's shock my brother." She laughed. "But we'd better hurry." She started pushing the chair. "He gets ornery if he's kept waiting."

Rolling her eyes, Melissa followed and replied, "Some things never change."

Chapter 13

The hum of the elevator drew Luke's eyes away from the medical journal he had been reading. His brows came together in a quizzical frown. *Anastasia?* She was the only one who used the elevator. But he couldn't remember the last time she'd come down to the first floor.

The elevator clicked to a stop, the door opened, and as Anastasia wheeled herself out, Luke sucked in his breath.

The faded gray housecoat she'd worn for ages had been replaced by a soft violet dress with white polka dots, a romantic summertime creation. Luke remembered it from before the accident. Her hair, which had been neglected for so long that Luke had forgotten the difference it made in his sister's appearance, was smoothly brushed and formed a soft, shiny frame around her face. She had even applied just enough makeup to off-set the pallor of her skin—the result of her self-imposed indoor exile.

"Anastasia," he said with a big smile creasing the corners of his face. He tossed aside the journal and stood up. He was speechless.

"Are you trying to suggest that I don't always look this good, dear brother?" She tilted her head saucily to the side, shades of the old Anastasia, and he wondered what had brought about this remarkable trans-formation. He'd often thought that if his sister ever changed from the frumpy recluse she had become, her coming out would be remarkable, given her flair for the dramatic. But seeing it now with his own eyes was beyond his wildest imagination.

He crossed the marble floor with a bounding gait and bent down to kiss her smooth cheek. "Um, no, I wouldn't say that." He scrambled to find the appropriate words. "You look. . ." his voice cracked with emo-tion as his eyes scanned her face, "like my sister again," he finished sim-ply, truthfully.

She rubbed her knuckles against his cheek, something she hadn't done since the accident. "Thank you, big brother," she said, and he heard some of the old jauntiness in her tone. Only the small lines that grief had carved around her mouth attested to how hard she was working to keep up the happy appearance. But the important thing to Luke was that for the first time since the tragedy, she *was* working at it. She was striving to live again.

She took his hand and held it tightly against her face. "For all that you've done for me, Luke, thank you," she whispered. "Maybe, just maybe," she lifted her green eyes to his, "I'm on my way back."

"I hope so, sis," his voice cracked. "Your daughter and I. . .we need you," he answered honestly and stroked her cheek.

The sound of Melissa's heels clicking down the stairs echoed in the marble hallway. Anastasia felt Luke tense, and he quickly stood up and brushed the wrinkles out of his slacks. With a sudden flash of insight, Anastasia understood exactly what her brother had given up to care for her. The woman he loved.

Granted, he and Melissa had broken up before the accident, but Anastasia was certain that if she hadn't needed him so much, Luke would have reconciled with Melissa long before now.

Melissa stepped into the room and both Luke and Anastasia looked at her with the same open expression of welcome creasing their faces.

Melissa paused. She knew that something wonderful was going on. She could feel it. The room did not feel as cold and sterile as it had before.

Anastasia smiled at Melissa but spoke to Luke under her breath in rapid Greek. "I think we both need this lady, big brother."

Luke turned startled eyes to his sister. She had just answered his question about her amazing turnaround. She had met Melissa and Melissa had won her over, every bit as quickly as she had captured his heart two and a half years before.

As Melissa stepped tentatively into the room, Luke left his sister's side and took a step toward her. If his breath had been arrested by his sister's change, it was punched clear out of him by the change in Melissa. When he had seen her earlier in the day, she had been tired and dusty and dressed in a simple cotton dress. Now she was impeccable, exquisite, and as stunning as the first time he'd laid eyes on her.

With his heart in his throat, he held out his hand to her, and without hesitation she reached for it.

He squeezed her fingers close to his.

She squeezed back.

And when their eyes locked, Luke knew deep in the center of his being that, given a choice, he didn't ever want to lose her again. "Anastasia," he spoke to his sister without looking away. "This. . .is Melissa."

Anastasia waved aside his senseless introduction. "Of course she's Melissa," she answered impatiently. "But what I want to know is why you didn't tell me before that 'the Castle Lady' was *your* lady?"

"*Castle Lady?*" Melissa inquired, saving Luke from having to answer Anastasia. Luke looked at her sheepishly and lightly ran his thumb over her wrist. "That's what Emilia, Anastasia's little daughter, calls you. We told her that a lady was coming here to visit Greece's castles and you've been 'the Castle Lady' ever since." He turned at the sound of small feet pitter-pattering down the hall.

"Ah. . .here's our little lady now, coming to say good night." He gently squeezed Melissa's hand before letting go to greet his niece. "I always tuck her into bed and then, about ten minutes later, I take her her favorite doll." He chuckled, sounding for all the world like an indulgent dad. "She conveniently forgets it at the dinner table every night."

Melissa heard the evident pride in his voice and remembered how dearly he had wanted a child—*their* child. Something inside of her almost cried at the thought.

"*Theo* Luke. . ." The little girl came running toward him, soft curls streaming out behind her and cascading down her back. But when her eyes settled on her mother, she stopped in her tracks. As if seeing an apparition, she stood and stared in openmouthed wonder as only a child would do. "Mamma. . .?" It was a question that spoke volumes about the suffering and loss she had endured since the accident. Tears gathered in Anastasia's eyes as she held out her arms to her little daughter.

Slowly, as if tiptoeing across a narrow bridge, Emilia walked to her mother's side. Tentatively, she reached out a small, six-year-old hand to touched the soft brightness of Anastasia's dress before moving her hand to her mother's hair. "Pretty," the little girl said in a tiny, awestruck voice.

"Do you want to sit on my lap?" Anastasia asked quietly.

Emilia looked up at Luke as if to get permission, but as soon as he nodded, she scrambled into her mother's lap.

"You smell nice," the little girl said as she buried her face in Anastasia's shoulder.

"Thank you. So do you," Anastasia replied, smoothing back her daughter's silky brown hair.

Motioning toward Melissa, Anastasia asked, "Do you know who this is?"

A gigantic grin flashed across Emilia's face. "The Castle Lady!" she exclaimed, and they all laughed.

Melissa left Luke's side and crossed over to Anastasia's chair. Extending her hand to the little girl she said, "Hello, Emilia."

The little girl took her hand and responded politely, "Hello."

"You can call 'the Castle Lady,'" Anastasia paused, and her eyes bounced mischievously between Luke and Melissa, "*Thea* Melissa."

Melissa glanced at Luke in time to see his eyebrows arch, and then her eyes turned back to Anastasia just as she was shooting her brother a cryptic, sisterly look.

Anastasia looked up at Melissa and explained, "*Thea* means aunt."

Melissa's mouth formed an *O* but no sound came out. Unlike Luke, Melissa wasn't surprised by Anastasia's cheeky suggestion. Apparently, Luke's sister was taking on the role of director by introducing a new plot twist to the unfolding "drama."

Turning to Emilia, Melissa said sweetly, "I'd like it if you called me *Thea.*"

"Me too," the little girl replied. "I've never had a *thea* before."

Melissa swallowed the lump that formed in her throat and avoided looking in Luke's direction. If they had married, Emilia would have a *thea* already. "Well, you do now. And you know what? This *thea* isn't only interested in castles made of stone. I like to make castles out of sand too."

"Sand castles! Hooray! Me too!"

"Maybe we can make one together," Melissa suggested.

"A big one?" Emilia asked.

"A very big one," Melissa agreed.

"When?"

"Is tomorrow soon enough?"

"I can't wait!" she exclaimed, and she snuggled closer to her mother. Anastasia's smile deepened before she leaned down and whispered something into her daughter's ear, something that made Emilia's head nod up and down in a quick, excited motion before she squeezed her arms even tighter around her mother's neck.

Pushing back from her mother, but with one little arm still around her neck, Emilia explained her excitement. "Mamma's going to put me to bed tonight! She said that I can ride on her chair with her!" But then, as if she suddenly realized that her uncle might feel bad, she said, "But you come too, *Theo* Luke. You can bring my doll."

"You bet," he agreed, emotion making his voice deeper than normal. "I'll be up later."

Amid happy giggles from Emilia, Anastasia started rolling the chair away. "I'll probably be awhile," she said over her shoulder. "You two start dinner without me."

A look of concern darkened Luke's face. "But you will come back down?" he asked, and there was no disguising how important her answer would be.

Anastasia looked at him over the top of her child's head. "Definitely." With a quick wink at Melissa she added, "After all, I don't want to miss the drama."

Melissa shook her head in amusement, but Luke looked confused. "That's an inside joke," Melissa said. "Girl talk."

"I see," he said, but it was obvious he didn't see at all. Luke and Melissa watched together as Anastasia and Emilia disappeared into the elevator.

The door closed and Melissa and Luke were alone.

As if in slow motion, Melissa saw Luke's hand leave his side and reach out toward her. When his fingers made contact with the back of her neck and he pulled her close to him, her knees went weak. "Luke," she breathed his name and rested her head on his shoulder.

"Melissa," he whispered as his cheek fell against the top of her head. "Thank you."

She tilted her head back and looked at him. "For what?"

"For giving my sister back to me."

"I didn't do anything."

"You did something very great," he corrected gently. "But how did you get her to dress and come downstairs? I've been trying to do that for such a long time," he sighed.

She shrugged her shoulders and answered as casually as she could, "We met on the verandah outside our rooms. I was playing my guitar. She said that if I promised to play for her after dinner, she would come down."

Luke was overcome by a rush of emotions that he couldn't even begin to identify. The only thing he knew for sure was that he felt happy for the first time in months—and he was willing to let the moment linger. He was almost sorry when Melissa tilted her head back and broke the silence.

"Luke, I had no idea about her accident. I'm so sorry." She noticed a momentary twitch in his jaw, the same little quirk she had noticed earlier in the day.

"Anastasia talked to you about it?" Anastasia hadn't talked to anyone about the accident. Not him, not Gabriel—no one. He was amazed that she had talked to Melissa, apparently within minutes of meeting her.

Melissa chose her next words carefully. "As you must remember, I suffered a similar loss as a child when I lost my parents."

Her parents. He berated himself for not recognizing a textbook example of recovery.

Melissa continued, "Well, Anastasia acted differently toward me the moment I told her about it. It was as if I was an example of a healed person to her. Plus, I think the timing is right. She's ready to try and live again."

He was amazed by her insight, but decided not to comment any further. Nodding his agreement, he pressed his hand lightly against the small of her back and directed her onto the verandah, where the table was set for dinner.

Melissa stood in wonder of the scene. It was elegant and regal in an Old World way. Candles were lit and several palm trees in the garden were spotlighted. Even the tower on the hill was lit up. The sea was calm, but its steady breakers whispered an age-old song into the soft and silvery summer night. "How beautiful. We're eating outside?"

"As long as it's not windy, I enjoy taking my meals on the verandah during the summer months and even on into early fall."

"Now I *know* I'm in Greece," Melissa sighed, as Luke pulled out the wrought-iron chair and seated her at the marble-topped table. He slid into the chair kitty-corner from her.

"Ah, here's Soula." He motioned to the older woman waddling through the French doors carrying a bread basket and water on a silver tray. The woman rocked back and forth on her legs so much that Melissa couldn't help but wonder how she kept from spilling the water. Standing, Luke took the tray from her. "Soula, I want you to meet Melissa."

Soula had kept her eyes on Melissa from the moment she walked through the door. With a broad smile she asked, "You are awake now? Did you sleep well?"

Soula had a heavy, but sweet, accent and Melissa liked her immediately. Returning her bright-toothed smile, Melissa replied, "Yes, thank you, the bed was wonderful after such a long journey."

"What? No," Soula very nearly clucked. "I saw you sleeping on the verandah."

Melissa laughed, and Luke remembered the familiar "chimes touched by the breeze" sound that he had always loved. "Oh, yes, that was nice too."

"Soula is my sister's housekeeper," Luke was quick to explain their relationship. "But more than that, she's our friend," he said, and he gave the large, but short woman, a kiss on her wrinkled face, which pleased her immensely.

"If you need anything else, you tell me," Soula instructed. She started to turn away, but Luke restrained her with his hand.

"Actually, Soula, we do need something. If it's not too much trouble for you, would you mind setting another place at the table?" Luke winked at Melissa. "Anastasia is going to join us after she finishes putting Emilia to bed."

The housekeeper gasped. "What?"

"I said—"

"Our Anastasia is putting Emilia to bed and she's coming to eat *here?*" Tears washed Soula's blue eyes and she crossed herself. "Thank God, thank God. But. . .how. . .?" she questioned Luke.

Luke motioned to Melissa. "It's all her doing."

Soula swiveled to face Melissa. "Bless you, child." She grabbed Melissa's hand and she kissed it before Melissa realized what was happening. "I knew while I watched you sleeping that I loved you."

"No, wait. . ." Feeling uncomfortable, Melissa gently pulled her hand away and said, "It wasn't me. It's all the love that both of you have given to Anastasia on a daily basis."

"Yes," Soula agreed without argument. "But it is you, too." She turned and scuttled as quickly as her legs would allow her to go back into the house.

"What a dear lady," Melissa murmured.

"She is," Luke agreed thoughtfully. "I don't know what I would have done without her after Anastasia's accident."

"How about your parents?" Melissa asked.

Luke made a bitter sound in his throat. "My parents. . .are. . .my parents. They haven't changed."

"Didn't they help at all?"

He shrugged his shoulders. "They were around for the first few weeks after the accident." He picked up the bread knife and slashed the loaf into slices. "But that was about it. End of discussion."

Melissa nodded. The topic of his parents had always been low on his list of favorites. They were rock bottom now. Leaning over, she picked up the rag doll that Emilia had planted strategically on the table. "Emilia is a wonderful little girl," she said, thinking that talking about his niece would be a safe subject. But it turned out to be an even more volatile topic than his parents.

Luke put down the knife and reached over to rub his hand across the rag doll's yarn hair. In the same motion he wrapped Melissa's hand in his and the two sat for a moment, clutching the doll together. "I had hoped that we would have had children by now, Melissa." He spoke with total honesty and the yearning in his tone brought tears to the back of Melissa's eyes.

"Luke. . ." She looked down at their hands still intertwined around the doll. "I wasn't ready for marriage then," she whispered, "much less children."

"And now?"

She looked up at him and searched his eyes for a clue to his real question. But he was veiling his emotions and his eyes were deep green pools of mystery.

"I could be," she softly admitted, but the anger that suddenly flashed in his eyes took her off guard.

With his lips barely moving, he ground out the question he most dreaded, and steeled himself for the answer he didn't want to hear. "Are you seeing someone else?"

Her eyes widened and Luke wasn't certain whether he saw guilt or merely surprise. But her reply was swift and emphatic. "Luke, since the night we met, there hasn't been anyone but you."

He clicked his tongue against his cheek. "That's not true, Melissa."

Her eyes closed and then widened again in disbelief. "Luke, it *is* true," she insisted and squeezed his fingers. "The man you saw me hugging. . . that day. . .was the pastor at my church—a friend only. I told you that." She couldn't believe that he might still harbor doubts, but she had seen a tiny quiver in the corner of his eye when she said *that day,* and she knew that he understood exactly which day she meant—the day they were supposed to have been married.

"There is no one but you," she insisted.

His mouth settled into a thin, dry line and, letting go of her hand, he reached to the back of her neck. With the soft touch of a surgeon, he pulled on the chain that held the object hidden beneath the folds of her silk dress. When the cross was free, he reached out and cradled it in his hand. "And your God," he said pointedly.

Melissa chewed on her lower lip. "Luke," she hesitantly began, but he silenced her with an upward jut of his chin, the Greek "no." Sighing, she lifted her hands to the chain to remove the cross from around her neck.

But letting go of the cross, he placed his hands above hers, once again stopping her. "No, Melissa. I don't want it back. I didn't want it a year and a half ago. I don't want it now."

"But, Luke, it's yours and—"

"As far as I'm concerned," he cut her off, his voice deep and biting, "it's your love for that cross that took you away from me."

She stiffened. "You're wrong, Luke. It's this cross and what it stands for that has brought me back to you."

The old, familiar rawness worked on his nerves and formed a knot in his stomach. He felt edgy. Shaking his head, he simply said, "I don't see it that way."

She bent her head and looked at the shiny metal. Twice she had tried to give it back to him; twice he had refused it. She wouldn't force it on him. "I told you on the day that you. . .gave. . ." she tried to explain, stumbling over the word, "the cross to me, that I would return it to you when I could tell you the meaning behind it." She moved her eyes away from the historic symbol of Christianity and looked straight at him. "I'm ready to tell you, but I can appreciate that you're not necessarily ready to hear. I'll wait. When you're ready to hear—when you're willing to understand, let me know." There was no rancor in her voice, but the message was clear. The ball was in his court.

He nodded and wondered bleakly how wanting her and blaming her at the same time could ever be worked out. "You might have a very long wait," he conceded.

"I'm willing to give you time." Again, her voice was soft and sweet and genuine, but the words pierced his heart. She was offering him the time that he had been unwilling to extend to her. Looking directly into his eyes, she lifted the cross and dropped it back inside her dress.

Luke's mind was a tangle of conflicting emotions. As much as he resented her fixation on the cross, he loved her and knew he didn't want to lose her. Not again. Grimly, he sat back and crossed his arms. The gauntlet had been thrown down, but he doubted there would ever be enough time to reach a genuine reconciliation. She might intend to stay for awhile, but eventually she would complete her study of the castles and then she would be gone.

She touched his hand and spoke soothingly, as if she were reading his mind. "Luke, this time around, we do have time."

"Do we?"

Her eyes shifted up toward the Byzantine fortress, silhouetted in the silkiness of the night, and she smiled. "Greece has a lot of castles. They could keep 'the Castle Lady' here for a very long time."

"And me?"

She reached out and rubbed her fingertips across his cheek. "And you, dear Luke, could keep me here for the rest of my earthly life."

His jaw tightened.

She closed her eyes and leaned toward him.

Luke didn't hesitate. His lips met hers in a sweet kiss of hope, desire, and promise. The hope of reconciliation, the desire for each other, and the promise to try to work it out.

Chapter 14

In the morning, the *meltemia*—the strong summer winds that usually fanned Greece around the end of July or early August—started to blow. Luke paused on the verandah, medical bag in hand, ready to leave for his rounds at the hospital. He glanced out over the dancing land and undulating sea. The long-awaited winds dusted a layer of dirt from the trees and swept the horizon clear of its hazy lines. The air was no longer oppressive, and Luke realized as he jogged down the steps to his car that his mind felt refreshed as well. Anastasia seemed to be coming out of her depression, and Melissa would still be here—waiting for him —when he got home.

Luke liked the idea. He liked it a lot, and as he fired up the powerful engine of his sports car, he decided that—at least for the moment— nothing else mattered.

✍

The days settled into a happy routine for Melissa and her newfound friends. Anastasia, Emilia, and Soula all took to Melissa like butter does to bread and Melissa grew to love them all.

In the evenings, she and Luke enjoyed long walks on the beach at sunset and candlelight dinners on the verandah—peaceful times of getting to know each other again. Anastasia always joined them for dinner and the happiness that Luke felt with his sister at the table was like a ribbon of joy that wound around them all.

Even though Luke had declared a truce, Melissa recognized it as temporary. She knew that his anger and bitterness were still percolating just below the surface of his smile and that one wrong word, one wrong movement, could elicit a new eruption. But she was glad for the reprieve. She needed the time to get her bearings and to pray.

And pray she did. Early each morning, to the sounds of seagulls playing tag above the shore and fishermen chugging home in their brightly colored boats after fishing all night, Melissa sat on her bedroom verandah, read her Bible, and prayed. And when the sound of Luke's high-powered car filtered up to her as he left for work, she would lift her head and offer up a special prayer for the man she loved.

With all of her being she wanted to go downstairs and see him off. But she didn't feel right about greeting him in the morning. Somehow, to wave good-bye to a man going off to work seemed more intimate than a candlelight dinner. She hoped that someday she would have that privilege, but for now, she would wait, and pray.

A few weeks after her arrival, she was at her usual place on the verandah listening to the last sounds of Luke's car fading away when Anastasia, more asleep than awake, appeared at her doorway. "I thought I heard you," she called to Melissa.

The sight of Luke's sister in a pretty pink nighty with her hair falling in silky, sleep-rumpled waves around her face, brought a smile to Melissa's face. Already, Anastasia looked so different from the woman she had met on the same verandah the afternoon of her first day at St. Andreas. *"Kali Mera,"* Melissa greeted her with the Greek words for "good morning."

"Kali Mera," Anastasia replied. Squinting against the brightness of the sky, she asked, "What are you doing out here so early?"

Melissa glanced down at the well-worn Bible in her lap. Remembering from their first conversation the negative way Anastasia had reacted to the mention of God, Melissa silently prayed that what she said would be well received. Training her eyes on Anastasia, she answered honestly, "I'm reading the Bible."

Anastasia dipped her head, shook it slightly, and when she lifted it again Melissa was relieved to see a slow smile gently lift the corners of her lips. "You and Gabriel. . .you're so much alike." There was wonder in her voice. "It's amazing, but. . .he reads his Bible every morning too."

Melissa didn't think it was amazing. The way she saw it, God in His wisdom was making sure that Luke and Anastasia were surrounded —and loved—by people who knew Him. From all she had heard about Gabriel Crown—especially from Emilia, who counted the hours until his next visit—he was definitely a believer. "I'm looking forward to meeting him."

"He should be coming this Friday afternoon," Anastasia volunteered, and in the timbre of her voice, Melissa was certain she detected the sound of a woman who was interested in a man.

"He's going to be very happy to see the change in you," she ventured to comment.

Anastasia nodded and a soft, attractive blush touched her cheeks. "He's been a very good friend to me."

Friend. Melissa remembered how she and Luke had started off. But Gabriel was a believer, and Melissa now knew that made all the difference to what might follow in a relationship. "Do I detect something more here than just friendship?" she asked coyly. Anastasia's blush deepened to the same soft color as her nightgown, confirming the budding romance Melissa had only suspected before.

"Like I said, Gabriel has been a very good friend to me. Tell me," she continued quickly in the same breath, obviously wanting to change the subject, "do you ever play your guitar in the morning?"

"Oh! All the time," Melissa said, "when I'm at home. But I haven't here, because. . .well, I've been afraid of waking you."

Anastasia rolled her eyes. "Don't be. I'd like to wake up to your singing," she assured. "In fact, play now if you want." Shielding her eyes from the glare of the morning sky, she started backing her chair into her room. "As for me," she said stifling a yawn, "I'm going to close these eyes for awhile longer."

"Pleasant dreams," Melissa whispered after her.

From then on, playing her guitar in the morning became a part of Melissa's daily routine, along with sharing a continental breakfast with Anastasia and Emilia on the western verandah, and then swimming and playing on the beach with Emilia.

One day, Emilia had just finished placing flags made out of seaweed on the four turrets of the largest sand castle they had made to date when the sound of a bee, just above Melissa's left shoulder, sent her scampering to her feet. She pulled Emilia up with her and protectively squeezed the little girl behind her while she backed away from the insect.

Emilia poked her head out from around Melissa's legs and asked, "Are you afraid of bees?" There was amazement in her voice.

"I suppose I am," Melissa admitted. Her heart was pounding, but she was trying hard to sound calm so as not to pass her fear to the little girl.

"Don't worry. I'm not." And before Melissa could react, Emilia slid out of her hold, stepped in front of her, and started fanning her little arms slowly and gently. "Shoo, shoo, go away, little bee!" The bee, evidently deciding that it would be best to leave such a brave little lady alone, buzzed quickly away, across the beach.

"My protector," Melissa laughed and chased the happily squealing little girl around the beach and then up the path to the house, where they ran smack into Luke.

"*Theo* Luke!" Emilia shouted out as he lifted her high into the sky, sandy body and all. "You're home early!"

"I thought I'd come and eat lunch with you today," he answered the little girl, but his eyes spoke on a different level to Melissa. She looked down and realized that she had forgotten to put on her beach cover-up before running up to the house. Not that Luke had never seen her before in her modest, one-piece swimsuit, but she suddenly felt more exposed than she ever had before. She quickly wrapped her towel around her shoulders and let it drape down around her.

When she glanced back at Luke, he was watching her with a small grin playing at the corners of his mouth.

"We were playing on the beach." Emilia wiggled out of his arms, totally unaware, as children can blessedly be, of the tension that was crackling in the air between the adults.

"I know. I saw you," he answered, and he ruffled his niece's hair, dislodging some of the thousands of sand particles stuck to it. As they fell, like bits of golden sun from the sky, Emilia tried to catch them.

"We built a sand castle and I chased a bee away. *Thea* Melissa's afraid of them."

"Is she now?" Luke asked his niece, but cocked his head toward Melissa.

"But I told her not to be," Emilia continued blithely along.

"Good advice," he said to the little girl. "But sometimes difficult to follow." He glanced again at Melissa.

"Where's my little lady?" An older man called out from the doorway.

"*Nono!*" Emilia exclaimed, and on feet that barely touched the marble she ran pass Melissa to greet an ageless man with snow-white hair, who was waiting for her at the other end of the verandah. Melissa watched as the man she assumed was Luke's godfather pulled a straight-back chair into the shade, dusted off Emilia's legs, sat, and pulled the little girl onto his lap. They looked like the best of friends.

Melissa turned back to Luke, then looked down at her sandy swimsuit and murmured, "I think I'd better get cleaned up."

His mouth tightened and he nodded. She started past him but his hand reached out, stopping her. "Melissa—"

She looked at him inquisitively. "Luke?"

"Seeing you like this," he nodded toward her swimsuit, "reminds me of our lazy days at Lake Breeze, before. . ." He frowned and stopped speaking, as though he wasn't quite sure what his point was going to be.

Melissa nodded her head and tried to reassure him. "You know, Luke. . .we haven't lost that much. Only a year and a half, and maybe this time—"

Luke's eyes instantly flashed with fire. "Maybe *we* haven't lost that much," he spat, "but Anastasia. . .she lost almost everything." He dropped her arm as if her skin were suddenly burning him.

Melissa's brows knitted together. "Luke? What are you talking about? What does Anastasia have to do with us?"

He whipped out his sunglasses from his shirt pocket and jammed them onto his face, shading his angry eyes behind the smoky gray lenses. "Ask her yourself." His answer was clipped and tight. Turning sharply on his heel, he walked into the cool darkness of the house.

Chapter 15

M elissa ran up to Anastasia's room, but when she didn't find her there, she decided to shower and dress. She had waited a year and a half to discover the core to Luke's anger. She could wait a few more minutes.

Melissa could see the back of Anastasia's wheelchair as she walked toward the verandah from the living room. On an impulse, she reached up to the chain hanging around her neck and pulled the heavy cross out from beneath her yellow sundress. Today seemed to be the day for revelations. Anastasia hadn't seen the cross yet. Melissa wondered what her reaction would be.

The sound of happy talking and a strange *click, click, click* sound came from outside the French doors. Melissa would have to wait to question Anastasia. She still couldn't fathom what Anastasia's situation had to do with her relationship with Luke, but knowing that she would soon learn something made her more patient than she normally would be.

"Here's the Castle Lady, *Nono!*" Emilia sang out, welcoming Melissa as she stepped onto the dining area of the verandah that was protected from the *meltemia* breezes by a glass partition.

Emilia and Anastasia, *Nono* and Soula were seated around the table. Luke wasn't there. Somehow that didn't surprise Melissa. He always went away when he was angry. This time, Melissa was almost glad that he had.

The strange *click, click, click* came from a strand of elegant Greek worry beads, *komboloi*, which *Nono* had twined between the thick fingers and the thumb of his left hand. He stopped twirling them when Melissa appeared, and rose to greet her. Melissa had never seen a more gallant gesture.

"*Nono*, this is Melissa," Anastasia introduced, "my almost sister." Melissa saw kindness in her green eyes, which only deepened her confusion about what Luke had said. "Melissa this is our *nono*," she reversed the introduction with fondness in her voice for the older man. "He is actually Luke's *nono*, which means 'godfather,' but we have all adopted him as our own."

The snowy-haired man held out his hand to Melissa.

"My dear, it's nice to finally meet you. Welcome to Greece." He had a distinguished accent, which almost seemed to come from another era.

Melissa took his hand and felt the warmth of his welcome, which was reinforced by the twinkle in his sagacious eyes. He was a big man—every bit as tall as Luke—and his many years had not diminished his stature. His crown of white hair was thick, and Melissa's mind went immediately to the words of Psalm 91, "with long life will I satisfy him." Melissa liked the old man immediately.

"Thank you," she said, and she sat in the cushioned chair that Soula indicated. *Nono* folded his body back onto the hard, cafe-style chair beside her and the clicking of his beads began again, a pleasant sound that was part of the Greek milieu.

"Luke has always spoken so highly of you, but tell me, please, what exactly is the role of a godfather here in Greece? I have the feeling that to be a *nono* in Greece is a much stronger relationship than a godfather would have in America."

"Oh, it is," Anastasia quickly confirmed. "In fact, in some cases a *nono* is like a second father." She looked fondly at the older man. "In our case he is like a first father."

The older man patted Anastasia's hand and turned to Melissa. "Between war and the plague, both of which Greece has suffered greatly through the centuries, the mortality rate was high, and godparents would naturally fill the role of parents if the need arose."

Anastasia nodded and continued, "It's kind of like the modern system of naming a guardian in a will today, only—" She stopped speaking as her eyes landed on the cross nestled in the folds of Melissa's dress. "Luke's cross," she whispered, and her eyes flicked up to Melissa's. Melissa almost cringed when she saw the sudden accusation in them. "He told me he lost it."

"He did lose it," Soula said quietly from behind Anastasia. Melissa swung her head around to look at the kindly housekeeper. "Symbolically," Soula finished.

"What?" Anastasia spat out like a recalcitrant child, her gaze returning to the cross.

"He lost it at the same time that he lost our dear Melissa," Soula explained, and Melissa felt as though she had just been touched by an angel. She had known that Soula was a friend, but she hadn't realized how dear a one until now. She sent her a smile of thanks.

But Anastasia was still bewildered. "I don't understand." Reaching out toward Melissa, she ran her fingertips over the cross and eyed it in the way that suggested she was evaluating its monetary worth.

"It's a long story," Melissa replied.

"It's pretty, *Thea* Melissa!" Emilia sang out, relieving the tension as only a child could do. Anastasia let go of the cross.

"Would you like to hold it, Emilia?" Melissa asked. When the little girl nodded, Melissa removed the chain from around her neck and handed it to her. She couldn't help but notice that Anastasia's eyes never wavered from the golden pendant.

"Do you have any idea how old—and valuable—that cross is?" Anastasia asked, and Melissa was sad to recognize a note of jealousy in her tone.

"Anastasia." *Nono* spoke firmly with a father's warning in his voice. "What you should ask is, 'Do you know the meaning behind that cross?' That is where its glory comes from. Certainly not from its metal or workmanship or age." He turned his wise old eyes toward Melissa.

Melissa met his gaze and it was as if a fresh springtime breeze—in contrast to the brisk, hot wind that whistled on the other side of the partition—had wrapped itself around them and bound them together in a sweet relationship that was far stronger than human emotions could express. Melissa knew—and so did *Nono*—that they were united in their love for the Lord.

"That's the reason I came," she whispered, and it was as if the two of them were all alone. "To tell Luke the meaning behind the cross." She motioned toward the cross that Emilia was turning over in her hand. "When Luke first gave it to me," Melissa continued, "I didn't understand what it stood for. And now that I do, Luke won't accept the cross. . .or its meaning."

Nono reached out and gently took the cross from the little girl. It was at home in his grasp. "I wore this cross for nearly seventy years, and my *nono* before me for nearly the same number of years," he said as he caressed the smooth metal. "For the first ten years that I wore it, I did so only to please my old *nono*," he admitted. He held the cross out to Melissa. "Its message is strong, but is best given slowly, and with love. His love."

Melissa reached slowly for the cross. "I understand," she whispered, and *Nono* let go of the chain.

"Put it on," he said gently. "Let it sit against your heart and give it to Luke when he accepts it."

Nodding her head, Melissa slipped the chain over her hair and let the cross fall beneath her dress as it had hundreds of times during the last year and a half. Then she hesitantly, warily glanced over at Anastasia.

"I'm so sorry, Melissa." Anastasia spoke softly with remorse in her eyes. "Please forgive me. Sometimes I can be extremely selfish. I always was jealous of that cross. I always wanted it," she admitted, twisting her lips wryly.

Melissa released the breath she had been holding. "Anastasia, if Luke never accepts it from me, then I'll give it to you. It belongs in your family."

"No, Melissa," Anastasia replied softly, and there was no mistaking the love in her voice. "You are the one who belongs in our family. How can I ever forget what you've done for me?"

"Anastasia is right," *Nono* pronounced, and placing his strong hand on Anastasia's slender shoulder, he gently kneaded it. "You've given us back our daughter, our sister, our mother. . ." He looked over at the happy face of Emilia and smiled. "We can never thank you enough."

Melissa shook her head. "It is the Lord who heals," she whispered to *Nono*, and he smiled. Then, bowing his head, he offered thanks for the meal that Soula had placed before them.

Melissa was surprised when she heard him say the Lord's Prayer. *Nono* spoke the prayer as the Lord Himself might have said it, with truth, meaning, and worship. She could have sat there all day listening to the wise old man pray, but when *Nono* had finished, they all dug in eagerly to the summertime feast of prawns, meatballs, and salad.

After the meal, when *Nono* and Emilia went to take a siesta, Melissa tried to help Soula clear the table, but the older woman wouldn't hear of it. "Stay and keep Anastasia company," she suggested.

"I'd like that," Anastasia quickly agreed.

"You aren't going to take a nap?" Melissa inquired.

"You know," Anastasia said with pleasure and awe mingled in her eyes, "I sleep so well during the night now that I don't even need to rest in the afternoon anymore."

Melissa smiled and the two women lapsed into a thoughtful silence as they watched the wind kick up whitecaps on the surface of the cobalt blue bay.

After a moment, Melissa spoke up hesitantly. "Anastasia, there is something that I need to talk to you about."

Anastasia looked over at her, her green eyes registering concern. "Sounds serious."

"I think it is," Melissa admitted.

"Is this the reason Luke left so suddenly?"

Melissa sighed. "Has he always gone away when he's angry about something?"

Anastasia mulled over the question, as if considering it for the first time. "You know, I think he has. That was one of the reasons he moved to the States all those years ago. He was angry with our father."

Melissa laughed and, rolling her eyes upward, suggested, "So maybe I shouldn't take it personally?"

"It's Luke's way of dealing with things," Anastasia explained, quickly defending her brother, but then she softened her words with a smile. "Let's move into the living room. I think the *meltemia* is blowing a bit too strongly for me," she declared, just as a particularly fierce gust of wind blew over *Nono's* favorite chair—the cafe-style one—that had been left at the edge of the glass partition. The two women laughed in unison. Releasing the brake on her wheelchair, Anastasia propelled herself toward the door. "See what I mean?"

Melissa nodded. She stepped into the exposed part of the verandah to retrieve the chair, struggling to keep her blowing hair out of her eyes. "Living room it is!" she agreed, and followed behind Anastasia.

Melissa sat in what had become her favorite chair. It faced the fireplace, had a reading lamp above it, and commanded the best view in the house. If she looked to the right, she could survey the vast expanse of the sea; and if she turned to the left, she saw the little castle on the hill.

Anastasia situated herself to the left of Melissa's chair, setting Castle Beauvoir in the background.

"Now, what was it you wanted to tell me?" Anastasia prompted after a moment.

Melissa brushed a stray strand of hair out of her eyes and began. "Things are changing between Luke and me. When I first arrived, I saw immediately that he still cared for me, but, at the same time, I also realized that there is something, or maybe many things, that are keeping him from caring too deeply. There is a restraint. I thought I was going to have to deal with it immediately, but," she smiled and reached out for Anastasia's hand, "after that first afternoon, we've all been basking in the euphoria of your recovery. Whatever was tormenting Luke about me was pushed aside."

"I'm glad," Anastasia said, squeezing Melissa's fingers comfortingly. "You needed the time to get to know one another again."

Melissa nodded, but then her lips pursed together in a straight line. "But like I said, things are changing. The time has come when we have to face what happened between us. And this is why I need to talk to you."

"Go ahead," Anastasia prompted.

Melissa let go of Anastasia's hand, stood up, and walked over to the fireplace. "Earlier, Luke said something that I don't understand, but which I think has a great deal to do with his anger toward me, and toward God." Melissa paused, and Anastasia's brows drew together in a thoughtful frown. "When I tried to tell him that we had lost only a year and a half—not that much in the scope of a lifetime, he cut me off and said that we—meaning he and I—hadn't lost much, but that you. . ." She turned to face Anastasia. "You'd lost almost everything."

Anastasia dropped her eyes and her lower lip came out in a sad pout, reminding Melissa of Emilia when she was told to go to bed and she didn't want to. But Anastasia's entire body shook, telling of much greater emotion.

Walking quickly over to her side, Melissa knelt down beside her chair and took her hands in her own. "Anastasia? What does he mean? He told me to ask you, otherwise, I wouldn't—"

"No, it's okay," Anastasia assured her, but when she looked up, Melissa was startled to see tears swimming in her green eyes.

"Anastasia—?"

Anastasia held up one hand, halting Melissa's words. "I realized when we first met that you didn't know," she began. "The woman I was then might have told you with spite, but. . ." She looked back at Melissa and there was no mistaking the love she felt. "I think that I was already beginning to love you."

Melissa squeezed Anastasia's hand. "Told me what?"

Anastasia took a deep breath and continued. "Melissa, the automobile accident that killed my husband and unborn child occurred shortly before Luke returned to Greece." She paused and spoke as gently as she would to her daughter. "Melissa, it occurred. . .on the evening of. . ." She paused again, and then whispered the date.

Melissa blinked and tears came immediately to her eyes. *It couldn't be.* But the stark realization of what had occurred swept over her like a tidal wave, and a nightmarish horror began to fill her heart. "That's the day that Luke and I were supposed to—" She choked back a sob, unable to complete her sentence.

Anastasia nodded and looked wistfully at Melissa, tears streaming down her face.

"And if we had gotten married," Melissa spoke the thought out loud, "you and your husband wouldn't have been here in Greece. . .but. . ." She stopped. She couldn't continue. The implications were too horrible. "Oh, Anastasia," Melissa wailed. "I had no idea." She looked down at the legs that would never walk again, and big tears of anguish spilled over and coursed down her cheeks in a raging torrent. She imagined the horror of what Anastasia and Luke had lived through. She had lost her precious husband and long-awaited son, and Luke had lost his bride, his brother-in-law, and nephew—and in a large measure, his sister as well.

The sudden onset of grief drove Melissa to her knees and, without thinking, she rested her head on Anastasia's lap.

"Shhh. . ." Anastasia soothed Melissa and stroked her hair, just as she might do for Emilia. "How were any of us to know?"

Melissa lifted her tear-stained face and stated the obvious fact. "I know that it wasn't directly my fault," she sniffled, "but Luke blames me all the same. I could see it in his eyes, and now I understand it. Deep underneath it all, he blames me for what happened to you."

Anastasia wiped a fresh tear from Melissa's eye. "He doesn't blame it all on you. He blames God, too."

Melissa breathed a long, sorrowful sigh and looked up at Anastasia.

"What about you?" she asked with a note of resignation. "Do you still blame me?"

"Oh. . ." Anastasia waved her hand above her head. "In my 'Why? Why? Why?' days, I suppose I did. For a while." When Melissa looked stricken, she quickly continued. "But I finally realized how silly that was. How were any of us to know?" she asked again. "We could just as easily have crashed on the way to the wedding."

Melissa squeezed her eyes shut. "Anastasia," she breathed out, "I am so sorry."

"All of our sorrow combined won't give me back what's been lost," Anastasia said matter-of-factly. "But, Melissa, when I saw the life and the joy in your eyes that first day you were here, it reminded me that life is still worth living. And when you told me about your parents, I knew that you understood me as few others can. As hard as it may be, we absorb our losses and try to keep going. You didn't say that with words, but I saw it in your eyes—and that's what saved me."

Placing her hands firmly on Melissa's shoulders, she sat up straight and tall in her chair, reminding Melissa of pictures she had seen of President Franklin Roosevelt. And like the great commander in chief from the Second World War, Anastasia issued her order. "Now you know what you're up against in Luke. He's a stubborn man, but even more he's a hurting man. I want to see my brother happy, Melissa. And ever since I met you, I have known that he will only be happy if he's with you. I want you to promise me that you will fight hard for him and not give up."

Melissa smiled and brushed away the last of her tears. "That's a very easy promise to make."

As if on cue, fighter jets from the nearby military base flew low over the villa, rattling the windows. "There's your air support," Anastasia said with a grin, and the two women fell into each other's arms, laughing. Melissa knew that she had support from an even higher source, and she resolved once again to trust God to change Luke's heart.

Chapter 16

Luke didn't come home until very late that night.

Melissa waited up for him.

The night wrapped around her like a cashmere sweater, soft and warm, as she sat on the same chaise lounge in which she had fallen asleep her first afternoon at Villa Beauvoir. While she waited, she prayed for Luke; she prayed for Anastasia; she gave thanks for the wonder of the stars as they twinkled in the infinite sky and for the soft melody that played over the still sea; but mostly she prayed that the Karalis family would soon know the completeness and happiness that only comes through a personal relationship with God.

She heard Luke's car pull into his parking place, and the throaty growl of the powerful engine fell silent. The door opened and slammed shut, and Melissa heard his footsteps climb slowly, wearily, up the marble stairs to the verandah.

In the darkness, he didn't see her.

She remained silent and watched as he leaned against the stone banister and stared out over the blackness of the nighttime sea. She heard him sigh as he lifted his head to gaze at the carpet of stars in the depths of the universe. The Milky Way cut across the sky like a ribbon of velvety light, as it had since before the dawn of mankind.

The muscles of Luke's back were tense and tight against the fabric of his shirt as he lifted a weary hand to rub his neck. Melissa wondered how she could be tough enough to love him the way he needed. Every fiber in her being wanted to go to him and massage the ache in his shoulders away. But she knew that the ache in his soul would remain. She had to love him enough to be firm, to be truthful.

"Melissa. . ." He suddenly, unexpectedly, spoke her name to the endless sky, capturing in that single word all the yearning, all the love, all the pain in his heart. She gasped before she could stop herself.

Luke spun around and peered across the dark verandah toward where she was sitting. For the longest moment, they just looked at each other.

To Luke's eyes, she wasn't more than a long, dark form against the paleness of the flowered cushion. But he felt her presence and he wondered how he had not known immediately that she was there. A wave of insecurity washed over him. It was as if she had a hold—a debilitating hold—over him. And he didn't like it one bit.

Sharply, harshly, almost rudely, he asked, "How long have you been there?"

Ignoring the tone of his question, she swung her feet to the floor and stood up. "I've been waiting for you."

"It's late." He turned as if to go into the house. "I'm going to bed."

Melissa decided that she wasn't going to let him run away from her any more. Not across an ocean, not to his office at the hospital, and not into the house right now. She blocked his path.

He stopped just before touching her and took a couple of steps back.

"You ran away today, Luke," Melissa softly accused. "Just like you did a year and a half ago."

He let out an impatient breath and turned his back. "Melissa—"

"No, Luke," she cut him off. "You should have talked to me earlier. You should have told me about Anastasia's accident and you should have told me when it occurred."

"So," he turned to her, "she told you." It was a statement, not a question. She nodded. "Why didn't *you?*"

"You broke up with me. Remember?" Sarcasm oozed from his words.

"No, Luke, I didn't want to break up. I just wanted more time. That was no reason to cut me so totally out of your life."

He laughed shortly and shrugged his shoulders, but kept his back turned to Melissa. "Well, Melissa, you've had your time. So has Anastasia. A bit different in degrees of enjoyment, but time spent nonetheless."

She knew that he was trying to provoke her. She wouldn't let him. Narrowing her eyes, she said softly yet firmly, "Luke, you're hiding behind this terrible coincidence."

He swiveled to face her and his self-indulgent sarcasm was replaced by anger. Melissa was glad. Anger demanded a response, and she was prepared for the challenge.

"And just what am I hiding, *Bee?*"

She winced at his caustic interpretation of her name, but tossed her hair and took a step toward him. "You're hiding your fear behind Anastasia's accident. You're using a sorry coincidence to justify your anger at me. . .and at God."

He heaved a weary sigh. "I used to understand the power of your stinger, Bee. I don't anymore." His voice was low and hard and unforgiving. She felt as though she were losing him, but she reminded herself not to trust her feelings. Rather, she would continue to trust God.

"Maybe because the so-called stinger that I carry now stings with the truth. And the truth hurts," she countered, but her tone was soft and caring.

Luke heard only the words, and that was enough to ignite his anger once again. "And what are you calling the truth?" he demanded.

Bulls-eye! It was exactly the question she had hoped he would ask. "The truth is. . .that all those years ago. . .you really wanted to be my. . . my savior."

"Your savior! Then *ise kalla,*" he mumbled in Greek, then translated the uncomplimentary phrase. "You're not well," he declared and turned his back again.

Melissa continued to speak as though he hadn't said a word. "You wanted to be the one to heal me and make me whole, to give me a life free from doubt and despair. And when I was alone with you, Luke," she whispered, reaching out to touch the back of his shoulder, "I think you were my savior. You did free me."

He pulled away from her and took another step toward the far end of the verandah. He didn't want her to touch him, didn't want to feel, period. And he remembered wryly that Gabriel had accused him of just the opposite. Gabriel had said that Luke wanted to love Melissa with all her faults but was unable to. Wouldn't someone in the role of savior be able to do that?

"I loved you and you rejected my love. That's all I know," he said.

"No, Luke. *You* rejected *me.* I never rejected you." She tossed the truth back to his unrelenting silhouette outlined in the faint moonlight. "When you saw that you couldn't be everything that I needed, and that the One who hung on that Roman cross nearly two thousand years ago could fill a part of me that you couldn't, you ran. And even more, you grabbed for every excuse to blame both God and me, so you could remain angry at us both."

"That's ridiculous."

"Is it?" she asked softly into the still night air. She shook her head sadly from side to side. "I don't think so." Sensing the need to draw his anger into the open where it could be confronted, she quoted one of her favorite verses from Psalm 62.

" 'My salvation and my honor depend on God; he is my mighty rock, my refuge.' "

It took Luke a moment to realize that she was reciting a Bible verse, but when he did, he lashed out with more angry words. "You're forgetting one thing, Bee," he rasped. "This God who is supposedly a refuge, a savior. . ." He spat out the words. "Where was He the night my sister lost so much?"

Melissa took a deep breath and spoke softly into the incalculable wonder of the starry night. "I don't have all the answers, Luke, and I won't insult your intelligence by pretending that I do. But I do know that God loves you, and He loves Anastasia, and He loves me. He cares for all of us. But it is our responsibility to respond to Him. He has spoken to us through His written Word, the Bible; through His Son, Jesus Christ; and through His Holy Spirit, His Comforter." She paused for a moment to let her words sink in. "Maybe He wants to tell you Himself where He was that night. But you refuse to listen. He's not going to force Himself on you. He's patient and He waits for us to turn to Him."

Luke shook his head in wonder. It amazed him how closely her words echoed what his good friend Gabriel had told him several times before. "So, is this why you left me? Is this what you needed to learn?" He couldn't hide the bitterness. He had worn it for so long that it had become an old, itchy sweater.

Melissa had finally had enough. She turned to him and the amber of her eyes flashed like topaz in the moonlight. "Let's get something straight, Luke, once and for all. *I* didn't leave you. *You left me.* And *yes,* I needed to learn about the love of God—the same love that my parents had shown me when I was a girl."

"I see." He spoke slowly, carefully, patiently, as if he were questioning a patient and trying to gather all the details he could about her medical history. "Then tell me, Melissa. Where was the love of God and your parents' protection the day they died?"

He knew it was a harsh question, and he instinctively looked at her eyes to gauge her response. By the light of the moon he saw the fire in her eyes settle into a soft and comforting glow. With a gentleness that suggested she was speaking to a child, Melissa said, "We don't know why certain things happen, Luke. But one thing I know for sure: I will see my parents again someday. One day, we will be reunited—and, until then, they are safe with God."

Luke felt her comforting hand on his shoulder, but this time he didn't move away. He needed her touch, needed her strength. He looked down at her and noticed that she was gazing out at the sea, which stretched before them like a carpet of pure satin. She began to speak again, and the words that came from her lips were like a soothing balm to his soul.

" 'If I go up to the heavens, you are there; if I make my bed in the depths, you are there. If I rise on the wings of the dawn, if I settle on the far side of the sea, even there your hand will guide me, your right hand will hold me fast.' " She licked her lips before continuing. " 'In you, O Lord, I have taken refuge; let me never be put to shame. Be my rock of refuge. . .' " She looked up toward the little fortress on the hill and smiled. " 'To which I can always go; give the command to save me, for you are my rock and my fortress.' "

She looked up at Luke and he saw the glistening of tears in her eyes. But they weren't tears of sadness or of pain; they were tears of joy that attested to her belief in every word she had spoken. "That's the truth, Luke," she whispered. "That's the truth."

Luke didn't know what to say, so he didn't say anything, but the angry wall of resistance inside his chest seemed to melt away. Gently, he placed his arms around Melissa's shoulders and drew her close to him. He didn't understand everything she had said, but he was more certain of one thing than he had ever been before.

He loved her.

And for the first time, he was willing to admit that he loved her exactly the way she was. Her firm belief in God was now part of the Melissa he loved. He ran his hand up and down her back, and when his fingers brushed against the chain around her neck, he paused for a second before resuming his caress. He knew that she felt his hesitation, because her breath seemed to catch in her throat. And he knew what she wanted. She wanted him to ask what the cross meant. But he couldn't. Not yet. Maybe not ever.

"Where do we go from here?" he finally asked, relieved that the nervous silence had been breached.

She tilted her head back to look up at him. "Well, I think we still need. . ." She paused and shrugged her shoulders, softening the word, "Time."

He looked deep into her eyes and then, slowly, their lips met in a kiss that united the past and the present in a commitment to make a new start. It was the kiss they should have shared in the cabin at Lake Breeze a year and a half before. It was a kiss that promised a love that could wait.

After a moment, with his chin resting on top of her head, Luke repeated his question, "Where do we go from here, Meli?" He honestly didn't know. He only knew that he didn't want to lose her again.

Stepping back, she shrugged her shoulders and looked up at the moonlit walls of the Byzantine tower. Gray and silvery, the ruins were romantically silhouetted against the depths of the night. "Well, I do have fortresses to research. I think I'll travel over to Acrocorinth tomorrow and then work my way across the peninsula."

"Not tomorrow," Luke spoke firmly, and she was sure that she heard fear in his voice.

Arching her brows, she assured him, "I'll be back."

He shook his head. "It's not that. It's the traffic. The roads are horrible on Fridays and the weekends. Visit Chlemoutsi tomorrow. It's only about fifteen minutes away."

And then she understood. He had been angry when she drove straight from the airport in Athens without resting. Anastasia's accident had put that fear in him. She could understand it. It was something like her fear of bees.

"Okay, Chlemoutsi it is."

"Besides," he said, "I'm going to close my office for a couple of weeks and I'll be happy to accompany you to all the fortresses you want to see."

"Luke!" Melissa exclaimed. "You can't do that. What about your patients?"

"I've already made arrangements. I planned this time away as soon as I knew you were coming—just in case."

Melissa threw her arms around his shoulders. "I had no idea!"

He chuckled. "Until this moment, I had no idea whether it was the right thing to do or not. But now I'm sure." He drew her closer to him. "I want us to try, Meli. I don't want to lose you again."

"Oh, Luke." She leaned up and kissed his chin. They had so much to work on. She knew that unless he became a man of faith she couldn't marry him, and his decision had to be genuine and uncoerced. He couldn't profess a faith in God just to make her happy. After all that they'd been through, she knew that Luke would never do that, and she resolved once again to trust God with the outcome.

"Meli," he started softly, a wistful quality in his voice and gentleness in his touch. "Perhaps I did want to be everything to you," he admitted. In truth, he still did. "But, is that so bad?"

"Oh no, Luke. I loved you for it then as I do now, but it's not a job that a human can handle. You're everything to me, as a man—I never want another—but you aren't God. And that isn't even a job you should covet—"

He stopped her by pressing his fingers lightly against her lips. "Not now, Melissa. You told me that you would wait until I asked. I'm not ready to ask that question, and I honestly don't know if I ever will be. I still can't help but feel that it was your sudden love for God that took you away from me."

She respected his honesty even though she wanted to argue with his conclusions.

"But there is one thing I do promise you," he continued as he drew her close to him again. "You are right. I do run away from situations that I find disagreeable. In some respects, it's amazing that I made it through medical school. But I promise you that I will never run away from you again."

Melissa squeezed her eyes shut. "Thank you, Luke," she whispered and nuzzled her nose against his neck, inhaling the masculine scent of the man she loved.

Chapter 17

Melissa spent the next morning at the Chlemoutsi Castle, and when she saw that she was running out of time to explore the fort, she obtained special permission from the guard to stay past the closing hour of three o'clock.

She was thrilled to walk among the walls of the crusader fortress. Melissa knew that the Fourth Crusade, which brought the Franks to Greece, was one of the greatest civil disasters in Christian history. One denomination, the Latin Church of the West, attacked and plundered Constantinople, the capital of the Greek church of the East. Yet she couldn't help but admire the Frankish Castle of Chlemoutsi.

Built between the years of 1220 and 1223 high above the Ionian Sea, it was a bulwark of strength and the site of many a great tournament. Melissa could almost hear the elegant cheers of the medieval ladies as they sat above the galleries and cheered on their favorite knights, who jousted and fenced on the grounds below.

The *meltemia* winds blew strongly and Melissa marveled at how they carried the heat away from the fortress on the hill. When it occurred to her that the same winds had blown during the time of the Franks, she felt a special connection with this historic site. The warm wind seemed to sing of the tale of the crusaders as it blew in and around the parapets and crenels, through the lancet windows and up the crumbling stairways.

As she stood among the massive walls of the man-made citadel, Melissa understood why King David in his psalms so often compared God to a strong fortress. There was something protective and reassuring about the gigantic walls of rough-cut, well-fitted limestone—something natural that was different from modern structures. The walls of Chlemoutsi were secure and firm even after more than seven hundred and fifty years of attacks from men and the forces of nature.

With the waning sun bathing the walls of the castle in golden hues of orange and red, she climbed the steps to the roof of the keep's galleries from where she had a panoramic view of her surroundings. Pulling her binoculars out of her backpack, she trained them toward the promontory to the south and the much older walls of the Byzantine Beauvoir. Below the edge of the rocky knoll sat Villa Beauvoir.

Melissa involuntarily sighed. She knew that she and Luke still had tall walls to scale in their personal relationship, but she was filled with peace when she acknowledged that they had made a good start at climbing them the previous night. Lowering the binoculars, she pulled Luke's cross out from beneath her T-shirt. It captured the rays of the setting sun and flashed in the palm of her hand. She squeezed it once before slipping it back inside her shirt, then gave one last sweeping look over the stupendous, unobstructed view before carefully picking her way back down to the entrance of the keep.

She walked through the deeply shadowed corridors and past the wide galleries. Night was beginning to fall on Chlemoutsi Castle, and although she carried a flashlight in her backpack, she didn't welcome the idea of getting caught all alone in the castle after dark. Stones and hidden foundations from fallen medieval dwellings littered the courtyard. By day, it was a mass of picturesque debris, but definitely not something she would want to traverse by the shadows of night.

Stepping out of the vaulted gallery, she approached the arched gateway of the keep. But the view framed by the stone arch caused her to pause. The sun was a gigantic orange ball, low in the fiery sky, and it highlighted the green of the fields below with a depth of color that an artist could only dream about. The walls of the old fort were nearly fuchsia in the light. Even the swallows flying to their nests above the arch seemed to trail fire from the sun in their wake.

Melissa couldn't resist watching the "show" from this vantage point. Dropping her bag against the wall next to a wild rose bush, she sat on the old stone walkway. With her arms stretched out behind her and her legs in front, she was wishing that Luke was with her to watch the sunset when the sudden intrusion of several high-speed military airplanes startled her. She quickly laughed at her jumpiness and waved at the second plane as it blasted past her. The lead jet was already over the fortress of Beauvoir and the villa fifteen kilometers to the south.

While she was waving at the second plane, she saw a black blur out of the corner of her eye circling her outstretched leg. In the split second that it took for her to recognize the blur as a bee, it attacked her and she felt the sharp pain of its stinger jabbing her ankle.

Jumping to her feet with a horrified shriek, she swatted and clawed at her ankle, clumsily dislodging the stinger in the process. Tears filled her eyes. "Oh, God! Help me!" she cried out and looked frantically around for help, even though she knew she was alone in the fortress. Looking down at her ankle, she watched in horror as it began to swell. She started breathing quickly and felt her body break out in a cold sweat. She knew that she was going into shock over being stung, but she also knew that she couldn't allow that to happen—not in a deserted castle with night quickly approaching.

Yanking her canteen out of her bag, she bathed her ankle with water. It was getting larger by the second and she knew that she had to get help. Grabbing her bag, she stumbled to her feet and rubbed her eyes. Even they felt heavy to her, as if they were beginning to swell too. She told herself that her imagination was working overtime now that she had finally been stung by a dreaded bee.

She stumbled down the ramp to the courtyard of the castle. It had seemed plenty big before, but it now looked like a continent. She didn't know how she would manage the uneven terrain.

The cross swinging freely from her neck caught her eye and called to mind the words of Psalm 18. " 'The Lord is my rock, my fortress.' " She took a step and looked around her. She knew that the fortress built by the hands of men couldn't help her—it was made of the inanimate stones of the earth—but the security she found in the fortress of God could. She took another step. " '. . .And my deliverer.' " She took two more steps. " 'My God is my rock, in whom I take refuge.' " She took three more steps and with each word she spoke, the panic that was threatening to overwhelm her was kept at bay.

" 'He is my shield and the horn of my salvation, my stronghold.' " Melissa knew as she forced one foot in front of the other that her Shield, her Stronghold was walking with her.

When she had finished reciting Psalm 18, she went on to some verses from Psalm 71. " 'In you, O Lord, I have taken refuge.' " She looked around at the castle's walls. People had taken refuge among these walls in ages past. She shook her head. They were like a prison to her now, a true testimony to the unreliable nature of the walls of men. " 'Rescue me and deliver me in your righteousness; turn your ear to me and save me.' " She paused and squeezed her eyes shut. They didn't feel right. She willed her feet to walk on. " 'Be my rock of refuge, to which I can always go; give the command to save me, for you are. . .' " Melissa stopped walking and inhaled deeply. But not as much air as she wanted was brought into her lungs, and fear started to inch its insidious way up her spine again. " 'You are my rock,' " she whispered, and forced her swollen foot to support her as she took another step, " '. . .and my fortress.' "

She reached the midway point and shrugged her bag off her back, unable to support its weight any longer. She found her flashlight in the side pocket and grasping it, she turned it on, just in case someone might come and see the wavering light in the deepening of the night.

She stumbled forward, willing herself to breathe slowly and carefully and not to let the walls around her, which had become looming shadows in the near darkness, scare her. Instead, she used them as a reminder of the One, the true Fortress, that protected her and loved her, her Fortress of Love. He was her Fortress inside this fortress and she would not let panic rule her. Only God.

The curtain loomed above her now, the friendly gray, sun-bleached wall of day was now a black monstrous form of incredible height. It had been about fifteen minutes since the sting, but it felt more like fifteen hours. Her face and eyes were definitely swelling, and Melissa knew that she must be having an allergic reaction to the bee sting. Her ankle was three times its normal size now, but it was the swelling in her face that concerned her. . .and her labored breathing.

The walk through the wall lay directly ahead and she squeezed her fingers tightly around the flashlight. The dark tunnel, which had been a haven of cool relief from the hot sun during the day, now scared her. Panic again gained a foothold in her mind. "Dear Lord. . . ," she whimpered, her strength almost gone, "please send someone to help me."

When she saw the light, she thought she was hallucinating.

"Melissa!" Luke's voice drifted out of the deep wall to reach her ears and she screamed, a scream of relief, a scream of terror that propelled Luke to her side within seconds.

"Luke! Luke!" She threw herself into his arms and cried.

"Meli! What happened?" He was kissing her but stopped when he felt the swelling of her skin. Training his flashlight onto her face, he sucked in his breath.

"I was. . .stung. . .by. . .a bee," her voice rose on a hysterical note, all the years of her fear sounding in it. "Luke," she tightened her arms around him and wailed out, "a bee. . . ."

It wasn't her fear that concerned him now. It was her labored breathing. "Where were you stung?" he asked firmly; his clinical skills took over and she became his patient.

Melissa took a wheezing breath and pointed to her leg. "My ankle."

Fear sliced through Luke like a cut from a scalpel. He quickly diagnosed an anaphylactic reaction to the bee sting. She needed help—and fast. He picked her up as if she weighed no more than Emilia and ran through the tunnel and out the castle wall.

He knew that the castle closed at three o'clock, so when Melissa hadn't been at the villa when he arrived home at six, he'd simply assumed that she had decided to spend some time in the vicinity of the castle researching the area. It had mildly annoyed him, because after the previous night, he had been looking forward to talking to her about her castle-treading day.

When she hadn't returned by seven, he'd become angry that the castle was apparently more important than spending time with him. But when Gabriel arrived an hour later, Luke's anger had turned to cold fear and they had immediately set out to find her.

For some reason, Luke hadn't expected her to be hurt. Even after they found her car parked outside the castle, he'd thought that she was just enjoying the sunset. It rocked him to his very core to find her in danger.

"Gabriel!" He shouted out to his friend who was looking for Melissa around the outside of the walls. "I found her! She's been stung by a bee. She's allergic."

Luke didn't have to say another word. Gabriel ran to the car, grabbed his Ana-kit, and sprinted toward the frantic sound of Luke's voice. Ever since he had discovered his own sensitivity to bee stings the previous summer, Gabriel had carried an antidote with him everywhere he went.

Luke covered the last twenty meters to his friend's side with Melissa in his arms. Gabriel coaxed Melissa to swallow antihistamine tablets while Luke injected her with adrenaline. "Let's get her to the hospital!"

Luke held her in the backseat while Gabriel drove and prayed.

Luke prayed too. *God. . .if you can hear me. . .please let my Meli be okay. I promise that I will ask her about the cross.* He knew in his mind that he was making an immature plea bargain with God, but it was all he could think to do.

Please, God, let her be okay.

Chapter 18

A s they drove, Luke didn't allow her to speak. He stroked her face and kept her calm. Her eyes, now only shiny slits showing through swollen flesh, never left his.

Her fingers moved weakly against the gold cross, drawing Luke's eyes down to it. He looked at the symbolic pendant lying in her hand. Slowly, thoughts and ideas that he had held for a lifetime shifted and moved, reorganizing themselves within his mind.

She had wanted to go to Acrocorinth that day. In a bid to protect her, he had asked her to go to the much closer Chlemoutsi.

He shook his head.

At Chlemoutsi, she had been stung by a bee. A tiny *melissa*, perhaps, but she was allergic. He wasn't able to protect her. Luke finally recognized the futility of trying to protect his loved ones from circumstances that were beyond his control. And for the first time ever, he considered that maybe, just maybe, God wasn't as far off as he had always thought Him to be. . .

Hadn't God protected his *Meli* today, by sending help in the nick of time? And not just any help, but a doctor and a battle-tested embassy official who carried a bee sting antidote. *The right help at the right time.* Luke mulled the words over in his mind.

Without giving it another thought, as if it were the most natural thing in the world for him to do, he reached down and wrapped his fingers around Melissa's—and the cross.

From within the hazy depths of her consciousness, Melissa noticed what Luke had done, and a tiny burst of joy pulsed within her heart. Unable to formulate any words, she lifted her thumb and rubbed it across the top of his hand. Feelings of peace, contentment, and satisfaction washed though her and she silently prayed that God would make her well so she could tell Luke everything. She closed her eyes and focused all her energy on breathing.

They arrived at the hospital just as Melissa started to turn blue. Her throat was constricted, but the emergency room doctors were able to insert a small tracheal tube, enough to relieve her lack of oxygen, and saved her from the trauma of a tracheotomy, which Gabriel had suffered the previous summer when he had been stung by a *sersegia*.

Luke sat by her side throughout the night, and as he watched the respirator breathe for her, his thoughts took him on a life journey to all those places and times when he had felt helpless: when he had been a child and his parents had given material blessings but neglected a hug or a smile; when Melissa's home had been broken into and he hadn't been able to do anything to prevent it; when Melissa had told him that she wanted to postpone their marriage; when Anastasia had lay broken and mourning the loss of both her husband and unborn child in a hospital bed not unlike the one he now sat beside.

When Luke returned to the present, he was amazed to realize that he no longer felt helpless. Although he knew that an allergic reaction to a sting could be life-threatening, he sensed for the first time that Melissa's care wasn't only up to him or the other doctors. Someone much stronger than any human physician was working to heal his *Meli*. He could almost feel the difference, taste the difference. It seemed to be in the air around her.

As he continued to review his life, he admitted that his idea of God had been shaped wrongly. He had always considered that God was like his father, a distant chairman of the board, sitting in a big boardroom in the sky, with no time for Luke or any of his concerns. He was beginning to realize that if he were to compare God to a father-type figure, *Nono* would be a much better representative.

He glanced down at the cross that now lay on top of Melissa's hospital gown in violation of the hospital's rule against patients wearing jewelry, which he had used his professional clout to circumvent. He remembered the look on Melissa's face when he had angrily thrust the chain over her head and insisted that she keep the necklace. What a fool he had been for blaming Melissa for postponing the wedding—and how unfair it had been for him to blame her for Anastasia's accident.

He had always known that he wanted to spend the rest of his life with Melissa. But this time, he would try to follow the path she had taken. It had changed her, yes, but for the better. He had to admit that the only changes he had made were for the worse.

He reached out and rubbed the smooth metal of the cross with his fingers. When she was able to tell him, he would listen to what she had to say about the cross. And this time his decision was what he really wanted, not a desperate plea bargain with God.

Early the next morning, Luke disconnected Melissa from the respirator and she was able to breathe on her own with an oxygen mask. By ten o'clock, she no longer needed the mask, and Luke leaned down and kissed her. "I love you, Meli. Don't ever leave me." His voice was low and husky with emotion.

Melissa reached out and ran her fingertips over the stubble of his beard. "I'm sorry, Luke. I didn't mean to scare you." Her throat, sore from the tracheal tube, produced a rough whisper that came out little more than a croak.

"I know," he said and kissed her lightly on the forehead. Her face was still swollen, her eyes mere slits of amber light between the puffy flesh, and his heart nearly stopped beating when he considered that her throat had been as swollen as her face.

She smiled, an ironic twist to her already alien features. "Can you believe it? All these years of being frightened of bees and I'm allergic to them."

Reaching for her hand and with a voice that nearly broke from remorse, he apologized, "Meli. . .I'm so sorry. . .I've. . ." He swallowed. "I've said some horrible things to you—about bees, I mean."

She squeezed his hand. "It's all forgiven and forgotten, Luke. All forgiven," she repeated, and he knew she really meant it. Though the swelling of her face made a mockery of her appearance, she had never looked more beautiful to Luke.

He reached down, and lifting the old cross from where it had been warmed by the beating of her heart for the last year and a half, he held it gently with his fingertips and said, "Maybe, when you're feeling better, you can tell me," he paused and smiled, "just what this means to you."

Her soul sang at the words she had waited so long to hear.

Without hesitation, she tilted her head to remove the chain from around her neck. Luke had to help her because it was tangled in her hair. He did so with infinite care.

She handed the necklace to him.

Without protest, he took it from her hand and placed the chain around his neck. The old cross settled, like a sigh, back where it belonged.

Melissa covered the metal pendant with the palm of her hand, touching it, and touching Luke at the same time. "The cross itself means very little," she began. "It's a beautiful piece of jewelry, a family heirloom that I have loved because it is yours," she whispered. "But it's the cross of Jesus that it represents that has true meaning, eternal meaning."

"The cross of Jesus," Luke repeated.

She nodded and her eyes filled with tears because it was the first time she had ever heard him say the Savior's name. It sounded so beautiful coming from his lips and she was glad that he had never spoken the Lord's name in anger or bitterness.

Sitting on the side of the bed, he leaned so close to her that their noses practically touched. "I realized last night, Meli, that anything important to you, is important to me. And that includes your belief in the cross of Jesus. I want you to tell me everything, but not here. At home, when you're feeling better."

She nodded and sank into the cool sheets. She didn't mind waiting to tell him. She closed her eyes and drifted off to sleep.

&

The days of Melissa's convalescence were joyful days for all the inhabitants of Villa Beauvoir. Gabriel and Luke were on holiday, and *Nono* finally gave in to the persistent entreaties of Emilia and Anastasia and agreed to close up his house in the village for the rest of the summer to stay with them. Soula was in her element catering to the many hearty appetites, and Emilia flitted among them all, like a butterfly that had just learned how to fly. Melissa and Gabriel, brother and sister in the Lord, became friends immediately.

Melissa was surprised at how long it took for her to regain her strength. She seemed to be tired all the time and spent many hours each day sleeping, either in her room or on the verandah. She would drift off to a happy sleep while conversations played around her and wake up an hour or two later to find herself lovingly covered with a nicely scented sheet, either alone or with Anastasia softly strumming the guitar Melissa was teaching her to play. Sometimes, Emilia was quietly playing with her dolls by her feet, or Gabriel was reading in a nearby chair.

Luke always appeared soon after she awoke, and he was as solicitous and caring as a prince in a fairy tale might be to his princess.

Melissa floated along on a cloud of happiness that took several days to reach the earth. What finally brought her back to earth was something that brought heaven down with it.

Chapter 19

Four mornings after the bee sting, Melissa awoke bright-eyed and feeling like her old self again—except happier. Checking her ankle, she was relieved to see that the swelling was finally gone. Only a head remained where the actual sting had occurred, but Luke had told her that it would go away with time as well.

Stretching, she was determined to start her days again with sitting on the verandah, reading her Bible, and praying. She hadn't been able to follow her routine for the past several days. Exhaustion, one of the after-effects of the sting, as well as medication, had kept her in bed until well after ten each morning.

She reached into the night table drawer for her traveling Bible, but it wasn't there. Sitting on the side of her bed, she remembered that she had last seen the Bible in her backpack the day at the castle. Gabriel had retrieved her pack from Chlemoutsi the following morning, along with her car, so she assumed that the Bible must still be in it.

Glancing around her room, she realized that she didn't even know where her backpack was. She was about to retrieve her father's Bible from the dresser drawer when the soft strains of guitar chords drifted into the room. Tying her silk robe around her waist, she padded out to the verandah and leaned up against her doorjamb to watch Anastasia. Luke's sister, dressed in a new, bright yellow dressing gown, started singing the hymn "Rock of Ages."

She sang softly in first soprano, but it was a voice that contained strength, and Melissa was sure that she would be able to fill an opera house with her notes if she wanted to. Anastasia was a gifted musician and Melissa felt privileged to have played a part in her discovering her talent.

Sensing Melissa's presence, Anastasia turned to her. A smile parted her lips as she started to sing the third verse of Thomas Hastings's song. Her shining, green eyes bored into Melissa's in a way that told Melissa more clearly than a million words ever could that her friend was singing her testimony!

> *Nothing in my hand I bring,*
> *Simply to Thy cross I cling,*
> *Naked, come to Thee for dress,*
> *Helpless, look to Thee for grace;*
> *Foul, I to the fountain fly;*
> *Wash me, Savior, or I die.*

Softly the strings faded into quietness and in answer to the wondrous question covering Melissa's face, Anastasia nodded her head. "We are truly sisters now, Melissa. I believe."

"Oh, Anastasia!" Tears filled Melissa's eyes. Running quickly to Anastasia's side, she knelt down and rested her head in her lap. "How?"

"How?" Anastasia repeated and laughed, a carefree, happy sound. "You, Gabriel, *Nono*, Soula, Emilia, Luke. . .but most of all, God. He didn't desert me, Melissa. Not ever. Not even when I was angry at Him and accused Him of not caring, and not hearing, and even, of not existing. He has always been close to me. I only had to answer Him. I finally did."

Reaching over to the table beside her, she picked up Melissa's much-used travel Bible. "I hope you don't mind, but when I saw that you weren't reading it these last few days," she paused, and grimaced, "I kind of borrowed it. Gabriel gave me a Bible a long time ago, but you know, there's something alive about reading a Bible that someone else has loved and written in, prayed and cried over."

Melissa nodded her head in understanding. "As your sister—your spiritual sister—I want you to keep it."

Anastasia's lips puckered together. She knew how much the Bible meant to Melissa. "That's one of many things I like about you, Melissa. You see past things to what is really real. The cross, the Bible, they mean a lot to you, but not as objects in themselves."

Melissa shrugged her shoulders and laughed. "It took me a long time to learn that."

"I will treasure it always." Anastasia held the book lovingly to her chest and they sat in companionable silence for several precious minutes. The same feelings of euphoria ran through Melissa that she would have felt if she had just been told that a much-awaited baby had just been born.

"Melissa," Anastasia began softly after a moment. "There's something else that I want to tell you."

Melissa knew from her friend's tone that it had to be something wonderful. Tilting her head to the side, her eyes flashed like topaz as she eagerly waited for Anastasia to continue.

"Now that I have accepted Christ as my Savior, Gabriel and I—we're going to be married!"

"Anastasia!" Melissa squealed and threw her arms around her. "I'm so happy for you."

"And I'm happy for you," Anastasia laughed, squeezing Melissa closer to her. "I think, that very soon, we are going to be sisters in more than just a spiritual way."

Melissa sat back and searched Anastasia's face with her eyes. "What do you mean?"

Anastasia looked like a cat who had just been given a sirloin steak. "Only that my Bible, the one Gabriel gave to me, hasn't gone unread these days."

Melissa's mouth opened, but it took her a moment before she could whisper her question. "Luke?"

Anastasia smiled. "I think you'd better get dressed and go find my brother. Most likely he's where he's been all week. In his office." She paused. "Uhh. . .studying."

≈

When she had showered and dressed, Melissa walked downstairs to Luke's office. Suddenly feeling shy, she knocked softly on the door. She had only been in the room on one other occasion and had been impressed by its beauty. The deep, rich brown of his oak desk and matching unit of shelves filled to capacity with medical books of all shapes, colors, and sizes, had impressed her. That Luke's brain could contain all that knowledge amazed her even more.

Luke opened the door hunched down to the level of a young child. "Luke?" Melissa laughed.

He straightened and smiled self-consciously. "Sorry. I thought it was Emilia," he said, confirming her suspicion. "She's always telling me that I'm too tall for her to see my eyes, so. . ." His voice trailed off.

"You are tall. . ." Her eyes twinkled with love. "But I like it."

He pulled her into his arms. "And I like everything about you, Meli, my love."

"Everything?" she asked.

Without saying a word, he reached for the chain around his neck and pulled the cross out from beneath his shirt.

When Melissa saw what was hanging on the chain with it, she drew in a sharp breath. "My engagement ring," she murmured. Amazement painted her features. She had assumed that he would return the ring after she gave it back to him at the cabin. She'd never expected to see it again. She looked at him with a silent question in her amber eyes.

He didn't make her wait for an answer. "I told you the other day at the hospital that I was ready for you to tell me about the cross." He rubbed his fingers over the pendant. "But, I've changed my mind. Instead, I'm going to tell you about what I believe. When I'm finished, I think you will agree that what I believe is the same as what you believe—maybe a little bit immature—but the same." His eyes looked very green to her and very, very deep.

"Luke," she whispered his name, and joy soared in her heart. She hardly dared to breathe.

Slowly, he began. "You told me, a long time ago, that the ring was because of the cross. And you're right. The ring *is* because of the cross, and anyone who takes the ring without first taking hold of the cross, starts off in a relationship that is crippled."

"You understand," she whispered.

He gazed for a moment into the amber depths of her eyes. They drew him in the same way they had at the Christmas ball the night he met Melissa. He nodded. "Your accident made me think, Meli." He walked over to the packed bookshelf and ran his fingers lovingly over the spines of the books. "I realized that I have read all of these volumes that describe everything we humans have discovered about treating diseases. But—" He walked back to his desk and picked up Anastasia's Bible. "I had never read the Book that tells the reason for diseases."

"Luke. . ." She took a step toward him but forced herself to stop.

"I don't want to be your savior anymore, Melissa. You've already got one." He paused and Melissa was certain she saw water begin to pool in the corners of his eyes. When he spoke, his voice was softer and tinged with love. "And so have I."

"Luke." She reached for his hands. "You believe?"

He nodded. "I believe that 'God so loved the world that he gave his one and only Son, that whoever believes in him shall not perish but have eternal life.' And I never knew this existed, but I have found 'the peace of God, which transcends all understanding.' And I am confident that this peace will guard my heart, and your heart, and my mind, and your mind, and everyone else who believes in Jesus Christ."

"Luke!" She fell into his arms and great big tears of happiness and relief welled from deep within her soul.

"You were right, Meli," he whispered, and she turned her face up to meet his. "It never would have worked before. We would have ended up a divorce statistic." He paused and kissed her lightly on the cheek. "Thank you for not accepting me as your savior. I never would have been able to finish the job."

"I know, Luke. But your heart was in the right place. It really was."

He nodded. He finally understood. "I loved you then and I love you now. But there is a difference, a gigantic difference. I now understand that love isn't what all the popular songs say. It isn't only tied up with our feelings and desires for one another. It's a meshing of all our parts—body, soul, and spirit—in line with God's spirit. God is Love, and only Love itself can guide us in how to be *in it*. Because to be *in love*, is to first be *in* a right relationship with God." Keeping his arm around her shoulder he guided her over to his desk and reached into the top drawer. Pulling out a carefully wrapped bundle, he handed it to her. "Open it."

With a questioning frown, she folded back the soft, blue felt. The little man-and-woman Christmas tree ornament that Luke had bought for their tree at the cabin stared back at her. Melissa looked up at Luke with wonder in her eyes. The last time she had seen the little carved couple, they had tumbled beneath the woodpile at the cabin after Luke had angrily yanked them off the top of the tree and thrown them across the room. She almost shuddered at the memory of that night.

"When I bought this ornament I hoped that we would eventually be like them," he admitted, and pointed to the happy expressions on the little wooden faces. "But I made a mistake when I put them on the top of our tree. The top should be reserved for a star or an angel, something that heralds the incarnation of Christ." He pointed to the Bible. "A star shone and angels sang that night as a way of declaring the wonder of God's Son leaving His throne in heaven and coming on a rescue mission to earth. This little couple can go on all of our Christmas trees, but not at the top," he declared. She nodded her head in amazement at how quickly he had grasped spiritual things.

"Melissa," he continued, "I'm only going to ask you this question one more time." With a big smile, he removed the heavy gold chain from around his neck and opened the clasp to pull off the engagement ring. Holding the ring between his thumb and forefinger, he said, "In Christ, we are both complete halves now. Be the half that makes me whole. Will you marry me?"

"Umm. . ." Melissa bit her lip and then dissolved in merry laughter. Without further hesitation, she reached out her hand to let Luke slide the ring onto her finger. "Dear, wonderful, faithful Luke, I would be honored to be both your wife and. . . ," her smile deepened as she considered how much her next words would mean to him, "the mother of your children."

He pulled her tightly against his chest. "A family," he murmured.

"*Our* family, Luke. *Our* family," she whispered. As she rested her head against his chest and listened to the strong, steady beating of his heart, Melissa glanced through the window at the little fortress on the hill and she smiled. Raising her eyes higher yet, to the soaring sky above, she gave thanks to her Rock, her Refuge, her Redeemer, her Fortress, for saving the man she loved.

Epilogue

"*Christos Anesti!* Christ is Risen!" the pastor shouted joyously to the congregation of believers from around the world who had gathered for the Easter sunrise service on Philopappos Hill in Athens. The Acropolis sat before them, silhouetted against Homer's "rosy fingers of light" as the dawning of the new morning, Easter morning, filled the sky.

"*Alithos Anesti!* Truly He is Risen!" the believers replied in unison. Luke drew his wife closer to him. His fingers touched the gentle fullness of Melissa's belly, where their long-awaited child was growing safe and secure.

Leaning over, in the great outdoor church with birds singing and fluttering above them and church bells ringing in the city below, Luke kissed the side of Melissa's head.

She looked up at her husband and smiled. No woman had ever been loved more. She had prayed that Luke's parents would spend Easter with them, and he had been amazed when they accepted the invitation. She had prayed the same thing about her aunt and uncle, but her petition had not been answered in the same way. She had received a nice card from her uncle, who said that he would come for a visit when the baby was born, but the note made it clear that he would be traveling alone. Her aunt's heart was still as hard and cold as ice, but Melissa didn't let that bother her. She continued to pray for her aunt's salvation. Melissa knew that miracles could happen if she lifted her requests up to God.

But as she surveyed the happy faces around her on the ancient hilltop, she rejoiced to see so many friends, including Jane and Dale from Virginia, and dear *Nono* and Soula, who had traveled with them from St. Andreas.

Luke nodded his head toward Anastasia as Gabriel pushed her wheelchair to the front of the congregation. Emilia walked next to them holding her mother's guitar.

"*Christos Anesti!* Christ is risen! Happy Easter!" Anastasia shouted, smiling broadly as the congregation replied in kind.

"My name is Anastasia Crown," she announce. She reached out for her husband's hand. "I've been asked to sing this morning, but before I do, I wanted to say a few words." The congregation hushed as they waited; the only sound was the chattering of the birds and the movement of the leaves on the trees.

"My name is of Greek origin and it means 'Who shall rise again.' " She motioned toward a stylish, older man and woman, who were standing, a bit uncomfortably, but proudly, next to Luke. Anastasia smiled, a gentle, forgiving smile. "I think my parents knew what they were doing when they gave me my name. Several years ago, I suffered a horrible automobile accident. I lost my first husband and my unborn son, and I was left paralyzed. But then a man came into my life," she looked up at Gabriel, "who slowly, with love, and much patience showed me that I was much more crippled in my soul than I ever would be in my legs. And then a sister," she looked over at Melissa and her smile deepened, "came into my life, and through her life, she showed me the same thing. Now, I am of the resurrection and I praise God daily for it. I would like for you to join me in singing 'Christ the Lord is Risen Today'!"

Programs flapped in the breeze as Anastasia strummed the first few chords of the song. She sang the first part of each line and the congregation joined in for the alleluias.

The beautiful Acropolis of Athens, one of the strongest fortresses made by men, stood in all its marbled splendor as the sun poked its golden head above the honey-scented mountains surrounding the ancient city. The rays shone on the believers—from Asia, Australia, the two Americas, Europe, and Africa—who were gathered together singing and celebrating the resurrection of the Son of God.

In the light of the newborn day, a bee buzzed in front of Luke's eyes. He squeezed Melissa closer to him and gently waved the insect away.

He would always protect Melissa, but it was a relief to know that he wasn't the only one who was responsible for her.

Luke Karalis smiled at the Easter sky, looked up toward heaven, toward his Savior, toward his Fortress of Love, and he sang, "Alleluia!"

ODYSSEY OF LOVE

To my dear husband George, with whom I travel. . .
"the path of life. . ." With love, Melanie

Chapter 1

The *tap, tap, tap* of Kristen King's high-heeled shoes irrationally irritated her as she crossed the marble lobby of the downtown San Francisco hotel where she worked as marketing director. The sharp repetition echoed loudly in the hushed elegance of the building and seemed an intrusion, an invasion of the refined surroundings, and even worse, it called attention to Kristen, something she avoided.

Kristen slowed her walk as she approached the reception desk and the tapping receded, relieving her.

But attention had already been drawn to her by the information receptionist who pointed her out to the tall man inquiring as to the location of her office.

Standing away from the information desk, hands in the pockets of his three-piece, ash gray business suit, the man named Paul Andrakos watched Kristen King with dark, assessing eyes.

Paul had not been sure what to expect when he had decided to travel the eleven thousand miles around the world in order to find his godmother's long-lost niece. But the refined, cool beauty of the tall woman leaning across the reception desk surprised him.

His eyes lingered over the shiny texture of her sable hair, pulled back into some type of skillful knot away from her face. Then they traveled down the long, shapely length of her body to the tip of her black leather pumps, and for the first time since his godmother, Aphrodite, had mentioned her wish to meet her niece, Paul felt the older woman had made the right decision. Kristen King was a woman Paul Andrakos wanted to meet as well.

Kristen turned away from the reception desk and walked in the direction of the imposing doors of the hotel. Paul fell into step behind her. She had the bearing of a queen and yet something about the nape of her neck seemed vulnerable to him. It was velvety and soft, and he found himself wanting to slide his face close to it, smell it, taste it, feel it. He wanted to remove the pins that kept her long hair tight against her head and cover her neck—protect it—protect her.

Paul breathed out deeply.

He had known more than his fair share of the world's beautiful, and so-called sophisticated women, and knowledge of them had made him cynical. The health of his bank balance and the mystique behind his profession attracted women like flowers do bees. And although most didn't know it, and even fewer would suspect it, Paul was stung to know that these qualities were his strongest draw to the opposite sex. What Paul believed and how he felt about things were both of minor importance to the women he had known. This experience had jaded him.

It had been a while since Paul had seen a woman across a room and felt that special urge to want to know her in that deep, giving way that made for a special relationship. It had been even longer since he had done anything about that urge, not wanting to chance being disappointed yet again. But watching Kristen as she strode, tall and elegant, purposefully in front of him, that desire was definitely there and it was signaling strongly for her. Paul especially liked the idea that Kristen King didn't know a thing about him, his work, or his monetary assets. For once, Paul felt at an advantage. He knew more about an attractive woman than she did about him.

But before he could think about her in those terms he had to ascertain if she was a woman to be trusted with knowledge about her Aunt Aphrodite, his godmother.

Paul's long stride brought him up next to Kristen.

"Excuse me? Ms. King?" he asked.

Kristen cringed inwardly as she heard her name called. Her thoughts had already walked out the hotel doors, if not her body, so to turn and confront an unknown and very attractive man, a man who already was doing something to her equilibrium, was more than she wanted to tackle at the moment. But business was business, she was still in the hotel, and even though she would have like to have avoided this gentleman, she had no choice but to respond to him.

"Yes? May I help you?" A frown cut across her pale forehead as she considered that he looked vaguely familiar, but just as quickly Kristen was sure that she had never before met him. With thick hair, the color of old gold, and eyes that were like finely polished chestnuts, he wasn't a man whom a woman was ever likely to forget—not even Kristen, who had been hurt badly by the man who widowed her, and who had subsequently avoided all involvement with men like one avoids a head-on collision.

"I'm Paul Andrakos." He extended his hand, and a collision was exactly what Kristen felt inside herself when she looked up his considerable height into the darkness of his eyes.

Kristen took Paul's hand. The embrace felt good, he had a firm handshake, a handshake to be trusted. But Kristen had not trusted anybody in a very long time.

"Andrakos? . . . A Greek name?" she questioned, quick to cover with small talk the attraction she felt for him. It was a skill she had perfected during the last few years of her twenty-eight years of life.

"Definitely," Paul affirmed and smiled, a friendly smile, and yet Kristen thought that it was a careful smile as well. Their hands parted but not their eyes. His continued to hold hers. They narrowed and made Kristen feel as if he were measuring her up, but not in an inappropriate way, and not in a business way either. This assessment did not offend Kristen, only puzzle her.

"I need to talk to you," he explained, "about family business."

"Family business. . . ," she echoed quickly, caught off guard. That was the last thing she expected to hear and her eyes widened as her mind started to run wildly through that all too familiar nightmarish maze which she thought she had left far behind her when she had left Virginia for good.

"You're from Virginia?" she asked, her deep voice little more than a whisper.

"No, from Greece," Paul replied, and only then did Kristen realize that his accent was not American. It was a lot like her father's had been, a mixture of Greek and English.

"My father was from Greece." She automatically made small talk, giving herself time to think. Her left hand moved to the gold chain hanging around her neck and she kneaded it between her fingers, something she did when agitated, frightened or confused. But there were very few people left in the world who knew that, and definitely not the man standing in front of her.

"Yes, I know," he replied flatly, his accent softening the definitive

145

knowledge of his words.

Startled, Kristen tilted her head, and Paul watched the changing expressions that crossed her face. First confusion, then fear, covered her clear, green eyes, but uniting them was strength. They combined to give her the appearance of a beautiful doe that wanted to run but was too curious and too smart to do so. And, as Paul watched her, he saw the exact moment when understanding replaced all other emotions.

"You're from my aunt," she pronounced. Kristen spoke the words slowly, knowing that there could be no other explanation, and Paul liked how it was a statement about something obvious and not an empty, airy question.

The corners of his mouth deepened. "Yes. Your aunt Aphrodite. Your father's older sister," he affirmed, and motioned over toward a secluded section of the lobby where comfortable sofas were discreetly placed among plants. He asked, "May we talk?"

Kristen nodded her head thoughtfully, and squeezing her shoulder bag close to her side said, "I think we'd better."

Turning, she led the way to the furthest, most private corner of the lobby.

The only connection Kristen had with Greece was this aunt whose existence she had only discovered while going through her parents' papers after their sudden deaths three months earlier. Kristen had called her, feeling that, regardless of the reason behind the siblings' decades-long estrangement, her aunt would want to know, indeed had a right to know, about her brother's death. Kristen hadn't talked to her aunt but to a man who had said that her aunt would get in touch with her. But as the long months passed and Kristen received no word, she'd assumed that her aunt didn't want anything to do with her and that the estrangement was to continue into her generation.

That realization had hurt.

Not having any other relatives in the world put an emphasis on blood relatives which most people ignored and made this surprise aunt of great importance to Kristen. Knowing that there was someone else in the world to whom she was related had given Kristen a warm feeling, a feeling that had died, however, with the passing of the days—days which had brought no word from her aunt.

Arriving at the plush, forest green sofas, Kristen sat in the corner of one, crossing her legs in front of her. She watched as Paul Andrakos folded himself into the close corner of an adjacent one. Again, that vague, nickering feeling that she knew him from somewhere crossed her mind. But she pushed the thought aside. It was unimportant; his reason for coming was all that mattered.

Life had taught Kristen to be direct, so she asked, "Mr. Andrakos, it's been nearly three months since I called my aunt. Why has it taken her so long to contact me?"

Paul liked her straightforward way of speaking so he replied equally directly, not bothering to mince his words. "She's been a very sick lady, Ms. King."

"Sick?" Kristen echoed dismay, as the fingers of her left hand again found the chain around her neck. In her insecurity, the thought had never occurred to her that her aunt might have been ill.

Paul nodded. "That's why I'm here, and not your aunt. Believe me, if she could travel she would be sitting here with you today, not me."

Kristen shook her head. After convincing herself that she was un-wanted and totally unblessed where family relationships were concerned, it amazed her to consider that there just might be a relative, someone who had the same blood flowing in her veins, with whom she could have a relationship. "I'm sorry. . .I had no idea. . .the man I talked to didn't tell me that she was ill."

The corners of Paul's mouth deepened. He loved his godmother with a love normally only reserved for mothers, but he was surprised to dis-cover that Kristen King's response to his next words was important to him for more reasons than just those pertaining to his godmother; it was important to him on a personal level as well.

"Ms. King, she wasn't sick until hearing that your parents had died." He paused. "It was that shock which caused her to suffer a heart attack."

Kristen's eyes shut for several moments and when she opened them, the pain that Paul read in their watery green depths was real, and it impressed him. It impressed him that she should feel so strongly for a woman whom she had never met; it impressed him more than a million words spoken on her behalf ever could have. As a result, that old cyni-cism that was as hard as a block of marble and had been a part of him for so long that he had thought it was a permanent trait of his personal-ity, started being chipped away at the edges. He liked the light way that it made him feel.

"I'm sorry. . .I had no idea," she finally whispered.

"None of us did," he stated simply. "If we had known that it would affect her so deeply, to the detriment of her health, we wouldn't have told her. At least, we would have found another way to do so," he offered. Kristen's reaction was far more caring and concerned than he had thought possible. But Paul was comparing her to the women he knew. And he was beginning to realize that there was no comparison. There was a lot more to Kristen King than business brawn and physical beauty and this thought pleased him.

"When I didn't hear from my aunt," Kristen hesitantly spoke in a voice lightly flavored with a soft, southern accent, "I thought that she didn't want to have anything to do with me. I'd resigned myself to the thought." Her shoulders shrugged minutely beneath her purple silk blouse and they seemed very fragile to Paul, as if they had carried too much weight for far too long.

And too, the vulnerability of her words amazed him. Vulnerability and humility. It was in her giving green eyes, in the softness of her deep voice, in the air around her, and with an insight born from years of reading people Paul was now quite certain that Kristen King would never do anything to hurt his godmother. Ironically, he found himself hoping that his godmother, a formidable personality even when ill, would never hurt Kristen.

As if he'd been doing it forever, he reached across the arm of the sofa and took her long slender hand in his own, gently squeezing it.

Kristen surprised herself by accepting his hand, accepting it as she might a gift. It was a natural reflex, born of an emotional moment and she pressed her fingers against the palm of his hand.

She liked the feeling. She needed it.

"Ms. King," he said leaning forward, "your aunt was pleased that you called her, but extremely saddened by your news. I don't know what it was that kept your father and aunt apart all those years, but did you know that they had resolved their differences and that your parents were planning a trip to Greece?"

She smiled, a small little smile that tugged at his awakening feelings for her. "I'm glad—glad for them all."

He nodded and expelling a deep breath, glanced at his watch. "I'd like to take you to lunch. There is much that we have to discuss. Can you get away?" He hadn't planned on asking her out, but neither had he planned on her affecting him the way she did.

Kristen nodded her head. "Yes, I . . . ," but then she stopped and shook her head. Giving his hand a quick squeeze, a sort of thank you, she let go of it and lightly touched her fingers to her hair. "I forgot. . .I have a hairdresser's appointment."

"A hairdresser's appointment?" he echoed. It seemed so mundane and out of place after the import of their discussion. "Why?"

"To cut my hair." She answered simply and thought how it was absurd for her to be discussing her hair with a man who was practically a stranger. Absurd. . .but kind of fun as well.

His eyebrows lifted and he gazed at her deeply and reflectively in a way in which a very close friend might.

It was as he looked at her so poetically that Kristen realized why he looked familiar to her. . .and she had to stifle a laugh as it dawned on her. The coincidence of it all was outrageous!

For Paul Andrakos didn't resemble anyone she knew; rather, he resembled a thing. . .a work of art. . .a statue actually. . . . He looked like her replica of the *Youth of Antikythera* which sat on her living room coffee table in her home across the bay.

The actual, life-size statue of bronze had been found in an ancient shipwreck off the coast of the little island of Antikythera in the Gulf of Crete, just northwest of the island of Crete, and was now displayed in the National Archaeological Museum of Greece in Athens. Kristen's good friend, Lottie, an archaeologist now living in Greece, had visited Kristen the previous summer and brought her an official replica of the museum piece.

Lottie faced life lightly in a fun, carefree way. Indicative of her personality, when she gave Kristen the statue she had declared, "Now all you need to do is find a real live fellow like this statue. . .or maybe one who has aged during the last twenty-four hundred years and is now a *man*, and not a youth of nineteen." She had laughed loudly, proud of her joke, and pointedly ignored the fact that they both knew that Kristen had absolutely no desire to get involved with a man.

But Kristen had accepted the gift in the spirit in which it had been given. Her friend had been trying to help her in the only way she knew how—in the humorous, light sort of way in which she herself faced life's problems, and Kristen had loved her for it.

Kristen remembered squeezing the foot-high statue to her chest and replying, "No, I think I'll just become friends with this little fellow. I already know that his heart is made of bronze so he can never hurt mine."

The funny thing was, in the months that followed, her little statue of the *Youth of Antikythera* had become like a silent pet to Kristen, a friend whom she talked to at the end of the day, kind of like most people talk to cats and dogs.

Looking at the man before her, Kristen decided that he could have been an older version of the model for the statue. His thick wavy hair and long straight nose and the sensitive set of his facial bone structure were identical with the statue's, but even more, the look he now sent to her was an eternal one, one which, like the *Youth of Antikythera,* tried hard to read the workings of another's soul. He wasn't trying to figure out how she would look with her hair down, but rather, why she would want to cut it.

"Don't cut it," he finally said decisively and Kristen couldn't stifle her laugh any longer.

She laughed, a light, carefree, bubbly laugh, and Paul laughed with her, and as they laughed Kristen realized that she hadn't enjoyed herself so much in a very long time. Before the fiasco of her marriage she had enjoyed a good time, good spur-of-the-moment fun, just as she was enjoying it now, immensely.

"Don't cut your hair," he repeated, his eyes still twinkling with laughter and his smile—a beautiful, dazzling smile, different from the one he had previously given—seemed to make the whole world right.

Grinning back at him, her mouth somehow unable to do anything else, Kristen wanted to ask "Why?" What possible difference could it make to him whether she cut her hair or not? But discussing her hair with a man who was still practically a stranger couldn't be any more odd than comparing him to her pet statue, and yet somehow it all seemed nice too. On the tail of such deep thoughts and questions about her parents and long-lost Aunt Aphrodite, frivolous thoughts were very nice and something Kristen hadn't had in a long, long time.

She rolled her eyes self-consciously, her lips still turned up in a smile. "Well, I won't cut it today anyway. Let me call and cancel my appointment and then I'll be right with you." She stood and his considerable height politely followed suit.

Reaching out, his fingers lightly touched her upper arm, detaining her. Through the silkiness of her blouse, his fingers felt warm to Kristen and nice. . .really nice.

"Thank you, Ms. King. Thank you for changing your plans." His voice was both husky and elegant, like a caress. And although the laughter was gone from his voice, something just as important, something even more important was now there. Now there was friendship, a new and budding friendship in his words.

Kristen shook her head. "No, I must thank you for coming." She licked her lips and continued hesitantly, wondering how much she should tell him of her feelings. But looking at him she felt that she could say what she really felt. So she did.

"I. . .was really sad when I thought that I had been ignored by my aunt. I don't have any other living relatives and, well. . .it's important to me to learn about my father's sister."

He nodded and she knew that she hadn't made a mistake in trusting him. "Your aunt feels exactly the same way about you, Ms. King."

"I'm so glad. . .but please, call me Kristen."

"Kristen," he repeated, as if he were tasting it, and the soft inflections of his accent made her name sound musical, magical to her. "A lovely name. And I'm Paul."

"Paul," she said and their eyes seemed to fuse together; deep brown ones merged with crystal green ones and with their merging Kristen's heart pounded against her rib cage. It wanted freedom from the prison in which she had placed it when her husband died a year and a half ago on their wedding day. A little freedom in that age-old game of male and female was all that it wanted, and Kristen decided as she stood there that for this one afternoon she would give it that freedom.

Paul Andrakos was safe after all. He lived in far-off Greece.

After today she probably wouldn't ever see him again. It was time for her to start trusting again; time to start, by trusting her own heart.

"I'll only be a moment," she said and, smiling, swiveled away from him to cross over to the reception desk.

This time the *tap, tap, tap* of her heels against the marble floor didn't bother her. And neither did she mind the idea of Paul Andrakos's eyes following her as she walked with the feminine tap across the lobby. She could feel his dark eyes on her back and a very womanly part of her, a part that had lain dormant for a very long time, hoped that he liked what he saw.

She reached for the phone at the reception desk and turned to watch the tall length of Paul Andrakos as he made a phone call from the telephone on the table next to the sofa. *Such thick golden hair and dark, dark eyes, eyes a person could trust, eyes a person's soul could fall into,* she thought. He was a golden Greek, just like her father had been before his head had turned white. But there the resemblance ended. The budding feelings she had for Paul Andrakos were definitely not like those she had had for her father.

She was attracted to Paul Andrakos in that age-old, inexplicable way that a woman is attracted to a particular man. She admitted it to herself, for she also reasoned that he was a safe attraction. He would soon return to his end of the world, and the only remembrances she would have of him would be of letting herself open up to the world once again and that of her little statue of the *Youth of Antikythera* on her coffee table in her home above the Pacific Ocean, who would from now on remind her of the real live 'Man from Greece' who had come with information about her aunt.

Yes, she thought, just before her secretary came on the line and she directed her to cancel her hairdresser's appointment, *Paul Andrakos was a safe attraction. . .for one afternoon.*

Hanging up the phone, she watched as he casually strode toward her. Squaring her shoulders, she took a deep breath like one normally does before plunging into a cold pool, and clutching her shoulder bag to her side, walked forward to meet him.

"All set?" he asked.

She nodded her head and breathed out. "Did you want to dine here in the hotel? There's an excellent roof garden restaurant."

"I just made reservations at a little restaurant I know of on the wharf. Is that all right with you?"

"What, with the competition?" she teased, and smiling, he took her hand and, as if he had been doing it forever, tucked it among the folds of his expensive suit into the crook of his elbow and guided her toward the massive doors of the hotel.

It surprised Kristen that he had taken her arm but she didn't feel offended. She knew from her father that it was a European habit. Her father used to always walk this way with her and her mother. Besides, it felt so good to have someone else directing her steps for a change. She'd been fending for herself for so long that even this one moment of following someone else was a treat, and the fact that her hand felt so perfect upon his arm, so natural and right, made it even more of one.

As they crossed the lobby, she took the moment to observe that he was tall and broad, but not like an American football player who is normally massive. Rather, Paul Andrakos was slender like a swimmer with a body that was shaped to knife swiftly through the water with the grace and ease of the clipper ships of old. She mused that the water, or something to do with the water, must be the natural setting for this man. It seemed to be a part of him.

So absorbed was Kristen in her thoughts that she failed to greet the two gentlemanly doormen as she breezed through on Paul's arm. Her transformation, however, did not go unnoticed by their ever-seeing, ever-observant eyes. They were accustomed to seeing the beautiful young executive with the sculptured expression nod an acknowledgement to them as she entered or exited the hotel. They gave one another knowing looks as she floated by with her escort and weren't offended that she failed to salute them. Her face was that of a woman now, one definitely not made of stone. It pleased the elderly gentlemen, who had always felt a bit sad for her.

Chapter 2

The warm summertime wind buffeted Kristen and Paul, and the traffic of the city roared around them as they stepped out of the protection of the marquee. It thrilled Kristen. She had loved San Francisco from the very first day that she'd arrived a little over a year ago. The city never failed to bring her senses alive with its vibrancy and color and Paul Andrakos seemed to combine forces with the city to doubly assault her.

Leaning close to her he spoke into her ear, and she felt her nerves quiver like a tuning fork just struck.

"Shall I hail a cab? Or would you like to walk and catch a cable car down to the wharf?"

Eyes shining, pleased that he would think to ask, she readily answered him, "Oh. . .I love cable cars!"

"I somehow thought you would." Paul smiled and started guiding her down the street.

She smiled up at him, and as the wind whipped the clean spicy fragrance of his aftershave around her, she found herself enjoying the manly fragrance that was him, masculine and fresh and nice.

Turning a corner, a gust of Pacific wind whipped through the tall buildings of the street like it might through a deep, deep canyon in the wilds, and Kristen's prim pleated skirt billowed out, soaring high above her knees. Startled, she frantically grabbed out for the wayward fabric.

Trying to be helpful Paul reached over to assist her, but when his hand inadvertently brushed against her leg, his help became much more than that, and with it Kristen's heart flew every bit as out of control as the silky folds of her skirt had.

Careful not to touch his hand, she relieved his long fingers of the material which he had captured. Their eyes, however, touched and held, became captive as they stood in the middle of the sidewalk looking deeply at one another.

Like in a melodramatic video clip, the multitude of people around them—those on the sidewalk walking, those in cars driving, and even those in a helicopter flying high in the sky above them—disappeared and only the music that came from their souls remained.

They were the only ones on that street, their attraction for one another was the only sound heard where man and woman recognized that there was something special between their particular souls, something very, very special.

With a silence that spoke loudly, the man called Paul and the woman called Kristen vaguely recognized that they needed one another to travel the path of life. The proverbial "love at first sight"—or at least almost first sight—had hit them.

But where this thought was appealing to Paul, it scared Kristen and she again reminded Paul of a beautiful doe unsure of the path to follow.

Wanting to relieve the fear he read in her eyes, he smiled, and reaching for her hand again tucked it in the crook of his arm and guided her down the sidewalk acting as though nothing had passed between them, as though nothing had happened.

"What a wind!" he expostulated.

"I. . .I normally wear tighter skirts or even slacks on days when the wind is blowing," she said, wanting to forget the moment, to forget the unspoken revelation which had passed between them.

He chuckled and pointed down to her skirt which was still trying to fly free of her hand. "I can understand why."

Relieved, she couldn't help the small laugh which escaped her lips. "But I like the wind. It's exhilarating."

"Then you would like Athens when the *Meltemia* starts to blow."

"*Meltemia?*" She tilted her head questioningly, glad for any conversation that might help calm her. The attraction that she felt for this man and which she was now certain he felt for her was a little bit more than she wanted to tackle at this point in her life. If she didn't know that he lived on the other side of the earth, and that she probably wouldn't see him again after today. . .well, she wasn't sure what she would do.

"*Meltemia* are winds that blow down from the cool zones of Russia to fill a vacuum created by the hot air rising over the Sahara Desert to the south of Greece," he answered. "They are a lot like your Californian Santa

Ana winds. They start blowing with the rising of the sun and end with its setting, acting as nature's fan to cool the earth and cleanse it."

"Winds from Russia. . .the Sahara Desert. . . ," she murmured. "Sounds so exotic somehow."

"Not any more so than your Santa Ana winds sound to me. In Europe, California—especially San Francisco—is thought of as paradise on earth."

Looking out over the Golden Gate, the entrance mouth to the San Francisco Bay, with the tall Golden Gate Bridge spanning it, and to the sailboats with their colorful spinnakers dotting the deep blue sea beneath it, Kristen couldn't help but understand people comparing it to paradise. It was one of the world's most beautiful locations and yet, even though her moving to its welcoming shores had helped to put her life back on track after the horrible events of her marriage, she knew that it wasn't paradise, and shaking her head thoughtfully she spoke softly, almost wistfully. "No. . .not even *this* is paradise. . .I don't think paradise is to be found anywhere on earth."

With matching seriousness Paul responded, "I quite agree."

Startled, and yet pleased, she turned to him. "You do?"

As they paused on a busy corner waiting for the walk signal to appear, he nodded and his mouth quirked slightly, in a way that seemed pessimistic to Kristen. "I've seen enough of life to know that what people run after all their lives—monetary success, social standing, good looks, holidays—doesn't bring the happiness people assume it should. But I believe that—" He broke off and flashed her a guilty smile. "I'm sorry, I didn't mean to bore you," he apologized, waving his response away into the wind as they started to cross the street.

"No. . .please go on," she encouraged him as they weaved around people in the crosswalk, and Paul was amazed to think that he had finally found a woman who was interested in what he believed, not just what he did for a living. A frown cut across his face as he vaguely wondered if she cared because she didn't know anything else about him, and he wondered if she would continue to care if she did know his financial status. The thought of never having monetary worries was very appealing to the women he had met. But then, remembering what he had learned about Kristen, he knew that money had never been a problem for her either.

Kristen misread his frown and thought he was embarrassed to speak his mind, so she again prompted him. "Please. . .I'd like to know what you believe."

"Why?" He looked down at her, his brow a quizzical line slicing across his forehead. "You hardly know me."

She knew that what he said was true, but she also knew that he would soon be leaving and that made such a deep discussion easier than it would be with a person who lived close by to her. She licked her lips and replied truthfully, "Sometimes, it's easier to talk to someone you don't know very well about really important things than people you do know. . .there are no preconceived notions to deal with, no histories to take into account. . . ."

He nodded his agreement.

"So please tell me what you were going to say," she prompted with a smile that made Paul feel more carefree than he had felt in a long time and happy to speak of his deep, deep yearnings.

"Well, I think that there has to be Something More, Something More in life which brings us a little bit closer to that Paradise which we all seek."

"I agree. . ." She frowned thoughtfully while tucking a wayward strand of hair behind her ear. "But what is that elusive 'Something More'?"

"I don't know. . .something to do with our souls, I think." He looked down at her and smiled sheepishly. "Sounds funny, I know. But it's something I'm determined to someday seek and find."

"That's something I'd like to find as well," she replied softly, truthfully.

He smiled and squeezed her hand as they arrived at the cable car stop and waited for the car to come. He didn't release her hand and Kristen didn't ask for it back. "You know, Kristen, I think you're the first woman I've ever met who feels as I do."

"Most likely other women have felt this need but they have superficially coated and hidden it with the things you mentioned before—monetary success, social standing. . . ."

"Have you ever done that?"

Have I? Kristen wondered as she let her eyes drift out beyond his shoulder over the busy street. Thoughtfully, she shook her head and turned her gaze back to his. "Not really, but I think this need was fulfilled for me by my parents. We were very close. After they. . .were killed in the boating accident. . .well. . .I've come to realize that there has to be, as you said, Something More in life. Something that doesn't depend on people. . .or things. . .or work. . . ." She shook her head and turned to look out toward the bay. "Something. . . ," she finished wistfully.

"Do you think that Something might be God?" he asked softly and she turned her eyes back to him.

"It might be. I just wish I knew how to find out."

Frowning, he replied, "I would say church but I don't know. I've been kind of discouraged by some people I know who go to church every Sunday and every religious holiday but then hurt their fellow human beings the rest of the time."

She remembered that her "almost" husband's family had been religious churchgoers and they had been the primary instigators in hurting her after Ted's car had run off the cliff the night of their wedding. They were the reason she'd left Virginia and missed spending the last year of her parents' lives with them.

She grimaced. "Yeah. . .me too."

He chuckled and squeezed her hand between both of his. "We're kind of a case of the blind leading the blind, I'd say."

She smiled in agreement and placed her other hand over his. "Well, we might be blind, but at least we know that we have to go somewhere—that there is Something Unknown which we must find."

"Maybe. . .we can grope our way. . .together," he said softly, his accent making the unromantic words seem more romantic than any she had ever heard before and because of this, more frightening as well.

As if his hands suddenly burned hers she let go of them and laughed, a fake sound even to her own ears, "How? By e-mail? You live on the other side of the world, remember?" And as the moment was getting to be too much for her, she was once again glad that he did. But his next words shattered her false sense of safety.

"Kristen. . . ," he spoke hesitantly, softly, and with hope in his dark eyes, "your aunt Aphrodite was hoping. . .that you would travel to Greece to visit her. . ."

"What?!"

He quickly continued. "This is why I've come. To ask you to visit her and to accompany you to Greece."

The *clang, clang, clang* of the cable car as it careened around the corner toward their stop wasn't any louder than the ringing in Kristen's temples. It wasn't that she didn't want to meet her aunt. She did. She just wasn't sure that she wanted to go any further with Paul Andrakos than to lunch at Fisherman's Wharf.

The safe world she had built for herself on the shores of the Pacific Ocean seemed to be rocking and swaying as if in a strong earthquake and, like one experiencing an earthquake, she wasn't sure which direction to go, if any, in order to escape it.

The cable car came to a stop in front of them. Rotely, she stepped onto the running board and, as she did so, she looked with longing back at the road she had just walked. She somehow knew that there was no going back. Her path had been mapped out for her and, unknowing as to how it was to change her life, she had walked it. As happy as the last few moments had been, she wished that she hadn't agreed to lunch with Paul Andrakos. She was terrified of the unknown and of being disappointed by people yet again.

"Kristen," Paul's voice came to her through the rattling of the car as it started to move away on its track. "You don't have to decide now."

She looked at him sheepishly, the wind from the moving car carrying her soft but truthful words back to him, "It's just that everything is happening so suddenly after months of nothing."

Without her intending it there was double meaning in her words and he realized it.

"I know."

She nodded and stepped inside to sit on a protected bench. He sat down next to her, draping his arm casually without touching her across the back of the bench. Wanting time to get her thoughts in order, Kristen decided to play tour guide. "Did you know that the first cable cars were built in 1873, and that they are still painted with the exact same colors as they were then?"

"More than a hundred years. . .that's quite a long time when you think that San Francisco isn't a very old city."

She laughed. "I guess by Greek standards it's a very young city."

"Young and beautiful," he agreed, and the look he gave her left no doubt that he was referring to more than just the city.

She quickly continued to find refuge in her role of tour guide. "Yes, well. . .there is a museum with an underground viewing room where people can observe the huge sheaves that guide the cable cars from under the street, too."

"They're amazing contraptions," he agreed, obviously amused by her travelog.

She smiled but boldly continued, "Well. . .Rudyard Kipling liked them. He wrote, 'They take no count of rise or fall, but slide equable on their appointed courses. . .turn corners. . .cross other lines, and for aught I know, may run up the sides of houses.'"

The car chose that moment to turn a corner sharply and Kristen was thrown against Paul. His hand grasped her shoulder to steady her, but when he didn't let go of her after the pace of the cable car evened out, she looked up at him questioningly.

"And how about you, Kristen? Do you slide equably on your appointed course?" His tone was serious—serious and caring.

"I. . ." She looked down at her hands and then back up at him. She wasn't sure how to answer the question. She decided to be truthful, something she was finding very easy to be with this man. "I don't know. I'm not sure what my 'appointed course' should be—I've always tried to do what I think is right. . .but it hasn't always been correct."

"None of us knows what our 'appointed course' is," he pointed out kindly.

"I know, but. . .at least some of us have an idea of where we're going and what we're going to do with our lives." She grimaced. "My life has made some strange and really nasty turns."

"Do you think going to Greece is a bad turn for you?"

She shook her head. "No. . .but. . .I'm relatively happy here."

"It's safe. Right?"

She lifted her head defiantly. "That's right. It's safe. It's a known in a world which is so full of unknown."

"But what about that Unknown, that Something More that you want to discover. Do you think you'll find it by just staying put?"

Tilting her head up, she replied, "I might."

He nodded. "Yes. You might." He lightly ran his thumb across her cheek. "But Kristen. . .maybe. . .maybe you are meant to travel to Greece . . .to meet your aunt. . .maybe it's all part of your appointed path. Maybe, by not going, you would miss out on the best path of your life."

She sighed. She felt defeated. "I know. I just wish there was someone whom I could ask."

The brakeman pulled the brake lever, bringing the cable car to a screeching halt at their stop on the wharf. Standing, Paul reached out to help Kristen alight from the car. His lips turned up into an amused sort of smile, and as she stepped down onto the sidewalk, he suggested, "Well. . .you could ask your aunt for advice."

She looked up at him in wonder. She liked the way that sounded.

It was nice to know that there was someone to whom she could turn. Smiling broadly, she replied, "Yes, I guess I could."

Chapter 3

The wharf was busy with tourists and businesspeople, with children riding bikes and with children being pushed in strollers, with street vendors and street performers, and after a woman carrying a "walk-a-way" shrimp cocktail nearly spilled it all on Paul, and a man balancing several huge crabs collided with Kristen, the two gave up talking until settled in their restaurant seats, which commanded a frontline view of the bay.

Kristen was surprised to hear the maitre d' address Paul by name but even more surprised to see several heads of well-known businessmen turn in their direction as they made their way across the plush lavender carpet to their table next to the window. "You seem to be known here," she commented as they sat down, and she motioned to a table where the people turned guiltily away as Paul's glance fell upon them.

"I probably just look like someone they know," he suggested.

She looked at him with curious interest, and picking up her linen napkin, she laid it across her lap and asked, "What is it that you do anyway?"

"Oh. . .a little bit of this and a little bit of that," he replied offhandedly.

She frowned. His answer bothered her. It was too vague, too glib, something he hadn't been before. Her eyes skimmed out over the busy wharf to the elegant Golden Gate Bridge and then back to the historic Alcatraz Island in the foreground before they again came to rest on the dark eyes of the man seated across from her.

"Paul. . .there's something I don't understand." She reached for the crystal goblet of water and sipped from it. "Why didn't my aunt just call and invite me? Why did you come in person?"

"I have business here in the city—" he prevaricated, but then, looking at her questioning eyes he knew that if they were ever to have a relationship, something he found himself wanting more and more with each passing moment, he'd have to be honest. He knew that the knowledge he

162

had about her had to be in the open between them. Clearing his throat, he sat back in his chair and admitted, "We had heard things—"

"What things?" Icy fingers of dread started to climb up Kristen's spine and she gripped the stem of the goblet tighter.

"We had read things—"

She waited. She knew what was coming and in spite of the air conditioning in the restaurant, she felt herself break out in a cold sweat. Was her almost-marriage to Ted to taint all her future relationships? She knew that the attraction she and Paul felt for one another was something special, something that went far beyond the physical to touch the deep yearnings of their souls. Now that Kristen wondered if she might lose Paul she recognized how desperately she didn't want to, how much she truly wanted to see him again and try for a future. . .together.

He watched the emotions that played across her face. She reminded him of the little tabby cat he'd rescued from the kicks and taunts of nasty children in the center of Athens the week before. Her green eyes were as wary, terrified, and vulnerable as that kitten's had been. The kitten had allowed him to pick her up and bring her home with him. He wondered if Kristen would allow him to do the same thing.

Somehow he managed to find the only words that could save their new friendship. "Kristen, if it makes a difference, I don't believe a word that was written in that newspaper. I don't believe that you were in any way responsible for the death of your new husband. He was drunk. He was driving. He ran off the cliff. Thank God you weren't with him."

She could tell that he meant it and the relief that she felt melted the icy fingers of dread away like the sun breaking out from the clouds on a cool winter day.

"Thank you, Paul," she whispered and wished that she could leave the subject alone but knew that she couldn't, not yet. "But. . .in order to know about. . .the events of my wedding day. . .you must have had me investigated." The idea was appalling to Kristen.

"Yes," he admitted. "You were investigated."

Her eyes flashed her anger. "What exactly is going on here?" she demanded, bringing her hand down hard on the table, rattling the silverware. She was terrified that she had once again been a bad judge of character. "Who are you," she ground out, "and what exactly is your relationship to my aunt? Are you her private eye?" she asked sarcastically.

His lips twisted wryly. He was amused by her question. "Well. . .I guess you could say that I am. . .especially where you're concerned."

His obvious amusement only served to further feed her anger. To think that people, people whom she hadn't even met, were spying into her private affairs bothered her. With her soft, southern accent smothering her anger she asked, "Oh. . .what else have you discovered about me?"

He shrugged his shoulders slightly. If he realized that she was angry, he deliberately ignored it and kept the conversation easygoing. "Nothing much actually, except to know that today is your twenty-eighth birthday." He picked up his goblet of water and flashing a smile filled with budding friendship, toasted her. "Happy birthday, Kristen."

In spite of herself her lips curved upward and she felt her anger fade away. She didn't think anyone in San Francisco would remember her birthday, and until that moment, she didn't realize how much it meant to her that someone did. It felt nice to be wished a happy one. "Thank you," she murmured and looked down at the butter on her bread plate, absently noticing that it was shaped like a conch shell. Feeling happy but a little bit uncomfortable, she picked up her dinner roll and asked, "But you still haven't told me what your relationship is to my aunt?"

As she stabbed the conch shell swirl of butter and started to spread it on her roll, she felt him bring his chair closer to the table. "I'm sorry, I should have told you sooner. . .you see. . .your aunt is much more to me than just a friend and a business associate. . .she's my godmother."

Kristen's green eyes widened in wonder. "Your godmother? She's your *nona*?" Her brows drew together as she remembered some of what her father had taught her about Greek traditions. "Isn't that what you call a godmother in Greek?"

A smile touched his mouth. "Exactly. She's my *nona*."

Kristen tilted her head, beginning to understand the situation better. "That's quite a strong tie in Greek society, isn't it?"

"It can be," he agreed, still holding her hand.

"Is it where your *nona*—my aunt—is concerned?" she pressed.

"Very." His tone left no doubt as to the love he felt for his godmother. "I love *Nona* like a mother. Since my parents died, she has been a mother to me." He paused, and squeezed her hand, this time reassuringly. "That's why I had to assure myself of your character before—"

"Before," she sighed and finished for him understanding everything now, "you invited me to come."

"Yes," he replied, nodding his head, relieved that it was out in the open between them. "*Nona* was too sick to allow someone to come who might upset her."

"And. . .after you read the accounts in that newspaper. . ." She let the rest of the sentence hang wryly.

"That newspaper did a hatchet job on you!" Anger flashed across his face and Kristen decided then that she didn't ever want to be on the receiving end of his anger. "Why? There must be some sort of behind-the-scenes reason. Was the owner of the paper related to your husband in any way?"

She smiled at his astuteness and let go of his hand. "You do know how things work." And then coming to a decision, a decision of trust, she said, "My father-in-law owned the paper."

"Ah. . . ," he sat back in his seat, "that says everything."

"Well not everything maybe. . .but enough for the moment."

He eyed her speculatively. He wanted to ask more but it was enough right now that she didn't seem upset with him for checking her out. "So you do understand why I had to come and see for myself what sort of person you are?"

She grimaced. "Well, I can't say I'm thrilled but—I do understand. I probably would have done the same thing had I read such things about someone. Even though I haven't met my aunt, Paul, I care about her. She's the only relative I have left in the world, unless. . ." She paused as it occurred to her that she could possibly have cousins through her aunt. "Does she have any children?"

"No," Paul tilted his head upward which Kristen knew from her father was the Greek expression for no. "She never married."

"Really. . ." Kristen frowned thoughtfully, more and more intrigued with this woman who was her aunt. "I don't claim to know too much about modern Greek culture, but isn't that a bit strange for a Greek woman of her generation?"

Paul's mouth tightened. "Yes, it is unusual, but then your aunt Aphrodite does not fit into the norm in any respect."

"Tell me about her," Kristen prompted.

"To understand your aunt, you must first know something about modern Greek history."

She sat back as the waiter brought their order of baked Pacific salmon and placed it before them. "Ummm. . .this looks delicious." She savored the lemony aroma and then looked back at Paul as the waiter departed. "Please tell me."

He nodded but motioned to her to eat. She picked up her fork and flaked off a bit of the tender fish, making a stab at eating while he told her about her aunt.

"It has only been a little over forty years that Greece has been without bloodshed on her soil. During Aphrodite's young adulthood, throughout her twenties, there was war on her doorstep.

"First there was World War II, the occupation, and then when most other European countries were pulling themselves back into being working countries, civil war broke out in Greece."

"Civil war? Like we had with the North against the South?" she asked and waited as he took a few bitefuls of the lemony fish.

He shook his head. "No, much worse. The dividing line was ideological, not geographical. It was a war against Communist takeover, and the Greek people—much to their credit—managed to keep it out of Greece, when much of Europe was cloaked by it."

"I didn't realize. . ."

"This war lasted an additional four years." He sighed. "It is very hard for me to even imagine what life must have been like during that time, but I do know that it had a profound effect on the way that the populace think and act even today." He paused and took a few bites of food.

"I just can't imagine anything so horrible as war at my home either. . . ," she murmured and toyed with her food, too interested in what Paul had to say to eat much.

"Well, most of the women survived by immersing themselves in their families. They were their men's companions and helpers and their children's teachers and caretakers."

"But my aunt?"

He smiled as he thought about the older woman. "Your aunt cast the traditional role from her life and put all of her energies into her work."

"Her work?" Kristen's eyes opened wide in surprise. "What does she do?"

Amazement lurked in his dark eyes. "You really have no idea?"

She shrugged her shoulders. "No. How could I? I didn't even know of her existence until recently," she reminded him.

"I just thought that your father might have said something—something about his past life," he prompted.

"No. Nothing. He never talked about Greece." She shook her head and waited.

Paul chuckled at her innocence. "Kristen, your aunt is one of the most successful persons in Greece. . .in Europe for that matter."

"What?" She was flabbergasted and repeated, "What does she do?"

"After the war she plunged into learning all she could about the family shipping business."

"Shipping business!"

He nodded, and speaking very softly, explained, "Kristen, you come from a very old and noble shipping family."

"I had no idea." She looked out the window, her savory lunch totally forgotten, and her eyes watched a ship as it passed under the Golden Gate Bridge with an interest she had never felt before. "My father never told me anything. . . ."

"Your father too had been trained in the business by your grandfather and he was to have been in charge. When he left, however, Aphrodite took over, although. . . ," his lips twisted, "not quite as easily as all that. Your grandfather thought a woman's place was in the home, definitely not in the shipping business."

Kristen rolled her eyes. "I can imagine. . . ."

With admiration in his voice, Paul said, "But your aunt is a fighter. . . ."

"But. . .what happened between my father and my aunt? Did it have to do with the business?"

"No. The only thing I'm sure of is that it didn't have to do with the business."

"Then why were they estranged for all those years?"

"Kristen. . ." He waved his hand out in frustration and sadly shook his head. "The only thing I know is what is common knowledge."

"Which is more than I know," she reminded him. "Please tell me."

He took a deep breath and sat back from the table. "Your father and his father, your paternal grandfather, had a terrible argument nearly thirty years ago, and immediately following the altercation your father left Greece, never to return again. Your aunt only discovered your father's whereabouts after. . .the events of your wedding made the papers."

"But how?" She shook her head, confused.

"Your name. Evidently your father anglicized his name after coming to live here. That's why your aunt couldn't locate him. But when she saw your name in the paper she put two and two together and came up with your father."

She shook her head. She was still confused. "I don't understand."

Paul patiently explained. "Your name 'King' is the exact translation of your Greek name 'Vasilias.' And your first name is a derivative of your grandmother's name, 'Christina.' It's the tradition in Greece to name children after grandparents."

She blinked and threw up her hands in total amazement, "I don't believe it. . .I was named for my grandmother and never knew it. . . ."

"It does seem unbelievable," he agreed.

Kristen shook her head. She was bewildered. It didn't fit with her father's character at all. "I just don't understand. My father was a wonderful man. I can't believe that he would cut himself off from his sister for all those years because of an argument he had with his father. I can't even remember my father arguing with anyone."

"And the same goes for Aphrodite," he said in defense of his *nona*. "She can be formidable, particularly in the business world," he admitted, "but she's a very lovely lady."

They sat in silence for several moments. The movements in the restaurant and the beat of the city outside ticked off the passing of time as Kristen tried to assimilate all that she had just learned.

"I wish I had the knowledge to tell you all that you want to know about the estrangement between your aunt and your father," Paul said, interrupting her thoughts, "but I'm afraid that I'm not privy to that information." His lips twisted at the corners. "It's a mystery to me, the one thing that *Nona* won't talk to me about." He paused. "But, maybe she'll tell you. Please come to Athens."

She smiled, a smile of wonder. "You know. . .it's kind of funny. . .so much has been pointing me in that direction."

Now it was his turn to be confused. "What do you mean?"

"Well. . .a really close friend of mine is an archaeologist living in Athens for the next several years, and a girl I went to university with has recently married a Greek man and is living in the Peloponnese. She's asked me to visit her several times."

"That's amazing," he agreed and then, lowering his voice, he referred to their earlier conversation. "Sounds like this is the path you are meant to follow, Kristen."

She looked into his dark eyes and nodded. "I think you may be right." She glanced down at her gold watch. It had been over an hour since she'd left the hotel. "I have to get back." She stood, and opening her purse, removed a business card and extended it to him. "Call me tomorrow, and I'll let you know when and if I can get away."

Paul nodded and reaching for the card, said, "Thank you, Kristen. You will make an old lady very happy."

They stood looking at one another for a long moment knowing that they would make themselves happy as well.

Finally, Paul leaned over and kissed Kristen in the European fashion of a kiss on either side of the face. The mild roughness of his smoothly shaven face rubbed against the smoothness of hers. Kristen closed her eyes and savored the moment. He smelled so good, so masculine and good.

"Let me see you back to the hotel," he offered, his voice deep with emotion.

Kristen shook her head. "I'd like to see myself back if you don't mind." She had a great deal to think over and she needed those few moments to be alone. On top of thoughts about her aunt, she needed to think about her feelings for this man, who she was now quite sure was meant to be in her life for more than just one afternoon.

He smiled and stood back for her to pass. "I understand."

She smiled up at him and then turning, walked toward the door.

As she went, Paul noticed that the back of her neck, which he had thought so vulnerable when he first saw her, was now covered with a few wisps of windblown hair. It seemed less vulnerable to him now, safer somehow, and he was glad. . .glad mostly to know that he might have the chance to get to know her, to care for her, to protect her from the hurts of the world. It was something that he wanted to do, something that he wanted to do very badly.

Chapter 4

Kristen stepped from her glass-enclosed shower stall that evening onto the white ceramic floor, feeling refreshed and revitalized. The chocolate cake she'd put in the oven before her shower tantalized her with its aroma as it wafted in through the open door of her bedroom and into the connecting bathroom.

Wrapping her head in a pink velour towel, she quickly rubbed her body dry with a matching one and reached for a red cotton T-shirt that had *Williamsburg, Virginia*, emblazoned across the front of it and a pair of jean shorts to go with it.

Even though it was her birthday, Kristen didn't dress up, as she was planning on spending the evening much as she passed every night. Alone.

Padding through her flowery bedroom with its large brass bed, into the living area, she pulled the towel from her head and absently rubbed the tangled strands of her dark hair, made darker now by being wet. She unlocked the sliding glass door, and using her hip, pushed open the door which commanded an eye-riveting ocean view.

A deep, contented sigh escaped her body as she appreciated the beauty spread out before her. She closed her eyes and inhaled deeply the sweetness of the ocean air. The wind was still blowing hard and whipped the salt spray from the foaming, churning ocean up to touch her skin, tingling it.

She walked forward to the wooden planter that ran along the length of the deck's railing, and bending, plucked a dried leaf from a red geranium plant.

Crushing the leaf in her fingers, Kristen held the grainy pieces up over the wooden railing and let the wind pick them up to carry them far away across the mighty ocean and she thought how those bits were just like her. She had been as dried out as that leaf after her husband's duplicity and death, but because of another man she was learning to be a person who could risk feeling, and a person who could risk crossing the ocean to meet her unknown aunt and to search for that Unknown, Something More that she knew was missing in her life.

Abruptly, she wiped her hand against her shorts, and tossing the wet towel across a deck chair to let it air dry, Kristen turned away from the view that had sold her the house, and strode purposefully back into the living room intending to go straight to the bathroom in order to comb out her tangled hair. But the aroma of the chocolate cake baking in the oven made her stop. It made her house smell yummy and cozy like a family home would.

And, it reminded her unmercifully of her parents.

Taking a deep, steadying breath, Kristen resolved not to let herself get maudlin. She wouldn't let it happen. Not today. Too many wonderful things had happened today and she knew that her parents wouldn't want her to feel sad on this, her first birthday without them.

She reached for the gold chain around her neck which glistened from its recent wash and absently rubbed it between her fingers. No. . .as much as she missed her parents, she wouldn't let herself feel sad today and she resolved to decorate her cake with icing and candles in keeping with their family tradition. The only thing was. . .her father had always iced her cake.

Squaring her shoulders, Kristen decided to leave those thoughts behind and was about to continue on her way to the bathroom, when from the corner of her eye, a movement captured her attention. Fluttering above her coffee table around her little statue of the *Youth of Antikythera* was a beautiful yellow butterfly.

Kristen turned to it slowly, not wanting to scare it away, and with cupped hands, walked toward it with the hope that the elegant insect would land within them. But the butterfly did not. Instead it chose to land on the long, straight, classical nose of the *Youth*.

Kristen laughed softly, sounding a bit like fine crystal tinkling in the wind. "Little butterfly, I see that you like my little statue, too."

As if in answer, the butterfly rose in flight and fluttered gracefully around the twelve-inch statue.

"I hope I didn't flutter around the 'Man from Greece' like that today," Kristen laughingly sang out and watched as the butterfly winged its way off toward the open door to the flowers beyond.

171

With the rays of the sun touching the tips of its wings, it was as golden as Paul Andrakos's thick hair, and Kristen thought how it seemed to gleam its joy in being free and alive. And she couldn't help but think that was exactly how Paul had made her feel today—free and alive, golden and warm.

As the graceful butterfly disappeared from sight somewhere over the bent sea pines, Kristen turned back to the statue on the glass-topped table. Plopping herself down on the floral sofa before it, she said, "Well, little *Youth*, I guess it's just you and me again."

She twisted her head like an artist sizing up a picture. "Seeing you close at hand, I have to admit that Paul Andrakos's hair isn't nearly as curly as yours. His is wavy. And his lips seem more straight than yours and, more, well. . ." Kristen tipped her head from side to side trying to decide. "Older." She finally decided that age was the difference.

"You are a youth after all, and he is a man. But except for your curly hair, if you were twenty years older, and alive, of course, you would be identical," she said and hopped up from the sofa. "I'm going to get a glass of milk. What shall I get for you, my quiet little one?" Kristen asked over her shoulder as she walked around the bar that divided the two rooms. "Perhaps a rag to wipe the dust from your handsome face?"

Reaching into the refrigerator, Kristen continued her one-sided dialogue. "Don't feel bad, little friend, but I think that I would much prefer the company of the 'Man from Greece' to yours tonight," she mused, and started to pour milk into a long-stemmed crystal wine glass. "And the nice thing is, I even think that I could handle it."

The doorbell chimed. Startled, Kristen slopped milk onto the counter. Leaving her glass in a puddle of white, she turned and walked hesitantly back into the living room toward the front door.

About five feet in front of it, she stopped, and rubbing her suddenly clammy hands against her shorts, she eyed the door skeptically, as if it hid a monster behind it.

Except for Lottie, and her uncle George when he'd been in town, Kristen hadn't had anyone else over to her house in the months that she'd lived there. It had been her refuge from the world, her place of healing, and acting in a way that was alien to her personality, that had been outgoing and sociable before Ted, Kristen had in fact become a recluse.

The doorbell chimed again, this time sounding impatient to be kept waiting.

"This is ridiculous," Kristen whispered, walking toward the door, finally realizing that her uncle George had probably sent her flowers for her birthday.

Lifting her eyes toward the little pinpoint of light filtering in through the peephole, Kristen spied the handsome face of Paul Andrakos on the other side. She jumped back as if she had been zapped by a laser beam!

"I don't believe it!" she whispered and quickly ran her fingers through her uncombed hair.

"Kristen?" she heard his deep voice call through the wood of the door. That melodious voice, that magical voice.

She glanced back at her little statue. It seemed to be grinning now.

"Well, little *Youth*, I think I'm about to receive my wish. The 'Man from Greece' is here!" Deciding that nothing else mattered other than seeing Paul Andrakos again, not her uncombed hair nor even her casual dress, Kristen slid the lock on the door, and couldn't help but smile at the thought that it was symbolic of sliding open her heart, too. She swung the door wide without hesitation.

"Paul! What a wonderful surprise!" she exclaimed and meant it.

"I hope you don't mind my just dropping in on you like this, but—" From behind his back he whooshed a dozen full-bloomed yellow roses set among innumerable buds. "It is your birthday."

"Oh!" She reached for the flowers, and cradling them in her arms, bent her head to inhale their clean honest fragrance. "Oh, Paul, they're beautiful! What a lovely surprise!"

She had no way of knowing how absolutely refreshing she appeared to him. Her hair in a damp tangle around her shoulders and her face clean of all makeup was as truthful an account of womanhood that Paul could ever remember seeing. She was beautiful but her physical beauty was only part of what he felt for her. He loved the way she opened the door to him even though she obviously wasn't dressed to have guests, and he loved the truthfulness that he read in her eyes every time she looked at him.

"When I selected them at the florist I intended to have them delivered, but then I got this crazy idea to bring them myself," he explained, but left off the jealousy he felt over thinking that an unknown deliveryman might tread where he, by convention, really should not have.

"I'm so glad you did."

"But just pretend that I'm the deliveryman. I'll be on my way now. I'm sure that you have plans for the night," he said and started to back away, all the while hoping that she would stop him. He felt like a lovesick adolescent.

"No!" she quickly shouted out. She didn't want him leaving. "I mean, I don't have any plans and I would love for you to come in."

"Are you sure?" He wanted to come in and spend the evening with her more than anything.

"Yes. I mean," she licked her lips, "we have things to discuss, and I have a cake in the oven. . . ." That wasn't what she wanted to say, but, if it kept him with her, she would say almost anything. "Do come in." She stepped to the side and motioned for him to enter.

He nodded and stepped past her. "The cake smells delicious."

"It will be ready soon." She looked down at her clothes and touched her tangled hair. She could feel his gaze sweep over her. If she were a person who could blush, she was sure that she would have then.

"I'll just be a moment while I change." Kristen placed the roses on the hall table. "Please, make yourself at home." She motioned toward the living room before turning on her bare feet to retreat to the bedroom.

As she closed the door to her bedroom, she saw Paul walk into her living room and she really couldn't believe that he was in her house, seeing her things. She knew that after tonight her home would never be quite the same. *But in a good way,* she thought, as a smile covered her whole face.

With super speed, Kristen tore off her shorts and T-shirt and selected from her closet a skirt with tropical flowers on it and a matching silk blouse which she had bought on an impulse two weeks ago but hadn't worn because of a lack of occasion. It was too feminine for the office, but perfect for tonight. She splashed on some mild perfume, whisked on a bit of rouge and a splash of lipstick. Her hair was practically dry so she brushed it until her comb could go through the thick strands, added a leather hairband, and donning her skirt and blouse and a pair of white pumps, quickly went back into the living room.

She couldn't help laughing softly when she saw Paul holding her little statue. He looked up at her and smiled. If he had thought that she looked sophisticatedly attractive at lunch and wholesomely honest just earlier, he now thought she looked alluringly beautiful. He liked

Kristen in every mode.

She saw Paul's appreciation and rejoiced in it. She had dressed for him just now and acknowledged to herself that it felt good to dress for a man once again. Meeting Paul was changing her back into the person she used to be before life took so many unpleasant turns.

He held up the statue. "When I was younger, my *nona* used to tease me and tell me that I could have been the model for this guy." He looked at the statue and frowned. "But I can't see the resemblance. Can you?" he asked, and Kristen had the distinct impression that he didn't like the idea.

"Perhaps when you were younger you did look similar," she offered diplomatically.

Paul held it in front of him, still frowning. "His hair's too wavy and—"

"He's very handsome, Paul." Kristen inserted.

"You think so?"

"Definitely."

"So," his dark eyes deepened and crinkled in the corners. "Does that mean you think that I am handsome?" Paul motioned toward the statue before he again put it in its place on the table.

"Paul?" She tilted her head over her right shoulder as she walked toward the kitchen, intending to test her cake to see if it was done. "You surely can't be fishing for a compliment?"

"I can."

She laughed and he liked the free way it sounded. In her home, Kristen was different, in a nicer, freer way, and he was very glad that he'd had the nerve to deliver the flowers himself. "Then, yes," she answered from the kitchen as he came to stand in the entranceway, "as you undoubtedly know, you are handsome." Kristen laughed again as she pulled a toothpick from its holder in order to check the cake and couldn't help adding impishly, "And I agree with your *nona*, you do look like you were the model for that statue."

Taking the toothpick from her hand, Paul chuckled, a deep and comfortable sound to her ears. "May I check the cake?" he asked, motioning toward the oven.

With a tilt of her head, Kristen stepped out of the way as he opened the oven door.

"Ummm, smells great!" He tested the cake. "And I'd say it's done, too," he pronounced, and reaching for her yellow potholders, removed the cake from the oven.

"You're very handy in a kitchen," Kristen commented, "especially. . .for a model of a statue," she teased. But at the challenging look that came into his eyes, she quickly held up her hand in truce and said, "I'm sorry, I shouldn't have started that again. I'll only say one last thing about the statue and then I'll leave the subject alone."

"And that is?" he prompted, understanding she was up to something.

"And that is. . ." She pinched a piece of cake from the top and blew on it before touching the tip of her tongue to it. "I was thinking maybe we could go to the National Archaeological Museum of Greece and see the real statue sometime—together."

"Kristen?" He waited without seeming to take a breath and the importance he placed on her answer impressed her and made Kristen feel wonderful.

She nodded her head affirmatively. "As of tomorrow afternoon, I'm on holiday for a month and free to leave for Athens whenever you say the word."

"Kristen," he repeated and moved toward her, and as his arms wrapped around her, she closed her eyes and savored the moment. It felt so right and so good to be held by a man after so long, but as Kristen rested her head against Paul's chest and smelled the essence of him, she knew that it was this man, and this man alone, whom she had only met this day, with whom it felt so right.

"I'm so glad." His voice was husky and deep, and very, very soft.

"Me, too." She looked up to his face and let her eyes roam around the classical planes of it before speaking. "I cannot wait to meet my aunt, and—"

"And," he prompted, following her eyes with his as they traveled his face.

"And," she continued, stepping back from him and whispering, "maybe. . .maybe we can start searching for that Unknown, Something More, together?"

He smiled a deep, warm smile that was glad for this woman who wanted more from a relationship than the superficial goals advertised so expertly throughout the world today. "I'd like nothing more, Kristen, than to go on that search together."

Paul didn't touch her again, but Kristen felt as though he had. There was a closeness growing between them that transcended the physical. Like the wind, it seemed to wrap around them and touch them, and weave them together with its invisible threads. "But. . .where do we start?" she asked.

He was unsure but he let common sense prevail. "Well, every search has a beginning, a path to follow. We just have to find that beginning and take it."

The doorbell rang, startling them both.

"I wonder who that could be?" Kristen asked as she walked toward the front door. Since Paul was with her she felt safe, so she didn't even bother to look through the peephole. She opened the door to a delivery-man who gave her a rather large package. She signed for it and kicking the door shut, read the postmark and exclaimed, "It's from my friend, Lottie, the archaeologist who is living in Athens!"

"Must be a birthday gift," Paul commented.

Running into the kitchen to get her scissors, Kristen nodded excitedly. "Last year she gave me the little statue." She ran back into the living room and sitting on the sofa, stared at the package for a moment before attacking the string with the scissors.

He laughed. "Wow, you do like opening packages!"

She laughed with him and nodded, unashamed, "I really do!" She tore at the brown paper until two gayly-wrapped packages appeared.

Paul picked up one of them and weighed it in his hands. "Feels like a book."

Kristen held the other one and nodded, "This one too. Oh, I love books and I imagine they must have something to do with Greece! Isn't that amazing, since I am going there soon!" She looked up at Paul, her eyes sparkling.

Paul laughed at her enthusiasm and handed her the package he held. "Quite amazing. Now why don't you open one and see exactly what it is."

Kristen sighed excitedly and looked from one to the other. "Yes, but which one should I open first?"

Paul pointed to one. "This one."

"Why this one and not that one?" she queried playfully.

"Because it says," he read the words written in among the stripes of the paper, " 'Kristen, please open this package first.' "

Kristen laughed and looked where Paul pointed. "Oh, I didn't see that!" She smiled up at him, then slipping her finger behind the taped end she carefully removed the wrapping. Flipping the book over, Kristen and Paul both gasped when they saw the book it was.

"A Bible. . . ," Kristen whispered and looked up at Paul.

"THE HOLY BIBLE," Paul read the words emblazoned in gold across the brown leather.

And they looked at one another in amazement.

Chapter 5

N o one has ever given me a Bible before," Kristen whispered and ran her fingertips over the smoothness of the gold lettering. Paul shook his head. He was amazed by the gift. "Me neither." With innate reverence, Kristen opened the book and read out loud the long inscription her friend had made.

To Kristen on her birthday,

The reading of this book has taught me that there is a birth even greater than the one you experienced twenty-eight years ago today.

It is the birth into God's kingdom which our Lord Jesus describes so nicely to Nicodemus in the third chapter of the Book of John and which I have been born into since coming to this ancient city of Athens.

I thought Athens was going to be good for my career; it has ended up being good for much, much more. No one ever knows what the future holds but I do know now that this Book is the key to life because it comes from God. In it, He talks to us all—a gift to be cherished.

There is a verse in the Book of Psalms which sums up what this Book has come to mean to me and which I hope comes to mean as much to you, Kristen.

"Your word is a lamp to my feet and a light for my path."

I hope your "path" brings you to Athens so that I may show you this wonderful city and even more, tell you in person about the wonderful knowledge, the wonderful news I have learned since coming here.

Your friend,
Lottie

179

Kristen stopped reading and slowly turned to Paul. "I have goosebumps breaking out on my arms. Can you believe the coincidence of it all?"

Paul took a deep breath and reaching for Kristen's arm, rubbed the goosebumps that had indeed appeared there. "I've never put much stock in coincidence, Kristen," he replied. "There's a power much greater than chance working here."

She slowly nodded her head and whispered, "You feel it too?"

"I feel it." He let go of her arm and reached for the Book. "And I think we have been given our starting place in our search for that Something More."

She looked back down at the Book. "I know some of the Bible stories but. . .I don't even know how to read this Book."

"Well. . .I guess as with anything. . .you start at the beginning."

He pointed at the other package which still awaited opening.

"Maybe that book will help."

Kristen turned to look at the package that remained unopened and nodding, reached for it. She was still excited but in a much deeper, more mature way that somehow knew that this moment of discovery was monumental to her life, and to Paul's life. She slipped off the bright wrapping paper and turning over the book, found that it was a Bible handbook and concordance. She flipped through its pages. "I guess it helps us to read the Bible. Look," she pointed out the headings, "it goes along with the chapters in the Bible. . .Genesis, Exodus. . .all of them."

He frowned, remembering something. "But they aren't called 'chapters,' they're different books that make up the Bible. The Book of Genesis, the Book of Exodus. . ."

She looked at him surprised. "You seem to know quite a bit more than I do."

"The Christian religion is a part of the Greek school curriculum." He smiled wryly. "I guess something had to sink in." He reached for the book and as she gave it to him a card fell out of the pages. Picking it up off the floor he handed it to her. "I have a feeling your friend has a few suggestions."

Kristen laughingly replied, "That sounds like Lottie!" Opening the envelope, Kristen removed a card which had a picture of the city of Athens on its front. "Oh, Paul, look!" she pointed out the picture. "It's your city! Can you see where you live?"

He took the card and pointed to the cliffs of the butte-shaped Acropolis, the ancient High City. There were numerous monumental buildings from Greece's golden past sitting upon it, including the world famous Parthenon, the temple that was built to honor the Greek god Athena. He explained, "I've recently refurbished a neoclassical home in Anafiotika."

"Anafiotika. . . ," she repeated the unusual name.

"It's part of the old town, built on the northeastern slopes below the Acropolis. My house is somewhere around here."

"Paul! I had no idea!" But she wasn't surprised to learn that he lived in the historical area. Somehow all that was modern and chrome didn't suit his personality. "It must be wonderful!" She scrutinized the card. "Can you see your house?"

He chuckled and tilted his head upward in the Greek expression for no. "I think it would take a magnifying glass to find it."

"It must be beautiful there," she said almost dreamily.

"It's home," he replied simply.

"I guess you can run up to the Acropolis anytime you want to."

He chuckled again. "Well—as a matter of fact—I do jog around its perimeters whenever there aren't too many tourists and whenever I have time, which unfortunately isn't often enough. Although I haven't been up to the Acropolis itself in years." He laughed. "I think the last time was on a high school field trip."

Kristen shook her head. "Imagine going on a school field trip to the Acropolis of Athens. . . ."

He smiled and pointed to the card again. "This picture was taken from the mountain behind your aunt's—and your father's—and your—ancestral home."

Kristen shook her head. "It's beautiful. . .I can't believe this is where my father grew up and where my aunt is today. . ."

"And where you will be in a couple of days," he reminded her gently.

She nodded almost in awe. "And where I will be in a couple of days. . . ."

She sat, entranced by the picture for a few moments until Paul said with good-natured impatience, "Come on. . .read what Lottie has to say."

She smiled up at him and opened the card. "I think you are as excited as I am."

"Maybe even more," he agreed. His tone was serious. "I feel as though the search that I have wanted to go on for so long is about to begin and it's amazing to think that its start is coming from a friend of yours who now lives in my city."

"It's like. . .something is weaving the fabric of our lives together. . ." She stopped and looked down at the card in her hand, suddenly embarrassed.

He gently touched her cheek with his thumb, silently asking her to look at him and his voice was deep with emotion as he spoke. "Perhaps. . .that Something More that we are looking for. . .?"

She bit her lower lip and nodded, "Perhaps. . . ," she agreed and started to read what Lottie wrote.

Dear Kristen,
  As you might know, Athens is a Biblical city.

Kristen looked over at Paul and frowned. "I didn't know that Athens was a Biblical city."

He nodded. "Many of the first Christians visited there. . .among them St. Paul. It's written about it in the Bible somewhere."

Kristen shook her head in wonder before continuing to read.

I think this fact has made Athens extra special to me. . .it certainly has inspired me as I discover the joys of being a new Christian in this ancient city.
  The Bible handbook and concordance will help you as you read the Bible. The handbook helps to explain the setting, mood, and history of what you might be reading and the concordance is there to help you locate certain subjects. Let's say you want to find all the verses in the Bible that have the word path *in them. Look up* path *and you will find them plus their location in the Bible.*
  Please come and visit me soon.

                              Happy birthday,
                                Lottie

Kristen fell silent. Her thumb rubbed lovingly over the words that her friend had cared enough to write to her.

"Path. . . ." Paul spoke the word into the wondrous silence that surrounded them.

Kristen nodded and looked up at Paul. "Path. . .my path. . .your path. . ." She took a deep breath and, unfolding herself from the soft cushions of the sofa, walked over to the window to gaze out at the setting sun. It hung over the churning ocean, like a lone Christmas tree ornament which someone had neglected to remove from the tree.

"You know. . . ," she began softly, "I think that I have always believed in the God of my ancestors. It's traditional." She played with the chain around her neck. "But. . . ," she turned back to Paul, "he has always seemed so remote, so unknown to me." She shrugged her shoulders, confirming the vulnerability Paul had thought to be hers when he first met her.

Rising, he walked over to the window to stand next to her. "I think I know what you mean."

She shook her head and turned to him. "No. . .what I mean is. . .I think that I have always blamed God for that. . .for the fact that He's unknown and remote to me. . .but I'm beginning to realize that it's my fault," she touched her palm to her chest, "my fault. . .that I haven't known Him better." She walked over to pick up the brand-new Bible from the table where it lay so quietly, so unassumingly, and yet, so forcefully. "How can I blame God for not knowing Him when I haven't even read this Book which is all about Him?"

Paul smiled wryly, guiltily. "I see what you mean. I think it's something many of us are guilty of in this day and age."

"Well. . .it's going to change for me." She plopped down on the sofa and with determination, seemed ready to start reading the Bible then and there. "I'm going to read this Book and see if it has some of the answers that I'm looking for."

Paul sat down next to her. "Good idea, but. . ." He touched her chin and turning her face to his, smiled that dazzling smile which made Kristen's insides turn upside down. "Do you suppose I could have a piece of that birthday cake before you start?" he asked. "It is rather a long Book."

She laughed softly. "Oh, Paul. I'm sorry." She put the Bible on the coffee table and hopping up from the sofa, walked toward the kitchen for the cake. "I have to decorate it first," she called back over her shoulder.

"What? Decorate your own birthday cake?" he questioned in mock horror, and standing, moved toward her just as the phone rang out insistently. "You answer that noisy machine and let me," he bounced his fingers against his chest, "decorate your cake."

She eyed him dubiously as the phone continued its demanding ring. "Do you know how?"

With mock exasperation, he asked, "Why is it that women always think men are so incapable in the kitchen?" He laughed and pushed her in the direction of the crying phone.

She paused and pensively replied, "Actually, I don't. My father was a whiz in the kitchen. In fact. . .he always made and decorated my birthday cakes. . .always. . . ," she finished on a sad note.

Paul felt her pain at not having her parents with her this year on her birthday and a part of him wanted to forget the cake, forget the ringing phone and go to her, wrapping her safely in the protection of his arms. But he knew that in the long run that action would only make things worse. Instead, he nodded toward the phone. "Whoever is calling you is going to hang up soon," he reminded her softly. The caring he felt was in his tone.

She nodded, and as Paul continued into the kitchen, she reached for the phone.

Paul found the icing supplies on the counter and began to ice the cake. He didn't mean to eavesdrop on Kristen's conversation, but with only a shuttered breakfast bar separating him from the living room, he couldn't help but overhear every word she said.

"Uncle George! What a nice surprise!" The pleasure in her voice was obvious but Paul frowned at her use of the title. He didn't think that she had any other living relatives, not even on her mother's side, and he wondered who this "Uncle" George could be.

"You will! Tomorrow night?" A pause. "That's great. And don't worry that you couldn't surprise me today, I've already had enough surprises for the day. . ." A pause. "Well. . .a man from Greece came today. . .from my aunt. . .she wants me to come and visit her!" She spoke excitedly but from the subdued sound of her voice when she spoke again, Paul was sure that this "Uncle" George wasn't too pleased with her news.

"No. . .I'm fine. . .and Uncle George. . .I'm glad. . .please be glad for me. . . ."

There was another long pause before Kristen again spoke words of reassurance. She seemed to be cutting her "uncle" off firmly but nicely. "Uncle George. . .don't worry. . ." A pause. "Because my aunt's been sick," she explained. "Well. . .I'm glad that you're coming tomorrow so that you can meet him and see for yourself. Don't worry. . .I'm a big girl now. . . ." She paused and Paul could tell from her voice that she was smiling into the phone. "I love you too. . .thanks for calling. . .bye. . . ." She hung up the phone just as Paul put the finishing touches on icing the cake.

Kristen strode into the kitchen and stood leaning against the door frame. "I hope you can come over tomorrow evening. A very dear friend is going to come to wish me happy birthday and I'd like for you to meet one another."

His back to her, Paul replied truthfully about what he had overheard. "I don't think your 'uncle' George is too pleased to hear that I'm here."

She arched her brows at Paul's use of her caller's name and looking at her over his shoulder, he explained, "Sorry, but I could not help overhearing."

"No. . .it's okay. If I had wanted privacy, I would have gone into my bedroom." She wiped up the milk she'd spilled earlier and opened the cupboard for two dessert plates. "Uncle George is a bit protective of me."

"Are you related somehow?"

As she placed the bone china plates on the counter she shook her head. "No. . .as I said earlier today. . .I don't have any blood relatives other than my aunt. Uncle George was a longtime friend of my parents. . .they were like siblings. Since they died. . .he has kind of watched over me."

"Sounds like a nice man."

"He is. I love him like. . .like. . . ," she fished around for a good way to describe her feelings for the older man and finally settled on the most obvious analogy, "a beloved uncle. I've known him all my life."

"And he's coming tomorrow night?"

She dipped the tip of her finger into what was left of the chocolate icing and licked it clean before explaining. "He lives in Virginia, in Richmond, where I used to live. He had planned on surprising me tonight. . .but he was unable to get away."

Paul placed the icing knife in the sink with a *plonk* and picking up the tubes of decorative icing and birthday candles said, "Well, I'm glad that I'll have the chance to meet him. But for now," he nudged her in the direction of the living room, "let me finish my job so we can eat this delicious-smelling cake."

"Can't I watch?" she asked impishly over her shoulder as she walked out of the kitchen.

"No way. . .it has to be a surprise. Now out!"

As she padded into the living room Kristen laughed, a happy, gay sound that only went a fragment of the way in telling how happy she really was that Paul had come to her house that night.

She couldn't help but think how differently the evening had turned out because of this man who had come from her aunt. Without him, she would have been alone and sad. With him, she wasn't sad and she wasn't alone.

Sitting down on the sofa, she reached forward and picked up the books Lottie had sent to her. She held both of them on her lap and inhaled the lovely scent that could only belong to new books. She listened to the sound of Paul whistling "Happy Birthday" as he worked in the kitchen. She watched the curtains as they danced to the beat of the strong wind blowing off the Pacific and she knew that she hadn't been happier in a very long time—in a *very, very* long time. The day had turned and twisted in such different directions from that which she had thought it would carry her when she had awoken to her birthday all alone that morning.

She put the Bible down and on a sudden impulse, leafed through the concordance in search for the word *path*. When she found it, she was surprised to see so many verses which included the word, and a little bit daunted. Since she wasn't sure where to start searching she began with the first one.

She read out loud, " 'Ps. 16:11 known to me the p'. . .*must be path*. . . 'of life'."

Picking up the Bible, she looked through the index, discovered that 'Ps.' stood for the book of Psalms, found the page number for the beginning of the book, turned to it, and from there turned the pages until she found the sixteenth chapter and then the eleventh verse. Her eyes lit up when she saw that she had found the correct verse.

She read, "You have made known to me the path of life. . ." She lifted her eyes to the mighty Pacific outside her window that was still visible in the lingering light of an already setting sun. But Kristen didn't see its beauty. Instead, the words she had just read made her see something within herself that was even more wondrous and mighty than the ocean beyond her window.

She looked back down at the book and slowly repeated the words, "You have made known to me the path of life. . .the path of life. . ." And she thought how magnificent it was that there was indeed a "path of life" and how it was something that could be made known to her.

"Are you ready?" Paul's voice boomed out from the kitchen, startling her.

Kristen wanted to share what she had just discovered with Paul, so she was careful to leave the Bible opened as she put it down on the coffee table before her. "I'm ready," she returned and as she smoothed out the folds of her skirt, thought that it was wonderful to feel happy again.

"Then here I come." He walked into the living room whistling "Happy Birthday" and holding the cake, now ablaze with candles, in front of him.

She laughed, delighted that he had filled it with twenty-eight candles instead of a token few. "Wow! It looks like a bonfire!"

"Well it just might become one if you don't hurry and blow them out," he admonished with a smile and placed the cake on the table before her. "*Hronia Polla*, Kristen. . ." He spoke the Greek birthday wish meaning "Many Years" which he'd written on her cake and she sucked in her breath when she saw the Greek letters. "It means—"

"Oh Paul. . ." She cut him off and her eyes, reflecting the light of her twenty-eight birthday candles, glistened with tears. "I know what '*Hronia Polla*' means. . ."

"Kristen—?" he questioned softly, concerned by the tears.

She touched the corner of her eyes with a birthday napkin and smiled, a sweet smile which held gladness in it. "Don't worry. . .these are tears of happiness. I thought I'd never see nor hear those words again." She paused and then explained. "You see. . .my father always wrote them on my birthday cakes, ever since I was a little girl. . .they're practically the only Greek words I know and they're very special to me."

Happiness filled him and he knew then that the best way for him to be happy was to always be able to make this woman happy.

Touching her shoulder in gentle understanding, he nodded toward the cake. "You'd better blow the candles out."

She squeezed her eyes shut and, looking to Paul like a little girl who was wishing with all her heart for her birthday wish to come true, opened her eyes and blew all the candles out at the same moment.

Paul clapped. "Bravo, Kristen. . .now your wish will come true."

"I hope so," she whispered and looked at him in a way that made him feel as though he were a part of that wish. "But for the first time," she continued, "my wish was more like a prayer."

"A prayer?" he questioned. That surprised him.

She reached for the Bible as he sat down next to her. "Look what I just discovered." She pointed out the verse in the sixteenth chapter of Psalms.

"'You have made known to me the. . . ,'" he paused as he silently read the next words before speaking them out loud, ". . .Path of life. . ." He turned amazed eyes toward Kristen.

She nodded. "See. . .my birthday wish—prayer—is that the 'You' in that verse makes known to me the path of my life and along that 'path' I hope that I can discover who exactly the 'You' is."

He nodded, and not wanting to discourage her, but also not wanting her to be disappointed, he felt that he had to remind her of a simple truth. "You know, sometimes our paths go in ways we least expect them to go and sometimes in ways we prefer them not to go."

"Don't I know that," she expounded, that old familiar bitterness creeping into her voice. "I thought that I would be happily married at this point in my life, maybe even a mother who could take her children to visit their grandparents. Instead, I'm legally a widow to a man who only meant to use me." She paused and breathed out in disgust, "Or, I should say, use my money—and even if I had children, my parents aren't living anymore to go and visit."

"Kristen. . ." He took her hand in his and gently squeezed it. That her husband had married her for her money was news to him and something that explained a lot about her and—it was something to which he could relate. It made him want to protect her more. If he thought that he had to go slow and easy with her before, he was now certain of it. She had endured too many hurts in her life and he wanted to do everything in his power to make sure that she wasn't hurt again.

An amazed frown drew his brows together in a straight line as it occurred to him that he felt this way because he loved her. He loved her. . .as he had never loved nor would ever love again. . .and he knew that he had loved her from practically the first moment he saw her.

She watched him frown and totally misreading his expression, was immediately disgusted with herself for letting him see her bitterness over the events in her life. She had already told him how confused she was about things. . .did she have to add bitterness to the list? Wishing she had kept her mouth shut, she withdrew her hand from his and asked brightly, too brightly, "How about a slice of cake?"

Still amazed by his thought, Paul absently nodded and Kristen escaped into the kitchen for plates and silverware and to regain her equilibrium.

Resting her forehead against the cupboard, Kristen squeezed her eyes shut and admonished herself for letting her bitterness over her disastrous marriage and her parents' deaths mar the evening. She didn't understand how it had happened but she knew that her feelings for Paul were running true and deep and getting deeper by the moment. She was looking forward to traveling to Greece to meet her aunt but somehow, in the course of the last few hours, she knew that it had become even more important for her to go to Greece in order to be with Paul. She hardly knew him and yet, somehow she felt that she knew him better than anyone else in the world. Her soul responded to his, and from somewhere the expression "soulmate" found its way into Kristen's brain and she smiled. For that was what Paul had become to her, and a part of her, a part that had been wounded and left bleeding for far too long, was mending and trusting and beginning to. . .love again.

That thought shocked Kristen and she banged her head lightly against the cupboard.

"Do you need some help in there?" Paul called out, startling her.

"No. I'm coming." But she was shocked by her thoughts. *Do I truly love Paul Andrakos?* she wondered as she absently rubbed her head and then quickly gathered the plates and silverware onto a serving tray. And how could it have happened so suddenly? Was it possible to fall in love with a man in only a few hours?

Squaring her shoulders, she walked back into the living room with the tray and sat next to Paul. She was aware of him in a way that was different from before, in a way that was both frightening and thrilling, and made her feel shy, like an adolescent. She was glad to have something to do with her hands and after removing the candles she sliced two big pieces of cake, one for each of them.

As she handed a plate to Paul she whispered, "Paul. . .I'm sorry for my outburst." She shrugged her shoulders, looking very vulnerable to Paul as she did so. "I guess. . .sometimes the anger I feel over how things have turned out. . ." Her voice trailed off.

Putting his plate down, Paul reached for her hand, quieting her with his touch. "Kristen, no. . .don't ever apologize for being honest with me."

She shrugged her shoulders again, making Paul ache over her vulnerability. "It's just that. . .I don't want you to think that I'm this bitter person who is obsessed with the past and angry all the time and confused the rest of the time."

Paul silenced her by lightly touching his finger to her lips. Her eyes turned to his and the agitation she had felt was squelched by what she saw written in the depths of his dark, warm eyes.

Slowly his mouth moved and the words which he spoke were like a soothing balm to her soul. "What I think about you is that you are lovely. . .both inside and out. We've only met this day but I feel as though I have known you forever."

"Paul. . ." She reached out and rubbed his face with her hand, a light touch of caring that made Paul, in spite of his resolve to go slow with her, unable to do so.

"Dear Kristen. . ." He placed his hand over hers and the sounds of the deepening night, the breaking surf, the wind above it, their breath and pulse beats, all combined to produce a symphony of sound, a symphony of life, that drew them together. "Dear Kristen. . . ," he repeated, "I never believed in love at first sight. . .until now. . . ."

"Paul. . . ," she whispered his name in wonder that he could possibly feel for her what she knew she felt for him. Her hand turned to hold his and he grasped her smaller one between both of his, gently bringing her closer to him.

His eyes spoke the words a moment before his mouth and Kristen had no doubts that they both spoke the truth, "Darling Kristen. . .as amazing as it might seem—I am falling in love with you. . . ."

Her eyes answered him before her mouth, but Paul too knew that they both spoke the truth, "And. . .I. . .am falling in love with you. . .Paul. . . ."

And their vow was sealed by a kiss, their first kiss. It was a simple kiss of love, of meaning, of two souls who had found one another and rejoiced in that discovery.

And Paul thought how a bond encircled them, a ring. It was something that neither of them had any part in making, but rather, something that had been ordained from the beginning of time and was meant to be.

And suddenly, Paul thought about the "ring of love," the name given to that very special ring of platinum and stone which his *nona* had given to him several years ago. The coincidence concerning its history and its future, in terms of the woman he now held in his arms, amazed him, a man who didn't believe in coincidence, and he squeezed Kristen closer to him, not wanting anything to ever twist that ring, that bond, which encircled them.

Chapter 6

I can't believe this is happening to me. . . ," Kristen whispered into Paul's neck and he sighed, a deep, loving sound to her ears.

"Well. . ." He paused for just a moment and lightly ran his hand over her cheek. "Perhaps love at first sight runs in your family," he suggested, startling her.

"What?" She sat back and her eyes darted around his face in curious question.

"Sudden and forever lasting love has been know to happen to ancestors of yours before," he explained.

She looked at him in wonder. "Ancestors of mine?" She had never thought consciously in terms of her ancestors before. But now, as she thought about it, she knew that it was something that was very important to her, especially since she felt that sudden and unexpected love for this man.

He nodded and was again amazed that her father had never told her anything about her family history or that she had never thought to ask. "Weren't you ever the least bit curious about your ancestors?"

"I was but. . .I was told that I had no living relatives. . . ." Her voice trailed off and she lifted her eyebrows in mute explanation. "But I'm very curious about these ancestors of mine who loved. . .as we love," she finished shyly and rubbed her fingertips over the back of his hand. "Please tell me?"

He lifted his hand to the smoothness of her face and rejoiced when her eyes closed and she rubbed her face against his hand. Whimsically, he was reminded again of his little tabby cat back in Athens. That was her way of demonstrating her love for him. He couldn't help but think how Kristen had many other more wonderful ways of showing her love. But that kind of thinking was dangerous, especially while in her house alone . . .and at night. . .and in love. . . .

Abruptly Paul stood, startling Kristen's eyes open, and she watched questioningly as he strode over to the window which now showed only the shadow of night. "Did I see a path leading down to the beach?" he asked and she nodded her head, wondering what he had in mind.

Walking back to her, he took her hand and gently pulled her up from the sofa and over toward the deck. "Then let's take a walk on the beach and I'll tell you the story of "The Ring of Love,' " he finished dramatically.

" 'The Ring of Love'?" she questioned as they walked out onto the deck and he slid the door closed behind them.

"Ah. . .Kristen. Didn't you know that all good love stories have a name?"

"True," she agreed and laughed as they walked down the steps of the deck to reach the short but overgrown path which led to the beach. "Then tell me, Paul. . .what will *our* love story be called?"

She tilted her head femininely to the side, wondering what sort of a romantic title he would come up with.

" 'The Grecian Quest,' " he pronounced without hesitation while leading her over protruding roots and around tangled branches toward the pebbly beach.

" 'The Grecian Quest'?" she echoed, dismayed by its lack of romance and in her disappointment she almost banged her head on a low branch.

"Careful," he admonished and pulled her around the branch and out onto the moonlit beach.

Turning to her, he watched as the long, silky strands of her hair were caught and played with by the strong wind. Lifted and twirled, her hair became a frame of motion around her face and he was glad that she hadn't cut it. He loved her hair and brought his fingers up to feel the strands as they danced in the wind.

But then, drawing his attention away from her hair to her eyes, he realized that she wasn't pleased about something. "Kristen? What is it?"

She shrugged her shoulders. " 'The Grecian Quest'. . . ," she repeated. "It's nice but. . .doesn't it sound more like the title for an adventure story than for a romance?"

Chuckling, he put his hands behind her neck and gently drew her close to him. "Ah. . .my sweet Kristen. But what could be more of an adventure than searching, finding, and learning all there is to know about our love?"

She sighed and smiled and let her head fall against his chest. The beating of his heart seemed to be one with the pounding of the surf. Together, they drummed out the rhythm of life, the adventure of life. The sea's steady rhythm brought with it the song of ages past and the man's heartbeat, the song of the present, and both told of people working and living and loving throughout time. As she stood and listened to the two together, the one with her right ear pressed against Paul's chest and the other with her left ear pressed by the sounds of the night, she knew that Paul was right. She was embarking on the greatest adventure of her life by traveling to Greece with him. And it would be an adventure meeting her blood relative, an adventure discovering if their sudden love was to be a long-lasting love, and most of all, an adventure that might lead to their finding out about that Unknown, Something More. . . .

"Besides, other than giving this love of ours a chance to grow, aren't we going on an even greater quest together in Greece—in search for that Something More in life?" he asked, echoing her thoughts and Kristen was surprised, not by the question, but by the note of vulnerability she thought she heard creep into his voice. Leaving the beauty that came from listening to his beating heart, she stepped back from him and looked up into the warmth of his deep, dark eyes, eyes that were as dark and as deep as the summer night that surrounded them, and she realized, with something close to wonder, that like her, he too felt vulnerable over falling in love.

And suddenly, "The Grecian Quest" seemed like the perfect name for the love story that was becoming their very own. "Yes, Paul." She squeezed him closer to her and whispered assurance into his ear. "The greatest quest of our lives. . .our 'Grecian Quest'. . .and ours alone."

His hands hovered above her back for a second before finally having their way and pressing themselves against her slender shoulder blades. He wanted to kiss her, he wanted to love her, but even more, he wanted to give their love the chance to grow straight and sure without any bends or twists from yearnings being met prematurely, to chance ruining it. Besides, instinct told him that even if he pressed his desire, she was of morals that didn't allow certain bounds to be crossed. And for this he was glad. . .very, very glad.

Stepping away, Kristen took his hand and led him over to her favorite thinking spot, a sea log that had washed up on the beach long before she had moved into her house. She pulled him down next to her. "Now tell me the story—'The Ring of Love.'"

"Curious, aren't you?"

"Definitely!"

Smiling, he began. "Several years ago, when my *nona*, your Aunt Aphrodite, was particularly concerned because I hadn't married, she presented me with a ring, a ring which has been in her family—your family that is—for over a century and a half."

Kristen hadn't remembered seeing a ring on Paul's hand but she felt along the knuckles of his hand anyway.

"No." He held up his hands for her to see that his fingers were void of rings. "It's not a man's ring. It's a woman's ring."

Her brows drew together in question. "Why would she give you a woman's ring?"

He smiled. "Its history will explain why."

"Sounds like it must have an interesting one."

"Believe me—it does." Paul took both of her hands in his.

"Especially interesting since you and I. . .love. Another event in the long list of events that shows that Someone—perhaps God—is orchestrating the path of our lives—"

"Tell me," Kristen whispered.

"I've told you that your family comes from a very old shipping family." At her nod, he continued. "Well, let's see. . .it would have been your great-great-grandfather, whose name just happens to have been Paul, who started the tradition of the ring."

"My great-great-grandfather," she repeated wistfully. "And his name was Paul?" He nodded and she smiled. "I like the name." She raised her hand to his face and moved it along the strength of his jawline.

He turned his head and kissed her palm before guiding her hand back down to his other one. "The story gets better," his eyes narrowed, "but you'd better sit still if you want to hear it," he warned.

Paul couldn't know how happy it made her to know that he found her so attractive. Ted's last words to her had been that she was an "ice queen, with a heart and a body made of ice." To know that Paul found her to be attractive and warm made her feel doubly so. But she wanted to hear the story so she primly folded her hands in her lap.

He nodded, satisfied, and continued. "During the golden days of

Galaxidi, which was one of the major shipping ports of Greece during the last century, your ancestor, who was a wealthy shipowner, survived a very dangerous trip around the Cape of Good Hope. By all accounts, he should have died. He had been injured, was taken sick, and the weather was supposed to have been fierce. But against all odds he survived the trip."

"Now that's an adventure!" Kristen interjected.

Paul smiled and continued, "Well, he was certain that he'd survived because of the prayers of his much loved wife back in far-off Greece, whose name just happened to have been. . .Christina."

"Christina! My grandmother's name! My name. . . ," she whispered in awe.

"Your name is a chain through the history of your family, Kristen. Remember how I told you that it's a tradition to name children after their grandparents. . .well, through your grandmother, you were named for the Christina of our story."

Kristen shook her head in wonder. "It's amazing. . . ."

He nodded his head in agreement and taking her hand in his and twining his fingers through hers, continued, "Even though their marriage had been arranged, as all marriages were in those days, they fell instantly in love with one another within moments of meeting." He paused and kissed her forehead.

Kristen nuzzled up against his shoulder. "Sudden love. . . ," she whispered.

"And forever-lasting love," Paul reminded her of the second part, draping his arm around her shoulder to gather her closer to him.

"Forever-lasting. . . ," Kristen repeated, her voice sounding like liquid crystal to Paul's ears. "Well, so far we have the sudden love, and our names in common with the hero and heroine of the 'ring of love'. . .the 'forever-lasting' must follow." She looked up at him and he didn't think that he had ever seen a more beautiful pair of eyes. *Emeralds, and that includes the unusual emerald in the 'ring of love,' would be lucky if they looked half as beautiful,* he thought and gently brushed his lips across the smoothness of her lids. She raised her lips to meet his but he turned away with a groan.

"Kristen. . .do you want to hear the story or not?"

She smiled and turning her face toward the singing sea, settled back against his side, determined not to interrupt again. But she reveled in

196

knowing that he found her attractive.

"Good," he cleared his throat and continued. "Well, the truth was, somehow Christina sensed that something was wrong with her beloved husband. And even when she was heavy with her surprise to him—their son—she was to be found, day and night, in the chapel of their home praying for his safe return. Paul survived that voyage and with practically all the money he earned from it he bought a ring, a most unusual ring. . . ."

"The 'ring of love'. . . ," Kristen whispered the words into the wind, which danced around their heads before being carried off into the windy night.

"That's right," Paul agreed. "And from the day Paul came home and put the ring on Christina's finger she wore it and your great-great-grandfather Paul always returned to his Christina from all his journeys to finally end his days a very old man at his wife's side, something very unusual back in those days of sailing ships and pirates. People always said that it was her love and her prayers for him that always brought him back to her when other women's husbands didn't survive."

"Oh, how lovely. . . ," Kristen said dreamily.

"The ring has come to symbolize their love and faith."

"But," she swiveled her head to look up at him, "I still don't understand why my aunt gave you a woman's ring?"

"There is more about the ring. It is to be worn only by married or engaged women of the Vasilias family and since I was a member of the family by being your Aunt Aphrodite's godson, and since she had no idea where you were, she gave it to me to put on the finger of my bride."

Kristen sat up straight. To fall in love in one afternoon was one thing but to talk about marriage all in the same afternoon was something entirely different, especially after the disaster of her marriage to Ted.

"Paul. . . ," she began, but he cut her off with a chuckle that instantly relieved her.

"Don't worry, Kristen. . .I'm not proposing. . . ."

She glanced over at him and at his warm smile and smiled self-consciously back at him. "It's just that. . .we have so much ahead of us. . . my aunt. . . our search. . ."

"I agree."

"You do? Honestly?"

"I do. Even though I know that I'm no longer falling in love with you. . . ."

She knew from his velvety-sounding voice with its magical accent that something wonderful was coming and with the patience of one hearing a fairy tale unfold, knowing that a happy ending was in store, she waited to hear him speak.

"Because you see. . . ," he rubbed her face with his hand, "I've already fallen. . .I'm there. . .I love you."

"Oh, Paul. . . ," she whispered as their foreheads touched. "I love you too." And then their lips touched, and then their souls, as they became one with the elements of the Pacific night.

"Darling Kristen," Paul whispered her name after a tiny moment.

"As the only direct descendant of Paul and Christina, the 'ring of love' is yours to wear upon your engagement—" he rubbed the fourth finger on her left hand, "but I hope—that the ring of love in your life—will include me—"

"Oh, Paul. . .I feel sure that it will. . .someday. . .it's just that. . .before I make any plans. . ."

"I know—" he cut her off. "And I agree." And before her amazed eyes he repeated the verse they had discussed earlier, " 'You have made known to me the path of life. . . .' "

Kristen nodded her head. "You really do understand."

"I think—somehow—that our quest is very important—to our love." He spoke haltingly but with such emotion that Kristen felt tears sting her eyes.

"Oh, Paul. . ." She gently went to rest her head against his chest, but a noise coming from the sea that was different from the pounding of the waves meeting land made her stop.

Both turned their heads toward the sound.

"Did you hear something?"

She nodded her head. "I thought I heard a cry—"

"Help. . .someone. . .help. . ." The faint cry came to them again above the pounding of the surf and both Kristen and Paul were on their feet and running toward the dark, foaming sea from where it came.

"Somebody's out there!" Paul, now a couple of strides ahead of Kristen, yelled into the wind.

"Help me!" The plea sounded again just as Paul flung off his shoes and jacket and dashed into the crashing waves to swim toward the unknown person.

Kristen kicked off her pumps and ran to where the waves beat against her waist but there she stopped, knowing that she would do more harm than good if she attempted to swim the turbulent sea. Unlike Paul, she was not a very good swimmer. She could barely keep herself afloat in calm seas, much less save someone else and in such turbulent seas. Watching Paul swim, now on top of the waves, then lost on the other side, she marveled at how on this night, the first where there had ever been a cry of need from the ocean below her home, Paul was there to help her. She didn't know what she would have done if she had been alone.

As it was, the waves pushed and pulled against her, threatening to lift her feet out from under her. Her flowered skirt billowed out in the waves, like a lifesaver. Kristen wished that it was one.

From the pale gibbous moon that was only now showing its face above Mount Tamalpais, Kristen watched as Paul closed the distance between himself and the man, and she could almost feel Paul's relief as he grabbed the driftwood which the man was clinging to and propelled him toward shore.

She watched and prayed, as all people seem to pray when they're frightened, whether they know God or not, and willed Paul to come to shore. Paul pushed through the water with his powerful muscles, man against the sea, now eight, now five, now three yards away to finally reach Kristen.

With his last ounce of strength Paul pushed the man, still clinging to the log, toward Kristen. "Get him to shore!" he yelled.

Kristen grabbed ahold of the driftwood and with all her might pulled the man the final yards to shore. Twice she fell down as the combination of the man's weight, the pounding waves, and the strong Pacific undertow all fought against her efforts. And when the driftwood slammed against her knees she had a moment of horror when she thought she was going to lose her battle, but Paul was now by her side and together they fought the water to get the man ashore.

"Dear God, help us," Kristen petitioned out loud and laughed giddily as a huge wave immediately surged against the driftwood and flung her, the man, and Paul onto the shore.

The three lay panting for a few minutes before Kristen raised herself to her knees and with all her remaining strength, pulled the man away from the waves and up onto the dry beach.

"Thank God. . . ," the man whispered as the dry sand touched his exhausted body and only then did he release his grip on the driftwood that had probably saved his life. "Thank God. . ." He looked up at Kristen, his eyes red and puffy, but much to Kristen's joy they were focused and alert. "After coming so far. . .I didn't have the energy to come ashore. . .I saw a light. . .and I prayed. . ." He coughed and Kristen helped him to discharge whatever of the sea he had swallowed. With a look that said he thought he was looking at an angel, he continued, "I prayed that you were on the shore. . .thank you. . ." He shut his eyes and Kristen gently laid him back down on the sand. He was exhausted and had already fallen asleep.

She looked over at Paul. Stumbling over to the man's side on legs that felt like jelly, Paul reached for the unconscious man's pulse and was glad to feel it strong against his numb fingertips, and quickly running his hands over the man's body, he confirmed that there were no broken bones.

He looked over at Kristen, and reached for her. "We make a good team."

She squeezed his hand and smiled and when he shook his head like a dog, the thought amazingly came to her that now that his hair had been touched by the sea, he was identical to the *Youth of Antikythera.*

She laughed, a light, free laugh of happiness, of relief, of joy that sailed off into the night like a seagull at dawn.

Paul smiled with her and looked down at the man. "I think he's going to be fine."

Nodding, happiness enabling her to stand on her wobbly feet, she said, "You stay with him while I call 9-1-1 and bring some blankets and hot soup."

"Soup. . . ," the man mumbled, opening his eyes a bit. "Sounds wonderful. . .so glad God let our paths meet. . . ," he whispered before drifting off into an exhausted sleep once again.

For just a second, Paul's eyes met Kristen's. They were both thinking the same thing. "The path of life. . ." How glad they were that they had walked the path down to the beach that night. . .for so many reasons.

"I love you," Paul mouthed the words and before Kristen dashed off to her house, she mouthed the words back to him.

And she had never meant anything more in her life.

Chapter 7

I can't remember when I've ever been so sore, Uncle George," Kristen said the next evening to the dignified man who sat on the sofa next to her in her living room. "But it's a good kind of sore," she amended and smiling, rubbed her stiff arms. Knowing that she had helped to save a man's life was a heady feeling.

"I'm proud of you, Kristy." George's voice was as dignified as his appearance. With a thick head of white—not gray—hair, and a tall, slender physique which men twenty years his junior could normally only hope to have, Kristen's Uncle George was a man the world took seriously. But right now his eyes twinkled as they always did for his best friend's daughter. That he loved Kristen as a beloved uncle might was readily obvious. "And your parents would be, too."

She looked down. "I wish they had been able to swim to shore. . .when their boat sank. . . ."

George reached over and patted Kristen's hand. She looked up at him and the sadness she saw there reminded her that he missed them as much as she did. And she didn't want him to be sad. Taking a deep breath that was meant to brighten the mood, she said, "Well, I'm just glad Paul was here. I never could have fought those waves and brought that man to safety alone."

When George cleared his throat and sat forward on the sofa Kristen knew that she had said the wrong thing. He had made himself clear on the phone the previous night that he didn't like the idea of her going to visit her Aunt Aphrodite, especially with a man who was a stranger. "Kristy, what do you know about this man?"

Kristen smiled, a secret smile which George saw and which did nothing to relieve his apprehensions. His frown lines deepened across his brow. That George was worried about Kristen traveling to Greece was obvious to her, so how could she worry him further by telling him that what she knew about Paul Andrakos was that she loved him, she needed him, she wanted to be with him always.

"What work does he do?" George persisted, cutting into Kristen's thoughts.

It amazed Kristen to consider that she really didn't know what job Paul actually did. His worth to her didn't come from his profession. It came from the man himself, that essence which was Paul Andrakos. But she knew that like her parents, her uncle George wouldn't understand that, so somewhat on the defensive side she answered, "Paul's a business associate of my aunt's. You do know what my aunt does?"

"Of course," he answered and Kristen lifted an elegant eyebrow at the defensive quality in his tone. It was an unusual timbre to hear in George.

"What else do you know? Did you know that my parents were planning a trip to Greece?" She pressed her advantage, both amazed and relieved to have shifted the direction of the subject. Uncle George was a lawyer who rarely lost the upper hand.

"Yes. I knew that there was some sort of reconciliation and that they were planning to visit your aunt," he admitted in his best lawyer's voice.

Kristen raised her hands in exasperation. "It seems like everyone knows things about my family and its history—everyone except for me that is!"

George ignored her outburst and remained calm and serious. "Kristen. . ." He caught her attention at his use of her full name and effectively cut off her exasperated anger. He rarely called her anything but "Kristy" and "Darling." For him to use her full name meant that the subject was of great importance to him. The last time he'd used it was to tell her that her parents had perished in a boating accident. "Don't go to Greece."

She took a deep breath and immediately softened toward him. The fact that her parents hadn't told her anything about her family wasn't his fault after all. He had always been a great friend to her, a man who had become a beloved uncle to her out of love for her and her parents, fulfilling a great need in her life. "Uncle George," she said, reaching over for his hand. "But why? Why don't you want me to go?"

"Kristy—" He paused and rubbed her smooth hand between both of his. He seemed to be weighing his words. "I don't think your father would want you to go."

Kristen shook her head. "I don't agree with you, Uncle George. I think that he *would* want me to go. . .as if I'm going in his place. And according to Paul, my aunt really wants to meet me."

"Kristy—" He seemed to be choosing his words carefully. "Sometimes friends are better than relatives. You haven't been around relatives so you've romanticized everything to do with them."

And with these words Kristen thought she understood what was bothering the older man. "Uncle George. . .are you afraid that my aunt might take your place in my affections? Because if you are. . ."

"No, Kristy. . .of course not," he denied hotly.

"No one could take your place in my life," she finished stubbornly. "You've been the greatest uncle a girl could ever wish for."

With a sigh, he pursed his lips together and sat back. "Kristy—I am not afraid of anyone taking my 'place.' However, I am concerned that you will be hurt." Reaching out for her hand, he squeezed it. "Darling girl, you have been hurt too much during the last couple of years."

She pulled her hand away and snapped, "And I have been a recluse because of it." Jumping up from the sofa, Kristen strode over to the window and stood looking out at the path which led to the beach.

She remembered all the times during the last year that she had walked that path alone. And then she remembered the previous night and how she had walked that same path with Paul and how they had talked about a path that might lead them to a future together and then, how their path had met another person's path which meant saving that man's life. *Not a bad way to start a life together,* Kristen thought, and turning back to Uncle George, she thought how she had done more living the previous day than she had during the entire previous year and a half.

"I'm going to Greece, Uncle George," she said with finality. "I believe it's what I'm meant to do."

Like a father who had tried to talk sense into his child but finally had to admit to the futility of it, George sighed and, standing, walked over to Kristen. Holding her shoulders lightly between his hands, he smiled down at her, a smile that told of all the love he felt for his best friend's daughter. "Then God bless, my darling girl." He grimaced. "I just wish that I didn't have to be in China during the next few months and in such a remote location."

"But why?"

"So that you could call me if you needed anything."

Kristen wrapped her arms around his neck and hugged him as she had hugged him ever since she was a little girl. "Uncle George! Don't worry, I won't need anything," she whispered and stepped away. "I'm a big girl now—remember?"

The doorbell rang and Kristen looked happily toward the door. "That must be Paul." She stood on her tiptoes and lightly kissed her uncle's cheek before hurrying toward the door. "You're going to like him," she threw back over her shoulder before reaching for the doorknob.

She opened the door and laughed delightedly as Paul presented her with a beautiful bouquet of fragrant roses, roses of every shade.

"Flowers again!" she laughed and nuzzled her nose among their silky folds. "But we're leaving tomorrow night. What will I do with them?"

"You will enjoy them until then and when we get to Athens, there will be a white bouquet for you," he said and kissed her in the European fashion of a quick peck on both cheeks. He wanted to do much more, but he could see the man whom he knew must be her uncle George from the corner of his eye.

"White roses?"

"Don't tell me that you've never heard of the white roses of Athens? There's even a song about them."

She laughed again. "Then you will have to sing it to me."

"Ah. . .no. Singing is not one of my talents. We'll leave the singing of that song to Nana Mouscouri."

"Nana who?"

"A Greek singer who sings like a nightingale," Paul explained as Kristen led him over to where George was standing by the window watching their exchange with interest and in spite of their restraint, with understanding. It would take a very obtuse person not to notice that there was more to Kristen and Paul's relationship than just friendship. And Kristen's uncle George was not obtuse about anything.

"Uncle George," she introduced the older man to the younger, "I'd like for you to meet Paul Andrakos." She turned to Paul. "Paul, this is George Lee, whom I fondly refer to as my 'uncle' George."

The two men shook hands and in the moment that it took to do so, they sized one another up as men all over the world do upon meeting. Both of them, in spite of their desires not to, liked what they saw in the other. This assessment was obvious to Kristen and made her very happy.

George's eyes narrowed. "Andrakos?" he questioned. "The Mr. Andrakos who just completed the amazing merging of Star with Achilles shipping lines?"

Paul smiled. He was surprised by the inquiry. "Yes, the same," he admitted. "But it's very recent. I'm surprised that you've heard about it."

"I'm a corporate lawyer," George explained. "I just read about the merging in yesterday's *International Corporate News* and I've always kind of kept an eye on the Achilles line," George explained.

"Achilles line?" Kristen questioned.

"One of your aunt's—and my—shipping interests," Paul explained to her but continued to look at George. "You know about Kristen's family?" he questioned.

George shrugged his shoulders. "Nick King, Kristen's father, told me a few things," he said carefully, *Too carefully,* Paul thought, and he wondered how much the older man actually knew. For some reason, Paul was quite certain that he knew a lot more about past events than he let on. Paul wouldn't forget this. Certain things were good to remember. This item was one of them.

"Why don't we all sit down?" Kristen suggested and the two men politely sat on opposite sofas. Kristen sat on the same sofa as Paul, which made him very happy. He wanted to reach across the small space and take ahold of her hand but with George Lee watching, he didn't. She smiled over at him and he could tell that she was thinking the same thing.

"Mr. Andrakos—" George began, "I have to admit that I'm not too pleased about Kristen traveling to Greece with you."

"Uncle George!" Kristen turned to him, totally surprised that he would say such a thing. It was so out of character for him to be so forward.

But he continued, looking piercingly only at Paul. "I don't want to see her hurt." That quality which made most people tremble when George Lee spoke was in evidence. But looking over at Paul, Kristen wasn't surprised to see that Paul neither trembled nor wavered but rather was a match for her uncle.

"Believe me, sir—neither do I," Paul answered politely.

"She has been hurt too much in the past—" George persisted.

"I will do everything in my power to make sure she is not hurt in the future," Paul declared.

But Kristen had had enough of them talking as though she weren't there. "Would you two stop. . .you're acting as though I'm a child."

Her uncle ignored her. He wanted some answers from Paul and he wanted them now. "But does her aunt really want to see her or just nurse her bad conscience?"

Paul smiled over at Kristen to assure her that he wasn't trying to talk over her and then answered George. "A lot of the first and probably a little bit of the second," Paul replied truthfully. "Who, when they reach the age of Aphrodite, doesn't want to assuage their conscience?"

Kristen watched her uncle. He liked that response and smiled. "Kristen said she'd been sick?"

Paul nodded. "Heart problems."

"Does she know that Kristen is coming?"

At that, Paul turned to Kristen. "I talked to your aunt earlier today." In spite of the watchful eyes of the older man Paul took her hand in his. "She is thrilled to hear that you are coming. She'll be calling you—" The phone rang out shrilly and Paul motioned toward it and smiled. "This evening."

Kristen glanced over at Uncle George. There was no condemnation in him. Since he couldn't change her mind he was now supporting her decision. She smiled her thanks.

As she walked over to the phone, she couldn't quite believe that this might be the phone call she had been waiting so expectantly for all those months. All of a sudden she felt very nervous and very shy. She placed her hand on the receiver and glanced over at Paul.

"She's a very nice lady," he assured her.

She nodded and picked up the phone. "Hello?"

There was a slight pause as the transatlantic connection was made and then Kristen heard her aunt's voice for the very first time in her life. "Hello. Is this Christina King?" The use of the name "Christina" threw Kristen for a moment, not because she was offended but rather because she liked the way it sounded. She was a descendent of the Christina in "The Ring of Love" and Kristen liked this link with her ancestry, this link through time.

She made a quick decision not to correct the older woman. "Yes, this is. Are you my aunt Aphrodite?"

"Oh my dear. . .I am. But I have waited too many years to hear that title." It was a cultured voice, a rounded voice, a voice of authority which was slightly accented by a multitude of languages.

"Aunt Aphrodite. . .I'm so glad you contacted me. . .I didn't know what to think when I didn't hear from you. . . ."

"Please forgive me," the older woman asked through the lines, and modern technology made it seem as though she were in the next room, not halfway around the world. "But Paul explained the circumstances?"

"Yes. . .don't worry. . .I understand. Just stay well."

"I'm trying, my dear, I'm trying. . .but Christina, your coming with Paul means everything to me. I would have come to you if I had been able to do so. Unfortunately, my mind is willing but my body is not. . . ."

"Well, both my mind and body are willing so I will see you in just a couple of days, Aunt."

"In just a couple of days. . . ," her aunt whispered, "after a lifetime."

When they hung up, Kristen looked at the two men who were looking at her so expectantly and smiled, a smile which her uncle George was familiar with but hadn't seen in a couple of years and a smile which made Paul feel as if the sun had come out after months of dark, dreary winter skies.

"I know that I've made the correct decision in going!" she exclaimed. "I can't wait to see my aunt!"

George smiled and stood to leave. "I'm glad."

Kristen walked over to him and hugged him. "You don't have to worry, Uncle George. . .that lady," she motioned with her head toward the phone, "loves me. She really wants to see me."

"I'm not worried, Kristy." He looked over at Paul. "I have Mr. Andrakos's word that you will not be hurt." He smiled at Paul. "And from all the years of following Achilles Industries, I know that Mr. Andrakos's word is good."

Paul stood and extended his hand. "Thank you, sir. Thank you for your trust."

That the two men trusted one another filled Kristen with gladness and she knew that the picture of them shaking hands would stay with her forever. That thought reminded her about actual pictures which she wanted to show her uncle.

"Oh! Uncle George. . .before you leave. . ." She walked over to an end table and opening it, reached for the four photographs which she had left lying conveniently on top. "When I went through my parents' papers, I found these photographs." She extended the pictures to him but frowned slightly at her uncle's intake of breath. She hadn't even considered that seeing the photos might upset him. "I'm sorry. . .I should have warned you," she offered.

He waved her apology aside. "No. . .it's just that these were taken," he paused and breathed out, "a lifetime ago."

"At least two lifetimes ago," Kristen whispered and pointed to her parents. "I recognize my father and my mother and you. . .but who was this man?" She pointed to a man with laughing green eyes and dark wavy hair who had his arm draped casually around Kristen's mother in three photos but was alone with her in the fourth.

"That," George paused as if remembering the man fondly, "was Raphael. He was from Spain and one of the nicest, most fun loving persons anyone could ever hope to meet."

"Was?" Kristen questioned.

George nodded sadly. "Unfortunately he was also one of the world's most daring men. He was a Rally racer. These pictures were taken in Monte Carlo where he was racing. He died the next day."

"Oh, how sad." Kristen pointed to the last picture. It was the one of just Kristen's mother, Jane, and Raphael looking at one another with a look that reminded Kristen of how she probably looked at Paul. She frowned. They definitely looked like they were in love, but not wanting to upset her uncle George, she said, "They look like they were very good friends."

"Even more than friends," Paul spoke Kristen's thought and she was glad for the chance to ask her uncle. That was what had bothered her since she had first found the photos.

"Were they, Uncle George?"

"No. No. Just friends."

Paul looked at the older man quizzically. He seemed to answer too quickly, as if he had something to hide.

"You know that your mother only had eyes for your father," George was quick to qualify.

Kristen nodded. "That's for sure." She handed the pictures to George, "Would you like to keep them. . .since you were there. . . ."

George took them and giving the top one another glance said, "We were all the best of friends. I miss them all and I would very much like to keep these photos. A remembrance of a very lovely day." He put them in his suit pocket. "Thank you, my darling girl."

George and Paul nodded at one another before Kristen walked with her uncle to the door.

"Thanks for coming. . . ."

George reached out his hand and rubbed her arm. "Couldn't let Jane and Nick's little girl's birthday pass without seeing her." He smiled and his lips seemed to move to control the emotion he was feeling. "Don't ever forget. . .they loved you more than anything. . .or anyone. . . in the world."

Kristen nodded. "I know. . .I won't forget." They kissed and then the older man was gone into the night.

Turning back to Paul, Kristen smiled. "That's my Uncle George," she said simply.

"A nice man." He walked toward her. "I think I had better be going too."

"So soon?" The disappointment she felt was in her deep voice.

"We have a plane to catch tomorrow," he reminded her. "Don't you have some packing to do?"

Kristen shrugged. "I guess. . ." She walked up to him and boldly put her hands around his neck. "But I still don't want you to leave."

Paul chuckled. "I think it's a good thing that you will be staying with your aunt in Athens."

"Why?"

He nuzzled his nose against her neck and sighing, gently stood away from her. "Because I don't think it's a good idea for us to be alone in an empty house, feeling the way we do."

"Paul—I've never—nor would I ever—" She stopped and looking at him realized that with him, she might. She had never felt such an attraction for a man before; in fact until Paul, she'd had no idea that someone could feel such desires. She stepped back from him. "I see what you mean," she whispered.

He smiled, a smile of yearning, a smile of want, but more than anything, a smile of love.

"I'll pick you up tomorrow at around three."

"You don't have to. I'll call a cab."

"Nonsense. I'll leave my rental car at the airport anyway." His eyes deepened along with his voice. "And besides—I want to start our quest together from your house."

"Me too." Her voice was deep and husky and if the phone hadn't chosen that moment to ring, Paul wasn't sure that he would have been able to prevent himself from going to her, empty house or not.

"I'll just be a moment." Kristen turned and reached for the phone. It was the man that she and Paul had pulled out from the ocean the previous night.

Paul looked over in interest when he understood who it was and asked, "Is he okay?"

Kristen nodded yes to Paul and continued talking into the phone to the man. "You're what?" she asked and it was obvious to Paul that she was surprised by something. "That's amazing. I'm going to be traveling to Athens tomorrow and Paul—the man who was with me—is from Athens." Paul looked at her in question. Her eyes were wide in wonder as she finished talking to the man.

"Well, be careful of wind surfing in Pacific waves, Dean, and I'm looking forward to seeing you next week."

"Next week?" Paul questioned her while taking the phone.

Kristen nodded and looked at Paul deeply, meaningfully. "You're not going to believe this. . .he's a pastor at a church in. . .in Athens."

"In Athens?" he repeated. She was right. He didn't believe it.

She nodded and motioned to the phone. Paul talked animatedly for a few moments, gave the man his address and phone number in Athens, and after hanging up, stood looking out at the ocean which was as calm today as it had been treacherous the day before.

Kristen walked up behind him. "Paul?"

He shook his head. "It's amazing. He again said something about being glad that our paths. . .met with his last night—"

"Paths. . . ," Kristen whispered and looked out at the calm, somnolent sea. "If it hadn't been windy yesterday—"

"He wouldn't have needed our help."

"Is he Greek?"

Paul tilted his head upward. "No. He's American. An American pastor serving at an American interdenominational church in Athens. I wonder if it's the one Lottie wrote about?"

Paul walked over to the coffee table and picked up the Bible Lottie had sent to Kristen the previous day. "Kristen. . .I found a Bible in my hotel room and read some of it last night. . .the part about St. Paul in Athens.

Kristen, do you know what he said?"

Kristen shook her head, wonder filling her eyes. "Tell me."

"'Men of Athens!' Men of Athens—" Paul repeated. "Kristen, I'm one of those 'Men of Athens'!"

"It's like he's talking directly to you—"

Paul nodded. "And something else. He said something about telling them about the God they worship as something unknown. . .something unknown. . ."

With an excitement Paul hadn't felt since he was a very little boy, he continued, "Kristen, when we get to Athens, I want us to visit the Biblical sites and find out where they are written about in the Bible."

Kristen nodded. "Our search."

"Our quest."

"Together. . . ," Kristen whispered and stepped into Paul's outstretched arms.

"The pastor will call me when he returns to Athens in a few days." He held her tightly against him for a moment and then stepping away, placed the Bible back on the table next to the little statue of the *Youth of Antikythera* and continued on toward the door. "Good night, my love. . . don't forget to pack your Bible," he said as he placed his hand on the doorknob.

"Paul!" Kristen ran up to him, surprised that he was really intent on leaving. "You really don't have to go so soon."

He turned to her and with a look that showed just what it was costing him to be near her, answered back, his accent making his words sound like a loving caress, a caress that touched her soul.

"Ah. . .my love. . .but I do."

Chapter 8

I don't think I've ever seen such a pretty approach to an airport," Kristen exclaimed nearly two days later as the jet she and Paul were traveling on made its descent into Hellenicon International Airport in Athens.

"Those islands look like the Titans." She glanced over at Paul. "The supposed parents to the Olympian gods," she explained, "dropped bits of earth on their way to making the mountains of Greece."

Paul chuckled and then frowned in concentration. "Except—if I remember correctly—the ancient Greeks never attributed the creation of the world to their gods. Rather, the gods were created by the universe."

Kristen answered thoughtfully. "Maybe that's one of the reasons Greece became a Biblical land."

"What do you mean?"

"Well. . .the Greeks already accepted that their gods were created by the universe. They were thinkers. Maybe they were ready to accept that the universe could not just come into being any more than. . . ," she paused, searching around for a good example, "one of their temples could just appear."

Paul tipped his head in appreciation of her analogy. "I see what you mean."

She continued her thought. "Maybe—they were ready to hear about Someone—a God—who claimed to have made the universe."

Paul took her hand in his and gently squeezed it. "Just like—we're ready to hear about that God too."

Kristen nodded and whispered, "So much has changed from one week ago." The sound of the jet engines using their might to slow the plane almost drowned out her words.

"But you're glad?" Paul asked. He wanted assurance.

Kristen moved her head up and down, slowly, thoughtfully. "So glad. . .

because of you. . .my aunt. . .our search. . ." She paused and repeated again, "And you. . . ," and then met him in a kiss, just a simple kiss but a kiss that held love, caring, and hope for a future together.

With their foreheads touching, Paul chuckled wryly. "Well, if I know your aunt, she's probably looking expectantly at the clock every few moments wondering if our plane has landed."

Kristen sat back. That surprised her. "Really? I pictured her as being totally cool and very patient."

Paul shook his head and his eyes widened at thinking about the older woman. "Not Aphrodite. Oh, she can be cool. In the business world no one ever knows what she's thinking," he amended. "But in her personal life, she's a mother hen who worries and clucks and drives James and me crazy."

"James?"

"Her best friend. An English lord, and nearly her own age. James is probably the only person in this world who Aphrodite listens to."

Kristen was very surprised by this character sketch of her aunt and it showed in her face.

"I've shocked you?" Paul inquired with a raised brow.

Kristen nodded. "I just pictured her. . .differently." She paused for a moment and then with a seriousness in her tone asked, "Paul. . . ?"

He looked at her in question, waiting.

"I've been thinking. . . ." She wasn't sure how Paul would take her next words so she spoke carefully, gently, and touched her fingers lightly to his arm. "Maybe we shouldn't let my aunt know how we feel. . .about one another. . .just yet. . . ."

"But why?" Paul's surprise over the suggestion showed in the sudden tilting of his head.

"I think. . .I think it might be too much for her. . . ," Kristen boldly continued, hoping that Paul would understand, "especially after you telling me how she frets about people whom she cares for."

Paul seemed to consider her words. "I don't know, Kristen—*Nona* knows me too well—I think she'll catch on pretty quickly."

"Well. . .let's try. . .at least for a couple of days not to let her know. I think it's important. . .to my relationship with her."

Paul's eyes scanned her face. He was amazed by Kristen's astuteness. Knowing Aphrodite as he did, he should have been the one to understand that detecting a relationship between Kristen and himself, immediately upon arrival, might be too much for the older lady. She and Kristen needed the time to forge a bond without any outside interferences. And Paul knew that seeing him in a serious relationship with any woman would be enough to excite the older woman. How much more with her own niece? He had no fear that his *nona* would mind him being interested in her niece, but he knew that Kristen was right in suggesting that they not hit her over the head with the knowledge.

"I love you," he finally whispered.

Kristen wrapped her arms around his neck and whispered into his ear, "Oh, Paul. . .I love you too." She raised her face to his.

"And you do understand?" She wanted to make sure that there was no misunderstanding.

He raised his brows self-deprecatingly. "I should have been the one to suggest it." He took her hand in his. "I promise. . .I'll try very hard to hide my feelings." He took a deep breath. "But, it won't be easy," he was quick to interject.

"I know. For me either."

"I do have a great deal of business to attend to these first few days. I'll use that as an excuse not to be around too much."

"Oh, Paul. . .I'll miss you."

"Hey! Only for a few days—Aphrodite will have to be told after that." Kristen nodded. "Thank you, Paul."

"No. Thank you, Kristen." He tapped her on the tip of her nose. "I want both of the women in my life, you and my *nona*, to be happy."

"We've had a few days to get used to our love. Let's give Aphrodite a few as well."

The plane tilted to the left and Paul's glance was pulled to the sea view out the window over Kristen's shoulder. "Look at that." He nodded out the little window. "I've flown all over the world but I've never seen bluer bodies of water than those found around Greece."

She followed his eyes to look down at the Saronic Gulf. It was the bluest sea she had ever seen, as blue as little children show seas to be when they color them with their crayons. "Such a deep shade. Almost cobalt," she agreed before wistfully adding, "my father's eyes were like that."

Paul looked at her in surprise. "Really?"

Kristen motioned down to the sea, which was getting closer and closer as the jet was about to land. "As blue as that water."

"Aphrodite's eyes are like that too," Paul commented.

Kristen shook her head in wonder. That there might be a resemblance between her aunt and her father wasn't even something she had previously considered. The thought thrilled her, especially since Kristen didn't resemble her father at all.

"I can't wait to meet her," she whispered and squeezed Paul's hand as the plane's landing gear made contact with the asphalt at Athens International Airport. After taxiing down the runway, the huge metal bird turned and followed the path to the terminal.

Kristen was on the same soil as her aunt now. She glanced over at Paul. She was in the "Man from Greece's" land. And she was glad with her choice to be there to discover her path in life.

❧

Kristen's first ride through Athens was a trip she knew that she would never forget. To say that the city was vibrant and alive would be only a half truth. It was more than that. It was dusty and hot, noisy and fast, and yet at the same moment it was clean and cool, serene and slow. Mountains encircled the city on the east, north, and west with the Saronic Gulf being the boundary on the south, making the plain of Athens a foundation for low buildings of concrete and marble.

People grasping plastic bags, and cars with honking horns seemed to be everywhere. And just when Kristen didn't think she could stand seeing any more nondescript, smog-dirtied, flat buildings, a twist in the road revealed the graceful columns of a temple from the elegant past as it rose, even with the road in front of her. She let out a gasp of pleasure.

"What is that?"

"The temple of the Olympian Zeus."

"It's beautiful."

"It is." Paul made a turn and pointed up and out the side window. "But it's nothing compared to that."

Kristen gasped again but this time it was a gasp of knowledge.

She had no doubt that what her eyes rested on was the Acropolis of Athens.

"Oh, Paul."

She didn't take her eyes off the flat mountaintop. Covered with some of the world's most beautiful architectural structures, including that most graceful and elegant of buildings, the Parthenon, it was a sight that held Kristen spellbound.

"Please. . .may we stop for a moment?"

He chuckled and pulled the car off to the side of the road next to the ancient theater of Dionysus. The sidewalk was filled with tourists from the world over—Asians, Europeans, Africans, Americans—all come to see the world renowned Acropolis, the High City, the citadel, that sat like a jewel above the modern city of Athens. But the commotion of people didn't bother Kristen in the least. She scrambled out of the car and stood, surrounded by the throng of holiday seeking people, hugging her arms around her.

Paul touched her. She had goosebumps on her arms.

"In this heat, you can't be cold."

Kristen shook her head but still didn't remove her eyes from the Acropolis. The Parthenon, that most beautiful of classical buildings, that was built during the golden age of Pericles, sat timeless and elegant against the blue of the Grecian sky.

"I'm. . .amazed. . .it's more beautiful than I ever dreamed. I could stand and look at it all day long," she murmured in awe.

Paul drew her close to him. "And I could do the same with you," he whispered. "But," he reached for the door handle of the car, his arm still around her shoulder, "I think that we had better go. Your aunt will be waiting for you and not very patiently."

Kristen smiled her agreement, turned away from the Acropolis and stepped into the car. She enjoyed sitting back and watching the modern city of Athens as it slid past her window. The center of Athens was a busy place with people going about their business much as they do in New York and London, Cape Town and Hong Kong.

Colorful kiosks selling anything from razor blades to newspapers were to be seen at practically every corner and motorbikes scurrying around like bugs on wheels scuttled between and around the cars, none holding a lane, and all terrifying Kristen.

After a few more minutes of congested driving conditions, Paul stopped at an overpass to turn off the main boulevard, and pointed ahead, "Your aunt's neighborhood is just over there."

"So soon?" Kristen was surprised, especially when she saw how different the suburb was from the city they had passed through. Quiet streets that were lined with trees and plants of a multitude of varieties surrounded her. Graceful and feminine eucalyptus trees swayed in the soft wind, hardy pines added their deep green color to the quiet streets, while oleander bushes, the size of small trees, scented the air with their pink and white flowers.

Kristen looked at Paul in amazement. "It's so peaceful here. I can't believe we're so close to the city."

"Old Psychikon, the name of this area, is the first garden suburb outside of the city, and a world all its own. *Nona* can't understand why I ever left it."

"You used to live here too?"

He nodded. "Like your father, I grew up here."

"This is where my father grew up. . . ," Kristen mused, and looking at the quiet streets, she tried to imagine him as a young man walking or riding his bike along these actual streets. But try as she may she couldn't. She didn't know enough about her father's youth to even begin to picture him as a young man and for all its beauty, it was too different from American neighborhoods for her to even try. There were sidewalks, but they were often uneven or overgrown with bushes or cut in the middle by trees. In many cases cars had parked up on the sidewalks as the roads were too narrow to allow them to remain parked at the side of the road.

Most of the houses had walls around them and those that didn't had bushes or trees hiding them from passersby. After a moment Paul turned into one of the sidewalks and paused in front of a large door. He pressed a button on the dashboard and the door started to slide back from the left.

"Welcome to your ancestral home, Kristen."

Like a curtain on a stage, the door slowly opened to reveal a large neoclassical home that immediately reminded Kristen of her parents' stately antebellum home above the James River in Richmond. Like her parents' home, it had grounds that were large and sloping and beautifully kept. She could envision her father at this home and it brought a warm feeling to her, brought him closer to her.

Paul put the car into gear and drove through the opened door and down the long circular drive toward the marble steps that led up to the majestic house. Kristen spied a swimming pool to the side of the house and a romantic pool house with a covered verandah close to it.

She couldn't help exclaiming, "Oh Paul, it's beautiful. . . I'm so glad I've come!"

Paul pulled the car to a stop in front of the marble stairs and pointed to the woman who was standing at the top of them. "Be sure to tell your aunt that."

As if she were the heroine in a slow motion film, Kristen turned her head to look at the woman who had commanded so much of her thoughts during the last three months and her eyes widened as she gazed upon her for the first time. Kristen's first thought was that if she had seen her aunt anywhere else in the world, she would have recognized her, for her aunt Aphrodite was the exact female representation of her father. And her second thought was how this woman could easily have been a southern aristocratic lady. Her bearing was regal, her expression grand, history and tradition were both worn comfortably by her.

With American impulsiveness, Kristen opened the door of the car, and with feet that seemed to have wings on their heels she sped up the stairs to the woman, and to the hands which were extended in welcome. Kristen took ahold of her aunt's hands and was surprised by their strength which was contrary to the small woman's fragile appearance.

And they smiled at one another.

Kristen noticed how her aunt's eyes crinkled at the corners just as her father's had when he smiled and she couldn't help but feel as though somehow, in her aunt's face, she was being given the gift of seeing her father again.

"Christina. . .my dear child. . .welcome home." Aunt Aphrodite spoke in a voice that quivered slightly with age and emotion.

"Oh, Aunt. . .I'm so happy to be here. . . ." Kristen leaned down and hugged the slight frame of the older woman and was surprised when her aunt turned her face and kissed her. Not a European kiss of a peck on both cheeks but a kiss of love, of joy for the return of a beloved family member. Kristen's eyes caught Paul's over her aunt's shoulders as he came up the stairs.

She smiled at him, a smile of happiness, of contentment, a smile of coming home.

He winked back at her. He was glad, very glad, to see that the woman he loved like a mother and the woman he loved as a woman were happy in their discovery of one another.

Chapter 9

Aunt Aphrodite finally pulled back. "Let me look at you," she said as her deep blue eyes, eyes that had lost none of their clarity through illness and age, and eyes which were indeed as blue as Kristen's father's had been, scanned her face.

Kristen laughed. "I'm afraid you won't find much in me that reminds you of my father."

"Ah. . .but that's not true." Aphrodite spoke softly, her accent more English than Greek and melodious in tone.

"It's true, you don't look like him physically," her blue, blue eyes roamed over Kristen's face, "but in a million other ways you resemble him. In the way your eyes open wide and in the way you tilt your head to the side." She looked down the length of Kristen's body and smiled. "Even in the way your left foot points off to the side when you stand."

Kristen laughed with pleasure. Her aunt described some of her father's characteristics perfectly. For her aunt to have remembered them through all the years of separation told more than any number of words ever could just how often she had thought of her brother.

"Yes, my dear child. . ." She finished her inspection of Kristen. "You look like your father in lots of little ways that speak of heredity without being overt."

Kristen smiled back at her. "Well, you definitely look like your brother. . . ," Kristen whispered and was rewarded with a bright smile.

"Yes. . .Nick and I always did look alike. Photos of us as babies are identical and of course, he was many years younger than I so—" She paused because of emotion. "I remember him as a chubby babe."

"I've never seen any photos of my father when he was a baby or when he was a child for that matter." Kristen wanted to relieve the emotion of the moment.

Aphrodite took her hand. "You will soon, my dear. You will soon. But first, I want you to meet my very dear friend." She turned to the silver-haired man who had stood off to the side watching the exchange between long-lost aunt and niece. "James. . .it's my niece, Christina. . .at last." The older woman breathed out as if she had been holding her breath for a very long time, and James put a supporting arm around Aphrodite's shoulder as he held out his other hand in greeting to Kristen.

"My dear," he turned one of the kindest set of eyes Kristen had ever seen to her, "we are very happy to finally meet you. I'm James Windsor."

"Mr. Windsor. . ." Kristen took his hand and was reminded of the stable friendship of her uncle George and she liked James Windsor immediately.

"No, please. . .call me James." Kristen nodded her assent as he continued with an admonishing glance at Aphrodite, "But shouldn't we be calling you 'Kristen' rather than 'Christina'?"

Kristen was pleased that he asked but waved all protest aside.

"No, really. . .I don't mind." She turned to Paul. "Paul explained how my name is derived from a long list of Christinas. . .I'm honored to share my grandmother's and my other ancestor's name."

Her response pleased Aphrodite who smiled at her before turning to Paul. The look she gave to Paul was one of a beloved mother to a beloved son, and Kristen knew that the love Paul possessed for his godmother was indeed returned, in full.

"And how are you, dear boy?" she asked softly and reached out her hand to bring him closer to her.

Paul bent down and kissed her on both cheeks. "I'm fine, *Nona.*"

Concern showed in his eyes. "And you?"

She laughed, a much deeper and fuller sound than Kristen would have thought possible to come from such a small body. "James is making sure I don't overdo and that I take all my medication."

She turned to Kristen and taking her by the arm led her into the foyer. "I hate taking medicine," she confided. "I hate even more being sick."

Then back to Paul she tossed, "Congratulations on the merger, dear boy. That's quite a coup."

"I learned from a pro," Paul said and glanced over at James, who smiled. The respect the two men felt for Aphrodite was obvious and Kristen felt very blessed that such a woman was her aunt.

The foyer was exquisite with brown marble flooring polished to a mirror finish and high windows that let in the afternoon light. The furniture was Italian antique and continued into the living room. One thing that struck Kristen was the lack of carpets. She was just about to ask about that when her eyes were caught by a painting on the wall which was spotlighted by a stream of sunlight pouring onto it from the outdoors. A soft gasp escaped her.

"What is it, my dear?" Aphrodite asked, but then understood when Kristen crossed over to the painting.

It was a small painting, but the mark of its artist was obvious.

"My father told me about this painting. . .he loved El Greco's work. He told me that he had seen it. . .he just forgot to mention that he had seen it in his parents' home," she finished wryly.

"Actually. . .he forgot to mention that he bought it. It was his painting," Aphrodite stated and Kristen, wondering if she detected a note of resentment or condemnation in Aphrodite's voice, turned sharply to her aunt. But one look at the older woman's face relaxed Kristen's fears and she knew that what she had defensively thought of as condemnation was actually only a wistful quality, a longing for something that wasn't, and now could never be.

"Didn't he tell you anything about his life here?" Aphrodite asked and sat in a chair that looked like it knew Aphrodite's body well.

Kristen shrugged her shoulders. She knew that the past had to be faced, she just didn't know if she wanted to face it now. The events of the last few days, the excitement of finally meeting her aunt, plus jet lag were weighing heavily on her and she suddenly felt exhausted. "Well, of course he told me that he grew up in Greece but. . .I guess I should have asked more questions. My parents and I were very close and well. . .I guess we were enough for one another. The past never seemed to come up." She looked again at the painting. She knew that her father had come from a wealthy family, but until this moment, she hadn't realized just how wealthy. "I guess. . .I was very naive."

"No, not naive, dear child." Kristen looked back at her aunt and was relieved to find no blame in her. "Just young."

Kristen thought she heard the voice of experience talking and after giving the painting one more glance walked over to sit in the chair facing her aunt.

Aphrodite continued. "We're all young and we all make mistakes because of our youth. It's simply a reality of life and the sooner people realize that, the happier they will be." Her gaze went past Kristen and Kristen thought it even went past the confines of the four walls, as the older woman seemed to look deep into the past. Both joy and pain flitted across Aphrodite's face as she looked into a past that was bridged with the present by the arrival of Kristen.

"Unfortunately though," she suddenly seemed to remember Kristen and continued, but with bitterness putting an edge on her words, "sometimes, our mistakes haunt us for many years." She looked intently at Kristen, so intently that Kristen felt a bit uncomfortable. "That's when naivete is to be feared."

"Now, Aphrodite," James interjected, "the child is here, and you no longer have to concern yourself with all of that. Heed your own words of a moment ago," he gently commanded and Kristen knew that what Paul had said on the plane was right. James probably was the only one who could ever sway Aphrodite.

"My words!" She looked reprovingly at James, but with deep affection, like a partner in a long-lasting marriage might look at the other. "You know very well, James, that I was only repeating the words you have spoken to me time and time again." She laughed, a deep clear sound without any sarcasm attached to it.

"Then heed what I say. You might be a couple of years older than I, but I have reached quite a stately age myself and have learned a few things in all these years." He glanced over at Kristen and smiled, a smile of comradeship.

Kristen returned his smile and at the same time was caught by a yawn. She covered her mouth with her hand and shook her head, embarrassed. "I'm sorry. . .I guess jet lag has caught up with me."

Aphrodite suddenly stood. "Dear me, what sort of a hostess am I? Let me show you to your room and I'll have a plate of refreshments sent up to you. You must be exhausted."

Kristen stood and smiled as she tried to repress another yawn.

"The last few days have been rather. . . ," she looked over at Paul and smiled, "eventful."

"It's not every day you discover a long-lost aunt," Paul commented carefully and smiled back at her. But his eyes told her that he understood that finding Aphrodite was just one of the many wonderful events to which she was referring.

Aphrodite stretched out her skinny arms, one reaching for Paul, the other for Kristen. "Well, I am a very happy old lady to have the two of you together. As Paul probably told you, I never had children of my own, but I feel as though God has blessed me in the two of you. My godson," she looked at Paul, "who has always been like a—son to me," she turned to Kristen, "and my niece, who I have always loved because. . .you are my brother's child."

She hugged them both close to her in the fierce sort of way older people have, as if with age she had learned the secret of time, that it passes so fast that all must hold tightly to those whom they love. "I love you both as if you were my very own children."

Paul looked over his *nona's* head to Kristen and motioned with his eyebrows that now might be a good time to say something to the older woman about their love for one another. But some instinct warned Kristen that he shouldn't say anything. She minutely shook her head. As far as Kristen was concerned nothing had changed since meeting her aunt. She still felt as though she needed time to get to know her without anything to complicate the process. Kristen was thrilled over her welcome. It was everything and much more than she had ever thought to receive from her aunt. But just because Aphrodite loved them like her children, that didn't necessarily mean that she wanted them involved with one another. . .not yet at any rate.

"Come," Aphrodite let go of Paul's arm but kept ahold of Kristen's as she guided her into the hall and to a door which looked to Kristen as though it might be a closet. She was surprised when Paul opened it.

"An elevator!" Kristen exclaimed.

"My father had it installed for my mother after Nick—" The older woman closed her mouth on the rest of the sentence but Kristen understood what she had left unsaid and finished it for her.

"After my father left?" she asked softly and Aphrodite nodded.

"My mother missed him very much. She was never the same after he left."

"Oh, Aunt Aphrodite. . .I'm so sorry. I don't know what happened in the past, but I'm so sorry that it happened."

"Dear child. . ." Aphrodite reached up and touched Kristen's face. "All of that has nothing to do with you. Nick and I. . . well. . .we finally realized that we were victims of circumstances. . ." She suddenly smiled at Kristen. "But you and I have time to talk. I promise that I will tell you all that I can but. . .slowly. . .over the next several days. . ." She looked suddenly sad but even more, old, to Kristen. "It's just too much to talk about all at one time. . .too many people's lives were upset by. . . those events. . ."

"*Thea.* . ." Kristen whispered the Greek word for 'aunt' which Paul had taught to her while on the plane and was rewarded by a wondrous look that replaced the sadness of the moment before. "All of that can wait. It's enough that I'm here with you and that we get to know one another."

"Dear girl. . .my brother and my sister-in-law were indeed blessed to have had you for a daughter," she said, and guiding Kristen into the elevator was about to press the button when Paul stopped her.

"Kristen. . .I'll probably be busy for several days, but I'll call you later." At Aphrodite's rather sharp look Paul was momentarily taken back. He addressed his godmother, a slight challenge in his voice, and as he did so he realized just how wise Kristen was to have suggested that they wait to tell the older woman about their relationship.

"Surely you don't mind if I show your niece around Athens, *Nona?*"

The older woman seemed to consider it for a moment, and Kristen saw something, like a shadow of fear, cross the older woman's eyes, before she shook it away and smiled. "Of course not. I think that would be very nice as long as. . . ," she paused and with a look of authority continued, "you remember that Kristen is my niece and that you are my godson. In the eyes of the church, that is as good as being my son and would make you two cousins."

This startled Kristen and she looked quickly at Paul to see his response. She was a bit relieved to see that he didn't seem to be in the least bit disturbed by her aunt's warning.

Paul smiled. "Don't worry. I won't forget that she is your niece. She will be safe with me." He kissed the older woman, winked at Kristen, and the door closed before Kristen could say another word to him. After traveling with him for so many hours, more than a day, she felt incomplete not to have him beside her, as if a part of her was missing.

She turned and looked at her reflection in the mirror which made up the back wall of the little elevator. Aphrodite met her gaze in the mirror.

Her cool, blue eyes collided with Kristen's soft emerald ones.

"You like Paul." It was a statement, not a question. And a statement that Aphrodite didn't seem too happy about making.

Kristen's lips turned up in a smile. "I'm glad you sent him for me. . . I like. . . ," the elevator stopped and Kristen pushed open the door and with a gentle squeeze, brought her aunt closer to her, "being here with you."

With a smile, a thoughtful smile that didn't quite reach the blue of Aphrodite's eyes, the older woman stepped out of the elevator and guided Kristen down the light and airy hall. As Kristen walked by her side, she was relieved that her aunt didn't ask her anything else about Paul.

The room she showed Kristen was enchanting. Lit by the late afternoon sun, it had high windows and ceilings and Kristen felt as though she had stepped back into Victorian times. It was decorated with muted shades of blue and rose. Fresh flowers were on the dresser and on the round table by the armchair. The bed was a four-poster and high with a lace covering to match the curtains at the window.

"This used to be my room. . .when I was a child and up to about your age," Aphrodite said.

"It's lovely." Kristen spied a huge eucalyptus tree swaying with the breeze outside the open windows. It seemed to be a part of the room, graceful and feminine and timeless, like the room.

Her eyes moved from the outside to the wall between the two windows. It was covered with reminders of people of the past. Portraits, at least half a dozen of them, covered the wall. Some were big, some were small, but all were framed in gold or silver and all were lovingly taken care of. Kristen walked over to the wall.

"Our ancestors." Aphrodite answered Kristen's unvoiced question.

Goosebumps covered Kristen's arms. She rubbed them and thought how she hadn't had so many goosebumps in her life as she had had during the last week. . .since meeting Paul. She pointed to the one in the middle which, from the manner in which the people were dressed, looked like the oldest one. A couple with a baby perched on the father's knee smiled with their eyes from the old canvas. The woman seemed to be holding her hands in a way so that the painter could capture the light in the ring, a very big circular ring, that was on her finger, and Kristen felt certain that she was looking at the hero and heroine of "The Ring of Love."

"They are the founders of our family's shipping business." Aphrodite confirmed Kristen's thought. "That portrait was done shortly after Paul, your great-great-grandfather returned from a very dangerous shipping venture. If he had failed in that journey, or died, as he almost did, then our family would not have been what it became."

"The path of life. . ." Kristen was surprised to hear herself whisper the words out loud and even more surprised to hear Aphrodite respond to them.

"Exactly."

Kristen turned to her. "Do you believe that there is a path of life?"

"I believe," the older woman began, then paused and took a deep breath, "that God knows what our path is but that it is up to us to find it and to follow it."

"Oh, *Thea*. . ."

"Just like. . . ," Aphrodite continued, her eyes moist, "I think that it was a part of your 'path' to come here and to be with me. Thank you, dear, for coming."

"Oh, *Thea*," Kristen leaned down and kissed the age-softened cheeks. "Thank you."

"Now, I will leave you," she said pointing to the wall of portraits and smiling, "with our ancestors." She walked toward the door and paused just before closing it. "Christina. . .I have always wanted a daughter. . .to love. You, as my niece, are that person."

Kristen watched in wonder as the door closed softly behind the rustle of her only living relative. And she smiled.

And later, after eating a dish of fresh fruits—grapes, cantaloupe, and figs—with an assortment of Greek cheeses, Kristen's eyes closed while gazing at the pictures of the men and women who made up her blood. And as the cicadas sang in the branches outside her window, and the breeze gently swayed the eucalyptus in time with them, and the red sun gave way to a silvery moon, she dreamed of Christina and Paul, of Kristen and Paul, and of the God who directed them all through time.

Chapter 10

The days passed for Kristen and her aunt as summer days of warmth and harmony are meant to pass. It was a time of discovery for the two ladies, a time of learning, a time of telling, a time of deepening friendship. But more than this it was a time of just being together, and of sharing their lives with one another without any interference from the past or from the present.

Of silent accord, the two women kept away from subjects of the past that could hurt and they dwelt instead on telling one another about the happy times. Aphrodite told Kristen about her childhood summers spent in the cool mountains of Greece back in the days when threats of malaria kept people with means away from its lowlands, and she told Kristen about learning French and the French governess she had as a child who smelled of garlic and wine, old books and velvet.

Kristen, for her part, told her aunt all about her life in Virginia, summers spent on the Atlantic coast, fall shopping trips to New York with her parents, Christmases in Williamsburg, and springtime strolling about the bountiful and flowerful dogwood groves above the James River.

Paul kept his word and except for a daily phone call to check on her and give her a dosage of love over the phone, he stayed away from Villa Vasilias. James too, even though he stayed at the villa when in Greece, kept away from the two women. But he would watch occasionally from a hidden spot behind a window or from a bench among the pine grove and be glad to see his best friend, Aphrodite, happy with her niece, and Kristen, whom he was coming to admire more and more with each passing day, happy with her aunt. James knew, perhaps even more than Paul, how important it was for Aphrodite to meet her brother's child. It was a need that had extended through the entire life of the child, now a grown woman, and further beyond.

For days, Kristen was content to walk the large grounds of the villa by her aunt's side and to sit and drink iced coffee and eat baklava and plates of scrumptious fresh fruit with her aunt under the shade of the house's many verandahs. She felt as though time had stopped or had even gone back to a more gracious era of living.

In the neoclassical home, with the silent staff around to take care of everything, and with her aunt to talk to, who seemed to know a lot about most everything, Kristen could almost imagine herself in Victorian times. They were cut off from the world; Kristen's reclusive life and demanding job in California now seemed like a distant memory.

She had called Lottie the first day she was there only to discover that she had been sent on an archaeological expedition to Santorini, the ancient island of Thera. Kristen had left a message and even though she wanted to see her friend, she had to admit to being glad that it hadn't been immediately upon arrival. She had time to get acquainted with her aunt and. . .to read the Bible Lottie had sent to her in California.

Kristen spent every afternoon, siesta time, when the old mansion was as hushed and as quiet as only the dawning of a new day is in America, poring through the Bible, as both owner and staff slept away the worst of the afternoon heat. After reading the Books of Genesis and Exodus, she'd skipped over to the New Testament. There was much she didn't understand but then again, much that she did, and the greatest revelation of all was coming to the understanding that Jesus was not only God's Son but God Himself. Somehow, she had missed that truth throughout her twenty-eight years that she was of the Christian faith on all official forms. Understanding it and learning it made her feel first amazement, then confusion, but then acceptance brought a clear understanding of the words printed in red, the words spoken by Jesus Himself in the first four books of the New Testament. She knew that it could only be the truth that Jesus was not only the Son of God but God Himself.

Finally, even though her days were all and more than summer days should be, the August morning came when the past and the present could not be put off any more than could the *Meltemia* which started blowing with the dawn of that day. Just as the cool north wind from Russia blew south in order to fill the vacuum created by the hot air rising above the Sahara Desert to the direct south of Greece, so Aphrodite's past had to be told in order to fill the vacuum left in Kristen's present.

The time of grace, the honeymoon period of getting to know one another, was past, and the two women recognized it when the subject turned naturally to the past which had kept them apart for more than two and a half decades.

Aphrodite had had a glass screen installed on the northern side of the verandah when she saw that the *Meltemia* was blowing. But when a chair toppled over in the strong wind, she laughed, her deep laugh which Kristen had grown so fond of during the last few days, and said, "Oh my, if it's a 'chair' wind here, imagine how the wind must be blowing on the islands of the Aegean—must be at least a 'table' wind, or maybe even a 'bell' wind."

Kristen got up and set the chair right. "A *what* wind?"

"That's how the islanders classify the strength of the *Meltemia*," Aphrodite explained. "It's either a 'chair' wind, a 'table' wind or a 'bell' wind, depending on what it causes to knock over or in the case of the bell, to ring."

Kristen laughed. "That's adorable."

"As long as you're not on the sea it's adorable. If you're on a ship, or heaven forbid, on a small boat, these gales can be dangerous."

"*Thea. . . ?*" Kristen wanted to ask about the estrangement between her father and her aunt now but wondered if, like a boat caught in the *Meltemia*, it might be too dangerous a question, dangerous to their relationship, dangerous to her aunt's health, to ask.

But her aunt was not to be put off. She seemed to know the direction Kristen's thoughts had taken. "What is it, my dear?" she softly prompted.

Kristen ran her tongue over her wind-dried lips and started carefully, "I know we haven't said much about. . .what happened to cause such a rift between you and my father. . . ."

The older woman nodded in agreement and surprised Kristen by standing. "It's time." She was subdued, but Kristen was glad to see that the subject didn't seem to bother her. "Let's go into the house. This wind," another chair toppled over, lending credibility to her words, "is a bit too strong for me today."

In the living room Aphrodite closed the doors, something she hadn't done before, and crossing over to her favorite chair, she sank gratefully into its folds. "I don't know how much you know."

"Only what Paul told me." For the first time in days, Kristen worried the gold chain around her neck as she told her aunt the extent of her knowledge. "That there was an argument between my father and my grandfather. But. . .what was the argument about? I have no idea."

Aphrodite took a deep breath. "The argument was because of your mother."

"My mother!"

Aphrodite nodded. "I hate to admit it but your grandfather simply didn't like the fact that your father had married your mother."

"What?" In all the months since Kristen had learned about her aunt and the estrangement between her and her father, she had never imagined anything so. . .so. . .unlikely.

"Your grandfather was a very good businessman," Aphrodite continued. "But. . .he had his failings in other areas. . . ." Her voice trailed off as she seemed to look into the past and remember some of those failings.

"But. . ." Kristen was aghast by the idea that someone, her very own grandfather, didn't like her mother. "My mother was a lovely woman. How could somebody not like her? Everyone liked her," she finished simply.

Aphrodite smiled, a sad smile that touched Kristen's heart. "I know. . . I met your mother. . .and I thought she would make the perfect sister-in-law. . .the perfect sister. . . ." There was a wistful quality to her tone.

"You met my mother? I didn't know that."

"Yes." That faraway look returned to Aphrodite's eyes. "When your father brought her here to meet us shortly after they were married, I met her. . .right here in this very room." She motioned with her hand. "She was sitting on the chair you are sitting on now and your father was standing by her side and my mother. . . ." Her voice trailed off and she visibly shook herself. She looked back at Kristen and spoke almost crisply as if that was the only way she could allow herself to remember. "Your mother was a lovely, gracious woman both physically and spiritually."

"So why didn't my. . .grandfather," Kristen almost choked over the word, "like my mother?"

Aphrodite stood and walked over to the mantel. Her steps were sure but her shoulders had lost some of their straightness. She was stooping just a little, as if the weight of remembrance was pushing her down, and remembering the heart attack the older woman had recently recovered from, an alarm went off in Kristen's head. She ran to her aunt's side and gently touched her arm.

"*Thea*. . .never mind. It's in the past. What's important is that I am here with you now and that you and my parents were reconciled to one another."

"Darling child." She touched Kristen's face, appreciating her concern. "Don't worry. I won't push myself. But I think. . .it's good for me to tell you the story, too. I don't want there to be any misunderstandings between us."

Kristen nodded and led the older woman back to her chair. "Fine. But you must stay seated and promise me that you will stop if it bothers you to retell it."

Aphrodite sat, nodded, and continued. "You have to understand that it wasn't your mother herself that my father objected to. If my father had bothered to take the time to look at your mother, really look at her and get to know her, he would have loved her, I'm sure. The problem was. . . she was a foreigner. She wasn't Greek."

"I see. . . ," Kristen said carefully but she wasn't at all sure that she did see.

"Like so many people the world over, my father was prejudiced. Oh, he didn't mind other people from other lands as friends, partners, or classmates. . .he wasn't as bad as many. However, he did *not* want his children marrying anyone who wasn't of Greek blood."

"And my mother was an American. . ."

"And. . .even worse. . .already married to your father."

"Worse?" Kristen couldn't understand how that made it worse.

Aphrodite nodded. "By that act, your parents had taken away my father's patriarchal right of giving his permission for his only son," she waved her arm around to include the opulent house, "and heir, to marry."

"But. . .if they were already married, why didn't your father understand that he couldn't do anything about it and just accept the marriage?"

"Because of the mentality of that time. It was a time when the father's word was the law of the family, no matter how old the children were. According to the way my father thought, your father and mother broke that law."

Kristen shook her head, trying to understand. "A different time entirely."

"Other than that, your parents weren't married in the Greek Orthodox Church, so as far as your grandfather was concerned the marriage was not even an actual fact. At that time, neither he nor the church would recognize any other marriage."

Kristen's eyes widened. "You mean, he tried to tell my mother that she wasn't married?" Kristen never knew a more moral woman than her mother so she knew how painful that must have been to her parents.

"Exactly."

They were silent for a moment, each deep within her own thoughts.

So much of what Aphrodite said explained Kristen's parents and their attitude toward one another to her. That Kristen's father had been devoted to her mother and her mother to her father was practically legendary in Richmond.

"But there's more. Are you sure that you want to hear it?" Aphrodite asked and lightly placed her hand on Kristen's shoulder.

Kristen nodded up to her.

"My father demanded that your father send your mother away, never to see her again or else. . .he would totally disown him and," she paused and squeezed Kristen's shoulder, "all his heirs."

"You mean. . . ," Kristen chose her words slowly and carefully, "it was my grandfather who caused the estrangement. . .not my father. . . ?" Kristen now realized that this is what had bothered her the most about the estrangement—thinking that her father had turned his back on his family when they had wanted him.

"Oh yes," Aphrodite answered quickly. "Your father begged him to reconsider. Your grandmother pleaded as well." That faraway look came into her aunt's eyes again. "And when I realized that your father had told my father. . . ," she reached out and ran her fingertips softly over Kristen's face, with all the love and longing she felt for her niece in the movement, "that you, my dear. . .were on the way. . .and. . .when. . .my father didn't care. . . ." Tears gathered in the older woman's deep blue eyes, making them shine in spite of her sadness. She took a deep breath and dabbed at her eyes with her linen handkerchief. "Well, your father took your mother and his unborn child. . .that is you, my dear. . .and left. Never to return."

From somewhere outside, the coo of a pigeon sounded and then the answering sound of its mate and Kristen considered all that her aunt had said. She was glad, more glad than she could recount, that her father had tried to avoid the estrangement. She was amazed to consider

232

that her grandfather, one of the ancestors on the wall in her room, hadn't wanted her. That hurt, but more for the old man than for herself. For someone to be so blinded by a sense of self-worth because of race, so blinded that he could hurt so many lives—his own and others— deserved, in Kristen's opinion, nothing more than her pity. And that's what Kristen felt for the man. To even consider that Nick would send his Jane back was the greatest mistake her grandfather could have made. For Kristen's father had been devoted to her mother all their lives, and it was almost a blessing that they had passed on together.

But one question bothered Kristen still and looking at her aunt, she was hesitant to ask, but she knew that she had to, so that the past could hopefully be left far behind them where it was meant to be. "But *Thea*, . . .why were you and my father estranged? You didn't agree with your father, did you?"

"Of course not." She held out her hands helplessly. "But I," she paused and the sadness and shame of that time made her strong voice sound weak, almost frail, "I. . .made the mistake of. . .remaining silent."

"But why?"

"I—" A knock at the door interrupted her. With her strong voice again in place she asked, "Yes?"

Kristen was surprised to see both James and Paul standing at the door. "Are we interrupting anything?" James asked as Paul's eyes found Kristen's where she was kneeling by her aunt's chair, and immediately understanding that something was amiss, asked with a tilt of his head if she was okay.

Kristen nodded imperceptibly that she was fine and stood as Aphrodite invited them in. "You are interrupting, but. . .you are also most welcome to come in."

Seeing Paul again after so many days made Kristen's heart feel light and happy in spite of the emotionally draining conversation she and her aunt were having. She wanted to run to him, be close to him, tell him everything, but she somehow sensed how detrimental to her relationship with her aunt that would be, especially at this critical time. Instead she smiled at him and walking over to the sofa, she sat down.

James took Kristen's place and stood by Aphrodite's chair. Kristen couldn't help thinking he looked like a cocker spaniel guarding his mistress.

Aphrodite reached up and took her friend's hand. "Kristen and I were just discussing the past." At James's quick look Aphrodite assured him, "I'm fine. It's good for me." She looked over at Kristen and smiled. "It's good for both of us."

Kristen returned the smile. "But, please. . .you don't have to say anything else. Knowing that my father didn't want the estrangement is the most important thing about the past that I needed to know."

"But don't you want to know why I remained silent?"

Kristen nodded yes and from the corner of her eye she noticed how Paul's attention was thoroughly caught. "But only if. . .you want to tell me. . .and if it's not too much for you."

"I want to tell you."

Kristen nodded and waited.

The older woman gathered her thoughts. "I was stunned by my father's behavior. That he didn't want your mother was one thing that could be explained, but not condoned. But not to want Nick's child. . .not to want his own legitimate grandchild. . . shocked me. I saw a side of my father—" She paused. "Well, from past experience I knew what he was capable of and I was afraid to cross him. . .afraid. . ." Her glance, a glance which Kristen could only describe as anguish and fear, fell on Paul, before sliding away to look down at the marble floor which had seen such history.

Kristen softly whispered. "It's okay, *Thea*. . .it's not your fault—"

"Your father left." She looked quickly back at Kristen and cut her off. "But he tried to contact my mother and me." Bitterness toward her long-dead father colored her words with pain and a hatred toward the man who had fathered her that she obviously didn't want to feel. "But my father never let me have any of the letters. Never," she repeated. "And I lost all contact with Nick until. . .I read about your wedding."

Wryly, Kristen commented, "So I guess something good did come out of that fiasco."

"Were you actually married?"

Kristen looked at Paul quickly before answering. "Ted. . .married me for money. . . . He was killed the day of our wedding. . . . Our wedding was never consummated. So. . .I guess you can't really call it a real marriage at all."

"I see. . ."

But Kristen wasn't ready to let go of the far distant past yet.

"*Thea*. . .I just want to know one thing and then we can let go of the past forever. . . ."

Aphrodite looked at her and Kristen thought she saw something close to dread or fear in her eyes.

"Did you explain everything to my father. . .did he understand why you were silent and why he never heard from you?"

Relief seemed to bring color back into Aphrodite's face. "Yes, my dear . . .I told your father everything. . .everything. . ." Paul frowned at the intensity of his godmother's look and that seemed to clear Aphrodite's expression. She turned back to Kristen. "He forgave me and your mother forgave me. . .and we were looking forward to seeing one another. We had planned on spending the entire summer together sailing around the islands of the Aegean. . . ."

Her voice trailed off and James noisily cleared his throat, bringing the discussion to an end. "Right. Well, I think that just about says it all. Shall I order tea?" An especially strong gust of wind shook the living room window.

Aphrodite placed her hand over her companion's. "I think I would like to go and rest for a while. All this talk about the past has exhausted me."

Fear jumped into James's eyes. "Are you not feeling well? Should I call the doctor?"

Aphrodite laughed. "Dear James. . .I'm only a bit tired, not sick." She glanced over at Kristen as she stood and smiled. "Believe me, it was worth it."

Kristen walked over to her and hugged the thin shoulders close to her, loving the jasmine scent that was the older woman's own special fragrance. "Thank you, *Thea*, for telling me," she whispered.

Paul walked up to them. "Well, I'm glad to see my two favorite ladies so happy."

Kristen saw the quick look of confusion that jumped into Aphrodite's eyes and motioned to Paul to be careful. Aphrodite still had no idea of the relationship and Kristen knew instinctively that now was not the time to tell her anything about it.

"My dear *nona* and my. . ." Paul paused for just a second as he looked at Kristen. "My almost-cousin," he explained and Kristen saw light come back into Aphrodite's eyes.

"And don't you forget it," Aphrodite admonished. "You must treat your," she faltered a bit at the word, "cousin—very nicely, Paul."

"And when do I treat women anything but nicely?" he kiddingly asked.

"Your string of women, don't you mean," she admonished, much as older people often admonish younger ones.

"Well, for today, I've come to ask your niece if she would like to do a bit of sightseeing with me this afternoon."

"Oh, I'd love to!" Kristen answered quickly. "Do you have time?"

"After one more meeting," he replied glancing at his watch, "which I have to leave for now, I'll be free for the next week to show you the sights and sounds of Athens."

Aphrodite turned suddenly to them and the look that filled the lines of her face could only be described as one of soul-stopping dread, as if she had seen a glimpse of the future and she couldn't abide it.

Paul saw it as well. "*Nona. . . ?* What is it?"

Aphrodite shook her head but still that look in her eyes held, a look that was now covered with yearning. But for what she was yearning, Kristen had no idea.

"What. . .I'm sorry?" Aphrodite asked.

"You don't like the idea of my showing Kristen around?" He sounded almost hurt and definitely confused.

Aphrodite's lips turned up into a smile, but Kristen saw that it was a smile that didn't quite wipe the dread away from her sharp eyes. "Nonsense. I think that would be very nice." She turned abruptly to James. "Do you feel up to continuing our novel?" To Kristen, she explained, "James loves to read out loud and I love to be read to, so we're the perfect pair."

"I think reading out loud is becoming a lost art," James commented as he escorted Aphrodite from the room.

Kristen and Paul turned to one another after the older couple left and forgetting everything but their need to be together, their arms wrapped around one another and Kristen rested her head against Paul's chest.

"Oh, but I've missed you," Paul whispered into Kristen's ear.

"And I've missed you."

"Now that you and Aphrodite seem to be such good friends," he laughed and squeezed her closer to him, "even to the point that she's worried about you going around with me, I think it's time to do all the things we've planned."

"Our search...," she murmured into the fabric of his shirt.

"Our search," he agreed and rubbed his hands over her back before stepping away from her. "Right now, I have to get to that meeting. I'll be back around six. And then I'm going to take you to a very special place."

"Should I dress up?" Her eyes sparkled in anticipation of their evening together.

"In your best walking shoes and jeans," he said, blew her a kiss, and was gone.

Chapter 11

"Best walking shoes and jeans," Kristen repeated, liking the idea of a date which required such apparel. She hurried over to the window to watch Paul as he walked down the marble steps to his sports car. The wind blew his hair in a wavy mass around his face and when he glanced up and waved, somehow knowing that she was watching him, Kristen felt a lump of pure happiness bubble up inside her. To think that handsome, wonderful, kind man loved her, Kristen King, was the most amazing thing Kristen could imagine. She waved back and watched until his car disappeared down the tree-lined drive and out onto the main road.

Kristen turned and looked around the room that had seen such drama throughout the years. So far, two of the things which she had searched for in traveling to Greece, finding a blood relative and finding out about the past, had been realized in this room today. She only hoped that her quest with Paul, as they learned about their new and fragile love and their search for that Something More in life which she was now certain had everything to do with God, would be equally successful.

Giving the room one more sweeping glance, somehow feeling not sadness but closeness, knowing that both her parents had been there, she walked out and was about to head up the stairs to her bedroom when, on an impulse, she decided to look around the library instead. Until Paul came for her at six, she had nothing to do, and she knew that she would be impatient at best. A stroll through the library would help.

Aphrodite had shown Kristen around the library on one of their numerous walks around the house and grounds. The library was her aunt's pride and joy, but James's domain. He lovingly took care of it, even to the point of being the one who dusted its numerous shelves. It boasted several manuscripts dating from the early Christian period and medieval times, and much memorabilia from the first modern Olympics held in

1896 in Athens, which the Vasilias family had helped to organize and finance and even had a family member participate in.

Kristen walked over to a manuscript in a glass case. It was a twelfth-century manuscript written in Greek which told about the conquest of Greece by the invading Franks after the fourth crusader's sacking of Constantinople in 1204. She knew that her college friend, Melissa Kincaid, now Melissa Karalis, was an expert on the subject of medieval Greece and probably knew what treasures the old manuscript held. She had tried calling Melissa several times at her Peloponnesian home but there had been no answer. As Kristen turned away from the treasured book to the next display, a Bible, she made a mental note to try and call Melissa once again.

Running her hand over the glass display case which contained a Byzantine Bible bound in enamel, she wished, like so many others before her, that she could touch the vellum pages of the ninth-century book and she thought how the Byzantine enamel work on its cover was probably as masterful as the little painting by El Greco which hung in the next room.

"Now there's a book I wish I could read!" she whispered longingly. But ancient Greek was a little bit more than she could tackle. At the moment, she was thrilled when she could correctly handle a phrase or two in modern Greek. Sighing, she turned away from the manuscript and started searching among the shelves. In several nooks and crannies, James had set up displays of books he found exceptionally interesting.

Kristen stopped in front of one. Another Bible, old and well-worn, but more from use than age. The oils of loving hands had turned the pages a rich gold along the edges. Carefully, Kristen turned the book to the title page.

It was written in English! And she gasped when she read the inscription. Written were the words:

> *To my dear wife Christina,*
> *All my love forever and ever,*
> *Your husband,*
> *Paul*
> *Galaxidi, Greece*

Kristen felt as if her breath had been knocked out of her. She couldn't believe it, but somehow she had found Christina's Bible! She tried to remember what Paul had told her about the "ring of love." Something about the ring having come to symbolize Christina and Paul's love and . . .faith.

Kristen picked the Book up and hugged it close to her heart. Now she knew just what their faith had consisted of and how deeply it ran. She also was beginning to realize that she had a lot more in common with her ancestors than just her name and her sudden love for her Paul. Handling the precious book with infinite care, Kristen carried it over to a table by the tall window and slowly, lovingly turned its pages. She let out a cry of delight when she discovered notes written with neat, very small letters in the margins. Even though the notes were written in Greek, it was a link with her ancestors and one which she knew that she and Paul would go over together and cherish.

She started to close the book but it opened of its own accord, as if it had been opened many times at a particular page. Kristen couldn't resist one last peek so she opened it wide.

She let out a gasp of delight when she discovered that it was the Vasilias family's Bible, its Record of Births. It dated from the time of Paul's and Christina's births and ended with an entry recording. . .her own birth. She read:

Christina Vasilias—Born July 20, 1967
(Richmond, Virginia, U.S.A.)
Daughter of Nick P. Vasilias and Jane Ann Pierce

Kristen sat and looked at that inscription. A tear, a poignant tear of happiness and of sadness, slowly fell from her long lashes to draw a line down her face.

"Christina?" Kristen looked up as her aunt Aphrodite walked on slippered feet over to her. Seeing the book her niece held, she understood her niece's tear. "So. . .you found the family Bible."

Kristen nodded. "I think. . .that this one," she motioned to the Book which she held open in her hands, "is worth much more than that one," she said looking over toward the Byzantine Bible that sat elegantly behind its burglarproof case.

"There are many different kinds of worth," Aphrodite agreed and sat in the chair next to Kristen. She pointed to the inscription that recorded

Kristen's birth. "My mother penned that the very day she found out about your birth. She sat right where you are sitting now and with tears in her eyes said, 'Praise God, my granddaughter has been safely born. I hope someday, Aphrodite, that I can give this Book, our family Bible, to her'."

Kristen's eyes opened wide in joy and wonder.

"In my mother's name. . .I present this family Bible to you, dear Christina."

"Oh, *Thea*. . . .I don't know what to say. . ."

Aphrodite continued. "All our ancestors have loved God. . .even my father did. . .at one time. He is the only one who didn't accept God's path for our lives. . .and look what grief his rebellion caused our family. I think. . .I think it had a lot to do with the two world wars and the Greek civil war. . .because he wasn't like that always. . . ," she spoke thoughtfully as though she had tried to understand a million times before. Maybe it had a lot to do with too much money as well. . .I don't know. . . ." She shook her silver head. Confusion was in its movement and Kristen felt a rush of love for this woman who had the blood of Paul and Christina running through her veins just as she did. Taking her aunt's hand, Kristen whispered, "I love you, *Thea*." It came out naturally and both Kristen and Aphrodite knew that it was true.

"Oh, Christina. . .I love you too, just as. . .your grandmother, your *yiayia*, did."

And their arms were around one another in an embrace of acceptance and understanding of the past that had, in spite of the rebellion of one man, been rescued by God to bring them all back together again. As the scent of jasmine wafted in through the open window to mix with that of her aunt, Kristen thought how the "ring of love," not a ring of substance, but the ring formed by God, wound around them gently, lovingly.

The housekeeper softly knocked on the doorjamb, bringing them reluctantly apart.

"Excuse me, ma'am," she addressed Kristen, "but you are wanted on the phone by a Miss Lottie," she said and left.

Kristen jumped out of her aunt's arms. "Oh my. . .Lottie! She must be back!"

"One of the friends you told me about?" At Kristen's happy nod she suggested, "Why don't you take the call in my study?"

Kristen started to get up but then stopped. She looked down at the

Bible, her family Bible, and then at her aunt. "Why don't we just leave this Book here in the library for now?"

Kristen could tell that her aunt was pleased with the suggestion by the way her eyes crinkled at the corners, just like her father's had when he was pleased. "I'd like that."

"Maybe," Kristen suggested hesitantly, "you should ask James to read it to you." At Aphrodite's surprised look, Kristen continued. "Lottie recently sent me a Bible for my birthday. I've been reading it. . .it's amazing!"

"Maybe I will." Aphrodite laughed her low, forceful laugh. "That is. . .if I can get James to stay awake long enough to read more than two pages."

"Is that what happened now?"

"He's snoring," she confirmed. "But I left him. He's leaving for a few days in England in the morning. At our age, you grab sleep whenever it graces you." She waved her hand. "Now go on with you. Your friend must be wondering what's happened to you."

Aphrodite's words were more than true. Lottie did wonder what had happened to Kristen, but also what had happened to make Kristen all of a sudden travel to Greece!

"I couldn't believe it when I got your message and they said that you were calling from Athens. What happened? Don't tell me you came to surprise me and then found me gone?"

Kristen laughed and could imagine her little redheaded friend through the wire. Lottie had always reminded Kristen of a miniature sports car of vivacious red coloring that was always trying to pass others and Kristen could tell, as she explained to Lottie about her aunt and Paul and their quest, that hadn't changed even though she had changed her way of thinking about life.

"Kristen. . .I'm. . .I'm so happy. . .I didn't know how you would react to getting a Bible for your birthday." She laughed, her deep hardy laugh that was so familiar to Kristen. "It certainly is different from the statue I gave to you last year!"

"Oh Lottie. . .I adore the statue. . .but the Bible. . .it gives so much!"

"It's life-giving," Lottie said, and Kristen was amazed to hear Lottie speak of things so deep and philosophical. Previously, she had always jested about people who became "deep and heavy" as she used to call it.

"It's life-giving," Lottie repeated, "and absolutely perfect for wherever you are in life."

Kristen nodded into the phone. "Your timing certainly couldn't have been better. . .just when Paul and I were wondering where to start searching for that Something More in life. . .the doorbell rang and the deliveryman handed me your package."

"That's something neat about God's timing, Kristen." She paused. "It's always perfect. . .just trust Him and He will lead you down the path that has been marked out for you since the beginning of time. It's a lot better than the path we mark out for ourselves. . .that's for sure! Look at me! I thought I'd be in Athens during my stay in Greece and suddenly this Santorini find exploded around me. And because I was already in Athens, the position was given to me by the university. It never would have been given to me otherwise. These super finds are too few and far between to be handed to a junior archaeologist."

"And you've always loved things to do with Santorini," Kristen commented, remembering the hours she had listened to Lottie talk about the lost civilization of Atlantis.

"It's what made me go into archeology in the first place. . .who knows . . .maybe I'll find the lost city of Atlantis after all!" She paused and with an inner peace Kristen had never heard in her friend before, she continued softly, almost reverently, "But you know. . .it doesn't even matter anymore. . . . I've already found the God who was lost to me. . .and that's the most important find I'll ever make."

Chapter 12

After hanging up the phone Kristen thought about her friend and the amazing events in her life and then she was reminded about her other friend, Melissa Karalis.

The events of Melissa's life were amazing, too. Kristen remembered that she had almost married her handsome Greek doctor during their university days, but then, something had happened to split Melissa from Luke just weeks before their wedding. Melissa had changed and from the deep recesses of her mind, Kristen vaguely remembered Melissa as having said something about discovering that she shouldn't rely on the man she loved to be her savior from all the hurts of the world. Rather, she had learned that there was One who she could and should rely on. . . .

Kristen shook her head and wondered, *Had Melissa meant God?*

Kristen picked up the phone and again dialed her friend's Peloponnesian home. She really wanted to talk to Melissa and she was thrilled when her efforts were rewarded by the phone being answered this time.

"*Embros.*" A woman's voice answered.

"*Yia Sas.*" Kristen was pleased that she remembered how to say "Hello" in Greek. "Melissa, please. . .*parakalo.*"

Understanding that the caller was English-speaking, the gracious woman answered in English. "Melissa isn't here. She's in Athens in the hospital."

"In the hospital!"

The woman laughed. "Don't worry. Both she and the baby are fine."

"Baby!"

The woman, who Kristen learned was Melissa's sister-in-law, Anastasia, laughed and was delighted to give Kristen all the particulars about the birth of her beloved brother and sister-in-law's baby, even to informing Kristen that the hospital where Melissa was staying was located very close to Kristen's aunt's home.

Kristen asked Anastasia not to tell Melissa that she had called, wanting instead to surprise Melissa in the morning with a visit.

Anastasia was thrilled with the idea and upon putting down the phone, Kristen felt sure that Melissa's sister-in-law, Anastasia, was a good friend to Melissa.

❦

Paul came and picked Kristen up at precisely six o'clock that evening. She was dressed in the requested jeans and walking shoes and was anxious to tell him all about the wonderful events of the day. As he drove through the quiet streets of Athens, which he told her were only so quiet during the month of August when most Athenians were away on holiday, she quickly and excitedly told him about finding the family Bible, about Aphrodite giving it to her, about her conversation with Lottie, and about Melissa's new baby.

When she'd finished he repeated the words Lottie had finished on.

"God's perfect timing. . .I'm beginning to believe in it."

The depth of feeling he put into the words impressed and surprised Kristen. She waited expectantly for him to continue.

He grinned, as pleased as a stray cat might be who had just found a T-bone steak. "You're not the only one who's been busy discovering new and wonderful things this week."

"What do you mean?"

"Well. . .when I haven't been attending to my job, I've been busy studying and reading the Bible and. . .meeting with Pastor Dean."

"What?"

"Well. . .we did come here to search for that Unknown, Something More, didn't we?" he gently reminded her. "And since we were literally thrown together with the pastor on that beach below your home last week. . . ," he said shrugging his shoulders, "when he called me a few days ago, right after he returned from San Francisco, I told him about our questions and search and. . .we've been meeting every night."

"Paul!" That Kristen was pleased was putting it mildly. She knew that he was serious about searching.

"Kristen, something you have probably guessed about me. . .when I say something or decide to do something, I'm serious about it. And I normally act on it immediately. Our search is. . .very important to me." He stopped at a light and reaching over, took her hand in his. "I think that it is very important to our love. . .one of the reasons our love is going to be the long-lasting kind. . .like Paul and Christina's."

"Oh, Paul. . ." She brought his hand up to her face and rubbed the back of it against her cheek. "I believe so too." After a moment of happy silence Kristen asked, "So. . .what have you learned?"

She was curious about his visits with the pastor.

Paul blew out a deep breath. "So much. . .but the most important thing is that we are on the right track. The Bible, known as God's Word, is the place to search. I've only read a small part of it, the four Gospels—the first four books in the New Testament telling about Jesus' life on earth—and the fifth book, the Book of Acts, which tells about the spreading of Jesus's message throughout the world. I feel almost certain that God, in the person of Jesus Christ, is that Unknown, Something More that we are searching for."

"Oh, Paul. . .I think so too. I haven't done too much reading but from what I've read and from talking to Lottie. . .I think so too," she repeated simply and felt joy, a joy unlike any she had ever felt before, fill her as the city slid past her window.

Paul left the modern city streets behind and turned onto the quaint small streets that made up the old town of Athens, called the Plaka. The buildings were built right onto the narrow roads and at a couple of points as Paul drove through the roads, careful of strolling tourists, it seemed as though the corners of the old buildings might possibly be clipped by the side of the car.

He drew her attention upward. Kristen gasped. "The Acropolis!" She swiveled around in her seat, cocking her head at an angle and back as far as it would go to see the ancient walls of Athens' High City. "It's right over our heads! Is that where we're going?"

Paul smiled, a smile that said "just you wait and see," and drove up and past the busy tourist section until he reached a quiet lane right at the base of the Acropolis's butte. Trees—pine trees, straight cypress trees, and olive trees—covered the slopes on the left side of the lane for several meters until the cliffs were reached.

He turned to the right and pulled into the driveway of a beautiful neoclassical house, and switched off the car.

And suddenly Kristen realized where they were. "It's your house!"

In all the excitement of the past week, she had totally forgotten about his house.

He led her to the side of the house, which was also the entrance, and to a gate which opened up onto a courtyard that was lovingly tended and filled with orange and lemon trees and with the delicate white blossoms of jasmine filling the courtyard with their sweet scent. Kristen breathed in deeply. "I think I will always associate jasmine with my aunt. . . ."

As if suddenly realizing it, Paul answered, "You're right. That is her fragrance."

Kristen smiled indulgently at him before turning her attention to the courtyard. She felt as though she had stepped into another world! Her aunt's house had the feeling of her parents' home. It was a big stately mansion. But Paul's home was something totally different. Swallows played under the eaves of the ceramic roof, bees buzzed busily, wanting to make their way home in the late afternoon sunlight, cicadas still ground their legs as they played their summertime song in the pine grove across the street. . . . It all combined to make Kristen feel as though she were a part of a fairy tale. She half expected Thumbelina to come riding by on the back of one of the swallows.

Kristen turned to Paul. She remembered reading that a home told a lot about one's personality. Knowing Paul as she did, Kristen knew that this home told clearly about the warm man she had grown to love. It was inviting yet stately, elegant yet cozy, old and yet new. "Paul," her green eyes sparkled out her joy in his home, "your home is enchanting."

He was pleased. "I'm glad you like it. I'd give you a tour but," he glanced at his watch, "if you don't mind, it will have to wait for later."

Kristen looked at him in surprise. "I thought this was it for tonight!"

"My dear Kristen. . ." He looked at her with those same dark eyes that she had wanted to fall into in San Francisco, and she now yearned to wrap her arms around him and to hold him and to love him and to keep him next to her always. He was the most precious person in the entire world to her.

He paused and felt the blood pound in his head as he easily read what was written in her eyes because it was a reflection of his own want, his own desire. But, ignoring his want, her want, he continued, "I don't think I would have asked you to dress so casually if I had only wanted to show you my house." He forced a chuckle and looked down at the smooth marble stones. "Neither the marble out here nor the parquet floors inside require walking shoes." He cleared his throat, respect in his tone. "But for a walking tour up to the Areopagus, the spot from where the Apostle Paul is traditionally thought to have preached to the people of this city, good nonslip walking shoes are a must."

"Oh, Paul, that sounds wonderful," she said, emotion lacing her voice, and she let her arms have their way and wound them around his neck. After a week of holding her emotions at bay, she just had to hold him for one moment.

Paul drew her to him. Their foreheads touched, their heartbeats ran together, and Paul whispered, his accent prominent and sweet with emotion, "I love you, Kristen. There's something very special between us."

Kristen shook her head. "No, Paul. . .I don't think there is something special between us. . . ." She smiled. "I think. . .that there is something very special among us. . .and. . .I'm beginning to believe that that special Something. . .is God."

"Kristen. . ." He pulled her closer to him, breathing in the scent that was all her own and sounding to his own ears more like Pastor Dean whom he had spent so much time with that week than himself, he said the unfamiliar words, but words he truly meant. "Praise God, I found you."

Their lips came together in a light kiss of sweet, growing love which promised a future of so much more.

Chapter 13

Holding hands, Kristen and Paul left his house and walked along the quaint roads that ran in and around the red-roofed buildings huddled picturesquely against the northern slopes of the Acropolis. The roads were actually little more than paths originally laid out in the days when horses and donkeys and human feet were the mode of travel. Cars weren't allowed on most of the roads, so pedestrians of all sizes, and of all nationalities, and of all ages filled the space as people wandered among the nooks and crannies, all enjoying the holiday atmosphere and checking out the many tastefully appointed tourist shops. Grecian urns, replicas of those found in the very location where tourist feet now trod, Greek worry beads, and T-shirts with anything from Plato to the famous Greek cats printed on the front, abounded in the shops.

Several times, young waiters dressed in dark pants and white shirts tried to escort Kristen and Paul into rooftop taverns for dinner, something Kristen found charming and that gave her the feeling of being more of an honored guest rather than a paying customer. But Paul politely declined in his own language and they moved on.

They skirted the upper slopes of the old town, with the grinding of the cicadas and the cooing of the pigeons accompanying them as they walked, and the ever-present *Meltemia* blowing everything in a symphony of sound and movement. Sidewalks of steep stairs led down into the gaily lit heart of the Plaka. Like a fair, the streets reminded Kristen of Disneyland and a recreated setting.

But a quick glance above her left shoulder to the majestic ruins of the Acropolis with the massive cyclopean walls dating from the late Bronze Age quickly confirmed that the streets were not a recreation. They were the real thing, with foundations that went back several millennia.

They left the commotion of the coffee shops and tourist shops and came upon the stone and concrete path, called Theorias Way, that cut through the ancient city of Athens like a pathway into another time. Turning around and around, Kristen sucked in her breath at the view that was before her, behind her, above her, and below her.

"It's beautiful, isn't it?" Paul whispered by her side.

Kristen nodded and thought how "beautiful" didn't go far in describing the view. Above her was the Acropolis sitting ageless and golden, below her was a land of ancient Greek temples and medieval churches, before her was an observatory and a bald, stony hill where people could be seen standing and sitting in the foreground, and behind her was the old town with its mixture of neoclassical buildings built in the protection of the fortress above its head.

"I'm not sure what I'm looking at. . .but it's one of the prettiest sights I've ever seen," Kristen finally breathed out. "I feel as though I've stepped into an epic film and I've gone back in time." She laughed and waved her hand to include all the buildings and constructions that spoke of so many different ages. "But which time period, I'm not sure."

Paul let go of her hand and opened one of the books he was carrying. "Well, how about if we go back to about the time of the Apostle Paul?" he suggested.

"Our quest. . . ," Kristen whispered and looked down at the guidebook he held and felt the thrill of discovery shoot through her.

"Our quest," he returned and pointed to a passage in the book. "You see, when the Apostle Paul arrived here in about the year A.D. 51, Athens' golden days were half a millennium in the past. The city," he pointed down to the ancient site below them, "the ancient *agora*—that is, marketplace—was said to have resembled an outdoor art gallery."

Kristen looked down at the ancient marketplace he indicated and laughed. "What it is now?" Even from about a hundred feet up she could see many statues and columns and altars and walls from ancient buildings filling the grounds. There were even a couple of temples.

Paul smiled. "Ah. . .this is nothing compared to what it was then. The city that was has been destroyed and set on fire many times by invading people—barbarians—that came swarming in from the north after the collapse of the Roman Empire." He squinted into the sun that was about two hours from setting and continued. "When St. Paul visited Athens it

250

was still the most respected center of learning in the world. Plato's University was still in session and the city was filled to capacity with altars and temples that were in use."

Kristen looked at him in surprise. "Really?"

He tucked her arm under his elbow as they continued to walk slowly down the old path. "I read," Paul explained, motioning to the book he carried, "how the Roman satirist Petronius, who was a contemporary of the Apostle Paul's, wrote that it was easier to find a statue of a god in Athens than a man."

"I wonder how that made St. Paul feel. . . ?" Kristen wanted to learn all she could about the St. Paul of the Bible.

Paul considered that for a moment before answering, "Well, his background was Jewish, his citizenship was Roman, his learning was influenced by the Greek world, and his thought had become Christian." He paused thoughtfully. "I imagine all the temples and altars that abounded probably offended the Jewish part of him, impressed the Roman part of him, were beautiful to the Greek part of him, and distressed the Christian part of him."

"What an interesting man. . .I didn't realize that he was anything but Jewish. . .and Christian, of course."

"Interesting doesn't go far in describing Paul. He was amazing. To leave his home and travel as he did, bringing new, but true, ideas to a place that had ancient ideas. . .he was not only a very learned man, but a brave one as well." He motioned down at the ancient marketplace and pulled from his back pocket a small New Testament.

"Paul!" Kristen exclaimed. "You've gotten a Bible!"

His eyes twinkled. "I've gotten several Bibles," he corrected and held the little Testament up. "This one goes with me everywhere."

Kristen watched him open the Book and thought how it added to his stature. *There is something masculine about a man handling a Bible,* she decided, as he opened it to a premarked page.

"I want to read to you from this spot what was written about Paul while he was in Athens, and in a few minutes, I'll read St. Paul's exact words from the location where he most likely spoke them."

Kristen felt tears, tears of wonder, tears of joy, tears of love build up behind her eyes for this man. To say that she admired Paul wasn't enough. And to say that she respected him still wasn't enough. He had something

251

special and, through his research, was acquiring something more every day that seemed to fill him and make him more of a man to be loved and cherished and adored and respected. There was so much more to him than just ambition and wealth and good looks. So much more simply because he knew that there was Something More in life than the empty demands made on men in the late twentieth century and he wasn't afraid to go out and find it.

The pages of the Testament ruffled in the ever-present wind that whipped across the path, and the paper seemed to demand its need to be read. Paul read, deeply, richly of the words. " 'While Paul was waiting for them in Athens'. . ." He glanced at Kristen and explained, " 'Them' being Silas and Timothy, his friends who were to join him, 'he was greatly distressed to see that the city was full of idols. So he reasoned in the synagogue with the Jews and the God-fearing Greeks, as well as in the marketplace.' "

"Marketplace!" Kristen exclaimed and looked down at the ancient site below her. "Do you mean there?"

Paul smiled. "Exactly."

Kristen looked at the site with new eyes. To think that she was looking at the actual place which was written about in the Bible, the actual site where the Apostle Paul reasoned with the Jews and the God-fearing Greeks, was almost too much for her North American brain to assimilate. She looked at Paul and hesitantly tried to explain what she was feeling. "Whenever I heard the Bible stories. . .when I was a little girl. . .they almost seemed like they were in fictional lands. . .but right now. . ." She turned and looked down over the ancient site below her, holding her windblown hair away from her face. "I'm looking at the actual place. . . the actual setting. . . ." Her words trailed off.

"I know what you mean, and I've lived here all my life," he replied in understanding before turning back to the ruffling pages of the Testament. He continued to read, " 'A group of Epicurean and Stoic philosophers began to dispute with him. Some of them asked, "What is this babbler trying to say?" Others remarked, "He seems to be advocating foreign gods." They said this because Paul was preaching the good news about Jesus and the resurrection. Then they took him and brought him to a meeting of the Areopagus, where they said to him, "May we know what this new teaching is that you are presenting? You are bringing some strange ideas to our ears, and we want to know what they mean." ' "

"I wonder what exactly he was saying to them?" Kristen interrupted.

"When I read to you from the Areopagus what Paul said to the Council of the Areopagus," he pointed to the bald hill that was before them, "I think you'll understand."

"Areopagus? Council of Areopagus?" The words were so foreign sounding to Kristen but the hill wasn't. It was the one that was straight ahead of them and filled with people.

"Known as the Areopagus or Hill of Ares, or by the time Paul arrived during the Roman period, the Hill of Mars, it was the site of the ancient council of nobles called the Council of the Areopagus," Paul explained and looked back down at Kristen. "In Athens' earlier history, it was both the senate and the supreme judicial court for Athens, but by the time of St. Paul's visit, the council had authority only in religious and moral issues."

"So. . .it was to this windblown hill that Paul was brought?"

Paul chuckled. "Well. . .they have found evidence of a structure having been there then. . .some sort of public building, I imagine."

"I always thought that he talked to the Athenians from the Acropolis." She motioned to the fortress that was about twice the height of the Hill of Mars and located to the east of it.

"He probably visited there," Paul conceded.

She turned back to the bald, unassuming hill. Somehow she felt drawn to it much more than she did to the world-famous Acropolis with its array of priceless temples and buildings. The wind seemed to be wrapping invisible threads around her and they were pulling her toward the hill's windy heights. She took Paul's hand and started walking along the path toward the stone stairs that led up to the rocky hill.

But Paul stopped her. "Wait." She turned and looked at him with questioning eyes. "Before we go up there and I read the words of St. Paul, I want to read one more thing which I found in the guidebook. I think it will help you to understand his speech better and. . .," he reached out and gently touched her cheek, "it goes along with what we said that first day that we met."

She tilted her head in question. "We said so much that day. . . ."

"About. . .that Unknown, Something More. . ."

Slowly, she nodded her head and thought how that invisible thread was now weaving itself around the two of them. "Tell me," she gently commanded and she felt as though she and Paul were the only ones on the path below the Hill of Mars. The sounds of the evening faded into the background and although they were surrounded by humanity, it was as if they were alone. But no, not alone exactly either. Something, Someone was among them.

"There was a Greek traveler and geographer whose name was Pausanius who visited Athens about a century after the apostle. He wrote in detail about everything he saw." Paul grinned. "I guess you could say Pausanius wrote the world's first guidebook. On the road from the port of Phaleron," he pointed off in the direction of the sea, "he reported as having seen. . . ," Paul looked down at the book and read, " 'altars of the gods named Unknown'."

"Gods named Unknown. . . ," Kristen whispered in awe.

Paul nodded and repeated, "gods named Unknown." He paused, and as he took her hand, they left the path and walked toward the stone stairs that led to the top of the hill. "So you see, Kristen—we aren't the only ones to realize that there is an Unknown, Something More in life than what our world would have us believe. Even in the ancient days which were filled with gods more personally named than ours of money and ambition and success, people knew that there was an Unknown, Something More to life."

Kristen squeezed his hand. Words weren't needed as that invisible thread seemed to wrap them tighter than ever together as they stepped, man and woman, simultaneously upon the bottom stone step that led to the summit of that unassuming hill from where the Apostle Paul was said to have spoken to the Athenians.

Kristen knew that she had learned more on their walk down the path that led to this hill than a month of lectures could have taught her. And some invisible force seemed to be telling her that she was about to learn more than she had learned in a lifetime of questions. She felt certain that the Unknown was about to be made known to her—and to be made known to her beautifully.

It filled her with excitement, excitement and peace.

Chapter 14

Sixteen stone steps, treacherous steps, old steps, maybe even ancient ones, cut out from the very substance of the hill, led to the top. Kristen counted them, one by one, as she ascended hand-in-hand with Paul and wondered if these were perhaps the very steps St. Paul had used.

If they had thought that the wind along the path had been strong, they realized that it was nothing compared to that at the top of the Hill of Mars. Kristen laughed into it and Paul laughed with her. It was more than exhilarating and more than invigorating. It was welcoming and somehow right, as if doldrums would have been all wrong and too tame for the hill that had heard the words spoken by that mighty man of God nineteen hundred years before the current world's population was born. The wind seemed to hold the words of the apostle in its ageless movement, in its whistling tune. They both felt it, they both loved it, and they were both anxious for Paul to read the actual words which St. Paul had spoken about the Unknown God from this very spot on earth.

At the top, Paul led Kristen over the jagged and slippery rocks and around people who sat upon smoother ones, to the gravelly section on the western side. There they found a stone and sat to look out over the city that sprawled outward to the mountains that encircled it on three sides and to the sea that hung like a sapphire from around its neck to the south. A fairy wind danced around Kristen's feet and a plastic bag, a sad leftover from somebody's picnic, was caught by the wind and pushed against a wild artichoke bush. Paul kicked it away from the thorny, purple flower with his foot and balling it up, stuffed it in his pocket to throw away later. A plastic bag was all wrong for what they had come to do.

That invisible thread, that which Kristen had felt on the pathway leading to the hill, seemed to bind them tighter and tighter as the wind encircled them. Kristen held tightly to Paul's arm. She loved this moment in time, she anticipated the next, and she hoped that the feeling she now possessed, the feeling of being on the brink of a wonderful discovery, would never leave her even after the discovery was made. Paul leaned closer to her as he reached into his back pocket for the little Testament.

"Can't you just imagine that St. Paul spoke on a day such as this one?"

Kristen looked out over the scene before her. Clouds danced in the sky above, swallows played in the wind all around, and the city, the beautiful and sprawling modern city of Athens hummed like an electrical wire below them. The people of the city seemed too busy to hear even itself, much less something as simple, but as magnificent, as words. But then, looking around her at the summit of the hill, Kristen was moved to realize that people, people representing cities and countries and continents from the world over seemed to have converged on the summit of Mars Hill. Black and white, yellow and red, tall and short, fat and skinny, old and young people were all atop the hill and were all somehow subdued, as if they too had journeyed to this spot to quest after Something, Something that only this spot on earth was meant to hand to them, a gift free of charge.

Looking closer at the people, Kristen drew in her breath and Paul turned to her in question.

"Look," she pointed. Many of the people seemed to hold books such as the one Paul now held opened to the seventeenth chapter of Acts.

"Bibles," Paul whispered and looked back at her with an expression of such tenderness and wonder that Kristen felt tears form at the back of her eyes. "Obviously. . .others feel. . .what we feel, Kristen."

"Oh, Paul. . ." She laid her head against his shoulder and was just enjoying the moment of revelation, of understanding that there were many other people in the world who were interested in searching for that wonderful Something More in life when her eyes caught such an extraordinary sight that she was sure it must be a figment of her imagination.

A man, dressed in the long billowing robes of Biblical days, with sandal-clad feet, appeared like an apparition from the west side of the hill.

Kristen blinked her eyes. If she had been asked to describe St. Paul as he might have been when he visited the Hill of Mars, she would have described him exactly as this man appeared. Robes flowing in the wind, red hair licking out behind him like a flame in the evening sky, and eyes, crinkled eyes that were kind, and yet disturbed for the intelligent people to whom he wanted to make known the Unknown God, would have belonged to St. Paul as they did to this man.

"Paul?" she whispered and squeezed his arm. But she didn't have to say anything. Paul had seen the man and from the whispered commotion which she heard coming from around her—Japanese spoken to her right, Spanish to her left, Greek all around, and a multitude of English-speaking accents that must have covered at least four continents—Kristen knew that all the people on the hill had seen the man.

"I don't believe it," Paul whispered.

"Neither do I."

The man, short of height and small in size, but seemingly bigger than life, stopped about ten feet from Kristen and Paul and with his back to the Acropolis, took a silent moment to gaze out over the city, over the world it represented. He closed his eyes and, as the real apostle might have done all those ages ago, he very obviously offered up a silent prayer for Athens and the people she contained.

When he opened his eyes, he looked directly at Kristen and Paul and smiled slightly, before encompassing all the people on the hill with the brilliance of his gaze. As he looked from face to face, all the languages that were spoken on that hilltop fell silent as the people gathered around the man. Kristen thought how they were all spokes of a wheel, while the man was the hub.

"Men of Athens!" the man's voice boomed out and Paul, a modern day man of Athens, understood immediately what this man dressed as St. Paul was about to do.

He put his arm around Kristen's shoulder and squeezing her close to him, said with the excitement he felt lacing his voice, "Kristen. . .he's going to recite St. Paul's speech!"

Kristen looked at Paul in amazement, her green eyes flashing in wonder. "Are you sure?"

"Listen," Paul instructed and trained his eyes back on the man. Kristen did the same.

The man continued, his voice clear and powerful and yet, with a love-sweetened sound that travelled with the wind to the hilltop's waiting ears. "I see that in every way you are very religious. For as I walked around and looked carefully at your objects of worship, I even found an altar with this inscription: To an Unknown God."

Kristen grabbed ahold of Paul's free hand and squeezed it. *To an Unknown God!* The words reverberated within her brain.

With caring and yet with challenge in his tone, the man, the wonderful man who cared enough to dress as St. Paul and reenact his words, continued. "Now what you worship as something unknown I am going to proclaim to you. The God who made the world and everything in it is the Lord of heaven and earth and does not live in temples built by hands." He motioned with his arm to the temples of stone which sat behind him on the high Acropolis and then down to the Hephaisteion, a monumental work of human art that had survived nearly twenty-four centuries, which sat below him. "And he is not served by human hands, as if he needed anything, because he himself gives all men life and breath and everything else. From one man he made every nation of men, that they should inhabit the whole earth; and he determined the times set for them and the exact places where they should live."

Kristen's nerves tingled. "The path of life. . . ," she whispered and Paul squeezed her closer to him, understanding and agreeing with her unspoken thought. They had walked more than just the little stone and concrete path of Theorias Way to reach this spot; they had walked a path from San Francisco to reach this windy hilltop and it was exactly where they were meant to be.

"God did this so that men would seek him, and perhaps reach out for him, and find him. . ." He closed his hands and brought them lovingly, as if he possessed the most precious thing in the world, close to his heart, "Though he is not far from each one of us."

His eyes, his hurting, caring, loving eyes smiled at them, implored them, and reached out to all the people of the world who were gathered on that hilltop. Kristen and Paul knew as the man continued to say the words of St. Paul that a force much greater than the wind was blowing around them. Something invisible, but Something tangible was binding them all together and instructing them and loving them. Kristen looked at Paul and Paul looked at Kristen, and they both knew that their quest for that Unknown, Something More had been realized on this windy hilltop.

And they knew that it was 'the God who made the world and everything in it' for whom they had traveled so far together to find. They had quested after Him and they had found Him on this beautiful Hill of

Mars above the modern and ancient city of Athens.

And, as the man concluded the speech of that great apostle to the Gentiles by gently bowing his head, Kristen and Paul knew that their lives would never be the same again.

With hands that shook slightly, Paul turned to the seventeenth chapter and read what was written after St. Paul's speech ended.

" '. . .At that, Paul left the Council. A few men became followers of Paul and believed. Among them was Dionysius, a member of the Areopagus, also a woman named Damaris, and a number of others.' " His words ended with wonder in his tone.

Slowly, Paul looked up and turning to Kristen, looked deeply into her eyes and said, "Kristen, like Dionysius of before. . .I believe."

"Oh, Paul. . .like Damaris of before. . .I believe too!"

With their hands clasped together they sat with faces that reflected their euphoria over discovering and recognizing the Unknown God—the God who made the world and everything in it.

People had started to talk and to move around on the hill again, but it was some moments before Paul and Kristen realized that the man who had reenacted the speech of St. Paul's so convincingly had moved next to them and was standing above them. The hem of his robe billowed out in the wind and brushed against Kristen's ankle.

Together, they turned to him and smiled. He returned their smile and said, "I feel that it is for you two that I was led to this windy hilltop today."

"Who. . . ," Kristen began and then pausing, licked her lips. "Who led you?"

"The same One who led you here," he replied simply.

Paul stood and pulled Kristen up with him. He towered over the smaller man, but the smaller man seemed every bit as big.

"We have been searching for Something More in life, Something that was Unknown to us. We now understand that that Something More is definitely God."

"Alleluia!" the man shouted out, surprising both of them. But rather than feeling embarrassed or ashamed by the outburst, both Kristen and Paul would have liked to have shouted out the same with him. Instead, they both grinned widely.

"But where do we go from here?" Paul asked.

"We have a Bible," Kristen offered.

"Several Bibles." Paul laughed and explained, "Until two weeks ago we didn't even own one."

"The Bible is the place to learn all about God. It is His word to us." He paused. "But first. . .how about if we pray?"

The man took both of their hands and there on the hilltop both Kristen and Paul asked the Lord Jesus to come into their lives and to live with them forever.

"Don't ever forget," the man reminded them after their prayer, "that Jesus came to seek and to save what was lost."

"I was truly lost," Kristen said, "and it wasn't a very nice feeling."

"But a feeling neither you nor I will ever have again," Paul said and squeezed her hand.

"Amen to that!" the man exclaimed and motioned over at a group of people that were obviously waiting to talk to him. "Forgive me. . .but I must move on. Maybe," he squeezed their shoulders fondly like a brother might do, "there will be another Dionysius and Damaris to be found."

Paul and Kristen shook hands with him. "Thank you. Thank you very much."

The man started to turn away but then he looked back at them and with a twinkle in his deep, deep eyes said, "You know, a good relationship with God is the cement that holds marriages together," and before either of them could comment, he turned away from them.

Kristen's mouth hung open in shock but not Paul's. Slowly, he turned to her and with infinite love radiating from deep within his being, he drew her close to his heart and gently cradled her within his arms. The wind whispered around them, caressed them, and seemed to push them together. But even more than the physical wind was that invisible thread, that spiritual force which they now knew was God, who drew them tightly together and bound them one to another.

And knowing that it was now right to do so, knowing from the deep groanings of his soul that had been answered by the man's words, Paul reached into his pocket and pulled out a small box that was delicately wrapped in silver paper with two white rosebuds made of the finest silk intertwined atop it. He handed the box to Kristen. "He's right, Kristen. A good relationship with God is the cement that binds marriages together. I've always known that our quest was important not only to our own personal lives but for whatever life we might share. . .together."

"Oh, Paul. . ." She held the box and looked from it to Paul. She knew what it contained. And she knew what he was about to ask. With her heart beating freely and more happily than she had ever thought it possibly could, she also knew what her answer would be.

"Kristen. . ." He paused and his eyes smiled, his mouth smiled, his whole being smiled at her. Her soul responded with a smile that brightly encouraged him to continue. "Would you do me the honor of becoming my wife?"

She threw her arms around his neck and together with the wind, whispered into his ear, "Yes, Paul. . .oh yes!"

He squeezed her to him. He felt as though his feet had left the earth and he was soaring through the evening glow with the swallows. The wind pushed them together and he knew that nothing could ever pull them apart. He loved Kristen with a love that he had never thought possible and he knew that it was because it was a love that had the backing of the One who was love. "Darling Kristen. . .so 'the ring of love' includes us after all."

Kristen stepped back from him to look into his eyes. "I think I knew that it would from the moment you told me the story. We just had to learn about God and accept His Son as our Lord before we could let our love become a part of the history of 'the ring of love.' It would have been. . ." She paused and searched around for the right words. "Kind of. . .backwards otherwise. After all, Christina and Paul loved God first and it was to God that Christina looked for the safety of her beloved."

"And it was because of her love and faith that he did return to her," he motioned to the package that still remained unopened in her slender hands, "and brought her this ring. Please open it."

Excitement bubbled up in her. The people on the hill faded into the background so that only she and Paul and the God who was no longer unknown to them remained. Slowly, knowing that this was one of the golden moments in life, she untied the ribbon, careful not to disturb the intertwined roses which she would keep forever, safe for her great-great-granddaughter, and slid her finger beneath the silver paper. But before she opened the lid of the blue jeweler's box, she looked up at Paul and said, "I love you, Paul. . .I always will."

He pursed his lips together in emotion and reaching out, he gently cradled her chin in his hand. "And I promise. . .never to let anything or anyone ever come between us. Not ever." She nodded, sure that he would always remain true to his promise, and looking back down at the box which contained the symbol of their love, the symbol of past loves too, she gently pushed back the lid and rested her eyes upon "the ring of love."

She gasped slightly but remained speechless. The circular emerald that glinted from the velvet box was warm and restful like a lazy spring day and yet as mysterious and timeless as the earth from which it was taken. It wasn't fiery but it was warm, and it wasn't icy but it was cool, speaking of all that must make up the love between a man and a woman. A temperance, a gentle sharing, a gentle love of giving and accepting one to the other. The emerald, flanked by diamonds and set among the strength of platinum, was an exquisite piece of jewelry.

"It's beautiful. . . ," Kristen finally whispered and removing it from the box, handed it to Paul. He looked at her in question.

"As my great-great-grandfather Paul did for his Christina, would you please put this ring on my finger?"

Paul took the ring and as it caught the setting rays of the giant sun as it set in the Grecian sky, he pushed the family heirloom onto the ring finger of Kristen's left hand. He looked from it to her eyes and knew that he hadn't been wrong in comparing her eyes to the emerald's beauty. But he also knew that the stone was a pale reflection in comparison. She had life in her eyes, something the stone could never hope to have. And with a longing that caught Paul almost unaware, he knew that he wanted to marry Kristen as soon as possible.

"Marry me, Kristen. This week."

With her left hand gleaming its joy in its new adornment she reached up and ran her fingertips across his cheek. "Yes, Paul. Whenever you want." She agreed simply and in so doing, knew that she was following the path of her life that had been laid down for her since the beginning of time. And as Paul wrapped her in his arms and they lowered themselves to sit and watch the sun as it slipped into its bed for the night, both reluctant to leave the wondrous site of their discovery of both God and one another, Kristen knew that she was doing exactly the right thing. For a fleeting moment, she wondered how her aunt would react to their news, but it was only fleeting, because to her, all that mattered at the moment was Paul and the God who had brought them together.

And she knew that if she could have, she would have married Paul that night.

Chapter 15

O h, Melissa. . .Luke. . .he's perfect!" Kristen said to the proud parents about the little bundle of baby boy she held in her arms the next morning. Walking over to Paul, she held the baby up for him to see and he automatically cooed a few baby phrases along with her.

Looking with love at his wife, Luke commented, "We traveled a very long road to become the family we are today. I really fought Melissa. . . and God." A sadness crossed over his face. "I fought Him and I blamed Him for things that I shouldn't have."

"How did you finally come to understand who He was?" Paul asked.

Luke laughed. "I finally realized that I had read every medical book I could get my hands on, tomes and tomes of books, hundreds of thousands of words, and yet, I had never read the Book," he admitted, looking over at Melissa, "that my dear lady here had been begging me to read." He turned back to Paul. "I finally read the Bible and I believed it. But," he laughed, "I don't know how Melissa had the patience to wait so long for me."

With love in her expressive amber eyes for the father of her child, Melissa softly replied, "Oh, I think you know very well where my patience came from."

Luke nodded and Melissa smiled at her husband before turning to Paul and Kristen. She stretched out her hand with its hospital bracelet dangling from her wrist to touch the ring on Kristen's finger. Kristen had told her all about Paul and her love and their quest before the men had arrived that morning, and Melissa was thrilled for her friend, especially since God was the foundation of their relationship.

"But you two are truly blessed to have your love happen so quickly and under such good circumstances. To have given yourselves to Christ and to become engaged all in one evening. . ." She shook her head, her long, nearly black hair shimmered like silk in the morning light.

"That's a miracle, I'd say."

Kristen grimaced. "I just hope my aunt thinks it's a miracle."

Paul drew his brows together. She had mentioned to him earlier her apprehension over Aphrodite's response to their engagement.

"Kristen—she will be thrilled for us." Paul had no doubts that what he spoke was the truth.

Kristen shook her head. She wasn't convinced. "I don't know, Paul. . .she wasn't too pleased with the idea of our spending an evening together. . . How will she react to an engagement?" Kristen just couldn't get out of her head that look of soul-stopping dread that had filled the older woman's face and her doubts wouldn't be relieved until after they told Aphrodite about their engagement, something they were planning on doing immediately after church.

Paul placed his arm around her shoulder and squeezed her close to him. "Don't worry. Nothing will ever come between us." Kristen smiled up at him. She wanted to believe that more than anything in the world. But as much as she didn't want to admit it, those old doubts of her being kept from happiness assailed her. Holding the baby close to her, she wondered if she and Paul would ever be so blessed as to have a baby of their own.

"Have you set a date for your wedding?" Luke asked, cutting in on her thoughts.

Paul and Kristen looked at one another and grinned.

"Well. . ." Kristen turned to Melissa. "That depends. . .when are you getting out of the hospital?"

Melissa's eyes opened wide. Carefully she answered, "Tomorrow morning."

Kristen looked at Paul and when he nodded yes, Kristen replied. "Well. . .we had thought about getting married a couple of days after you are released from the hospital. So I guess we'll be getting married on Friday."

"What?" Melissa's eyes opened wide in wonder and joyful surprise.

"I do need a matron of honor, after all." She put the little baby into her friend's arms.

"Oh, Kristen. . .I'd be honored!" She looked up at her husband and exclaimed, "What a week this has been! First our little baby is born, then Kristen's surprise visit, and now a wedding!"

Luke smiled, a special twinkle in his dark eyes for his wife.

"I'd say it's a week of miracles."

Luke and Melissa grinned at one another. They both knew that there was a time when the scientist in Luke would never have said such a thing. They both now rejoiced in his belief. It was the greatest miracle of all.

≪⬧

Kristen observed the pastor standing below the stained glass window that depicted the life of Christ and the spreading of His news into the world, including a panel of St. Paul preaching to the Athenians on the Areopagus. She could hardly believe that it was the same nearly drowned man whom she and Paul had pulled from the Pacific Ocean just a few short weeks ago.

With sandy blond hair and all-American good looks, Pastor Dean was a remarkably handsome man. Tall and husky, and built like an American football player, Kristen was amazed that she had found the strength to pull him onto the beach below her home. But smiling to herself, she now understood fully where her strength had come from. Her eyes moved again to the stained glass window above the pastor's head. God had been with them on that beach and He had saved not only the pastor from the waters of the earth's biggest ocean, but Paul and herself from the world's biggest lie, that made people believe that they could live a full life without God.

Kristen knew better now. And she smiled as she thought about Pastor Dean's message this morning about the brotherhood of all believers; it had touched a sensitive chord in her heart and it was as if he had spoken right to her. That need to have blood relatives which had been all-important to her a few weeks ago was now washed away in the understanding that all believers were her relatives. She was still very glad to have her aunt, a blood relative by human consent, but she now understood that she had a multitude of other relatives in the Lord to whom the blood of Christ bound her, brothers and sisters in Him.

She glanced up at Paul and then down at the ring that glittered on her finger. Paul, the wonderful man sitting at her side, had put it on her finger not twenty-four hours before. It was a symbol of their love and a symbol of the love of others of her blood who had loved before them. She rubbed her finger over the hard smoothness of the circular emerald. "The

Ring of Love." Their quest had made them a part of that circular "ring of love."

Seeing the direction of her gaze, Paul reached over and placed his hand over hers and together they rubbed the historic stone. She looked up at him and they smiled at one another. Kristen never before realized that people were allowed to be so happy.

Around them, people stood for the benediction. Paul and Kristen stood with them and, bowing their heads, prayed. Music played as the service ended and Pastor Dean smiled at them as he passed them on his way down the aisle. A soft murmur started as the congregation greeted one another with smiles and good cheer and slowly moved down the aisle to exit the church.

Kristen and Paul stood off to the side and waited for the congregation to greet Pastor Dean before greeting him themselves. He finished greeting the last person and with a beaming face, reached out his hands and enfolded Kristen in a hug such as a brother might give his much-loved sister.

"Kristen, Paul told me all your news on the phone this morning. Welcome, my dear sister in Christ."

Kristen pressed her check to his. "Thank you, Pastor Dean."

Pastor Dean laughed an infectious laugh. "No, it's me that's happy to finally be able to thank you in person for pulling me out of the Pacific Ocean. How can I ever repay you?"

Kristen tilted her head to the side and, casting an impish look at Paul before turning back to the pastor said, "Well. . .how about officiating at Paul's and my marriage next Friday?"

Dean smiled. "To officiate at your wedding would be my honor, Kristen." He turned to Paul and took his arm above the elbow in a heartfelt shake. "My honor indeed, Paul."

≫

It was hot and windy by the time Kristen and Paul turned into the driveway of Aphrodite's neoclassical mansion. The cicadas were grinding their feet and making a racket of sound in the pine trees that was nearly deafening. For the first time since coming to Greece, Kristen felt the heat and thought with longing about San Francisco's notoriously cool summers. She remembered how Mark Twain had written that the coldest winter he ever spent was one summer in San Francisco. She smiled at how apt a description that was as she dragged her heat-drained body up the marble steps that seemed to have heat radiating up from them, like bricks in an oven. Not even the strong *Meltemia* could ease the furnace-like heat of the day. It felt as though someone were fanning flames over the city.

But Kristen was honest with herself and knew that more than the heat, it was the dread she felt over telling Aphrodite about Paul's and her engagement that made her feel tired and lethargic, and if the truth were to be known, downright scared. Some instinct seemed to be trying to warn Kristen that the older woman was not going to take the news with joy. She paused on her climb up the stairs and lifted her hair off of her shoulders. The wind brushed against the damp curls and cooled her slightly.

"Is the heat getting to you?" Paul asked as he came up next to her.

Kristen shook her head. "It is hot today but. . .mostly, I'm apprehensive about telling *Thea* about us—"

"Kristen—" He smiled at her crookedly and reaching out for her hand, helped her to the top of the stairs before turning her to face him. "There will be no problems. Aphrodite will be thrilled to learn that we are to marry."

But doubt remained in Kristen's eyes. "I don't know, Paul. . . ."

"Didn't I tell you that no one would ever stand between us?"

Kristen hesitantly nodded.

"Well. . .that includes my godmother, your aunt. If she does try to cause a problem—something I feel certain she won't do—we will still remain together and we will be married next Friday."

Kristen bit her lower lip in apprehension and as he guided her into the coolness of the marble hall, she leaned her head wearily against his shoulder. "I hope you're right."

He tapped the tip of her nose and smiled. "I'm sure that I am."

He directed her toward the living room. "Now go sit down and cool off. I'll go find something cool for us to drink and be back in a minute. When Aphrodite wakes up from her afternoon siesta," his eyes seemed to dance his delight over the news they had to impart, and Kristen was sure that as much as she was dreading telling Aphrodite about their engagement, Paul was looking forward to it, "we'll invite her to our wedding."

Kristen took hope from his words and as she wandered into the living room she began to feel as though she were being ridiculous.

Her aunt had no reason not to be thrilled over their news. What could be more to the older woman's liking than to see her much-loved godson marry her long-lost niece? Aunt Aphrodite had been the personification of kindness since Kristen had come to visit, and Kristen felt as though her search for a blood relative had been fully realized in the person of her aunt. That the older woman loved her was obvious.

Kristen wandered over to the little painting by El Greco and she thought about the history that had taken place in the very room in which she now stood. Her father had grown up here. . .he had celebrated holidays and birthdays and graduations in this room. He had tried to celebrate his wedding in this room, but that celebration had led to his leaving the room, the house, and the country, never to return.

Kristen sighed.

Maybe, Kristen thought, *by telling of my and Paul's desire to marry, all that had been made so wrong all those years ago could finally be made right.*

She held up her left hand and ran the fingers of her right hand over and around the perfect workmanship of the round emerald that flashed in the afternoon light with all the brilliance of the God-made earth in its color.

The "ring of love". . .

Perhaps the ring of love had finally come full circle and the daughter of the woman that had been spurned was to weld it back together.

Kristen held the ring higher. The sun caught its angles and flashed.

Too late, Kristen realized that it was flashing a warning. With a voice barely able to contain rage, her aunt walked up to her side and exclaimed, "What are you doing with that ring?"

Chapter 16

Kristen whirled to face the older woman. Even more than the anger that was detectable in the older woman's voice was the soul-stopping dread that was now openly visible in her flashing eyes. *"Thea. . . ?"*

"I asked you a question." Her voice was like steel, and for the first time, Kristen understood precisely what went into making her aunt the formidable businesswoman she had become. "What are you doing with that ring?"

Kristen looked down at the ring. The platinum now seemed to burn into her flesh. She berated herself for not listening to her instinct. She had known, had sensed somehow, that Aphrodite didn't want Paul and her becoming more than just friends. The question was *Why?* It was that answer that now began to terrify Kristen. Why was Aphrodite so afraid of them becoming close? She looked back at the older woman. All traces of love and friendship and family ties seemed to have been wiped clean from the older woman's face. Kristen could only think that her grandfather must have looked the same when he sent her parents away.

That thought sent chills down Kristen's spine.

"Did Paul give you that ring?" the older woman ground out between lips that were white with anger.

"I did." Both women heard Paul answer from behind them, and Kristen couldn't have hidden the sigh of relief that emanated from her if she had tried. She was grateful when he placed the drinks he was carrying on the coffee table and came to stand by her side.

Aphrodite's eyes flashed in pain, in anger, but mostly in dread, up to Paul's. She reached for Kristen's hand and pulled it roughly with a strength Kristen didn't know the older woman possessed, up for them all to behold the offending ring. "What does this mean?" she demanded.

Paul gently removed Kristen's hand from Aphrodite's grasp and held it lovingly in his own. "It means exactly what you think it means, *Nona*." He spoke softly and in marked contrast to the savagery in Aphrodite's face and in her voice. "Kristen and I are to be married."

"Married!" the older woman spat out. "How dare you get involved with my niece!"

Paul's eyes narrowed. He was confused. And getting angry. "What. . . ?"

"I trusted you with my niece," she shot out.

Paul smiled and the anger he was beginning to feel vanished as suddenly as it had appeared. He thought that he now understood what she was concerned with and he was glad that he was honestly able to relieve her fears. "Then you have nothing to fear. I know it's an old-fashioned term but—" Paul looked over at Kristen and smiled. "I respect your niece. Nothing has happened between us that should only happen after marriage."

"Thank God. . . ," the older woman breathed out and, walking heavily over to her favorite chair, sank into its protective comfort.

Paul put his arm around Kristen and smiled reassuringly down at her as if to say, "There. The problem is solved." But Kristen didn't feel reassured. She only felt as though history was about to repeat itself and for some deep reason that only the past and Aphrodite knew, she was going to be kept from happiness with Paul.

Paul explained to Aphrodite, "Kristen and I fell in love while we were in California."

"So suddenly."

Paul grimaced and calmly responded, "Sudden love has been known to happen in your family before, *Nona*." He indicated the ring on Kristen's finger. "Remember—Paul and Christina."

Aphrodite nodded and seemed to be looking into another time.

"Yes. . .Paul and Christina. . .and. . .others. . ." Then she looked at Paul and the anguish in her eyes was real and strong and sliced through Kristen's heart. Her words made the cut even deeper. "But why didn't you say anything to me about your. . . ," she looked from Kristen to Paul, "your . . .relationship? I might have been able to prevent so much unhappiness."

"What do you mean?" The steel in Paul's voice was ominous. He didn't like the direction the conversation was taking again.

Aphrodite looked at Paul with that determined quality, that formidable quality that brooked no argument, that steel-like quality which was a match for his own. He saw it and recognized it for what it was.

Kristen saw it and quaked. She knew that somehow, something that the woman was going to say was going to keep her from a future with Paul. She could feel it in her very being.

Finally the older woman spoke, but that instinct Kristen should have listened to before was now warning her that her aunt was prevaricating and trying to hide the truth. "You are my godson. In the eyes of the church that is the same as being my son. That makes you. . . ," she seemed to stumble over the word and swallowed, "cousins. A marriage between the two of you will never be permitted."

Paul laughed. "That's archaic."

Aphrodite's eyebrows cut a straight line across her face. Paul's cut a straight line across his in answer.

"Nevertheless. . .marriage between you two will not be allowed." She spoke as if she were the empress of the land, decreeing their lives.

"Aphrodite. . . ," Paul began slowly. If she were the empress, he was the emperor. Tone for tone, steel for steel, soul for soul, Paul matched Aphrodite, and Kristen thought that it was as though they were the same person.

And it was then that Kristen understood.

It was then that she finally understood the truth.

And the knowledge of it sliced through her heart with all the pain of a dull blade and even as she heard Paul tell the older woman in no uncertain terms that they were going to be married the following Friday, Kristen knew that it was the older woman who spoke the truth.

She and Paul would never be allowed to marry.

Not in any church.

Stepping back from Paul, Kristen raised her hand to her mouth and bit deeply into her finger to try and keep from crying out. But she could not have muffled the cry that came out of her with anything. A strangled cry, it was a cry that came from her soul, a cry of anguish for a love that could never be.

"*No!*"

Paul was by her side. "Kristen. . .darling. . .don't. . .it will be all right." He looked over at Aphrodite, imploring her to stop hurting Kristen and as Aphrodite looked back at him, obviously wanting with all her might to stop her hurting words, Kristen wondered, through the cloud of pain that enveloped her, how she hadn't seen the resemblance between the two of them immediately.

It wasn't anything physical because by some trick of genetics Paul didn't resemble Aphrodite in the least. Rather, it went deeper than looks, it was as if their souls were the same, the parts that think and act and reason were identical.

Aphrodite looked away from Paul and met Kristen's eyes. In them now there was no empress. Just an old woman that was sorry—very, very sorry for the hurt history had to inflict on the two people she loved most in the world. Kristen saw it and reached out her hand to her. She somehow knew that the older woman, the woman who had never relied on anyone's strength but her own, needed her strength now, the strength Kristen was able to give only because of her new faith in God.

"Oh, *Thea*. . . ," Kristen whispered and gently squeezed the frail hand of her aunt, "I don't know why I didn't see it immediately." Tears formed in Aphrodite's crinkled eyes as she realized that Kristen had guessed her secret. "I'm so sorry Christina. . .so sorry. . . ," she croaked out in a voice that was little more than a whisper.

Kristen nodded and motioned to Paul. "You must tell him. . . ," she whispered.

"Tell me what?" Paul ground out and turned to his godmother. He was angry now, angry and confused.

Aphrodite suddenly looked old. Like an old warrior who had fought her last battle. In truth, she had battled throughout life so that this moment would never have to be faced. She glanced down at the ring on her niece's hand, the "ring of love." It had turned and twisted to bring them to this moment, this moment that Aphrodite had hoped never to arrive at.

"Tell him," Kristen gently prodded and squeezed her aunt's hand to give her the strength to speak the words that would forever keep Kristen from the man she loved.

"Tell me what?" Paul ground out again.

Aphrodite turned her tired old eyes to Paul. "That I'm your biological mother."

❧

Kristen pushed the door of her home closed against the cold and wet

November wind that blew off the Pacific Ocean. Crossing over to her living room, she placed her briefcase down next to the coffee table, intending on going over some papers during the long Thanksgiving Day weekend. Her glance rested on her little statue of the *Youth of Antikythera* before sliding away to the well-worn Bible that rested beneath it. Because of the Bible, Kristen was able to smile at the little statue.

When she'd first returned to California after learning that Paul was her first cousin, Kristen had hidden the statue away in her closet, the memories it invoked too painful for her to face. But gradually, because of the Bible, she was able to bring the little statue out and look at it and remember Paul, her aunt's son, with joy.

She no longer talked to the little statue as she once did. Rather, because of the quest she and Paul had taken together, their search for that Unknown, Something More, she now talked regularly to the God who was no longer unknown to her. Kristen knew that without her wonderful life-saving, personal relationship with God that was growing deeper and more precious with each passing day she would never have been able to survive leaving Paul. That she was related by blood to Paul was one of the great ironies of life. She had been desperate for blood relatives, had yearned for them. But finding out that Paul and she were too closely related to marry brought a sadness unlike anything she had ever known before. And she still couldn't quite believe it. Her feelings for him had never been cousinly.

Kristen kicked off her shoes and sat heavily down on the sofa, her wool suit bending with her, and reaching forward, she picked up her Bible. Holding it as one would hold the most precious, most redeeming, most comforting thing in the world—which it had become to her—she let herself remember that last day in Athens.

After her aunt had told Paul that she was his biological mother, she had gone on to explain how she had fallen suddenly and very deeply in love with Paul's father, whose name had been David. As might be expected, Aphrodite's father was against her marrying David from the start, even though David's family was one to be admired and one which had a long-standing political friendship with the country of Greece. But despite all their pleas and all David's promises to cherish and adore and keep Aphrodite safe and happy, Aphrodite's father had adamantly refused her permission to marry the handsome Englishman.

274

"War raged around us." Aphrodite's tired old voice had trembled as she told about her love for Paul's natural father. "It was a time when young, healthy people were alive one day," pain gripped her face at the remembrance, "and dead the next. So many friends. . .dead. . . ." Her voice trailed off, remembering that sad time of war.

"Tell me—" Paul swallowed a lump which had formed in his throat as he tried to assimilate that this remarkable woman was his blood mother. A part of him admitted that he had always known that Aphrodite was his mother and her pronouncement really didn't surprise him. What was confusing him now, however, was that that same part was crying out that Kristen was not his first cousin. Something didn't seem right about that and even though his heart was breaking thinking that there was nothing he could do to change the flow of mutual blood that filled their veins, he somehow felt that he had to learn all he could about the past, about his biological father, about Aphrodite and her family, in order to search for that missing something.

Paul Andrakos would not, *could not,* accept that Kristen and he had no future together. He would not accept it until he had searched and learned all that there was to know about that time and the people of that time.

Aphrodite looked at Paul and she reached out and rubbed her hand across his face as only a mother is allowed to rub her grown son. She smiled and Kristen felt that she said the words that she had longed to say for all the years of Paul's life.

"You are the image of your father," she laughed lightly. "I used to tell him that he resembled the statue of the *Youth of Antikythera* also." Her eyes sparkled as she looked back at Paul. "And he hated it too."

Paul smiled at that. Even though many men would feel anger and hurt and confusion over being told that their lineage was not what they had thought it to be, Paul loved and respected his *nona,* his biological mother. He felt certain that she had done the best she could with the situation she had found herself in all those years ago, and so he was able to sit and wait for her to tell her story and the story of her love for the man who had fathered him.

Her face turned grave with sadness. "My father would not give David and me permission to marry," she explained, looking at Paul with a degree of that formidable spirit which was so familiar to him. "But I loved David and he loved me so we did marry. We exchanged our wedding vows in a little medieval church overlooking the Aegean Sea. An American serviceman, who was a clergyman, officiated at our wedding but," she looked deeply into Paul's eyes, "the marriage was not one which the state of Greece, at that time, would recognize."

That news didn't bother Paul. He was sure that the marriage was legal in the sight of God and according to the American clergyman. "What happened to—my father?" he asked. That was important to him.

Sadness washed over Aphrodite's face, making her look old and frail and very, very tired. "We had one wonderful week together and then. . . he became a casualty of that dreadful, dreadful war."

Paul squeezed her hand and she looked up at him with brightness shining in her eyes. "But David left me with a gift. . .the most wonderful and beautiful gift he could have given me. He gave you to me, my son."

Tears swam in Paul's eyes as he pulled his mother into his arms and held her, as she held him, for the first time ever, as mother and son.

She pulled back after a moment to continue the story. Having begun it, she had to finish it now—all of it. It was a secret she had held for too many years and it weighed heavily upon her.

"I told my father about my marriage and about you and he was. . ." She glanced up at Kristen. "Well, let me say, he was even angrier with me than he was when Nick brought your mother to us years later, Christina."

"Oh, *Thea*. . ." In spite of her pain, Kristen felt for the older woman.

"But. . .how did my adoptive parents come to be my parents?" Paul needed to know. "You were all so close, such good friends."

Aphrodite nodded. "Our being good friends was a miracle. Your parents had been married for many years, and were still without the child they longed for. My father was an associate of your father's and knew of their desire. When he learned that I was pregnant he arranged it so that both your mother and I would go to live in a village. Supposedly, I went to care for your mother who, everyone was told, was finally expecting a baby. Of course, it was the other way around. But when we returned to Athens everyone thought she was the mother and I was the godmother of her beautiful baby boy. I loved your adoptive parents dearly, Paul. They were not only wonderful to you, my dear son, but wonderful to me. They knew the entire story and insisted that I be a part of your life," she grimaced, "much to my father's chagrin."

"I can imagine."

"The only time that my relationship with your parents—for they were your parents, Paul, in every way but blood—was in danger of faltering was when," Aphrodite looked up at Kristen and smiled sadly, "your father returned to Greece with his bride. I was appalled by my father's behavior and told him so. He warned me that if I became involved and sided with Nick and Jane in any way that he would tell Paul, who was just a young boy, about his parentage. So when my father demanded of your father that he give up his Jane and his unborn child, I was unable to come to his aid. Too many lives would have been hurt if Paul had been told about his lineage then."

"But. . .why didn't you tell my father the truth?" Kristen wailed. "So much pain would have been avoided."

Aphrodite shrugged her shoulders. "Looking back, it seems that would have solved many problems but at the time. . .I don't know. . .my father was formidable and had a mean streak in him that he never hesitated to use when crossed. All I knew was that I couldn't chance my father telling Paul. I just couldn't let that happen."

Tears fell down the lines of Aphrodite's face, following a course Kristen was sure they had followed many times before. "I just couldn't hurt your dear mother that way. . .nor your father. . .nor you." She looked over at Kristen. "So I remained silent when Nick looked to me for help. I remained silent," she repeated and looked across the room, across space and time to that moment, before looking back at Kristen. "And I'll never forget your father's look. To say I hurt him. . .it's not enough. I think that. . .I must have killed something within him with my silence."

"But you told him everything when you made up," Kristen reminded her, her own eyes wet with tears.

"Oh yes. . .I told him everything." She looked up at Paul. "Even that he had a grown nephew."

❧

"A grown nephew. . . A grown nephew. . ." The Pacific wind seemed to shout it out as it pushed pellets of rain up against Kristen's window and made Kristen aware of the cold November day once again.

She got up and crossed over to her patio door. The Pacific Ocean was a swirling mass of water and foam, gray and foreboding, dark and cold. Kristen shivered slightly. It was exactly how she had felt that hot August afternoon when she and Paul had said good-bye.

She had accepted the news of their close blood tie almost fatalistically, as though she had been expecting something to keep her from happiness with Paul.

But Paul hadn't.

"Kristen," he had ground out by the car that was to take her to the airport and away from him, "I don't believe that God would give us to one another only to have our relationship end so tragically."

"Paul. . ." She shook her head and tried to keep the tears from falling. But it was useless, as useless as their planning a life together had been. "Paul. . .it's hopeless. . .we. . .are cousins. First cousins. We just have to accept it."

"I do not accept it," he stated. "I will not accept it," he said more softly, "until I've searched all angles and found out everything that there is to know about that time. Something just isn't right. Something just doesn't fit."

Kristen looked down at her hands. "It's us that doesn't fit together," she said, and through eyes swimming with tears that blurred the emerald on her finger and made it seem bigger and more defused, Kristen tugged on the ring to remove it from her heat-swollen finger.

Paul looked at her aghast. "What are you doing?"

"Returning your ring."

"No!" He stilled her hand with his own but then quickly removed it from hers. Whenever they touched, it was as though they burned one another. "It's your ring," he reasoned. "Regardless."

She nodded. She couldn't fight him and he was right. As the only female descendant of Christina's and Paul's, the ring was hers.

But she really didn't want it. It mocked her love for Paul. "The 'ring of love'. . . ," she whispered. "I guess it doesn't include us, Paul," she said and stepped into the airport limousine.

Paul leaned his forehead against the window. "But it will, Kristen. It will. Something is wrong. Something. . .I will search and find out what it is. Please don't take the ring off until I'm satisfied that we have no future together."

She smiled bravely and nodded. If he didn't want her removing the ring, it was something she could do for him and she would do it. But she was quite certain that unlike their last search together, this one would not yield satisfactory answers.

Kristen shivered again. She wasn't sure whether it was from the cold November day or from her thoughts, but she walked over to the thermostat control and reaching out with her left hand, turned on the heater. The emerald flashed on her hand. Paul had asked her to wear it until they saw one another again. And she would. But she still thought it was useless.

She was not only cold but tired. She went into the kitchen, opened a can of tomato soup, made a grilled cheese sandwich, and then put herself to bed.

She fell asleep on that Thanksgiving Eve with a simple prayer on her lips. "Please, God. . .make everything right. . .please. . . ."

Chapter 17

I f possible, the day Kristen awoke to was even grayer and even wetter and colder than the one which she had fallen asleep to. She looked at the clock and was shocked at the time. It was past ten o'clock!

Her eyes traveled over the photos that were in silver frames on the table. In the one Melissa held her three-month-old baby boy high in the air in a happy moment of motherhood and in the other, Lottie and the new man in her life were posed romantically beside the world-famous cliffs of Santorini.

Kristen sighed and pushed back the down comforter that had kept her warm and toasty all night. The house was cold again so she quickly washed and dressed in comfortable but warm old jeans and her sweatshirt that had *Williamsburg, Virginia,* emblazoned across it.

She made coffee, switched on the TV to see which of the numerous Thanksgiving Day parades she could find, but paused in front of the set when a news story captured her attention. A reporter told the sad story about a promising athlete who was going to miss competing in the Olympic Games the following summer because of an automobile accident which had severely broken her ankle. What made the story extra sad was that it would make the third time in twelve years of trying that the runner, Niki Alexander, who had set a new world record the previous summer in middle-distance running, was going to miss out on the Olympics because of injury or illness. Kristen sighed. She could feel for the girl. Such a disappointment. A disappointment which was similar to her own simply because. . .it was a deep and cutting disappointment.

Flipping the channel, wanting the happy sounds of a parade to fill the house, Kristen walked into the kitchen and got busy with making the four pumpkin pies she had promised to make for the church-sponsored Thanksgiving dinner she was going to attend later in the day.

She had found a lovely church home after returning from Greece, one which was similar to the one in Athens in that it was filled with people who loved the Lord and loved one another like one always believed blood relatives should, but often didn't. They were Kristen's relatives now, relatives given to her through the blood of the Lord rather than through the blood of ancestors and in them Kristen knew that she had finally found the relatives for whom she had been craving.

She loved her aunt Aphrodite dearly, but she knew that it would be unwise for her to ever return to Greece. She loved her aunt's son too much for that. And not as one should love a cousin. She mixed the shortening, flour, and the salt together for her homemade pie crust and was vigorously slicing through it, her emerald ring flashing like green lightning as she worked, when she thought she heard the doorbell chime.

She paused and tilted her head to the side and waited. She wasn't expecting anyone and thought perhaps it was the TV playing tricks on her. But when it sounded again, she quickly wiped her hands on her apron, removed it, and rushed through the living room and over to the door.

She glanced through the peephole.

And *zap!*

She jumped back as though a laser had struck her!

Paul, the Paul who should have been *her* Paul, stood on the other side of her door.

She looked down at the ring on her finger and was amazed that at a time like this she should notice the bits of flour that were stuck to it. She was sure that Paul had come to tell her that his search had proven that it was time for her to remove the ring, and she just didn't know how she could bear the pain.

She squeezed her eyes shut on the pain that threatened to overwhelm her and prayed, "Dear God, help me. . .help Paul," as she slid the security bolt free of the lock and swung open the door to the man she loved.

"Darling Kristen," he reached out his hands and took hers in his and spoke the words she had longed to hear but had thought she never would. "We are not related to one another in any way."

"What?" she breathed out the question. It was as if the days, the weeks, the months had never parted them. They were continuing their parting conversation as if it had occurred only moments before. "We aren't blood relatives?"

His dark eyes swam with moisture as he pulled her gently to him and whispered into her ear. "The only blood we share is the blood of Christ which binds all believers together in a Christian family of brotherhood."

"Oh, Paul!" The relief she felt trickled out of her eyes as all the tears of sadness gave way to tears of joy as she nuzzled her nose against the warmth of his neck, savoring the scent of him, the feel of him, and knowing that there would be a future for them after all.

"But how? You aren't Aphrodite's son after all?" And she held him closer, wondering what traumatic discoveries he had made during the last few months.

He took a deep breath and gently tilted her head to look at him. "I am Aphrodite's son."

She frowned in puzzlement. "But if you're Aphrodite's son. . .and we aren't first cousins. . ." The possibilities were staggering and she let them dangle in the wind as she hesitantly considered them.

She didn't hear the older man step up behind her until he spoke. "Hello, Kristy."

"Uncle George?!" Kristen whirred around, totally shocked to see her uncle standing behind her. "What. . . ?"

Uncle George smiled and with a twinkle in his eyes asked of Paul, "Do you want to give her these now?" From behind his back he brought out a beautiful bouquet of red roses.

"Oh, they're beautiful!" Kristen accepted them and cradled them gently in her arms before looking at the two men in total confusion. "What's going on here?"

"Let's go in the house and we'll tell you," Paul said, and putting his arm around her shoulder, he guided her into the living room.

She put her roses on the coffee table next to her Bible, took their coats, and asked of her uncle George, "I thought you were supposed to be in China through the new year?"

"It will probably extend longer than that. I'll be returning tomorrow."

"Then why. . . ?" She looked from her uncle to Paul. "What's going on?"

Paul took her hand in his. "Remember how I told you something just didn't seem right about. . .our being cousins?"

"Yes, but. . .I don't know how you even got that feeling."

"Well. . ." Paul smiled and reached out to rub her face as only a man

282

who loves a woman can. "Other than not having cousinly feelings for you, something seemed wrong, like there was something important missing from the puzzle of our past which our ancestors had put together."

"Like what?"

"Like. . .how could a man reject and disown not only one, but two grandchildren, especially when that was all he had?"

"What do you mean?"

"I mean. . .my grandfather didn't want me because his daughter, Aphrodite, had married without his permission and had married a foreigner at that. And in the intervening years, she had made it very plain that she wouldn't ever marry again nor have other children. Then, one day his son arrives, married to a foreign woman who is expecting their first child. It just didn't make sense to me that our grandfather would make the same mistake a second time. . .unless. . .there was something more, another much bigger reason for him in his narrow-minded, bigoted way not to accept that second grandchild."

Kristen's eyes opened wide at the implications. Since Paul was Aphrodite's biological son, the only way for them not to be cousins would be if Aphrodite and her father weren't siblings or she wasn't her father's biological child. The thought was staggering. She turned amazed eyes to her uncle George, understanding now why her uncle was here.

"Uncle George? Is there something I should be aware of?"

Uncle George cleared his throat and looked uncomfortable, a trait Kristen had never seen in him before. "I wasn't sure whether I should tell you or not. I thought about it on your birthday," he said, reaching into the breast pocket of his coat, pulling out an envelope and handing it to her, "especially when you gave me these photos. But you seemed so happy for a change and I had no idea then that Paul was your aunt's son and that there might be a problem if you two became involved so—" He paused and shrugged his shoulders much like an adolescent might when explaining why he had returned home too late, "I adopted a wait-and-see attitude."

Kristen opened the envelope and the picture on top was the one of her mother with the man with laughing green eyes and dark wavy hair who was looking at her mother as if she were the woman he loved.

And then Kristen knew.

She knew why she and Paul were not first cousins.

She knew why her uncle was there.

She looked up at George, her eyes wide and questioning. But she wasn't questioning what she had already guessed. She was questioning the how of it all.

George nodded. "Raphael was your biological father." He confirmed her knowledge. "He and your mother were to be married the week after this picture was taken. Their love was one of which fairy tales are made. They loved one another dearly and you were the product of that love, conceived, your mother told Nick and me, the day before he was killed in that Rally race. She and Nick thought of you as a gift from Raphael. . .and from God. Even more as the years wore on and they were never able to have children, most likely because of the malaria which Nick suffered when he was a teenager."

"But. . .my parents, Nick and Jane," she qualified, "loved one another dearly. I know they did."

"Yes, they did." He paused and then continued. "You see Kristy, when Raphael died in that auto crash, Jane confided in Nick that she was pregnant. It was then that Nick told her of his love for her. He had always loved her, but because of his friendship with Raphael he had kept his love to himself. He begged Jane to marry him, promising to love and cherish her—and her baby—forever."

"He certainly did that." Tears swam in Kristen's eyes as she thought about the two men whom she could call father. The one had given her life, the other had sustained her life. Her mother had loved them both and so did she. It was as simple as that.

She looked down at the picture of her mother with the man who had fathered her. That her mother was in love with him was now obvious to Kristen's enlightened eyes and she was certain that she would have liked the fun-loving daredevil whose looks and blood she had inherited.

She turned to the next picture that showed the four friends all together and ran her fingertip lightly over the old photo, with a special pause for the father who had cherished and adored her and given up his family because of his love for her and her mother.

"I think I have been blessed in my fathers, in my mother, and," she looked up at the white-headed man who still looked so much like the laughing youth in the photo and putting her arms around him, squeezed him as she had always done and whispered, "in my uncle."

"Dear Kristy," he said patting her back, "both your fathers would be proud of you."

She looked back at the photo of her mother and Raphael. "I look like my. . .father. . .don't I?"

George nodded. "You're the image of him. Your eyes, particularly."

"I always wondered where I got my green eyes from." But now her green eyes looked at George in hurt. "But why didn't my parents tell me?"

Uncle George shrugged his shoulders. "I don't know. Probably, they wanted to. But they just kept putting it off until—"

"It was too late." She finished the sentence for him and at his sad nod, she smiled. "But you know, Uncle George, at this point it doesn't even matter. In fact, the news that they had probably dreaded telling me has become the best news I could ever have. It doesn't change at all how I feel about my parents, except maybe to love them even more now that I understand what they had to go through in order to have a life together. And best of all. . .it means that Paul and I can marry!"

"And that will be accomplished within the week," Paul was quick to reassure her. "Your aunt Aphrodite and James are planning a fabulous wedding reception."

"But not the wedding?"

"No. That she's leaving to us. She wants it to be our moment, our service, and held in whichever church or spot on this wonderful earth that we desire."

Kristen smiled but then a cloud passed over her face. "But she's not really my aunt."

Paul didn't say a word but rather reached for his briefcase and pulled out a box. He handed it to Kristen. "This is from your aunt. She said that you forgot it."

Kristen looked at him in question. He shook his head and motioned for her to open the box. She did, and gasped when she saw the old leather of Paul and Christina's Bible.

Paul took it from her and opened it to the family registrations of births and deaths. Above her name had been added Paul's name, his date of birth, and the name of his biological and adoptive parents. And next to her name was added the name of her biological father, Raphael Tores.

"In every way but by blood," Paul explained, "you are her brother Nick's child. She loves you as such and," he glanced at his watch, "she'll be calling you later to tell you."

"Oh, Paul. . ." Kristen could hardly believe that all she had hoped for, all that she had prayed for, was coming true and in a magnificent way whereby nobody got hurt. She put her arms around his shoulders and let herself lean against him. This is where she belonged and this is where she would stay forever.

Through a fog of happiness, she heard Uncle George clear his throat. "Well, I'm glad that I rented my own car. I'm going to leave you two lovebirds and be on my way."

Kristen turned to him. "Oh, but Uncle George. . .it's Thanksgiving. Won't you celebrate with us?"

He reached out and rubbed her cheek. "Darling Kristy, I think I just did." She smiled as the two men chuckled and shook hands.

"Thank you, sir, for all your help," Paul said.

"I still don't know how you tracked me down. I was quite literally at the end of the earth."

Kristen laughed, that light tinkling sound that made both men happy. "Believe me, Uncle George, when Paul goes on a search, he doesn't stop until he's found what he's looking for."

After her uncle left, with promises to try and attend their wedding, Paul took Kristen's hand and walked with her to look out at the churning ocean. His thumb played with the emerald ring on her finger, hers joined in with his.

Kristen spoke softly. "I've often stood here and thought about Christina and how she probably stood looking out at the churning sea below Galaxidi, turning and twisting her ring and wondering whether she would ever see her Paul again." Kristen took her eyes away from the sea and looked up at Paul, her green eyes soft and full of light. "And I wondered the same thing. . .whether I would ever see *my* Paul again."

"Darling Kristen. . ." He pulled her tightly against his side. " 'The Ring of Love' has turned and twisted to finally include us in its loving history—for that we have only God to thank."

Kristen nodded and rested her head against his chest. "Only God, Who showed us our paths—"

"And made our paths run together."

RACE
OF LOVE

To my wonderful children, Sara and Jay,
With many thanks for your help. . .and love. . .
May you always run with perseverance the race marked out for you!

Chapter 1

Niki Alexander leaned heavily on her cane as she trekked around the Olympic stadium. The pain in her ankle was great but it didn't come close to the throbbing in her heart. The injury to her leg was physical and understandable, and the pain was slowly diminishing with each passing day. But the pain in her heart was something complicated, made up of anger, bitterness, and disappointment, which was growing into a monster, consuming more and more of her with each passing day and turning her into a person she didn't recognize and didn't much like either.

She paused in her hobbling to pull her pink ski parka tighter around her waist. It was cold—freezing—and as a particularly strong gust of wind raced down from Mount Kronos she shivered and let loose with a cry that echoed the cry in her soul.

"Why God. . . ? Why. . . ?"

The wind took her mournful words and swept them sadly across this ancient stadium that had meant so much to so many people throughout recorded time. To run around Olympic Stadium, the Olympic stadium in Olympia, Greece, was a dream that Niki had held and cherished—a sweet reward for herself—for as many years as she could remember.

On that wonderful day in her dream, she ran the track to the cheers of a crowd of summertime visitors to Olympia, with at least one Olympic gold medal dangling from her neck.

But dreams are different from reality.

In reality there was no summer warmth and, except for a solitary man at the other end of the stadium, she was alone on this cold winter day. Very, very much alone. Instead of an Olympic medal swinging around her neck, keeping rhythm with her run, she swung an aluminum cane in a steady arc to support her lumbering gait.

She hadn't traveled to ancient Olympia as a reward for becoming an

Olympic winner but rather as a way of saying farewell to her dream, to the dream that God had given to her so long, long ago. . .before He'd deserted her. . .and taken her dream away. . . .

She shook her head and compelled her throbbing leg to take another step and then another, and another.

Forcing her body beyond what it wanted to do was nothing new to Niki. In order to set a world record in the eight hundred meters, which she had finally accomplished last summer at the World Games, she had pushed her body onward countless times when all it had wanted to do was rest. Now, however, she was pushing herself to do what was normal—simply to walk.

She paused and laughed mirthlessly, a bitter vibration that sounded her disappointment. She was listed in all the current record books as the fastest female middle-distance runner in the world today, yet she could hardly walk.

"What a joke," she grumbled to the crowdless stadium. Swinging her cane forward, she stumbled into the homestretch of the track.

The swirling dirt crunched beneath her orthopedic shoe, a far different sound than that made by running shoes—a heavier sound, an earthbound sound that mocked her laborious steps. How she wished that she could fly around this stadium as she had others barely two months ago. To feel her muscles stretching and striving to move her 120-pound body as fast as it could go, the pounding of her blood as it pulsed vibrantly on its way to her brain, the straining of her neck toward the finish line and the cheers of the adoring crowd.

In spite of the ache in her leg, Niki's body responded to the stadium like a bear to honey. She longed to run the last length of the ancient track, to be one with the wind as it pushed behind her, to be one with the athletes of old as she ran.

Her muscles twitched to do what she had been doing forever. To run.

She swung her arms a little faster, flexed her knees a little higher, but when her injured foot came down hard on a hidden stone she cried out, dropped her cane, and would have fallen if strong arms from behind hadn't miraculously caught her.

"I've got you." The words were spoken calmly as if by a loving father. Through the pain—a moment that felt as though the pins holding her ankle bones together had been yanked out of her—she thought they could be the words of her heavenly Father, words she'd been too angry to believe during the past two months. She trusted in them now as she clung blindly to her rescuer. Her leg hurt too much for anything but trust.

She felt her feet leave the ground and the relief from not having to support her weary and hurting body outweighed the embarrassment and fear of being carried across the stadium by a stranger. Without a glance, she knew he must be the man she had seen at the other end of the track.

Instinctively she wrapped her arms around his neck and rested her head against his broad shoulder. His strength comforted her and did more to relieve her pain than a shot of painkillers ever could. He was warm, and safe, and human, and he had been in exactly the right place when she needed him.

With infinite gentleness, her deliverer lowered her to the banked hillside that surrounded the stadium. As he stood above her, Phil Taylor watched the steady rhythm of her breathing. He had seen her hobbling down the backstretch when he'd entered the stadium and he wondered why someone with a cane would be so determined to circle the track on this freezing day. He looked at her face. It was white with pain and a film of perspiration had formed above her upper lip.

"Hey! Are you okay?" he asked anxiously.

The concern in his voice forced Niki to open her eyes. At first, she couldn't focus. She had to shake her head, blink several times, and rub her fingers roughly over her lids before her eyes consented to bring the man who leaned above her into focus. Like fine-tuning on a TV screen, his features slowly took form: thick hair the color of a blue-black summer night sky, and eyes as blue as a sun-filled summer day. Niki was sure she had never seen a more handsome man, and for the first time in two months, the throbbing in her leg and—even more importantly—the personality-changing hurt in her heart receded.

He looked like a movie star or, better yet, against the backdrop of ancient Greek columns reaching through time to show a glorious past, he looked like a handsome Greek god. *He could easily pass for Apollo or Hermes,* she thought whimsically.

"Are you okay?" Phil asked again. Her expressionless stare was beginning to worry him. "Shall I go for a doctor?"

Niki sat up and shook her head. "No, I'm fine. . ." Grimacing, she leaned down and rubbed her ankle. "This leg of mine. . ." She looked at him and smiled.

As her lips curved upward, Phil noticed how pretty she was. Strawberry-blond hair curled gently around a lovely, oval face and olive-green eyes sparkled between a fringe of dark lashes. Phil realized he had managed to assist one of the most attractive women he had ever seen.

"Thanks for catching me. . . . That was pretty great timing."

Phil chuckled. He felt light and happy now that his sudden companion seemed to be okay. "God's timing—it's always perfect," he responded automatically.

The serene curve of Niki's lips turned into a downward frown. A muscle jumped in her tightened jaw. Shifting her gaze away, she looked out over the stadium to where she had dropped her cane. The aluminum stick lay in the dirt, a silent but forceful reminder of her doubts. Absently, her fingers opened and closed on the grass by her side as she pulled at its roots.

"I used to believe that," she finally said in a voice that was unable to mask her bitterness, "but. . .I'm not so sure anymore."

Following the direction of her eyes, Phil knew that the confusion and doubt that now filled the air around them must have a lot to do with the cane. Leaving her side, he walked to the middle of the track, retrieved the cane, and brought it back. "We might not know the reason some things happen, but I do believe that God's timing is always perfect," he said as he set the cane on the ground next to her.

Niki took the cane and frowned stormily at it. For all her hard work and all her efforts to be cut off just when they were about to bear fruit did not seem like God had such great timing to her. But as she looked up again at the kind man who towered above her, she didn't want to get into all that, and when he extended his hand to help her up from the ground, she gratefully took hold of it.

"Well, it certainly was perfect today," she conceded as he eased her gently to her feet. "Thanks again for catching me."

He smiled and Niki liked the way his eyes crinkled at their corners. "Phil Taylor at your service, *Thespinis*." He bowed slightly, theatrically, and Niki was glad that her knowledge of Greek extended to the word that means "Miss."

"And I'm Niki Alexander."

Phil frowned quizzically at her name. He thought he had heard it somewhere before but before he could question her, she asked, "Do you speak Greek?"

He shook his head as he replied, "Just a few words. But I'm trying to learn it. My mother's parents were from Greece."

"So were my mother's!" Niki exclaimed. "Is that why you're here in Greece?"

"One of the reasons," Phil replied offhandedly. "And you?"

"I needed a change. My—" She started to say "coach" but quickly changed her mind. "That is. . .a friend of mine has a sister who owns a hotel near Corinth, in Cenchrea. She offered me a place to stay for a few months." She glanced down at her leg. "To recuperate."

"Cenchrea?" Phil pulled a New Testament out of his jacket pocket. "Do you mean the Cenchrea mentioned in the Bible?" Excitement laced his words.

Niki looked at the Bible and smiled in understanding. "You must be a Christian."

Phil nodded and asked quietly, hopefully, "Do we have that in common as well?" Her answer was suddenly very important to him. When she gently, almost reluctantly nodded her head, something in his soul jumped with gladness, and a smile split his face—a beautiful smile that made Niki feel as though the sun had suddenly come out on this bleak, gray day. She found herself grinning back at him.

Even though she was upset that God had allowed her leg to be broken at the worst possible time, she knew that to turn her back on Him would be very wrong.

Niki loved God, but she didn't know how to stop being angry with Him. She had always trusted Him and quite simply felt as though He had let her down. Her dream had been to win an Olympic gold medal and through it to witness to people around the world. It seemed as though God had taken her Olympic aspirations and had deserted her before she could "finish the race and complete the task." Her burden was too much to unload on her new friend, so she simply said, "Yes, I'm a Christian. I have been for many years. . .but. . .well. . .I have some things to work out."

Phil clicked his cheek. "I think we all do." He held up the pocket New Testament and continued, "This is the Book to help us though."

Niki set her cane purposefully before her and avoided his gaze. More than anything, she didn't want to admit to this obviously gung ho Christian that she hadn't read her Bible in more than two months. She had picked it up several times, but each time she had angrily tossed it back on her desk.

"Are you okay for walking?" Phil asked as he slipped the Bible back into his pocket. As she tentatively put weight on her injured ankle, he reached for her elbow to support her. She grimaced, but nodded.

"Yes. . .I can handle walking," she looked up at him and moved her lips wryly, "or my current variation of it. But I'd better leave jogging for another couple of months." Phil wanted to ask why she had been walking around the stadium on a broken leg but he sensed that she wasn't interested in talking about it. Instead, he kept his hand on her arm and as they walked slowly down the rest of the track he asked, "Where are you from?"

"Virginia." She turned her eyes up to his, acutely aware of his hand on her arm but glad at the same time, and not just because of the physical support. "And you?"

"Maryland," he replied, and he shivered as an icy gust of wind swept past them. "And except for the style of architecture to be seen here," he waved his arm toward the columns that were visible in the distance, "I feel as though I'm there now!" He pulled up the collar of his sheepskin jacket. "I thought Greece was supposed to be warm!" he complained goodnaturedly.

Niki laughed and as she did she realized that she hadn't laughed—really laughed—since her accident. "It is. . .in the summer."

Phil laughed with her, a happy sound that to Niki's ears seemed to celebrate life. She smiled at him and his eyes gleamed. In that moment a bond, a mutual thankfulness that they had met, was kindled between them.

"Well, Maryland is warm in the summer!" Phil finally said as they stopped in the shelter of the stone walls of the stadium's once vaulted entrance. Niki shivered and nodded her head in acknowledgment. Without the wind to buffet them they were warmer but still not warm enough for Phil. He had been at the ancient site since early that morning and he was ready for a hot meal. "How about we go to the modern village and get something hot to eat and drink?"

"I'd like that, but. . ." She looked longingly over Phil's shoulder toward the ruins of the Altis, the sacred grove where columns, walls, and stones lay scattered. "It seems a shame to come so far and not see anything other than the stadium."

"You went to the stadium first?" He was surprised. In order to reach the stadium, one had to pass the Altis. Phil had assumed that Niki would have toured the Altis on her way to the stadium, especially given her bum leg.

Niki shrugged her shoulders. "I. . .this was what I mainly wanted to see." She looked down at her leg. "I had to make sure I could make it, so I came directly here." She spoke softly, so softly that she almost wasn't audible over the wind. Phil began to realize that her visit to the stadium was some sort of pilgrimage, which explained her determined, hobbling walk around the track. Her head stayed lowered and Phil had to fight the urge to reach out and touch the silky strands of her hair as they played chase in the wind. Something about this woman tugged at his heart in a way he had never felt before. Maybe because he was a Christian now and hadn't met such an attractive woman—who was also a Christian—since he committed his life to Christ. No woman had ever moved him as much as this girl did. When at last she lifted her head and looked at him with her deep, intense eyes, he no longer felt the biting cold that whipped around them. Inside he felt warm and cozy and very, very happy. He smiled at her, a lopsided, questioning grin and motioned toward the historic site that had once held one of the Seven Wonders of the Ancient World.

"Do you think you can manage to walk it?"

The obvious joy in his smile reminded her of a world she once enjoyed without anger darkly coloring it. She returned his smile.

"I can—if I have a brother in the Lord to lean on," she answered before her nerve left her. She couldn't remember ever being so forward, but she really did want to see the ancient ruins and she knew she couldn't do it alone. But even more, she realized that she wanted to spend more time with this man. Phil held out his arm and the crinkles around his eyes deepened along with his smile. "At your service, *Thespinis*."

Niki giggled—something else she hadn't done in a long time—as she grasped his offered arm, and together they stepped away from the protection of the stone walls and out into the icy world of ancient Olympia.

"I really appreciate this," she shouted above the force of the wind that seemed intent on pushing them back against Mount Kronos.

"Appreciation not necessary." Phil leaned closer to her in order to be heard. "You're a sister in the Lord, a fellow American and," he looked at her with a look that turned her insides upside down, "best of all, you just saved me having to devise a way for us to get to know one another better." She dipped her head in acknowledgment, and her heart quickened with excitement that he felt as she did.

Her steps fell softly beside his and, for the first time in two months, Niki felt light and carefree. With Phil's hand on her arm, it was a revelation that she felt the joyful, free way that only running had ever made her feel before—as though the elements of the earth couldn't hold her down.

Chapter 2

Was there anything in particular that you wanted to see?" Phil asked as they walked through the romantic valley of classical ruins, surrounded by tall pine trees but no other people.

"Well. . ." Niki glanced up at him before continuing. The wind chose that moment to push his thick, longish hair—now several weeks past needing a barber—away from his face, showcasing his strong chin line, chiseled nose, and sensitive mouth in a most appealing way. Niki had met many handsome men during her twelve years in the sports world, but Phil was definitely one of the most attractive she had ever seen. But there was something more, something that went beyond the physical, something that reached toward the deep, inner part of her soul that made it throb with awareness. A feeling of completion, as if—

"Yes—?" Phil nudged her back to reality. Niki blinked her eyes and hoped that her cheeks were already red from the chill in the air. But Phil saw her blush and knew that it wasn't because of the cold. There was something special happening between them that was obvious to him, and the look of wonder that crossed his face told Niki all she needed to know. With this man by her side, in this place, she felt like she was on recess from the cares of life, the hurts of life. A fresh chill ran down her back as she realized that she felt just as she had always imagined she would feel when on her honeymoon. The implications of such a thought, with a man she had only just met, brought another blush to her face, and she quickly took refuge in playing the tourist.

"I'd like to see the statue of Zeus. Isn't it one of the Seven Wonders of the Ancient World?"

Phil's eyebrows rose and he smiled, a knowing smile that made Niki wonder if he could read her thoughts. "The statue was one of the Seven Wonders of the Ancient World—but it no longer exists," he finally answered.

She looked at him quizzically, trying to keep her mind on the subject of Olympia and not on him. "I didn't know that. What happened to it?"

"It was carried off to Constantinople some time in the second half of the fifth century and it disappeared in a fire shortly after that."

"A long time ago," Niki mused, shaking her head at the mystery of passing time. Often during the past few months she had thought about how life didn't need years or centuries in which to change, but only a twinkling of a moment. Whether it was a famous statue being moved, an accident, or a chance encounter with a man. . .

"That's the foundation of the temple of Zeus," Phil said, once again bringing her back to the subject at hand, "where the statue was housed." He pointed to a large rectangular base of stone.

"Wow!" she walked closer to the elevated site. She couldn't help but be impressed by its awesome dimensions. "Wasn't Zeus the king of the mythical Greek gods?" She tilted her head to the side, trying to remember her high school literature class.

Phil nodded. "He was the guy in whose honor the Olympic Games were held."

Niki shook her head in amazement. The columns of the once magnificent temple now lay on the ground like Tinkertoys without the middle stick holding the drums together, *As if,* she thought whimsically, *they had been pushed outward from the temple by the mythical god Zeus himself.*

"Do you know what happened to it?" she asked Phil, who seemed to be a walking encyclopedia.

"A combination of earthquakes, fires, and floods happened to it." He pointed in the direction of a river that was barely visible through the trees. "And during the Middle Ages, the Alpheus River changed direction and covered the entire area for centuries."

"Amazing. . .what a glorious place it once must have been," Niki murmured, trying to keep her mind on the ancient city. But with this man who did nice things to her equilibrium standing by her side, her mind wouldn't stay on Olympia. It didn't help that a gust of wind kicked up the golden dust of the ancient land around their legs, enchanting and sparkling. Ancient Olympia was transformed in that moment into a magical place where God had brought two of his children together to laugh and talk and play among the ancient stones and whistling wind.

Niki drew her eyes away from the once-upon-a-time city and met the silent calling of Phil's gaze. She felt the allure of the moment tighten around them, binding them with the dancing twirl of "fairy dust." Her natural inhibitions fled as she gazed without coyness or hesitation up at Phil.

Phil felt it too, the God-given magic of all that was good and right, as it wrapped its way around them. With a certainty he didn't question, he knew that he was looking at a woman who had very quickly come to mean a great deal to him.

The wind whooshed Niki's hair around her face and she watched as if in slow motion as Phil's hand reached out to tame it. As if she had been doing it forever, she turned her cheek to meet his hand. His eyes widened in surprise. He was glad that he hadn't resisted the urge to touch her this time, and he gently ran his fingertips over her cheek as if she were the most precious person in the world. For the first time, Niki felt cherished—cherished and adored—by a man.

She smiled at him and he looked quickly toward the horizon. "Come on." Phil's voice, husky and low, finally cut into the moment. "There's something I want to show you." With one last feathery touch on her cheek he lowered his fingers to hers, intertwined them, and started guiding her down the pathway. Trusting him totally, she walked beside him. The wind sang around them, now stronger than before. It played a wintertime symphony through the olive trees and around the fallen columns, but Niki hardly noticed. She was far too absorbed in her own storybook moment.

"I'm so glad God brought our paths together, Niki." Phil leaned over and spoke into her ear. "Thank you for not remaining a stranger for long."

She rejoiced as his words nearly echoed her thoughts, but when a gust of wind whisked his hair hard against his forehead, she took refuge in a laugh. "Are you sure you're not too cold?"

He gently nudged her closer to him. "Funny. . .but I don't even feel the cold." His voice was deep and masculine, with a hint of challenge to it. "How about you? How's the leg holding out?"

"What leg?" she answered airily, with an honesty Phil appreciated. He pulled her closer and pointed to a structure of stonework unlike anything else Niki had seen at the site. Not only was it built of different materials, but it still boasted walls as well as a definite shape. "What is it?" Her curiosity was piqued.

"This is the site of Pheidias's studio."

"Pheidias's studio?" She tilted her head inquiringly.

"The craftsman who sculpted the statue of Zeus," he explained.

"But. . ." Her eyes drifted again over the brick masonry of the building in front of her, "Why is it so different from everything else here? It seems—I don't know—newer somehow. . . ."

"Probably because it is. What you're looking at is an early Christian basilica that was erected over what was once Pheidias's workshop."

"Over his workshop. . ." Frown lines creased her forehead. "But why would people build a church over something as interesting as where Pheidias sculpted one of the Seven Wonders of the Ancient World?" She shook her head in dismay. "So many wonderful things must have been destroyed."

"Well, my own personal thought is that the early Christians constructed it because they felt as though the people of the land were still too closely linked to the ancient Greek ways and their array of Olympian gods. Maybe they wanted to honor God by building a place of worship for Him in the place where one of the most famous statues of a false god had been crafted."

"Maybe," Niki grudgingly conceded, but she hated the way this discussion was quickly destroying the magic of the place and turning the "fairy dust" back into plain, old, ordinary dirt. "But I don't think they should have destroyed Pheidias's workshop in order to build a church. God can be worshiped anywhere. In a church, a cave, a field, on a mountaintop, in the ruins of an ancient temple. . ." She pointed back toward the temple of Zeus. She remembered reading that throughout Greece, during the Middle Ages and after, ancient temples had been converted into Christian churches. The beautiful Parthenon of Athens was the most famous of all.

"I couldn't agree more." Phil left her side and walked up to what had once been the apse of the church and ran his hand across the stones. They were rough and cold beneath his touch, yet comforting to his soul somehow. "I wonder though. . .whether worship was even the main reason for the building of this church. I think. . .it was probably some early Christian's way of claiming, as it were, this land for God."

Phil's observation broke the magic of the place completely, like a mirror shattered into a thousand pieces. His choice of words couldn't have been worse. She understood what Phil was saying about the early

Christians claiming the city of Olympia for God, but all she could think about now was how God had "claimed" her Olympic dreams three times in a row. Not just once—not only this year—but during the two previous Olympics as well. The first time, it was an injured knee during tryouts; the second time, it was the flu; and now this stupid ankle. Anger filled her like the flash floods that had once filled the very valley where she now stood.

Her face lost all animation and became as hard and unbending as the ancient stones that surrounded her. She turned away from the church and Phil and hobbled as fast as she could over to a low wall. She sat heavily onto the stone and grimaced sourly as her leg—protesting her quick pace —shot painful waves from her ankle into her entire body.

The change that swept over her took Phil by surprise. He frowned at her, gave one last, friendly pat to the building that had impressed him so much that he had spent most of the morning there praying, followed her to the wall, and dropped down next to her.

The very air around her had changed, now charged with negative feelings that once again made Phil acutely aware of the cold winter day. The warmth that Niki's presence had brought to him only moments before was now gone. With the way she now stared icily down at her cane, Phil knew that her withdrawal had something to do with her injured leg, and something she had admitted she was trying to resolve earlier at the track.

"Niki?" He softly spoke her name.

She heard the concern in his voice, just as she had at the stadium. Squeezing her eyes shut, she endeavored, with all the determination that had made her a world-champion runner, to clear them of the misery that had claimed her. Thinking she had succeeded, she lifted her gaze to Phil. Sparkling eyes, that Niki hoped would mask the ache in her heart, beamed up at him. But the brightness didn't fool Phil. He knew that her eyes were too bright, too brilliant to be filled with real happiness.

"You know what I would really like to see?" She spoke in a tone that perfectly matched the false look in her eyes. "And then we can get that hot food and drink you've been wanting. . . ." Phil wanted to ask what or who had hurt her, but their friendship was still much too new for a question like that.

Ignoring the mood that had come over her, he smiled, shook his head, and said, "What would you like to see?"

"The place where the Olympic flame is lit for the modern Olympics." She paused and licked her lips. "Do you know where it is?"

He nodded. "I found it earlier."

"Would you please take me to see it?"

Her request surprised him almost as much as her hobbling around the stadium had, but quick to grab the opportunity to chase her black mood away, he stood and stretched. If Niki had known him longer, she would have recognized the mischievous glint in his eye and been prepared for what came next. In an instant he reached down and lifted her into his arms as if she weighed no more than a feather quilt.

"Phil! What are you doing?" she squealed, instinctively wrapping her arms around his neck.

"Taking you to where the Olympic flame is lit," he replied, blatantly ignoring the fact that he was carrying her. He was very pleased that his impromptu act had dispelled whatever had been bothering her—her amazed and amused laughter proved that.

"Phil!" she squealed again but in a delighted sort of way. "Put me down! You're going to hurt yourself."

"Relax. I grew up carrying boxes of books that weighed much more than you. I've developed 'carrying muscles.'"

"Carrying muscles!" she exclaimed, and in spite of herself, she relaxed in his arms. "Never heard of them."

He smiled down at her. They were so close now that Niki could feel his frosted breath against her face and smell the manly scent of his after-shave. She liked both sensations.

"They're muscles that enable a rather large man like myself to carry damsels in distress across Olympic stadiums and ancient cities," he explained.

"Phil. . .are you sure?" She felt so comfortable being literally in his arms that she really didn't want him to put her down. And if she needed an excuse, she had to admit that with all the walking she'd been doing that day, her leg was tired and was hurting quite a bit.

"I'm sure, and besides. . .boxes can't hold on to me. Having your arms around my neck really makes carrying you much easier." He wanted to add, "And much more pleasant as well," but he didn't.

It was totally out of character for Niki to rely on someone else, but she found that she liked stepping—or, in this case, being carried—out of what was her normal self. Reassured, she settled down in Phil's arms and rested her head against his shoulder with a familiarity normally reserved for longtime friends.

Meanwhile, Phil couldn't help but notice that her hair smelled like springtime and her body, wrapped in her pink, down-filled jacket, was soft and warm against his chest. He was glad that his arms were occupied with the task of holding her. If she had been walking beside him, he was sure that he would not have been able to keep from embracing her anyway. Being a Christian certainly hadn't diminished his masculine desires in any way. It had taught him, however, that the physical union between a man and a woman was something sacred, given by God, as a trust to be enjoyed and cherished between a husband and a wife only and not something to be treated carelessly as he had in the past.

Niki was not a person he would ever treat carelessly. In the course of the last few hours, Phil had realized that he didn't want to let her slip away, and he was slightly startled when the thought occurred to him that he would rather carry her forever than risk losing her.

Niki clung to him with closed eyes. The security she felt, the warmth, was unlike anything she had experienced during her adult life. His walk was smooth, his movements measured for her comfort, and she felt herself drifting into a never-never land of emotions where the magic of before was recaptured. It was almost a miracle that she was letting a man whom she had only just met carry her around ancient Olympia. Niki Alexander—the same Niki Alexander who had always been so self-sufficient, so capable, so determined—now admitted that, for the moment at least, she relished her dependence on this man. She didn't want to analyze her feelings—for once, she just wanted to be happy. She closed her eyes, and closed her mind to all thoughts.

A few minutes later—or was it a few hours or a few days?—Niki heard Phil ask, "Hey, are you asleep down there?" She blinked open her eyes to find Phil's grinning face only an inch or two from her own. She couldn't believe that she had actually fallen asleep, but she had felt so warm and so comfortable that her tired, aching body had switched off in response.

"I think I might have drifted off," she admitted self-consciously. His smile widened in mirth, his eyes crinkling even more at their corners, and Niki knew that if she wasn't careful, she would lean forward and kiss him on those friendly lines. The thought shocked her and her face burned!

Phil stopped walking. She looked away and her eyes scanned the graceful columns of what had once been the aqueduct of Herodias Atticus. She wiggled for him to put her down. Slowly, reluctantly, Phil lowered her to the ground.

"I've been here," she said as her feet touched the earth.

Hand in hand, they surveyed the location. With a tilt of his head, Phil indicated the entranceway of the stadium.

"You passed it on your way earlier."

Niki nodded. She had her bearings in Olympia once again, but as she looked down at their hands intertwined together, she wasn't so sure about her bearings where Phil was concerned. She quickly decided that she wasn't going to dwell on it. She had let him carry her, not once but twice, and had even fallen asleep in his arms. The parameters of their friendship were already far different from the normal. Smiling softly up at him, she simply said, "Thanks for carrying me."

He rubbed his thumb against the sensitive part of her wrist. "Anytime."

She squeezed his hand in response and with her other hand pointed up at the temple that was beside them. "That must be the Heraion, the temple built to honor Hera."

Phil nodded. "Zeus's wife. It's the oldest temple in Olympia." He pulled a set of postcards out of his pocket and showed them to Niki. "There aren't any signs marking the location of the lighting of the Olympic flame, but I figured it out from looking at these."

Niki glanced down at the pictures that showed the ritualistic ceremony. Modern women dressed in the ancient Greek style of dress solemnly lit the flame from a sun dish and then passed it on to a twentieth-century athlete. Niki didn't need to look at the postcards closely because she had watched the dignified ceremony via satellite during the previous two Olympics. Looking around, she knew that this was definitely the spot. A lump formed in her throat as she remembered the hopefulness she had felt both times she had watched the flame spring to life from the heat of the sun. She had already decided that she wouldn't watch the ceremony this time. She wouldn't even think that it was happening a short two hours away by car from where she would be staying. Abruptly, she let go of Phil's hand, and with a muffled groan she turned away and started the long walk back toward the entrance of the ancient site.

The wind was strong and biting. Niki wished that she could run. She hadn't missed running more than at this moment. If only she could use her legs the way they had been trained, she knew she would have been capable of breaking her own world record. Instead, each step took the energy of three and acutely reminded her of her pain: The pain in her heart was again far greater than that in her leg. She had hoped that coming to Olympia would ease the pain, but it had only intensified it.

"Niki?" Phil called after her and in a few quick strides he caught up to her. Her mood had plummeted once again, just like at the church and at the stadium before that. She turned to him but this time her eyes were bright with tears that swam in their sadness. He pulled her to himself and she was glad and relieved to lean against him. "Niki. . .what is it?"

She shook her head against his shoulder. She wanted to tell him, but she was afraid that if she did she would break down completely, and she didn't want to do that. "Please, Phil. . . ," she whispered against his ear, "take me away from here."

Phil didn't need to hear another word. Gently, reverently, he lifted her into his arms and began to walk. He was impervious to the wind as it pushed against him. His desire to protect Niki was stronger than any gale. Neither said a word as they passed the ancient temple and the site of the ancient gymnasium. For Niki, words would just bring more tears. All she wanted right now was to get away from this place of pain, this place of disappointment. But through her tears, she also realized that Olympia was the wondrous place where she had met this wonderful man. She buried her face in Phil's sheepskin coat and recalled the words he had spoken at the stadium: "We might not know the reason some things happen, but I do believe that God's timing is always perfect." The words echoed in Niki's mind. As she clung to Phil's neck, she had to admit that God's timing seemed perfect today. She didn't know what she would have done if Phil hadn't been in the stadium this morning. He had rescued her both physically and mentally. She only wished that he could rescue her spiritually as well.

Chapter 3

A crackling fireplace welcomed them to a restaurant in the tourist town of modern Olympia. It was warm and cozy and just what they needed. In an atmosphere of warmth and good cheer much like a Christmas Eve, Niki and Phil thawed their icy fingers and toes. They talked for more than an hour as the fire blazed and the sky outside finally decided to send flurries of fluffy snowflakes upon the ancient land. As they chatted, Niki and Phil discovered some tangible reasons behind their mutual attraction. It wasn't that they were exactly alike, but their interests hovered in the same vicinity.

Niki learned that Phil loved working with young children and that his dream was as simple, and as difficult, as wanting to be an elementary school educator. It was a dream that had been thwarted countless times, however, because of the demands placed on him by his father, who expected Phil to follow him into the family business—the bookselling business where Phil had developed his "carrying muscles."

Phil loved books; he just didn't want to sell them. Instead he had spent years procrastinating at the university and had become a perpetual student. He earned his MBA and a doctorate in literature to appease his father, but Phil was the most pleased when he received his simple teacher's certificate, and it was that credential that he hoped to use once he returned to the States from Greece next summer.

Phil learned that Niki was pursuing a master's in sports education but that she was taking a break from school and planned to spend the next few months at her friend's hotel in Cenchrea. Phil mentioned that he had spent the last few weeks cycling around Greece, but when he asked Niki about her sports interests she quickly changed the subject and asked him, "Where are you going to be cycling to next, Phil?"

Frown lines crossed Phil's forehead at the way Niki sidestepped his question, but he quickly decided not to challenge her. Niki had been deeply hurt—as her mood swings during the day had confirmed—but he knew that it was a subject she would have to freely broach on her own. He wasn't going to push her. He liked her too much to push and risk losing her.

"I've gone all over the Peloponnese," he finally answered. "So I think I'll head up toward Patras, take the ferry across the Corinthian Gulf and go to Delphi before settling down in—" He paused and the name of his destination slid off his tongue as a question: "Cenchrea?" He was asking her not only if she would like to see him again but if she would like to give their quick and extraordinary friendship a chance to grow into something more.

Phil didn't realize that he was holding his breath until he saw the light of joy that jumped into her eyes. He finally exhaled as his soul sang in tune with her obvious pleasure. He wished that he could always be the one to put gladness into this woman's eyes.

"Do you mean it?" She reached over and took his hand in hers. She was thrilled at the prospect of seeing him again. Now she could look forward to developing their friendship and—even more exciting—she could look forward to feeling wonderful again because he would be with her. She had dreaded saying good-bye. Just knowing their "farewell" wouldn't be final filled her with the hope that her future wouldn't be ruled by unwanted anger and bitterness.

"I have to settle somewhere," he pointed out laughingly. "It's about time I thought about making a little bit of money. I've heard that English teachers are needed everywhere in Greece, and. . ." He looked at Niki with eyes that were suddenly soft with caring and appreciation. "And. . . I like you very much, Niki. If you're sure you don't mind my coming to Cenchrea—?"

"Mind!" She laughed gleefully. "I couldn't be more pleased!"

Phil's eyes crinkled at the corners in the way she had grown to love. He was quiet for a moment before he spoke in a tone that was serious and almost reverent. "Somehow, Niki. . .I think God brought us together today for a very definite reason."

"Oh, Phil. . ." She didn't know whether he was right or not but she wanted to believe that Phil would play a bigger part in her life. She liked the person that she was when he was around. Squeezing his hand, she softly replied, "I hope so."

He rubbed his thumb across the knuckles of her fingers. He knew it was a cliché but he couldn't help feeling as though he had never really been alive before. He was nearly thirty but he had never truly cared for a woman who wanted more than just a quick fling or someone who just wanted him to spend lots of money on her. Niki seemed real to him. She was alive in a way that the women he had spent his time with before he gave his life to Christ had never been. Not even close.

It was obvious that Niki was hiding a lot of pain, yet she was still a lady. She was a lady who had the imprint of her Lord stamped into the fabric of her life, and nothing would ever change that. It would be an understatement to say that he was pleased that she wanted him to come to Cenchrea.

"Tell me," Niki cut in on his thoughts, "is there a reason why you chose Greece to cycle around? And why now? It's winter after all." She laughed and pointed out the window at the big, fat snowflakes that danced to the earth like celebrating fairies. "And I've already seen how much you dislike the cold!"

Phil returned her smile but as he turned to look out the window, a grave expression covered his face, effectively removing the cheerful lines from around his eyes. He appeared to be watching the fluffy flakes of snow falling on the street but Niki was sure that he didn't see them.

After a moment he expelled a deep breath and said, "Something happened a couple of months ago—many things actually—" He flashed her a self-conscious smile. "And well—I thought it was a good idea to leave home for a while. I came to Greece for many reasons, not the least of which is the fact that I have a great-uncle who lives here who I really wanted to get to know. He's a fantastic man."

Niki wanted to ask more about the mysterious something that had happened a couple of months before, but she didn't want to pry. Instead, she asked about his great-uncle.

"Tell me about him," she softly prompted. "Is he a relative of your mother's?"

Phil nodded. "Her uncle—her father's brother." He glanced down at his watch as if the mention of his uncle suddenly reminded him of something. "I'll tell you about him sometime, but there is one more place I wanted to visit today. It closes in an hour. Are you up to it?"

Niki glanced at her watch. "I don't know. . .is it close by?" She had arranged for a taxi to wait for her and she pointed now to the short, balding driver, who she had discovered had a heart as big as his gaily decorated cab. "With this weather my taxi driver will probably want to leave soon."

"It's not far. Just around the corner and up the block." Phil vaguely waved his hand in the general direction.

"Well, what is it?"

"Let me surprise you." With her background in sports education, Phil was certain she would enjoy a visit to the museum he had in mind.

"Okay," Niki agreed, ready to go anywhere with Phil in order to prolong their time together. "Let me just ask my cab driver if he minds waiting a little bit longer." Reaching for her cane she stood and walked over to where the man sat drinking coffee and playing backgammon with a fellow cabby. Her driver didn't mind waiting, but he cast a concerned glance out the window at the weather and asked where she was going so that he could collect her afterwards rather than making her walk back in the snow.

Niki motioned to Phil. "Unless you're planning to carry me all over modern Olympia as you did ancient Olympia, I think you'd better tell him where we're going."

"I don't mind carrying you," Phil responded in the playful manner that Niki was coming to expect from him. Rolling her eyes, she motioned to the cab driver who was watching their exchange with interest.

"Honest, I don't," Phil said with a slow smile but he turned to the driver and said, "The museum here in the town. Take a left at the second corner and it's the large building at the top of the road."

"Okay, okay. . .I will come soon," the cabby said in heavily accented English. Just then, a gale-force wind hit the building, rattling the windows and sending a puff of dark smoke shooting out from the fireplace. The driver jumped up from the table with more speed than his rotund body seemed capable of, grabbed his coat, and said, "No. I take you now!" He pointed to Niki's foot. "It might be slippery."

Phil took a quick dash outside to check the conditions. It was snowing but it wasn't sticking and it wasn't particularly slippery. After a lively negotiation with the cab driver, who was treating Niki more like a beloved daughter than a paying fare, they agreed to meet the cabby at the museum, and Niki and Phil took off on a walk through the streets of modern Olympia.

Niki enjoyed gazing in at the various tourist shops, but she wasn't looking at the statues of Hermes or the souvenir plates displayed appealingly in the windows. Instead she was looking at Phil's and her reflection in the glass and she couldn't quite believe that she was the girl with the handsome man's arm around her shoulder. At twenty-seven, Niki had never been in love. Oh, she had had boyfriends, mostly other athletes who understood the demands on time and energy that competing at a world-class level required, but never anyone who made her breath catch, or that her body thrilled to be close to, or someone who made her want to watch his reflection in a window.

Phil guided her around a corner and—whoosh! Niki's cane flew out of her hand and she staggered in the forceful wind that hit her squarely in the chest. She was sure that she would have fallen if Phil hadn't held her tightly against his solid body.

"Wow! This is amazing!" she laughed, thrilled as a little child might be as snowflakes ran wildly before them like white mice in a maze. "I have to admit I always pictured Greece as being sunny and warm, too. . . ." She shivered deeper into her bright pink parka.

"Ha!" Phil bellowed out above the wind. "The truth comes out at last. And here I thought I was the only one who was surprised by such arctic conditions!"

"But I love it!" Niki was quick to qualify. "Who would ever think that Olympia, home of graceful Greek antiquity, could be painted with snowflakes?"

"Well, much of Greece is on the same latitude as Washington, D.C., so I guess cold weather should be expected."

"And most of the country is mountainous," she pointed out the obvious.

"Don't my cycling legs know it!" he laughed and indicated a white building at the top of the road that was just about lost in the dizzy dancing of the swirling snow. "We're almost there."

"Does this museum have finds from the ancient site?" Niki looked quizzically at the unassuming building.

"No." Another gust ripped down the street and Phil pulled Niki even closer to him until he was practically carrying her again. "This museum has 'finds' from the sites of all the modern Olympics."

"The modern Olympics. . ." Niki mouthed the words into the collar of her coat and the roar in her ears had nothing to do with the wind but everything to do with the pain in her heart. She gaped at the building before her. She had known that there was a museum honoring the modern Olympics in the vicinity, but she had thought it was near Olympia, not in the town itself. She had purposely ignored its existence. With both resentment and fear coloring her vision, she continued to stare at the building before her.

"It's the Museum of the Modern Olympics." Phil proudly recited the name. He had wanted to visit the museum ever since he arrived in Greece and, caught up in the excitement of the moment, he was totally oblivious to the frozen expression that now covered Niki's face. "It has the most extensive display in the world of stamps commemorating the Olympics. I wanted to look at the ones from the 1936 Olympics. . . . My uncle participated in them and there's even a picture of him hanging in here."

Niki's head swiveled to him. "Your uncle?" she asked, surprised. A combination of the swirling snow and Phil's totally unexpected words made her feel as though she were floating in a surrealistic world where coincidence laughed at her. Snow in ancient Olympia and now this? *But what should I expect?* she thought ruefully. Of course other people who had some connection with the Olympic Games would travel to where they all began. Wasn't she being egotistical to believe that she was the only one? And why not snow? Greece wasn't a tropical country, after all.

"Yes. . .the one who lives here in Greece. My great-uncle," Phil said with obvious pride that stood in stark contrast to the pain that Niki felt at the thought of going into the museum. She didn't want this pain. Walking around the Olympic stadium was supposed to have helped it go away. It hadn't. Would a visit to the museum help? She looked at the building with a mixture of resentment and curiosity. She had never been jealous of fellow athletes' successes because she knew how much hard, grueling work went into being a winner.

Squaring her shoulders and drawing on some of the strength and determination that used to get her out of bed an hour before dawn every morning in order to train, she decided to go into this museum and try for a moment to forget about her own attempts to be a part of it. Instead, she would concentrate on Phil's uncle and all her friends who were Olympians. With her newfound determination she quickly, almost demandingly said,

"Tell me about your uncle." Phil's sharp look told her that her conversational timing was off. Taking a deep breath she forced herself to speak more slowly and calmly.

Pasting a smile on her face, she prompted, "The 1936 Olympics. . . Berlin, right?"

"Right." Phil nodded, but fingers of apprehension tickled the back of his neck. Carefully regarding her, Phil saw that her eyes were too bright and her smile didn't quite jibe with the look in her eyes. He was certain that she was once again trying to mask a deep hurt.

"I've always admired Mr. Owens very much," she continued, bravely trying to fight with chitchat the anger that was threatening to explode from her like a volcano. "He won four gold medals and humiliated Hitler in the process. Your uncle was very lucky to have been a part of that Olympics. Did he win any medals?"

"No, he didn't. . ." Phil decided it was best to follow her lead for the moment. "But. . .he told me that he won just by being there—by taking part."

Niki sucked in her breath as if someone had hit her in the stomach. Startled, Phil turned to face her. Part of him was glad to see the too-bright mask slip away but the rest of him was hurt terribly to view the naked pain that had been hidden beneath it. Gathering her close against his body, he wished he could protect her from whatever was distressing her. "Niki? What is it?" he begged her to tell him.

"I'm sorry, Phil. . . ," she spoke dejectedly into the fleece of his jacket as she pointed an almost accusing finger up at the museum. " I. . .I don't want to go in there."

"But why?" he asked with more demand in his tone than he had intended. He took a step back when a challenging spark suddenly replaced the despair that had been in her.

"Why?" she trembled with anger. "I'll tell you why! Because when I was driving my car home from. . .from training. . ." She stumbled over the word so she didn't notice how Phil's eyes widened or that the blood seemed to drain from his face, "Some partying. . .fools. . .crashed into me. . .and did this to me." She pointed with her cane down at her injured ankle.

"Training?" he questioned through a throat that had suddenly gone dry.

She nodded and sharply tapped her hand to her chest. "I was an

Olympic contender." She jerked her thumb toward the museum. "I was going to participate in this year's Olympics."

"The Olympics!" Like fission tearing the earth apart, Phil felt himself tremble. "Dear Lord—" he breathed out.

"Yes. . .dear Lord!" Niki shot out sarcastically. Bitterness toward God, bitterness toward the beer-drinking fools who had rammed into her, bitterness toward her life as it now was, all gave force to her words. Turning suddenly away from Phil, she limped toward the taxi as it drew up to the curb. Phil reached out and caught her arm. He couldn't let her go like this. He needed some answers. She turned to him and frowned at the confusion that she saw in his eyes.

"When did it happen?" Phil finally asked, an effort that brought sweat to the hollow between his shoulder blades.

Niki couldn't understand why it mattered to him but she managed to croak out, "Last November the third."

Phil squeezed his eyes shut. He felt as though someone had just kicked him in the gut. When he opened his eyes, the pain in Niki's face was now mirrored by that in his own. But where her pain was flavored bitterly with anger, his was saturated with guilt.

"Niki," he finally spoke, "I'm so sorry. . ."

"Yeah. . .everyone always is." Bitterness made her speak through her teeth, through trembling lips. "Except for the beer-drinking fools who did this to me," she spat. She turned back toward the cab. Through a fog Phil watched her go. Stunned, his feet wouldn't move. It wasn't until he saw her open the door and struggle to get into the cab with her cane and with snow falling like bothersome bugs all about her that he realized that she was about to leave; about to leave his life.

He ran to her side, sliding slightly on the wet sidewalk.

"Niki. . .?"

She turned to him and it nearly tore him apart to see that her too-bright smile was back in place. He understood now what was behind it—and he wished that he didn't. "I'm sorry, Phil. . .it's not your fault. . . ." He stiffened at her assurance but she was so intent on trying to make up for letting her bitterness come into open display that she didn't notice it.

"Are you. . .will you still come to Cenchrea?" Her eyes scanned his with hope. She feared that her outburst might have destroyed whatever chance they had of a future together. *Will I come to Cenchrea?* Phil questioned ironically in his mind. Knowing what he now knew, nothing could keep him away. He nodded. "Soon," he assured her and watched mutely as she nodded and then lowered herself into the backseat of the car. There was so much that he wanted to say, so much that needed to be said, but he knew that it would have to wait—until Cenchrea.

As the cab crunched away from the curb, Niki watched him through the back window standing by the cold, wet curb. She was disgusted with herself. More than anything, she was afraid that clinging to her Olympic dream had destroyed her one chance to get to know the first man she had ever loved. As the taxi moved down the road and she watched Phil grow smaller and smaller in the distance, she knew that she had indeed fallen in love with him. She leaned back in her seat as tears of pain mingled with tears of the loss of love.

Chapter 4

P hil watched the taxi as it drove down the road. The gray sedan gradually blended with the gray of the sky and the gray of his thoughts. Niki's pink ski parka, now barely visible through the back window of the cab, was the only spot of color in Phil's suddenly gray world. And when the taxi turned the corner and took Niki away, that little bit of color was gone too.

On legs that felt like jelly, and blinded by the swirling snow, Phil turned and stumbled up the marble stairs of the museum. It was only when the guard looked at him strangely that Phil realized that it wasn't the snow but tears, now coursing down the strong lines of his face, that blinded him.

Swiping at his eyes with the back of his hand, he walked into the warmth of the museum. But he felt no warmth. He was freezing, much colder than he had felt all day—even in the icy, swirling winds in the ancient stadium.

He trudged through rooms filled with memorabilia from every modern Olympiad, from the first, held in Athens in 1896, through the present day. Medals, pictures, even the torches used to bring the Olympic flame into the Olympic stadiums around the world over the past hundred years were there. Phil sighed, found a bench in a secluded corner and sank his suddenly exhausted body onto it. Now he understood why Niki had walked around the Olympic stadium and why she couldn't bear to stay where the flame-lighting ceremony took place. He understood too well, much more than Niki could ever know.

Reaching behind his head, he laid his fingers against the long scar concealed by the thick hair on the back of his head. Yes, he definitely understood.

He rested his head against the cold wall behind him and his mind drifted back to that morning—the morning that had changed his life.

He had awakened in a hospital bed. . .his head felt like it had split wide open or was ready to split open at any moment. The glare from the overhead lights thwarted his attempts to open his eyes.

He heard rustling in the room and moaned crossly, "Mom. . .what are you doing? Turn off the lights and leave me alone."

"Well, now—" an unfamiliar woman's voice replied.

Phil's eyes flew open in spite of the misery it brought to his senses. The room around him wasn't his own and the woman dressed in white standing over him was most definitely not his slender, small-boned mother.

"As you can see, I'm not your mother and as to leaving you alone, it's my job to be here with you." She paused and Phil's eyes finally focused on a large, black woman who stood by his bed, thermometer poised and ready in her hand. "Now I can either take your temperature with your help or—" She glanced down at the sheets that covered his lower body, leaving little question as to her intent if he didn't open his mouth.

Phil opened his mouth.

He was able to open his mouth, but his brain refused to work. He looked again at the huge, rawboned woman. After a moment, she removed the thermometer and grunted her approval.

Phil touched his head and discovered it was bandaged. "What happened?" He looked around the room. "How did I get here?" he demanded autocratically, which was his normal tone of voice.

"You don't remember a thing." The way the big woman stated it made him feel about the size of an ant. Phil started to shake his head but the motion made him nauseous. His lips twisted in pain.

"Nothing."

"Probably due more to your hangover," she spat out as if it were the most offensive word in the dictionary, "than to the bump you took on your head."

"What happened?" he demanded again. "And where are my parents?"

"Your parents are probably trying to keep you out of jail, and as to what happened, you were in an automobile accident late last night."

Phil squeezed his eyes shut, trying to recall. He couldn't remember the crash but he remembered the car. "I wasn't driving," he said, as if to justify himself. His voice had the fractious tone of one who was accustomed to blaming others for his actions. "Why are my parents trying to keep me out of jail?"

With sudden insight he remembered his partying friend, John. His eyes stretched wide in panic, and fear made him oblivious to the pain that sliced through his head. "John! He wasn't. . .I mean. . .he's okay. . . isn't he?" The fright that now laced his voice took away its antagonistic force. In the very long moment that it took for the nurse to answer, Phil knew an anxiety unlike any he had ever experienced before. He knew deep down that if John had been killed in the accident, Phil was to blame. It had been his idea to go out that night. John had wanted to stay in front of the TV and watch a football game. Phil had been the one to insist on picking up a six-pack and going to discos and barhopping.

"Yes. . .he's fine," she finally grunted. "Your friend didn't even get a bump on the head. He went home last night."

Phil's relief was immediately overshadowed by the selfish anger he felt toward this woman for scaring him as she must have known her silence would. "Why did you let me think that something bad had happened?" he lashed out. His head pounded back at him as if a million drums were beating.

The nurse's dark eyes hardened and became as piercing as a laser. For the first time since he was a little boy Phil quivered under the mantle of authority. "Something bad did happen. Oh, don't worry. . .*your* friend is fine. But the girl. . ."

"Girl. . . ?" Through the haze in his throbbing head, Phil tried to remember if they had picked up a girl along the way. It had happened before. But, try as he would, he couldn't remember anything other than the wind in his face and the ever-present feeling of discontent that had fueled his beer-drinking binges since he was a teenager. "What girl?" He hated that he was at this woman's mercy.

"The girl that your car smashed into."

Phil sucked in his breath and, for the first time, he truly felt the weight of his fast life. To have been hurt himself didn't bother him much. But to have hurt a girl—an innocent person—to know that someone else was injured by his lifestyle struck terror into his heart. It scared him a million times more than if John had been hurt. His anxiety was almost unbearable. "You mean. . .we didn't hit a tree. . .or a sign?" he asked weakly.

"No. No tree or sign—like the previous times." Revulsion radiated from her, as though Phil had some foul disease, and he wondered vaguely whether she knew about the other two crashes. "No, this time you had to smash into a twenty-seven-year-old girl," she spat out.

Phil struggled to remember the accident. Had they run into another car? Or. . .a pedestrian? A fleeting image of the night before scared away all of his antagonism and selfishness and left behind a raw human being, shaken beyond belief. "Is. . .is. . .she. . .alive?"

The woman grunted. "She's alive."

Relief flooded Phil's mind, but with it came an egotistical anger that this nurse would have deliberately upset him and put on such an attitude toward him. Wasn't it her job to comfort him?

"She suffered a severely broken ankle." Phil closed his eyes and grimaced. "Thank God," the woman continued, "she was wearing her seat belt." The way she said it sounded to Phil like she really was thanking God. "She didn't need to get smacked on the head too—unlike somebody I know."

Her jab only served to further irritate Phil. He opened his eyes and looked at her crossly, his fear and regret forgotten as quickly as a high-school algebra lesson. "So, she's okay. She'll recover?" After thinking that he and John had killed someone, a broken ankle seemed like a joke. If the girl played her cards right she might even collect big money from his father.

"Oh, she'll recover—" the nurse shot out, jarring him away from his self-serving thoughts. "The question is. . .will her dream ever be recovered?"

Phil looked at her as if she were crazy, and with disdain bending his otherwise handsome features, he demanded, "What are you talking about?"

The nurse's disgust for Phil was as stark as her white uniform. "I'll tell you what I'm talking about, young man! You and your drinking buddy managed to break the ankle of an Olympic hopeful. That girl won the world championship for middle-distance running last year. She was going to win a gold medal for this great country of ours—that is, until you and your friend stole it from her, and from the American people."

"Oh!" he groaned. Athletes and teachers were the only two groups of people that Phil admired. To think that he had been responsible for hurting an Olympic runner, well, he actually did feel some true remorse.

"Yes, oh, God. . . ," the nurse agreed, and this time Phil had no doubt she was speaking literally. She turned to the dresser and picked up the Bible that was supplied by the hospital. With what Phil could only describe as reverence, she laid it across his stomach and said, "Maybe you better read about Him. . . . He's the only one who can give you what you need. . . ," she picked up his chart and read his name, "Mr. Theophilus Taylor." She seemed surprised by his name, which was no surprise to him. He hated the name Theophilus. It was a throwback to some ancient relative whom his mother adored.

"The name is Phil," he corrected her irritably.

The nurse confounded Phil by smiling, and he was amazed to see that she actually looked human. He had begun to think she was a tormenter that his brain had conjured up in its pain-filled state. She picked up the Bible and flipped through its pages with a familiarity that seemed very religious to Phil. She opened it to a certain page and grunted in amazement at something she read there. "Maybe you should start with the Gospel of Luke and then the Book of Acts—*Theophilus.*" She put special emphasis on his much despised name. "Looks like it was written to you." She handed the open Bible to him and with a curious chuckle following behind her big frame, she left the room.

Phil's eyes rested on the Book. He came close to angrily flinging it onto the cold, linoleum floor, but his curiosity won out. He picked up the Bible and scanned over the first few words of the text. His eyes hurt and he wondered what sort of nurse would suggest that a person with a head injury should read. Nevertheless, he was determined to find out what she found so funny. He read the first few words but his brain couldn't or wouldn't assimilate anything.

He started over and read out loud from Luke 1:1–3: " 'Many have undertaken to draw up an account of the things that have been fulfilled among us, just as they were handed down to us by those who from the first were eyewitnesses and servants of the word. . . ,' " Phil mumbled. He still didn't understand a word of what this first-century religious man was writing but he forced himself to continue. " 'Therefore, since I myself have carefully investigated everything from the beginning, it seemed good also to me to write an orderly account for you, most excellent. . .' " Phil's voice faltered as the next word jumped out at him: " 'Theophilus. . .' "

Phil looked away from the Book to the brightness of the window. He understood the nurse's mirth. "Theophilus. . . ," he murmured. He had no idea that one of the Gospels had been written to a man who shared his name. Phil had to admit that he was pleased. It seemed such a silly thing, as silly as when children feel a special kinship with one another when they discover that they share the same name or the same birthday, but something within him melted. For the first time he could remember, the dark despair of living a life that seemed senseless—a life that now had destroyed the dreams of a girl who had some goals and direction—began to lift.

Phil continued to read, eager now to discover what this man named Luke had written to his friend—Phil's namesake—Theophilus.

He read until his eyes began to blur from fatigue that evening. The next morning, he grabbed the Bible first thing. He went from the Gospel of Luke to the Book of Acts, which he discovered was also written by Luke to the man named Theophilus, and then on to the other three Gospels of Matthew, Mark, and John. But it wasn't until the third day, when he read from the Book of First Corinthians, "Therefore I do not run like a man running aimlessly; I do not fight like a man beating the air," that the book, the Holy Bible, that most wonderful of all books ever written, became more than just a book to Phil, more than just a work of literature. On that third day it became a way of life for Phil. After three days of reading, really reading and paying attention, Phil called out to God to save him as he now believed from reading the Bible that God would.

Before that moment, that wonderful lifesaving, soul-satisfying moment, Phil knew that he had spent all the years of his miserable, bored life senselessly beating the air and aimlessly racing through each day to arrive nowhere. And he didn't want to live that way any longer. After reading the words of the Bible, after thinking about them and believing them, Phil was ready for the new life it offered.

The guilt he felt over destroying the young Olympian's dream weighed heavily upon him and he knew now that the only way to deal with it was to become a new person in Christ. He couldn't wear his old self any longer without sinking under the weight of its guilt so he grabbed hold of the promises of the Bible, like a drowning man clinging to a life preserver, and let God pull him out and far away from his aimless life.

With deep remorse he asked God, the God who had changed his life, to let him somehow make it up to the girl whose dream he had destroyed.

He didn't know how God might accomplish it, but even though Phil's faith was new, it ran strong and true, with a resilience that many long-time Christians could only wish to obtain. Phil harbored no doubt that someday God would show him the path to take that would let him help the woman whose dream his old life had destroyed.

Phil left the hospital with a bandaged head but with a heart that was totally different. It was as if his heart had been transplanted, a transplant that required no bandages. He kissed the wonderful nurse who had cared enough about one miserable rich man's son to point him toward the correct path in life. He understood the tears of joy that sprang into her eyes, and his eyes shone with tears of his own.

Telling his mother about all the changes that had taken place in that hospital bed was easy. She didn't understand everything but that didn't diminish her joy. She thought that the change in her son was nothing short of miraculous and secretly wondered if the nurse was an angel. His mother was thrilled by his decision to travel to Greece and encouraged him to get in touch with her uncle Theophilus.

Phil had smiled over that. To meet his namesake was the main reason Phil had chosen Greece over any other location. That, and a deep desire to study and learn more about his God in the land where many Bible events had taken place. To visit ancient Corinth, Cenchrea. . .Athens! The places where some of the apostles had actually walked would inspire and stimulate Phil's Christian walk. He decided that he would cycle around Greece in order to be a little bit closer to them, closer to the land where those men of faith had walked.

Phil's father was livid when he heard of Phil's proposed trip. The changes he saw in his son after the accident had led him to believe that Phil might finally be ready to take his place in the family business, but Phil had used the accident as an "excuse" to totally alter his life. When Phil informed his father that after his Hellenic travels he would be following his dream of becoming an elementary school teacher, his father had laughed—a savage, hard, bitter laugh.

"And what mother would trust you to teach her little darlings?" he had sneered, his face a distorted reflection of the son who was formed in his image. "When they discover your reputation—for women—for drink—ha! They'd never trust you."

With a grimace, Phil remembered when he had acted just like his father. But now, out of respect for the man who had fathered him, Phil spoke gently, as a son should speak to his parent. "Dad, I'm not like that anymore."

But his father didn't believe him. Even more, he didn't want to believe him because, as strange as it might seem, the one thing Phil's father had always admired in Phil was his quick, partying lifestyle. Phil's father took a perverse pride in knowing that his son was able to have any girl money could buy. When he threatened Phil with cutting off his allowance if he didn't stop "playing Christian," Phil responded with a gentle smile.

"Thanks, Dad. . .I wasn't quite sure how to tell you that I didn't want an allowance any longer."

When Phil left Maryland and flew to Greece, all that he took with him was his new Bible, a mountain bike, a knapsack with a few clothes, and lots of dreams and prayers. His mother saw him off with a few of her own prayers and Phil had the satisfaction of knowing that at least one of his parents was happy over the changes God had wrought in his life.

Phil cycled around the country of Greece, or Hellas, which was the official name of the country, the name by which the Greeks knew their country. He went up one mountain and down the other, and the one after that, and the one after that, and the one after that. He had time to think, time to pray, time to simply be.

Phil became close to his Maker and, for the first time ever, he became close to himself. With slow understanding he came to realize that he had spent his life in senseless activity in order to avoid being alone with himself. But he didn't have to do that anymore. He found that he actually liked himself. He could easily sit under an olive tree for hours as the sounds of nature played around him. One day he sat on a boulder in a hidden cove and watched the waves as they lapped against the ancient shore. He could do it for an hour, for two hours, or even an entire day and never grow tired of the experience. Phil discovered, as he peddled his bike around the Peloponnese of Hellas, that he was never truly alone. His God was with him everywhere. And Phil thought that was miraculous.

Phil visited his old relative and was not disappointed. Great-Uncle Theophilus lived near the top of one of the many mountains in Greece. He lived in a little stone house that had running water and electricity but only an arched fireplace to chase the cold of winter out of the air.

"Wood heat. It's good for the bones," the old man said as he pushed the end of a long log into the flames, and Phil thought there must be something to it. He'd been with his uncle for about two weeks and had discovered in that time that the old man, at eighty, could still run races around most of the world's population. And that wasn't just in walking. Great-Uncle Theophilus was a giant of a spiritual man. He too had been very impressed at a very young age to learn that Luke had written his two letters to a man named Theophilus.

"You know. . .here in Hellas names are a chain that runs through time. I was named for my grandfather, he was named for his grandfather, and so forth. I kind of like to think that it was an ancestor of mine to whom St. Luke penned those two letters," his crusty old uncle admitted.

Phil had never considered his ancestry before, but he did now. "And I was named for you. . . ," Phil quietly responded.

The old man nodded. "It's quite a legacy we carry, boy. . .quite a legacy." To say that the old man had been happy to see Phil would be the understatement of the year. When Phil had pedaled up to his uncle's mountaintop village and his uncle had beheld him for the very first time, a light had jumped into the old man's eyes.

"I've been waiting for you," the old man had said and Phil was sure that he had. Phil had sat with the old man on his old stone verandah for weeks and they had talked about everything under the sun. Great-Uncle Theophilus was the father that Phil's own father had never been. A man of knowledge, a man of philosophy, a man of God, Great-Uncle Theophilus taught Phil as God had intended old ones to teach young ones from the beginning of time. Phil learned about the spiritual world and the natural world from that wise old sage, and when it was finally time for Phil to continue on his way, it was with the understanding that Phil always had a home with his uncle.

The old man watched with his cronies as Phil cycled out of their village. The look on his weathered face was one of knowing his namesake would return and so, as he turned away from the wild and free view of mountaintops undulating in the distance, he smiled the satisfied smile of a man who has found his son.

Phil visited ancient temples and medieval castles before turning toward ancient Olympia, a place that meant so much to his great-uncle. . .

And. . .to Niki.

Phil sat up and away from the cold wall. The museum guard was standing in front of him. "Sir. . .we close now." The man spoke in broken English. Phil nodded and stood, stretching his legs out in front of him.

As he walked toward the door of the museum, he paused as he realized that he hadn't even seen the picture of his uncle that he had wanted to see. But one glance at the face of the guard, who obviously wanted to go home and eat his midday meal, convinced Phil that Uncle Theophilus would have to wait for another day.

Pulling his collar up around his neck, he stepped out into the cold of the January day. It had stopped snowing and, amazingly, the sun had even come out to warm the earth. Phil paused on the steps and smiled into the bright rays. It wasn't a thin, wintery sun that covered his face but a strong sun of strength that warmed the blood beneath his skin.

Phil smiled. *What humor God has to take a day and give it so many different feelings,* he thought as he walked down the steps and toward the center of Olympia.

And what humor God had to bring Niki and him together in such a way. He had asked God while still in his hospital bed to let him someday help the girl his old life had cost so much, and here God had placed them together, the only two people to visit ancient Olympia this day.

Phil threw back his head and laughed. "Thank You, God," he shouted to the deserted streets. "Thank You," he whispered with respect for God's mysterious ways. Phil knew where he was going. First he would return to his great-uncle's mountaintop retreat for a time of Bible study and prayer. Then Phil was going to Cenchrea—to help the woman he loved.

Chapter 5

In one fluid, smooth motion Niki rolled out of the shoulder stand she had held for several minutes and onto her bare right foot, gracefully holding her injured leg off to the side.

"Are you sure you're a runner and not a gymnast?" Niki heard Mary, her coach's sister, ask from the doorway of the hotel gym. As Mary walked across the gym, she glanced around the room with the practiced eye of an entrepreneur, looking for anything that needed repair or attention. Flashing a quick smile, Niki turned to greet her friend. At forty-five, Mary was a stunning woman. Tall and slim, with just a few strands of silver highlighting her long, chestnut waves, Mary was a study in grace and peace. She kept her hair pulled back at the nape of her neck with a colorful scarf, which brightened the traditional black worn by widows in Greece. Mary was a woman of faith, looked up to by those around her, and Niki loved her like a sister.

Mary's husband, many years her senior, had died suddenly the previous year, leaving the resort hotel for Mary to manage. Though grief-stricken, Mary had not wallowed in self-pity. Instead she worked doubly hard to make the resort a success for herself, her eleven-year-old son, and the sundry people like Niki who needed a home. Normally, the winter and spring months were too slow to warrant keeping the hotel opened, but Niki was amazed by all the paying guests who were there for extended stays. Niki admired Mary immensely.

"There's poetry in all forms of sport," Niki finally answered as she started rotating her waist from side to side as far as she could go, her legs slightly apart.

Mary's amused laughter followed her as she bent down and rubbed her hand over a small section of the carpet that was unraveling. Niki was certain that by the following day the carpet would be mended to look like new. Mary kept the hotel in tip-top shape.

"You sound just like Bill," said Mary, referring to her brother and Niki's coach. Niki smiled again. To find the music in sports, and the ballet to go with it, was the essence of Bill's coaching. And it worked. Niki had found the music to match her strides at the championship races the previous summer and she had won. She flicked a sudden, angry glance down at her still slightly swollen ankle. If only it hadn't betrayed her. Following the direction of Niki's eyes, Mary spoke quickly to encourage her.

"You've made amazing progress, Niki. You walk easily without a cane now and I haven't seen you limp in over a week."

"Until the pins are removed," Niki huffed as she continued to exercise, "I'm not allowed to put too much pressure on it. Walking is about the only thing that is allowed," she said with disgust. To a runner, walking is akin to crawling.

Mary frowned. "Is it permissible for you to be exercising in this manner?" she asked, and Niki couldn't help but smile at her correct manner of speech. Although Greek was Mary's mother tongue, she spoke English more precisely than most native speakers.

"It is permissible," Niki replied, using Mary's word. "But floor exercises and swimming are best." To make her point, Niki lay down on her back and went into 'The Plough.' She slowly raised her legs straight up and over her head, touched her toes to the floor behind her head and held the position. "But I'm so out of shape." She twisted her head to the side to look at Mary. "I get so winded doing things that were nothing just a few weeks ago."

Mary smiled. Niki didn't sound winded to her. But she didn't challenge her. "You have to be patient, Niki. You're doing very well."

"I'm doing lousy," Niki bit out, but she immediately felt bad. She hated the self-pity that assailed her practically every moment of every day. Who was she to feel such anger compared to the trauma that Mary had gone through during the last year? First, Mary's husband had died, and then her eleven-year-old son, Stavros, unable to come to grips with the loss of his father, had developed phobias that manifested themselves in tics and fears for his mother's safety, which were just about to drive Mary crazy.

Niki breathed out deeply and, lifting her legs above her head and back to the floor in front of her again, she stood and walked over to Mary. "I'm sorry. I didn't mean to sound so egotistical."

"I know. . ." Mary gently touched her hand to Niki's shoulder in understanding. "But you are doing better," she insisted.

Niki nodded but didn't say anything. For someone recovering from a severely crushed ankle, she knew that her recovery was far better than average. But for an Olympic contender it cut deeply to know that she was definitely out of the running. She sighed audibly. Mary's problems, her problems, they were sometimes too much for her to think about. She was glad for the excuse Mary's presence in the gym gave her to change the subject.

"So, what brings you down here?" Niki knew that Mary would have to have a definite reason to leave her busy office at this time of day. Mary slowly intertwined her fingers in a way she did whenever she was hopeful or thoughtful about something.

"Well, I do have a favor to ask. . . ."

"Anything." Niki was curious. So far, Mary had refused her numerous offers to help out at the hotel in any capacity. Mary gave Niki a long, thoughtful look before plunging in with her request. "When some of the hotel guests learned that a world-champion runner was staying here, they wanted me to ask if you would mind organizing an exercise program for them."

Niki sighed again. *Anything but that*, she wanted to say. But she didn't. She owed Mary too much to turn her down, plus she knew that Mary hadn't asked lightly. Mary never did anything without thought. But oh, how Niki would have preferred to wash pots and pans or clean every toilet in the hotel for a month rather than organize an exercise program for guests.

Reading Niki's thoughts, Mary quickly continued, "I know how you feel, Niki. I know how hard it is for you to be constantly reminded of what you lost out on, and doing something like this will be a reminder, but—" Mary turned away and wrapped her arms around her chest in a way that could almost be defined as defensive as she looked out at the sea that shimmered beyond the little whitewashed chapel on the hotel grounds. Mary's dark eyes focused on the chapel—where she had been married, and where her husband's funeral had taken place. She breathed out deeply and looked back at Niki, refusing to dwell in the past.

"Sometimes, Niki, the best way to help yourself is to help others."

Niki's lips curved into a sad, little smile. "Is that what you do, Mary?" Niki asked quietly, respectfully.

Mary nodded and the pain of the past year made her softly accented words sound husky. "It keeps me remembering that I'm not the only person in the world with a problem."

Niki knew that the problem she was referring to now was her son. The death of her husband was something she couldn't do anything to change and though she missed him terribly, Mary had the believer's comfort of knowing that he had been a Christian and that he was now safe with God. But Stavros and his personality change was something that could and must be dealt with. Bright and cheery before his father's death, the little boy was a worried, pale reflection of himself these days, and he seemed to be getting worse rather than better. For the last week, getting him to go to school was like going through a war.

"Did Stavros get off to school okay today?" Niki asked.

Mary sighed almost helplessly. "He yelled and screamed and finally made me promise him that I would be alive." She paused. *"Alive,"* she repeated with sad emphasis on the word, "when he returned from school." She shook her head. "He never used to yell before—he's just so afraid."

Niki made a frustrated sound. "I've tried to get him to open up to me. He's polite but. . .he just isn't interested."

"I know you have. And I thank you. Believe it or not, he likes you."

"He does?" Niki found that hard to believe. The boy had all but ignored her.

Mary took a deep breath and tried to explain the problem as prayer and patience had shown it to her. "I think my son's inability to cope with his father's death is because he not only lost his father when Nikos died, but he lost his best friend as well."

Niki sucked in her breath. That wasn't something she had considered before, but it made perfect sense. Carefully, she replied, "Mary, I think you might be on to something."

Encouraged, Mary breathed in deeply and continued to share her thoughts with Niki. "So I thought that what Stavros needs is a father–friend type of figure. . .a sort of big brother." Her face brightened as she continued, "And I think that I have found just the right man."

Niki's eyes widened. "What do you mean?"

"I interviewed an American man this morning about giving Stavros English lessons, and—I don't know—something about the man made me feel as though I could trust him. . .so I told him about Stavros's problems. . . ."

"And. . . ," Niki prompted eagerly.

"And. . .he agreed that if Stavros responds well to him that he would become his companion and spend more time with him, all under the guise of teaching him English, of course."

"Oh, Mary!" Niki clapped her hands together. "That's perfect! I hope he works out."

Mary smiled, the calm smile of a mother who hopes but doesn't presume to hope too much before the situation has had a chance to develop. "We'll see. Now, about those exercise classes. . ."

Niki smiled crookedly. The last thing she wanted to do was to hold exercise classes. But because Mary had asked, she wouldn't refuse. "Of course I'll do them. I'll make up some posters later in the day."

Mary gave her a quick hug before leaving Niki to the completion of her routine and her thoughts. But the only thoughts Niki had were of Phil. She hadn't heard a word from him in the four weeks since she left Olympia. But—she reminded herself as she stretched out on the floor to do another exercise—he had told her that he would come to Cenchrea, and Niki felt certain that Phil's word would always be enough and that he would come, if not quite as soon as she had thought, then soon enough.

The afternoon was peaceful and calm, a time of day that Niki loved. Wrapping her parka tightly around her and waving good-bye to Mary from across the marble lobby where the entrepreneur was busy at the reception desk, Niki walked out of the hotel and into the brightness of the crisp, winter day. She passed the swimming pool—heated now for wintertime swimmers like Niki—crossed over the green lawn, walked past the whitewashed chapel with the almond trees surrounding it, past the children's park, and finally around the headlands to her favorite location in Cenchrea—perhaps her favorite place in the entire world.

She had first found the clump of stones after returning from Olympia. Ancient and square cut, the huge blocks formed a platform in a nook above the waters of the Saronic Gulf, backed by low sea pines. Niki had asked Mary about the stones and was amazed to discover that they were the foundation stones for the lighthouse of the ancient town of Cenchrea! The actual lighthouse! The harbor of Cenchrea had been in use from very ancient days, from the Hellenistic period of history, but it was during the late Roman and early Christian periods that buildings were constructed alongside the harbor, which accounted for the foundations still visible today.

Niki shaded her eyes from the glare of the sun on the water's surface and looked toward the site of the ancient city. From walking the grounds, she knew that most of the building's foundations were visible under the shoreline, although a few columns and foundations were scattered across the water's edge as well.

The Port of Cenchrea had been Corinth's east port and thus a very busy place. Goods bound for Corinth or for the western part of the Hellenic world were unloaded here, hauled across the narrow isthmus on the ancient road called the Diolkos, and then reloaded at Corinth's western port, Lechaeum. But in spite of all its amazing history, Cenchrea's main claim to fame as far as Niki was concerned was that it was a biblical site. She remembered reading about it in the Book of Acts when she was a young girl and it thrilled her to think that she was now living here just as the apostle Paul—the man of faith whom Niki most admired—most likely had. Niki sighed. She wished that she possessed just an ounce of that saint's faith.

Climbing up onto her favorite sitting stone, she looked away from Cenchrea in the west to the scene directly before her. The mountainous Epidaurus peninsula stretched away to the southeast like a blue ribbon flowing gracefully through the sky. But if the mountains were blue, the hue of the sea redefined the color. Never had Niki seen such deep blue seas as those found in Greece. Indigo, royal, sapphire—no single word described the blue of the Grecian sea. It was a combination of all three and yet still something more, something that was totally Hellenic. Today, both the sea and the wind were calm so that the waters of the gulf sat like a mirror reflecting and enhancing the blue of the sky above. It was cold and crisp and if anger hadn't burned in Niki's heart, the day would have been perfect.

She sighed and picked at a shell that was embedded in the stone beside her. This anger was wearing her out. Mary had so much more to be angry about, and yet she wasn't. Niki sighed and as she stood she looked to her right toward the ancient site of Cenchrea again. It was hard to believe that so much history had occurred at this very location. It was so rural and deserted now with only colorful Greek fishing boats, not mighty Roman and Byzantine merchant ships, bobbing against its shore for company.

A different time, Niki thought. *But then, that's how time is: things change. Except for God of course*, she tightly amended, and scooped up a fistful of loose stones. *He was good at giving people dreams—and even better at taking them away.* In her frustration, Niki flung the stones into the sea where they plopped upon the surface to immediately sink into its deep, dark depths. The bitterness of her thoughts almost frightened her and she wished that she could throw her thoughts as easily and as far away from her as she did the stones.

She shivered, but not from the cold. The anger she felt over her broken ankle hadn't gotten better with time as so many had predicted it would. On the contrary, as the date of this year's Olympics drew closer, her anger seemed to flare within her. Trying to calm herself, Niki lightly ran her fingers over the wall that had once been part of the port's much-needed lighthouse. Now it was nothing. Just a clump of stones that caused her to think, to remember, to feel. . .

To think about the people of almost two thousand years ago, about the apostle Paul who had most likely gazed at the light that shone from this very spot. . .to remember how she had felt just last year when she had broken the world championship record. . .

To feel Phil's arms as he had carried her around ancient Olympia. . .to feel her heart pound at the sound of his voice as he called to her. . .

As he was calling to her now!

"Niki!"

It was his voice!

Swiveling, she saw him walking toward her, with the same sheepskin jacket that she remembered so well from Olympia keeping his body warm and those same expressive eyes smiling up at her. Those eyes, those wonderful eyes that reminded her of a summer day, that reminded her of life without anger.

Stepping gingerly down from her perch on the old foundation wall, she went as quickly as she could toward him, feeling every bit the heroine in a romantic story and loving every moment of it.

"Phil!" she laughed as his arms wrapped around her and she buried her face against his shoulder, as she had several times before. "You came," she whispered into the fleece of his jacket. She felt the anger in her heart slither away as his arms held her and squeezed her tightly.

"Of course I came," he managed after a moment. "Nothing could have kept me away." The emotion Niki heard in his voice was like a balm to her senses. She tilted her head back in order to look into his eyes.

"Phil. . ." She was amazed by what she saw there. Caring, hope, and maybe even love was in the intensity—the brightness—of his gaze. "You really missed me. . . ?"

"I missed you," he quickly admitted and squeezed her close again. "Oh, how I missed you."

A laughter of pure delight bubbled out of Niki, who felt cherished and adored. His declaration couldn't have pleased her more, but before she could stop herself, admonishing words tumbled out of her mouth, "Then why did it take you so long to come?" A blush crept over her face. She didn't mean to sound like a demanding, longtime girlfriend, but she hadn't realized until this moment just how much the delay had bothered her. "I'm sorry, Phil—I just thought you would come within a week or so after Olympia."

"No—it's okay," he assured her, but the same grave expression covered his face that had swept over it at the cafe in Olympia when she had asked him about his reasons for cycling through Greece in the winter. He motioned her toward the stone wall, which she had just vacated, and they climbed up and sat side by side.

She looked up at his strong profile as he gazed out over the sea and she berated herself, wishing that she had kept her accusing question for another time or, even better, had never asked it. But when he turned to her, relief washed over her like a warm summer wave as she realized that rather than being annoyed, his eyes seemed to beg her to believe him and trust him, something that Niki found no trouble at all in doing. She trusted him here in Cenchrea just as she had in Olympia. Implicitly.

"I wanted to come sooner," he admitted and Niki felt her spirit soar like the seagull that was playing far above their heads, "but I had some things to work out." He paused before continuing and ran his hand through his newly barbered hair. "I had to get away to a quiet place to pray and think and listen before I—" he reached out and touched his fingers gently to her cheek, a caress that Niki savored, "before I could come to you."

Niki briefly covered his hand with her own and smiled. "I understand," she murmured and she thought that she really did. Phil had feelings for her just as she had for him and he had needed the time to work them out before coming to see her. Now that he was here beside her, she had to admit that she had needed the time as well. Theirs was a deep and true friendship that hadn't evolved slowly, as such friendships normally do, but rather one that had fallen as unexpectedly and delightfully upon them as the snow on that magical winter day in Olympia.

Before their relationship went any further, Niki felt she should explain her emotional farewell in Olympia. Hesitantly she began, "Phil. . .about what I told you. . .about my having been an Olympic contender. . ."

Phil expelled his breath, cutting her off. "Niki—" He wanted to tell her that their parting in Olympia was what he had been thinking about every moment during the last month. But in order to tell her that he would also have to tell her about the part he had played in her accident. After much prayer, God had led him to believe that he should wait to give their friendship a chance to grow deeper roots before telling her that he had been one of those beer-drinking fools who had crashed into her car.

"I'm really sorry. . . ," she pressed on, saying the very words Phil yearned to say to her, "about how I acted—"

"Niki—" he tried to cut her off. He was the one who should be apologizing, not her.

"No—please." She wanted him to know what sort of a crippled Christian he was getting involved with. "I think you should know that I've got a lot of anger in me about the accident. A lot of anger—" she repeated and looked down at her ankle.

"You're angry with the—fools—" he stumbled over the word, "who ran into you. That's understandable. Being a Christian doesn't make us immune to anger."

Her gaze swiveled back to his. "Of course I'm angry with them!" she shot out with eyes that looked like hot bits of coal. "But even more, I'm angry with God for allowing it to happen."

Chapter 6

Phil squeezed his eyes together and thought, *So that's how it goes.* At that moment, Niki thought that she had lost him.

Phil's second thought was that he now understood why God had instructed him to remain silent for a while about his part in her accident. With deep remorse he realized that the accident had done much more than rob Niki of her Olympic dream; it had robbed her of her faith as well. And that was the worst robbery of all.

He shook his head. It amazed him to consider that the accident that had shaken her faith in God was the very one that had led him to God. Niki watched the emotions flicker across his face and her distress grew as the moments ticked by. Misunderstanding his expressions, she rushed on with an explanation.

"I'm telling you all this so that if you don't want to get. . .involved. . . with someone who has such doubts or anger or—"

Phil raised a finger to her lips, quieting her. "Niki. . .stop."

She heard the soft command in his voice and stopped talking. When his eyes crinkled at the corners in that way she had fallen in love with in Olympia, she knew that she had been right to trust him.

"Niki," he repeated her name and smiled, a whimsical, marveling sort of smile. "Do you know what your name means?"

She did know. Bill, her coach, had reminded her of it practically every day for years. She nodded, amazed that Phil seemed to know it's meaning as well.

"It's a Greek name that means 'victory,' " he said, answering his own question.

"That's right, 'victory.' " Niki watched in wonder as the lines of Phil's face became etched with determination, the type of determination that only good friends can impart to one another.

"Niki, you will be victorious. You will overcome these feelings of anger.

334

And you will have spiritual victory." The conviction behind his words filled Niki with hope.

"Oh, Phil. . ." She sighed, both relieved and comforted by his words, and as if she had been doing it forever, she leaned her head wearily against his shoulder. "I hope you're right. I hate feeling the way I do. . ." she paused and licked her lips before admitting, "and it's only when I'm with you. . .that these feelings. . .leave me at all." He pulled her closer to him, amazed that she would feel this way, that he who had caused her such injury might somehow be allowed to help her.

"This anger is turning me into a person I don't like, Phil," she continued. "I can't pray, I can't read the Bible. . . ." She clenched her fist against her leg. "I feel as though I'm angry with my best friend—I don't want to be, but I just don't know how to stop!" she admitted, helplessly slamming her fist against her thigh.

Reaching out, Phil stilled her hand in his. He liked the way it felt—soft and warm, yet capable and strong, just like the girl. A crushing need to apologize now filled him—for all the pain, for all the changes to her life that his careless action had caused. Although he understood why God wasn't allowing him to relieve his conscience with a full confession right now—which would help him but not her—knowing that he had hurt her was a heavy weight to bear and he still had to apologize. "Niki—" His voice broke.

"Phil?" she tilted her head in question and waited for him to continue.

"I'm so sorry for—" He paused. It was on his lips to say, "For hitting your car, for hurting you, for breaking your leg," but he didn't.

"Sorry? About what?" she prompted, totally perplexed by his obvious, emotional struggle. It was almost as if he felt guilty about something.

"For all that you've had to go through because of the accident." His voice was sandpaper rubbing against silk.

Her eyebrows knitted together in confusion. It sounded to Niki as though he felt personally responsible. "It's not your fault," she said.

He let go of her hand and turned away to look out over the sea that seemed as never-ending as his guilt sometimes felt. He wasn't sure that he was up to keeping this heavy secret. It was so much harder than making a swift confession. "Oh, God!" he mumbled, not an oath but a prayer for help.

Niki was completely baffled. Phil had gone tense, his back to her like a rigid wall. Tentatively, she placed her hand against the tightness of his shoulder.

"Phil?"

He turned back to her, the determination in his eyes now mixed with need. "Niki, you will be victorious in this. I promise you," he said after a while, and Niki thought that she understood.

She smiled, a wise woman's smile. *He is such a strong Christian that it bothers him to think that I am so weak.* She reached up and lightly, reassuringly, touched her fingertips to his face.

"With you as my spiritual coach, I think there's a chance that I might live up to my name." When Phil sucked in his breath, she laughed and explained, "I am used to having a coach, after all."

"But, Niki—" His brows came together in a straight line that cut his forehead in two. He needed to set her straight about his spiritual walk. "I'm not the spiritual giant that you think I am. I'm a very new Christian actually—"

She stopped him with that same wise smile. "Sometimes, new Christians can see things and discern things we older Christians can't. It's kind of like children who often understand and accept deep concepts more readily than adults."

"But, Niki. . ." He reached out and rubbed his knuckles across her cheek and wondered how she would take the truth when he told her. "You know that I want to help you in any way that I can—"

"Good," she interrupted decisively. Those who knew her well would recognize her tone as being final and, even though Phil hadn't known her long, he understood. "Because somehow. . .I think that you are the only one who can," she admitted with a challenging tilt of her chin.

Phil looked at her for a moment, then threw back his head and laughed.

Totally bewildered, Niki blinked her eyes. "Phil. . .what's so funny?"

He stopped laughing but mirth remained in his eyes. "Tell me something. Have you ever thought about God's humor?"

"What?" She was really confused now and even a little hurt. She couldn't understand what God's humor had to do with what they were discussing. And being pretty low on God lately, His humor was the last thing she'd been considering.

"God's humor," he prompted. She made an aloof sound but, sensing that he wouldn't leave the subject alone until she replied, she gave him a pat answer: "If you look at some of the animals God made, it's obvious that He has a sense of humor. . . ," she admitted. "But what has that got to do with what we're discussing?"

"A lot," he said. Then, to Niki's relief, as abruptly as he had broached the subject, he dropped it. Standing suddenly, he pulled her up with him and draped his arm around her shoulder. "It's beautiful out here." He swept his arm out to include the panoramic view of sea and land before them. "I want to see it all, Niki—ancient Corinth, Isthmia, ancient Cenchrea, the Corinth Canal—"

Until this moment, Niki hadn't given much thought to sightseeing, but with Phil by her side, she knew that she wanted to see it all too. Looking out over the Hellenic beauty before her she sighed. "Me too."

"We'll do it—together."

"Together. . . ," she agreed and smiled up at him. She liked the way that sounded. She liked it a lot.

"We'll do everything together, Niki, and—" He came to a sudden decision about their other discussion. "I will be your spiritual coach," he agreed, understanding that God was leading her to want him to be her spiritual guide. It was all part of His wondrous plan and Phil knew better than to try and buck it.

Niki felt a relief lighter than she had felt since their day in Olympia. "Thank you, Phil," she whispered. She needed this man and she needed to know that he would be around. "Then—you'll stay for a while?" she hesitantly asked. He pulled her close against his side and said the most beautiful words in the world to Niki. "I'll stay for as long as you want me."

She smiled, a smile of wonder, for within her heart she knew that she wanted to answer, *Then that would be forever.* But it was still too soon for such declarations. Instead she asked, "Have you found work then?"

"Yes. As a matter of fact, I'm going to be teaching English to several of the children in the area."

"Phil!" she exclaimed. He must be the American man Mary had been so impressed with. How many American men were to be found in Cenchrea, Greece after all? "Are you going to be teaching Stavros Passos? Mary Passos's son?"

"The lady who owns this hotel?" He waved his arm back toward the hotel. "Yes. In fact—" he glanced at his watch, "I have a lesson with him soon."

Niki smiled broadly. "Oh, Phil. . .I'm so glad! If anybody can help Stavros. . .it will be you."

Phil frowned sadly. "The little guy's gone through a pretty rough time since his father died."

"When he left for school one morning, his father was doing all the normal things he always did. . . . When he came home. . . ," her voice trailed off into a sad whisper, "he was told that his father had died."

Phil clicked his cheek. "That's got to be one of the hardest things."

Niki nodded thoughtfully as he helped her down from the wall and guided her toward the hotel. "One of the hardest," she murmured and was again disgusted with herself for being angry over missing the Olympic Games. It seemed silly and so unimportant compared to what Stavros dealt with daily. Holding tightly to Phil's arm, she resolved then and there that she would try very hard to get rid of her anger. She glanced up at Phil's strong profile. With this man to help her, she knew that she could do it.

He looked at her and smiled. Pointing to her leg, he commented, "You're walking without a cane now."

She teased back, "Worried that you might have had to carry me around Cenchrea?"

"Wouldn't bother me if I did." He flexed his muscles. "Carrying muscles—remember?"

She laughed. Oh, how she remembered!

In the hotel lobby, Mary looked up from talking to her son as Niki and Phil walked in, hand in hand. The shocked look on her face was almost comical.

"Mary. . ." Niki glanced up at Phil who was equally amused, "You didn't tell me that Stavros's English teacher was my friend Phil Taylor." Mary quickly recovered and her eyes showed her delight over this development.

"Well, you didn't even tell me that you had a friend," she paused over the word showing that she understood very well that they were much more than just casual friends, ". . .named Phil Taylor. Imagine my surprise when the teacher I hired to teach English to Stavros," she patted her son's shoulder, "arrived early and asked where you might be found."

Phil smiled at both women. "I'm only glad you knew where she was." He turned to Mary's son who was watching this exchange through thick, but attractive glasses. "How do you do, Stavros?" Phil extended his hand. "I'm Theophilus Taylor, and if you agree, I would like very much to be your English teacher."

Stavros, a tall boy of eleven with his mother's handsome, Mediterranean looks, ran his eyes over Phil, as if he were sizing him up. He shook his head in a way that was obviously a tic; then, taking Phil's extended hand he smiled, a smile that transformed his serious expression —much too somber for such a young man—into that of a playful kid. "I've never had a man English teacher before," he said.

"I hope you don't mind?" Phil asked.

"No," Stavros quickly answered. "I like it. . .especially if. . ." He looked at his mother and paused.

"What? *agape mou*—my love," Mary prompted her son to continue.

Stavros licked his lips. "It would be nice, Mamma, if we could have some lessons outside—doing different things."

Mary smiled, a smile of a prayer answered; but keeping it hidden from her son she casually answered, "If Mr. Theophilus doesn't mind, then I don't."

"Sounds great to me," answered Phil. "Conversation is a great teacher. How about if you show me around today, and we can look over your books during the next lesson," Phil suggested to Stavros.

Behind his glasses, Stavros's deep eyes fired with life, a life Niki was shocked to see. In all the weeks she had been at the hotel, she had never seen such light in his eyes.

"Yes!" He looked at his mother. "Can we go now?"

Phil smiled and tapped the top of Stavros's head. "Number one English lesson, Sport—it's *may* we go now?" Phil corrected him.

Stavros smiled good-naturedly and repeated, "May we go now, Mamma?"

Mary shrugged her shoulders. "It's fine with me." She smiled at Phil. "I trust Mr. Theophilus implicitly. Whatever he says."

"Let's go then," Phil said to Stavros. Then, turning to the two women, he said, "Excuse us, ladies, but Stavros and I have some exploring to do."

Mary and Niki watched the two go. The shy, reclusive boy Niki had come to expect was gone and in his place was a boy, full of animation and excitement, who was intent on giving Phil the full tour of his domain. Niki glanced over at Mary. Tears of relief were gathered in the corners of

Stavros's mother's eyes. Niki pulled her friend close to her in a hug of happiness and whispered, "Now that Phil's here—I'm sure that everything will be fine with Stavros."

Mary nodded and dabbing at her eyes quoted, "Do not forget to entertain strangers, for by so doing some people have entertained angels without knowing it." As she turned to Niki, her dark eyes were dancing a dance of joy just as her son's had a moment before. "If you didn't know that man, I would be quite sure right now that he was an angel," she whispered before turning to help a guest who was motioning to her from the reception desk.

Niki walked over to the big picture window and watched as Phil and Stavros stood above the swimming pool talking. The change in the boy was a miracle.

And Niki wondered herself, *Was Phil an angel?* The first time they had met, he had miraculously caught her from behind as she was falling onto the track at ancient Olympia. . . .

She shook her head as quickly as the thought occurred. Phil couldn't be an angel. He had to be a man. She heard Stavros squeal with delight and brought her mind back to the present just in time to see Phil swing the boy high into the air as if he were going to throw him into the pool. When Phil put Stavros back down, the boy was laughing the sweet, sweet laugh of a child. Niki smiled and shook her head.

Phil acted like an angel. But he couldn't be one. Stavros and she both needed the man too much.

Chapter 7

The weeks passed for Niki, Phil, and Stavros in the sweet companionship of growing friendships and growing love. They became a threesome, the "N.T.S. Team" was how Mary joyfully dubbed them as she waved them off on adventure after adventure. Stavros bloomed under Phil's watchful eye and, seeing the regard Phil held for Niki, the little boy finally opened up to her. The three laughed and sang and visited many of the ancient and medieval sites in the greater Corinth area—all those that Niki's leg would permit.

The ancient city of Corinth was sunk several feet below the modern town, in what looked like a large field. They all decided that it resembled a gigantic jigsaw puzzle that was beautiful in spite of its many missing pieces. Still green from winter rains when visited by the N.T.S. Team on a glorious early spring day, it was a special place where the three roamed in and around what remained of the architecturally magnificent temples, public buildings, and shops of what had once been one of the capitals of the ancient world.

Niki held tightly to Phil's arm. Loose stones and uneven terrain were still the enemy of her injured foot, but they both rejoiced that he didn't have to carry her as he had in Olympia almost two months before.

Stavros buzzed in and out of all the different ruins, as a boy at play should. Full of adventure, he climbed and jumped and pretended to be an ancient Greek soldier, a hoplite, at battle. He was a totally different child from the taciturn and tic-ridden boy of just a few short weeks before.

Corinth's citadel, Acrocorinth, stood behind the city like a baldheaded sentinel, 575 meters tall. Since prehistoric times it had been a landmark for both land and sea travelers. Visible for miles around, it looked like a clump of dirt that a mythological creature might have dropped while on a stroll to the sea.

When Phil pointed out to Niki how Acrocorinth was most likely the inspiration behind St. Paul's famous words, written to the Corinthians—"They drank from the spiritual rock that accompanied them, and that rock was Christ"—she was flabbergasted. She had grown up and lived her life far away from any biblical sites, and it had never occurred to her that St. Paul might have used landmarks from the actual cities of the people he wrote to in order to better explain the gospel truth.

But standing in the ancient city of Corinth, with the Hellenic wind blowing the silver-winged olive trees musically around her, and with the soft scent of early spring flowers tantalizing the air, she could understand the impact such an analogy would have had on the early citizens of this famous city. The "rock" of Acrocorinth, with its fortress walls and its life-saving spring—a spring that still bubbles today—had always protected the Corinthians. It was ever with the citizens of this town just as God is ever with the citizens of His kingdom.

Stavros begged them to visit the fortress. Maneuvering the little red car, which Mary had placed at their disposal, up the steep mountainside, Phil drove them as far as the road went. Niki sighed when she saw that an arduous walk of about a quarter of a kilometer was yet necessary in order to reach the castle. Three massive gates leading to the final entrance had to be passed, and the walk became steeper and more difficult with each succeeding gate. It was obviously a citadel that in ancient times had made siege warfare difficult, if not impossible. None but the most hardy would climb it even during peaceful times!

Niki was disappointed that she wouldn't be able to handle the trail, but she encouraged Phil to take Stavros to visit it while she waited in the lovely, though deserted, little cafe below.

"You guys go. I'll be fine," Niki assured Phil as she sat at a table that commanded a panoramic view of the Gulf of Corinth and its surrounding, rich farmland below. Above loomed the impressive fortress. The view was a fantastic slice of the old world. As she looked down at the gulf, where it split the mountains of mainland Greece from those of the Peloponnese, Niki felt as though she really could see forever.

"Are you sure?" As far as Phil was concerned, there were plenty of other sites in the area that Niki could navigate. Every moment away from her was a moment he didn't like. "Let's go someplace else," he decided and placed his hands on her shoulders to guide her up.

Niki felt the warm glow of being cherished envelop her like a cloud of fine perfume and she looked up at Phil, smiling. She didn't want him to go, either; she hated being apart from him for even a few moments, but one glance at Stavros, standing in the parking lot gazing up at the castle with longing, was all she needed to see. "He's aching to go and pretend that he's a medieval knight out to slay a dragon." She placed her hand on Phil's arm. "And besides. . .it's good for you to have some time alone with him."

Phil turned toward the boy and a grin of extreme contentment, a feeling that was still new to Phil, split across the fine lines of his face. Stavros's tics had slowly disappeared during their days together—no more shaking of his head, no more blinking of his eyes. Phil knew what a great relief it was to Mary and to all the people at the hotel who cared about the boy, but none of them knew just what the boy's recovery meant to him. For the first time in his life, Phil felt as though he had made a difference, a good difference, to another human being. For once, his being on earth was of worth to others. It was a heady feeling, a life-giving, spirit-renewing feeling. If there were any lingering doubts about following his dream of becoming an elementary school teacher—and he had questioned himself after his father's hateful words—they were long gone. After being with Stavros and teaching English to several other children in the area, he knew that to make a difference in the life of a child was how he wanted to spend the vocational part of his life.

He turned back to find Niki's deep-green eyes studying his face, and he sucked in his breath. He knew that making a difference in the life of this woman—a good difference—was, next to God, the very most important thing in the world to him. He ached to hold her, to love her, to be just the person she needed him to be. Still, he knew that much needed to be conquered on both their parts before they would ever truly be together.

Although his hand wanted to slide beneath her hair to find that silky, feminine spot on the back of her neck, he took a deep, controlling breath and forced himself to wave in Stavros's direction instead. "Praise God— he's doing great," he stammered huskily.

With a gentle nod, Niki looked toward Stavros before turning back to Phil, with a mischievous twinkle in her eyes. Her look brought his brows together in curiosity. "You know," she finally spoke with a playful smile curving her lips, "Mary thinks that you're an angel."

Phil's blue eyes sparkled and, without saying a word, he slowly leaned down and met her lips with his own. On an evening sortie, they had shared their first kiss at the ancient lighthouse of Cenchrea two weeks before, with only the strong winter wind, the salt spray from the bay, and a lone seagull as witnesses. Since then, Niki had lost count of the number of their kisses—those above the hundred-year-old canal, those above the sea, those at the door of her room each night—but one thing was certain: Phil's kisses were definitely those of a man.

"Ummm. . ." She softly sighed, not wanting the kiss to end as Phil straightened away from her.

With a husky timbre that made his voice sound extra warm, he said, "Please tell Mary that I am most definitely a man, complete with all the needs," he breathed out deeply, "and desires of a man."

Niki wasn't sure how to respond. Her eyes widened as she admitted to herself that she had needs and desires as well.

"Mr. Theophilus!" Stavros's impatient call interrupted them, saving Niki from having to reply.

"Mr. Theophilus. . ." Niki nodded toward Stavros as she mimicked the name that Phil had come to be known by. The old names were very much kept alive in Hellenic culture and the name Theophilus slid easily off their lips.

"That's my name," Phil said proudly and turned to watch Stavros as he came rushing into the cafe. As much as Phil had disliked his name before, he now liked it. To be a "friend of God," which was what his name meant, was something he was now proud to be.

Stavros ran up to Phil and motioned to his digital watch as he spoke with all the eagerness of a normal eleven-year-old, "Come. Let's go up to the castle. My mother's expecting us back in an hour and a half."

Phil fondly smoothed the boy's windblown hair, managing to tame it for a moment, then turned back to Niki. "Are you sure you don't mind waiting?"

Stavros shot an alarmed look at Niki, his eyes looking huge through the lenses of his glasses. "You're not coming?" Up to this point, the three of them had done all their adventuring together.

Niki shook her head and, reaching down, rubbed her leg. "I think it will be too much for my ankle," she explained. "Besides," she glanced at Phil and smiled, a poignant smile of finally admitting to a need, "I wouldn't mind looking up that verse about 'spiritual water' if you think you could part with your little New Testament for a while."

Phil reached into the breast pocket of his jacket. "It's found in First Corinthians, the tenth chapter," he said and handed the Book to her. The evident gladness in his voice made her feel special as she fingered the little Book that meant so much to him, the man who meant so much to her. The Book's brown leather was warm from lying against Phil's heart. She fanned her finger over it, gathering in his warmth. Finally, feeling the eyes of both the man and boy on her, she looked back up. The sad, puppy-dog look in their eyes told her they were ill at ease about leaving her alone.

Laughing, she flung her hand out in front of her and good-naturedly shooed them away. "Off with you two! I've got reading to do. . . ," she paused and her eyes softened as she admitted to Phil, "and thinking. . ."

Nodding, Phil reached for her hand and gently squeezed it. She squeezed his back before letting go of it to give Stavros a friendly jab in his tummy. "And you've got a castle to explore, young man!"

"Yahoo!" Stavros yelled. He yanked his Charlotte Hornets cap out of his jacket pocket and plopped it on his head, all the while pulling Phil toward the door of the cafe. "*Ella*, Mr. Theophilus. Come on!"

Blowing a kiss to Niki, Phil challenged Stavros to a race as they ran out the door. As Niki watched them go, a satisfied and yet thoughtful look covered the soft planes of her face. She could understand how Mary would consider Phil to be a real angel. He was almost too wonderful to be true. . . .

She ran her thumb over the cover of the New Testament before placing it softly onto the top of the wooden cafe table. She was soon lost in her thoughts, musing about how her consuming anger, the anger that had been eating away at her and devouring all her thoughts with a corroding passion for so many months, had abated since Phil had come to her. She knew she was ready to try to read the Bible—and maybe even to believe it again.

She placed her elbows on the table, rested her head between her hands and looked out the window, down toward the Gulf of Corinth. It was a clear day. The wind had swept the often-present haze of white that lent an air of mysticism to Greece, clear out of the sky, and she was able to see all the way to where the earth rounded on its way toward Italy. Her eyes slowly followed the progress of a luxury cruiser as it glided over the deep waters of the gulf, until she forced herself, not accepting any more procrastination, to move back to the Book that rested on the table in front of her.

She picked it up and held it lightly in her hands. The last time she had tried to read this Book she had slung it angrily away. This time, she was relieved to feel no anger, but she did feel dizzy. She squeezed her eyes shut against the burning brightness of the gold engraving. The blood vessels in her temples started to pound as if she were running a hard race, and her leg started to throb in sympathy. Abruptly, she dropped the Book onto the table with a thump, and regarded it with a mixture of wonder, horror, and interest all mingling to make the lines of her face bend and pull into a look she might wear if an unwanted insect had suddenly appeared on the table before her.

She continued to stare at the brown leather. Sitting up straighter, she took a deep, composing breath, picked up her injured leg to gently rest it on the chair across from her and forced her reluctant hands to reach for the Bible once again. Breathing with the controlled rhythm that years of training on the track had taught her, she ignored the buzzing in her head and with her thumb against the Book's edge, she twirled the pages. A frown deepened the lines of her face when she saw the rainbow of color that greeted her. Stopping on a random page, her eyes carefully scanned the spectrum of colors. She felt daunted as the realization of what Phil had done hit her. He had taken markers and had color-coordinated most of the verses in the book according to their themes. She had heard about people doing it but she had never actually seen it done before.

Flipping first to the front and then to the back of the Book, she searched for a key. She found it at the end of the Book. The color red was used for verses pertaining to "healing," green was for those about the "Word," yellow for "salvation," and so on. But when she found the final color-coordinated title her eyes stopped on the entry as if in a trance. With the color pink, Phil had underscored all the verses having to do with "running a race" or "racing." She read the key while trying to control the shudder that racked her body. She knew all those verses by heart. She had lived by them for years. And after missing out on the Olympics for the third time in a row, she had decided that they had all lied to her. God's Word had lied to her, which was the seed from which all her anger had sprouted—and that hurt. To accuse God of lying struck at the very core of her belief. It was something she couldn't tolerate. Something she wouldn't believe.

She placed the Book back down on the table, but she didn't release her grip on it. A great sob escaped her which was followed by another and yet another. As her head dropped to her arms in exhaustion she wept—the sweet, deep, cleansing cry of a soul that had passed the numb stage and could bear to address the hurt and maybe, just maybe, tread the path that would lead to recovery.

By the time the last tear ran its path down her check and into the soft folds of her pink ribbed sweater, she had fallen into a restful sleep, with no dreams, but more importantly, with no anger. A rejuvenating sleep of the nicest kind.

Almost an hour later, Stavros and Phil returned full of high adventure and with a thirst that seemed as though it might be capable of consuming the entire Gulf of Corinth. Niki had awakened before their return, feeling refreshed and revitalized. Now that the shock had worn off she felt touched that Phil had cared enough about her to underscore the verses concerning racing. She didn't want to look at them yet, and she certainly didn't want to discuss his reasons for underscoring them, but she was relieved that she had progressed to the point of being content to sit and hold the Bible in her hands as if it were a friendly companion. She didn't feel close to God, as she had in previous years, but she did feel close to Phil, the owner of the book, and somehow, his faith seemed to bring her closer to God. It was as if she were somehow justified through him.

"I don't know how people make that climb in the heat of summer," Phil wondered out loud as he downed a large, icy can of cola.

"They take a bottle of water with them," Stavros answered between sips of his orange juice.

"They'd better take two," Phil uttered good-naturedly.

"I thought there was a spring up there," Niki said.

"There is, but we didn't walk very far up into the fortress and I'm not sure if the well is even drinkable today anyway."

"The castle's big!" Stavros interjected. "And even when you climb all the way up through the last gate you still have to climb more once you get inside the fort."

"Really?" Niki looked up at the fortress with interest. "Was it pretty?"

she asked wistfully, wishing that she had been able to visit it.

Phil drew an appreciative breath. "Beautiful," he replied, but not in the direction of the castle. Niki felt his eyes on her and adrenaline coursed through her veins as she realized that he meant her. She was beautiful. That cherished feeling was hers again and it felt wonderful.

"An American lady we met up there. . . ," Stavros cut in, oblivious to the adult exchange in the innocent way of children, and both adults reluctantly turned their attention back to him as he blithely continued, "said that in ancient days, Acrocorinth could communicate with the acropolis of both ancient Mycenae and ancient Athens." He pointed up to the fortress above them, then off toward the south and toward the east.

"Really?" Niki eyes turned to the castle again but she wasn't sure what interested her more: the communications abilities of this ancient fortress or the fact that there was an American lady close by. She all of a sudden realized how much she had missed her friends from home.

"I hope you don't mind—but I invited Kristen and her husband, Paul, to come to the hotel for dinner," Phil said. Niki looked at him with obvious pleasure, and he was glad that he had acted impulsively to invite the other couple.

"Mind! I'm thrilled!"

"They struck me as a very nice couple."

"Will we wait for them here or. . ."

"No. They want to spend some more time in the fort," Phil twitched his eyebrows at Stavros. "And they came prepared with canteens and food. Didn't they, Sport?"

"Thank goodness. . ." Stavros rolled his eyes in a comical way that suggested he had almost been ready to expire from the lack of provisions. "They shared juice and cookies with me." He looked at his watch and suddenly became serious. "May I go wait by the car?" Niki and Phil exchanged amused smiles. Wherever they had gone exploring, Stavros had been very careful of the time. He never wanted his mother to wait a minute past the time they were due back.

"Sure." Phil ruffled Stavros's hair. "We'll be right out."

They watched him walk out the glass door of the cafe, doffing his Charlotte Hornets cap as he went.

"You've been perfect for him," Niki said sincerely.

Phil's eyes crinkled at the edges. "He's been perfect for me," he admitted quietly, but he didn't give Niki the chance to ask him what he meant as he quickly added, "Well, I guess we'd better go." He stood, but as he did his eyes fell onto the pocket Testament in silent question.

Rubbing her fingers across the burnished leather, Niki picked it up and handed it to him. "Thank you," she softly murmured.

Phil took it. He didn't want to pry but he needed to ask, "Did you look up that verse in Corinthians about spiritual water?"

"No, I. . ." Niki paused and licked her lips. She really didn't want to get into any sort of discussions about the whys and wherefores of his underscoring all the verses pertaining to racing, so she said, "I flipped through it and then I. . .I—" She paused. A part of her wanted to tell him how she'd cried cleansing tears, but another part of her didn't. She settled for telling him what happened afterwards.

"I slept."

"You slept?" he repeated, amazed.

With a secretive smile, a smile that Phil understood meant a lot more had transpired than what she was telling him, she rose from her chair and flicked a challenging finger against his shoulder.

"Yes. I slept."

Chapter 8

Kristen and Paul Andrakos were newly married and newly Christian, and they were a delight to be around. They met Niki and Phil at the hotel for a dinner of moussaka, an eggplant casserole with cheese and meat, followed by baklava, the famous Greek pastry made with honey and nuts. The two couples hit it off as if they'd known each other for years.

Mary and Stavros joined them for dessert and Mary insisted that the newlyweds stay the night rather than driving back to Athens that evening. In Paul Andrakos, Stavros found yet another father-type friend, who could help the boy over the ache of losing his father, and Mary could not, nor would not, let the opportunity pass for their friendship to develop.

Finally, after an hour of laughter and fun when there was a lull in the conversation, Mary put on her best authoritative-mother tone, took Stavros's Hornets cap from his head and lightly tapped him with it. "It's way past your bedtime, young man. Off to bed with you now."

Stavros turned beseeching eyes to his mother, "*Se parakalo* Mamma, *ligo acoma?*" he begged for a little more time as children around the world are known to do at bedtime.

"Do as your mother says, Stavros," Paul gently urged him. "We'll see you in the morning before you leave for school."

"Really?" Stavros looked at him in wide-eyed wonder.

"Really." Paul's deep chestnut eyes twinkled at the boy and Stavros beamed, a smile that cut across his narrow face like a happy clown's smile.

"Are you sure that you will be up in the morning before I leave?" He wanted reassurance.

"Most definitely." Paul patted the boy's shoulder. "You have school tomorrow and I have work. I must get up early in order to get to my office on time."

"But you didn't go to work today, and I went to school," Stavros pointed out logically.

"Ah. . . ," Paul explained, "but I went to work last weekend and the weekend before that. I was on a business trip and I promised my wife that I would take her someplace special in order to make up for it." Paul looked over at Kristen with an expression that left no doubt how much he loved her. "Little did I know that she would choose a castle!" He laughed while continuing to look at Kristen in that way all women wish for a man to look at them. Paul still couldn't believe that they were actually married and he loved to refer to her as his wife. It made it all seem more real.

Kristen was beaming back at Paul. "I have a very dear friend from home who married a Greek man about a year and a half ago. Melissa—that's her name—is an expert on medieval Greece and, well. . .she's been after me for months to visit Acrocorinth. When I awoke this morning and saw this beautiful spring day, I knew that today was it."

"And good for all of us that you did," Niki inserted. "Otherwise, we might never have met."

"Oh, I don't know. . ." Kristen tilted her head sideways and with her deep voice, lightly flavored with a southern accent, spoke almost sagely. "I've learned. . ." She reached across for her husband's hand and squeezed it while amending her words. "That is, we've learned that God always makes the paths of those He wants to meet run together. I truly believe that there is a path for each one of us—we have only to tread it."

Paul squeezed his wife's hand and murmured, "The path of life."

She nodded, a special nod of remembrance. They were remembering how in their lives God had certainly made it true.

Phil looked over at Niki and repeated practically the first words he had said to her the day they met in Olympia. "God's timing. . .it's always perfect."

"Amen to that," Paul agreed.

"Amen. . . ," Kristen softly chimed in.

Niki pursed her lips together. She could admit that God's timing was perfect about certain things perhaps—about her meeting Phil, about meeting this wonderful couple—but how could His timing have been perfect where her accident was concerned?

Phil heard the denial in Niki's silence. It shouted out to him. She had borrowed his New Testament earlier in the day, and that was a step in the right direction, but he knew that it was only a step, a small, hobbling step along a very long and rocky path at that. And he knew that he had an equally long and difficult path of patience to travel alongside her.

Standing abruptly to escape his thoughts, Phil reached for Stavros's hand and asked Mary, "May I have the honor of putting this son of yours to bed tonight?"

Mary smiled and nodded. Phil didn't even have to ask.

"Zito!" Stavros cheered, the Greek child's equivalent of the English "hurrah," as he bid everyone a good night. Planting a small kiss on his mother's cheek, he turned to Phil and pranced happily around him as they walked toward the large bungalow that was home to Mary and her son.

"What a nice boy you have," Kristen commented as she watched the man and the boy walk out of sight.

Mary smiled with poignancy. "He has blossomed under Phil's friendship. I don't know what I would have done if he hadn't come." She turned to Niki and her smile deepened. "And you too my dear. You are the reason Phil came here, after all."

Niki smiled in answer. She too was glad that Phil had come. Glad for them all.

"How did you happen to come to Greece anyway?" Kristen asked Niki. "Sorry, but I'm always a bit nosy about how foreign women end up in Greece. It seems like so many women from around the world live here."

The question took Niki by surprise. She opened her mouth to answer but didn't know where to begin. It seemed so long ago now since her coach had suggested she come, and her reasons for coming were all mixed up with her reasons for staying. Her ankle, the Olympics, Phil, Stavros, Mary—she shrugged her shoulders helplessly. It wasn't that she didn't want to answer, it was simply a case of not quite knowing what to say.

Mary caught her eye and tilting her head toward Kristen, she asked, "May I tell her?" Niki nodded and Mary smiled before turning back to Kristen.

"Several months ago, Niki suffered an automobile accident. My brother, who is Niki's coach, thought that it would do both her," she paused, "and me, a lot of good for her to come and stay here for a while." Smiling, she reached for Niki's hand and squeezed it. "I think he was right on both counts."

352

"Coach?" Kristen asked and knitted her brows together.

"Niki Alexander...," Paul whispered to himself, and then he looked at Niki in amazement as comprehension suddenly dawned on him. "I knew I'd heard your name before! Niki Alexander. Of course! You broke the world record for the eight hundred meters last summer at the world championships."

Niki smiled and nodded her head. She couldn't help but feel satisfaction that he knew about that race. But right on the tail of satisfaction came a wave of anger that there would most likely never be another race like it. Not for her anyway.

"You didn't just break the record—you blasted it apart! I saw you do it! You're the number one contender for the Olympic gold this summer in both the eight hundred meters and the fifteen hundred meters!" He continued on as excited as a young boy.

Kristen, meanwhile, was looking down at her unusual emerald and platinum wedding band, and as she slowly twirled it around her finger, she thought back to how she had felt last November. At the time, she was brokenhearted because it seemed that the past was going to keep her from happiness with Paul. She was crying and watching TV when a story came on the news about a girl who was also brokenhearted—not because of a human love lost, but because of a longtime dream that was lost, something very similar, in Kristen's opinion.

For the girl on the news, an accident was going to keep her from competing in the Olympic Games. What was so unusual was that it would make the third time in twelve years of trying that something had happened at practically the last minute to prevent her from running in the Games. Kristen remembered how she had sympathized with the athlete even though she didn't know her. Such a disappointment, a disappointment that was similar to her own, simply in that it was deep.

Kristen looked up from her ring into the deep sadness in Niki's lovely green eyes and knew that she was looking at that girl. She squeezed Paul's hand in that way a wife has of getting her husband's attention. Her serious look sobered his enthusiasm faster than a pail of icy water ever could. He looked at Kristen with a "What did I say?" look of questioning confusion.

Niki spoke up. Her voice sounded to her like it was coming from somebody else. She wished that it was. "I won't be competing this summer. . . I. . .the accident. . .if the accident had happened even a month earlier. . . ," she rambled, "maybe. . .but now. . . ." Her voice trailed off. It was only the second time she had spoken about her loss. Phil had been the first. She couldn't go on.

"Niki's anklebone was severely broken," Mary explained as Niki re-arranged her napkin in her lap. "It won't be in shape in time to compete in the Olympics this year."

Paul exhaled audibly and turned to Niki with eyes filled, not with pity, but with a compassion that Niki could appreciate. "That's hard. I'm really sorry. I was looking forward to watching you run."

"You and the rest of America," Kristen qualified.

None of them heard Phil return nor did any of them see the look on his face as he paused several feet away in the shadow of a potted rubber-tree plant. He heard the tail end of their discussion and shame swooped in on him like a mugger. He wanted to scream out to all their disappointed faces that he was responsible. . .he was the one who had cost Niki her dream and America its little darling. . .

But he knew that God didn't want that from him. He couldn't let his "guilt" sin destroy that part of Niki that his previous "drinking" sin hadn't reached. Deep prayer and the study of God's Word had taught him that God wanted no man to wear guilt like a mantle. The weight of that mantle was too heavy for a man to carry and survive. Phil reminded himself that Jesus had died so that all men's sins could be forgiven. He had asked God's forgiveness and it had been granted as all who ask are forgiven. Phil had to remind himself continually of that truth and he knew that he would have to wait a little bit longer before he could ask Niki for her forgiveness as well.

He started walking toward the table again, casting his eyes over Mary, Kristen, and Paul, and he was glad to know that Niki would at least have some good friends to lean on here in Greece when he did tell her that he had been in the car that slammed into her, and that he had been the one to suggest a six-pack and a tour of the bars that night.

Phil sat down and reached for Niki's hand. It was cold, freezing, almost lifeless. He covered it with his own hand to warm her, but at the moment there was no warmth in his own hand to give.

With a quick smile of acknowledgment to Phil, Mary continued her explanation. "After the pins are removed, Niki will be able to start running again. According to my brother, she still has what it takes to be a world-class runner."

"When will the pins come out?" Kristen asked Niki.

"Around Easter," she answered.

"Will you have them removed in Greece or return to the States?"

Niki sighed. "I don't know. My doctor gave me the name of a good specialist in Athens. . .but I'd have to be in the hospital and then stay in Athens for a few days afterwards and I don't know if I want to do all that alone."

Kristen glanced at Paul, who nodded imperceptibly. Reaching out, Kristen took Niki's hand. "You won't be alone. I will stay with you at the hospital and then you will come to our home and be our guest until you are ready to return here."

"Definitely." Paul immediately seconded the plan.

Niki looked at them with happy incredulity covering her face.

"Thank you, but. . .I. . .I couldn't ask you to do all that."

"As your sister in Christ, you most certainly could ask me," Kristen pointed out. "But you don't have to ask because I'm offering. Besides, my aunt Aphrodite would love to show you her collection of memorabilia from the first modern Olympics. One of our ancestors competed in it and another helped to organize it."

"I. . .I don't know what to say." Niki lapsed into silence. The idea of traveling all the way back to the States just to have her pins removed had never appealed to her and yet, at the same time, she didn't want to impose on these people whom she had just met. In spite of her reservations, however, she was surprised to hear herself ask, "Are you sure you have room?"

Paul and Kristen laughed and their eyes twinkled in amusement. Aunt Aphrodite had a large, neoclassical home in Athens where they all lived together.

"Dear girl, we have room for you and everyone at this table, maybe even everyone at this hotel!" Paul assured her.

Phil squeezed her hand. "I think you should take our brother and sister in Christ up on their very heartfelt offer," he encouraged. "I really don't want you traveling all the way back to the States either." Then he softly spoke the deciding words for Niki, "I'd miss you."

Music seemed to sound in Niki's ears at those words! Phil would miss her! She had been waiting, hoping, to hear those words, and joy filled her heart as she gazed into his summer-blue eyes.

After a moment, Niki tore her eyes away from Phil and looked back at Kristen, who eagerly nodded her head in encouragement. "I really would love to have you. I love having houseguests!"

"She really does," Paul agreed.

Niki smiled, a deep smile that banished the shadows from her face. "Then how can I refuse? Thank you."

"Good!" Kristen clasped her hands together. "Just call the doctor and let us know when the appointment is set for."

"Terrific." Paul clapped his hands together. "Now that that is settled," he stood and stretched, "is anyone in the mood for a walk down by the shore?"

With unanimous acclaim, they piled on their heavy coats and headed for the door. Although the day had been warm, the breeze that had arisen with the setting of the sun reminded them that it was spring only according to the date on the calendar. They walked and laughed and threw stones into the lapping sea, returning late to the hotel for a short night before they had to face the next day.

True to their word, Paul and Kristen didn't keep Stavros waiting in the morning. They were up and ready for the hour-long drive back to Athens before Stavros came bounding into the lobby. As a special treat, Paul asked Mary if he and Kristen could drive Stavros to school that morning. Stavros was thrilled to drive away in Paul's fancy sports car while Mary, Phil, and Niki waved them off.

Mary turned away as the sleek car disappeared down the eucalyptus-lined road and sighed, a mother's relief that her child was happy and healthy. "So, what are you two doing today?"

Phil put his arm around Niki's shoulder. "Well, I don't have any lessons until the afternoon, so I thought I'd take this lovely lady to visit ancient Isthmia."

"Oh, I'd love to," Niki readily agreed. The idea of spending the day alone with Phil was very appealing. As much as she loved having Stavros with them, she also wanted some time alone with Phil. Her shoulders sagged as she suddenly remembered, "But I can't. I have an exercise class at ten."

"Don't be silly," Mary quickly interjected. "I didn't mean for these classes to keep you from enjoying yourself. I'll let the word out that the exercise class won't start until," she cocked her head questioningly, "two? When Phil has his lesson with Stavros."

"Great," said Phil. Niki beamed her agreement and he started walking toward the kitchen. "Go get a light jacket just in case it turns cool while I get some munchables, and meet me back here in five minutes."

As he disappeared around the corner, Niki and Mary laughed at his take-charge attitude. "Nothing better than a man who knows what he wants," Mary said with a smile and started to turn toward her office.

"So. . ." The teasing tone in Niki's voice brought Mary's eyes swiveling back to hers. "You do believe Phil is a man now. . .and not an angel?" The light in Niki's eyes matched the banter in her voice.

Mary surprised Niki by laughing. As she started again to walk away, she threw over her shoulder, "No angel could look at you the way that man does." She flashed Niki a knowing smile and disappeared into her office.

Niki's smile mirrored Mary's and she shook her head at the wonder of it all. It was fantastic to know that Mary was absolutely correct. Phil did look at her as if she were the most important person in the world to him. It was a heady feeling, a wonderful feeling, and the feeling was mutual. Clasping her hands together, Niki was as excited as a little girl on Christmas morning. Being with Phil made her feel as though she always had Christmas packages to open. Today she was going to open Isthmia with him! She told herself that it didn't bother her one bit that in ancient days, Isthmia had been the site of famous athletic games.

No, it didn't bother her a bit. . . . *They weren't the Olympic Games*, she reminded herself as she started off across the lobby; and besides, that was back then. This was today. And today, she would have gone most anywhere in the world with Phil.

Chapter 9

Niki loved the short drive to ancient Isthmia. Lined with Mediterranean pine, cypress, and olive groves with peekaboo views of the deep Saronic Gulf as it flowed toward the Corinth Canal, it was special in that old-world sort of way, where the stones of centuries-old farmhouses seemed to grow out of the ground. Plane trees and oak, poplars, and walnut all seemed to sprout leaves overnight, scenting the land with their freshness and softening the hard lines of winter into the more gentle ones of spring.

"When my pins come out," Niki spoke after several moments of companionable silence, "I'll have to make this road into one of my regular training routes." It was the first time that Niki had talked to Phil about running again and he wanted to shout with happiness but, following her lead, he curtailed the euphoria that coursed through him and, instead, he nonchalantly replied, "Good. I'll ride my bike alongside you."

"Afraid to run?" Niki taunted.

"Hey. . . ," he laughed, "you're a world-champion runner. . .give me a break."

"Correction. I *was* a world champion." Hurt and anger yanked the serenity off of Niki's face, and her voice sounded as if a ton of bricks had been dropped on it. Phil's happiness from the moment before was crushed along with it. "How I run after my pins come out," she flicked her hand contemptuously down toward her ankle, "remains to be seen."

Phil bit the inside of his cheek to keep from speaking. There was so much that he wanted to tell her, to confess, but he knew that now wasn't the time. He didn't say anything, and by the time they reached the Isthmia and parked outside the little museum, the peace and serenity of the Hellenic countryside had worked its magic on Niki's spirit and she was almost a carefree tourist again, out to enjoy the wonders of the land. *Almost*, Phil said to himself as he helped her from the car, *but not quite*.

They walked through the entrance hall of the museum to the verandah that overlooked the site. "Not much remains of the ancient temples
and such," he said, pointing out the obvious. Niki gazed out over the arid
area of what had been ancient Isthmia and even though she knew that
she should be disappointed in the dust-laden site before her, she could
only muster up relief. Despite her brave thoughts at the hotel, she was
glad that, unlike ancient Olympia, it was difficult to even begin to make
out the magnificent sports center that had once been here.

Craning her neck, she searched for a track. She was relieved not to
find one. "It looks more like the grounds of a country fair right after the
fair pulls up stakes and leaves," she murmured, and smiled when Phil
chuckled. "There's hardly anything left." She waved her hand out over
the site. "What happened to all the buildings? Not even fires, earthquakes, or floods managed to ruin ancient Olympia this badly."

Phil chuckled again. "No. Something much more fierce destroyed this
place." She looked at him quizzically, and he said, "Man."

"Man?"

He nodded. "But it was for a good cause. The stones of the buildings
and sanctuaries were removed one by one in order to build that." He
pointed to part of an old, but very solid-looking wall, which was barely
visible near the bottom of the site.

Niki squinted her eyes. "A wall?"

Phil nodded. "Justinian's Wall."

"Justinian?" The name was unknown to Niki, but very exotic sounding.

"He was a Byzantine emperor who lived in the fifth century. He
ordered the wall built across the isthmus in order to check the aggression
of the Slavs against this part of Hellas all those years ago."

Niki looked out over the beauty of the green and golden land to the
rust-colored walls of the centuries-old canal that divided mainland
Greece from the Peloponnese. "Did it work?"

Phil chuckled as he pulled her toward the museum. "Not for long."

The museum was small and friendly, with approachable caretakers
who were proud of ancient Isthmia's treasures and pleased to give
impromptu tours, which Niki found quaint and refreshing. There were
little terra cotta vessels from the archaic temple at Isthmia that, although
thousands of years old, looked like little knickknacks that belonged on a
modern living room shelf. Niki and Phil agreed that a large terra cotta

sprinkling basin that resembled an elegant birdbath would look beautiful on the lawn of Mary's hotel, and they couldn't help chuckling at an ancient stone bathtub, completed with a seat and a deeper basin for the feet, that sat on the museum floor. But it was the finds from Cenchrea, which this museum housed as well, that most interested them.

A wooden door—a very unusual find because wood normally disintegrates over time—that they discovered in the cellar of the temple of Isis at Cenchrea, caused Phil to reflect. "Imagine the people who opened this door. . . ."

Niki nodded and looked toward the next display.

"It was probably a working door when Cenchrea looked like this," said Niki as she pointed at a masterfully crafted mosaic of vivid, colored stones, which portrayed the shore of ancient Cenchrea.

Phil whistled. "Would you look at that," he said as he read the placard. "Shore Vista, A.D. fourth century."

Niki nodded. "Amazing to think that our quiet Cenchrea was actually a major metropolitan city at one time."

Phil ran his hand lightly over the glass case that protected the beautiful mosaic. "But this proves it. It's like an eyewitness account of the city."

"Ancient man's answer to the photograph," Niki murmured as they left the museum, and walked like happy, carefree tourists toward the ancient site.

Phil took Niki's hand. "Come here. There's something in ancient Isthmia that's like an eyewitness account of what this place actually was too."

"What?" she asked cheerfully.

"The old running stadium's starting gate."

"Starting gate?" Apprehension shot through Niki like a popping balloon.

"It's been unearthed." He paused and tilted his guide map this way and that before finally pointing in what he thought must be the correct direction. Niki sighed as he pulled her along. To see where the runners of the ancient games had actually started off somehow made the ache in her soul flare up again. But she followed along behind Phil, reminding herself that these were the Isthmian Games, not the Olympic Games. She'd never even heard about the Isthmian Games until she came to Cenchrea. *It's different,* she reminded herself.

"Here it is!" Phil walked onto a flat surface that was in the shape of an isosceles triangle. There was a curious, circular pit at the apex of the triangle.

"Very interesting," Niki said dryly. She looked down toward what she supposed would be the track but she couldn't find one. "A starting gate without a track. . . . Those ancients must have run some race." She was using sarcasm to cover her pain.

"Niki—this is the older of the two ancient stadiums here at Isthmia. Buildings and such were built over this track when it fell into disuse," he patiently explained. "But look, this is what I wanted you to see." He jumped down into the circular pit, which was just wide enough to fit a man. "See. . .the starter stood here and held onto ropes—"

"Ropes?" she interrupted, continuing her sarcastic line. "Were they footraces or horse races?"

"Ropes," Phil patiently continued as if she were a mule-headed sixth grader, "which were connected to bars, which the runners stood behind. When the starter released the ropes, the bars fell, and the runners ran."

"Like you said. . .unique." Niki knew that she was being difficult but she couldn't seem to help it. Without really meaning to, she blurted out the question that had been lying in wait on the fringes of her mind since the previous day. "Tell me, Phil—why did you underscore every verse in your Bible that pertained to racing? You know—the verses highlighted in pink?" she reminded him unnecessarily.

Phil breathed out deeply before climbing out of the pit. He had been waiting for that question, both hoping for it and dreading it. He considered that he had probably brought her to Isthmia in a subconscious bid for the subject to come up.

Guiding her over to a fallen pillar, they sat and he pulled the little New Testament out of his pocket. Flipping through it, he smiled at the rainbow of color that greeted him. "I used pink because it reminded me of you—your parka."

"So you did underscore them after meeting me." It was meant to be a question but it came out as a demanding statement. She couldn't understand why she was suddenly feeling antagonistic, but she couldn't help it. Her glance jumped quickly over Phil's shoulder to the starting gate behind him, before bouncing back again to his face. She decided that it was probably the setting. Games again. . .

Phil reached out and gently ran his fingers across her cheek. "Of course I marked the verses after meeting you," he softly admitted.

"Why?" In spite of the battle warring within her, she really wanted to know.

"Because racing is important to you and there are so many verses in the Bible that use racing as an allegory—"

"I know, I know, I know—" She cut him off as bitterness asserted its ugly tone in her. "Believe me, Phil. . .I know them all!" Before he could say another word, and with all the anger she felt toward God for deserting her and her dream—for lying to her—she quoted the lines from the Bible that had inspired her for years:

" 'Do you not know that in a race all the runners run, but only one gets the prize? Run in such a way as to get the prize. Everyone who competes in the games goes into strict training. They do it to get a crown that will not last; but we do it to get a crown that will last forever. Therefore I do not run like a man running aimlessly; I do not fight like a man beating the air. No, I beat my body,' " she hit her fist against her chest for emphasis and spoke through clenched teeth, " 'and make it my slave so that after I have preached to others, I myself will not be disqualified for the prize.' "

She leaned her head forward. It was as if she had given a great theatrical reading, but Phil knew that it wasn't theatrics. It was something that came from her heart, and the pain she felt exhausted her.

"Niki. . .?"

She looked at him. He saw the anger that was in her even more than he had in Olympia, when she had first told him about her accident. He saw the anger that was consuming her, hurting her, destroying the woman he loved.

"Niki," he said her name more forcefully and took hold of her shoulders as though to prevent anger from holding her.

"I did it all, Phil. . ." She spoke quietly but with rage in the timbre of her words. "I did it all. . .I beat my body and made it my slave. . .but I was disqualified anyway. All that hard work. . .for nothing. . . ."

He squeezed his eyes shut and touched the scar on his head that was hidden by his hair. He remembered back to his hospital bed, and to the first time he had read those words.

"Those verses mean a lot to me, too." The gentleness in his voice met the gentleness of the spring day like a melody meets its lyrics and, in spite of her anger, Niki listened.

"More than any other verse in the Bible," he continued, "it's the one that convinced me that the life I was leading before giving my life to Christ was one of running aimlessly and of doing nothing in life other than beating the air."

"Oh, Phil—" Niki stood and with her hands spread out imploringly before her, said, "I know the verse doesn't refer to only racing as in a running race—but don't you see how it could?" she finished with a stubborn whisper.

He looked almost hurt to her and she shook her head, suddenly realizing that Phil was telling her something really important about himself. And here she was, only thinking about herself. She pressed her fingers against her forehead as if to push out the anger, reseated herself next to him and took his hand in hers.

"But please—" Her voice was as soft as the breeze that fluttered off the canal a half mile below them. "Tell me how this verse spoke to you."

Phil squeezed his eyes tightly shut. He was hurting, but not for the reason that Niki thought. Phil was hurting because that old, demanding guilt came running in, like a mugger demanding money. Money would have been easy to give. The guilt demanded his soul. How Phil wanted to tell her everything, but he knew that now still wasn't the time. Niki needed him right now. His need—to have her know all and, he hoped, forgive all—would have to wait.

He turned to her and rubbed his fingers over the smoothness of her cheek, rejoicing that he could touch her.

"Darling Niki—that's another story—my story, and a story I want to tell you, but—"

For a moment as he looked into her wondering eyes he was tempted, very tempted, to tell her how his story collided with her story to make him the man he was today. But with renewed determination and a quick prayer to again give his life-consuming guilt to the only One who was capable of taking it from him, Phil guided the conversation back to Niki and to her feelings.

"Right now," he spoke with conviction, "we're discussing you and how you feel." He picked up the little New Testament from his lap and motioning to it, finally answered her question from a few moments before.

"Yes, Niki, I can see how easy it would be for you to take these verses to literally pertain to racing—"

"Good," she cut him off abruptly. Once Phil agreed that she could take the verses literally, she felt as though she had a platform to stand on. He could be her cheering section, the one to feed her conscience as friends often do.

"But, Niki," he quietly continued, "I think that you are wrong to do so."

Her eyes widened as she felt her figurative platform slide out from under her.

"Niki—don't you know that St. Paul used the allegory of racing because it was something the Corinthians would understand? They were so involved with sports because of this," he spread out his arms to include the ancient site, "their very own Isthmian Games."

"It's possible," she conceded, looking out over what at one time had been a fantastic sports center.

"Niki, in the ancient world, sports played an even bigger role in the lives of the people than they do in our world today. The ancient Hellenes had major sporting events every year."

"So I've heard," she conceded. "But first were the Olympic Games." She felt the need to defend the Games that meant so much to her; but even as she did, she hated the way it made her sound like a little girl.

"First were the Olympic Games," Phil agreed with a smile. "They were the oldest and the most famous, but the Isthmian Games, held right here where we are now sitting, were very important and second only to the Olympic Games. They were, in fact, probably one of the main reasons that St. Paul left Athens somewhat abruptly and traveled to Corinth." His eyes wandered over the dusty site as his imagination filled in the details of what had been magnificent structures of marble and stones.

In spite of herself, Niki was interested. Things about St. Paul always interested her. She looked back at Phil.

"I didn't know that."

Phil nodded and shifted on the ridged column to find a more comfortable spot. "See, back in ancient days, the games weren't just athletic events." He chuckled and waved his hand up to the verandah from where they had first looked out over the site. "Actually, you weren't far wrong when you said that it resembled a country fair that had just vacated the grounds, because the games back then were like a fair. It was a time when historians read their works, playwrights read their plays, and people came from around the world to hear the latest news."

"So—?" She spread her hands out impatiently.

"So," Phil patiently continued, "when Paul wrote these verses to the Corinthians, he was living in Ephesus, a Greek town on the eastern coast of the Aegean Sea, and he was trying to teach the Corinthians about the Christian life by using examples of things they were familiar with. Like Acrocorinth, the rock, the Isthmian Games were known to the Corinthians as well. You see, the people he wrote to weren't necessarily athletes. In fact it's possible that none of them were."

Niki knew that what Phil was saying rang true but the anger within her wouldn't let her accept it for herself. Stubbornly, she shot out with another verse. "What about, 'Let us run with perseverance the race marked out for us'?" she asked impatiently. "I always did just that, Phil! I let go of everything else—cheerleading, drama club, going out and eating pizza with my friends, and every other normal activity teenagers do in order to run that race that was marked out for me."

"But Niki. . .are you sure that you didn't get your races confused? Are you sure that it was a running race and not a different, perhaps much greater, race that this verse was speaking to you about?"

Her jaw tightened. "What do you mean?"

"Don't you realize that you are running your greatest race right now? This very minute even as we sit here. . ." He pushed ahead, even though he saw anger filling her again.

She glared at him as he gently explained, "Your Christian race. The life of a Christian is a race that we run until the day we die and you are running it now."

Niki heard his words but her ire wouldn't let her listen to them. Shaking her head, she spat out another quote, " 'You were running a good race. Who cut in on you and kept you from obeying the truth?' "

"Niki—"

"I'll tell you who cut in on me!" she shouted, her green eyes flashing, not giving him a chance to speak. "God cut in on me. He cut in on me when He didn't protect me." Her voice was dry and hoarse. She wondered if it would ever feel normal again.

"But don't you see, Niki—God did protect you."

"What!" She was incredulous.

"He protected you. Look at you, Niki—you're fine—you're whole—you're alive!"

"But I'm going to miss the Games because of the accident," she wailed. "My ankle might be well again someday, but not in time for these Games."

Phil smiled sadly. "Listen to yourself, Niki. . . ."

She shook her head in angry confusion.

He explained using one word. "Games. . ."

Her eyebrows knitted together in disbelief. To think that he was putting down the Olympic Games was almost like blasphemy to her.

"Niki—" he pressed on, "they're only games."

"The Olympic Games," she countered, almost livid that he would dare belittle them to her.

"Yes. The Olympic Games." He agreed to their importance and then shrugged his shoulders. "But games nonetheless. . ."

She stood and walked a short distance away from him before spinning back around. "How can you make so little of something that's so important to me!"

He walked over to her, stopping just a handbreadth away, and repeated another verse in the Bible, " 'Do you not know that in a race all the runners run, but only one gets the prize?' " He paused and exhaled audibly. "Niki. . .if you are going to take all the verses referring to races and racing literally. . .then take that one too. There was no guarantee that you were going to be the one to win the Olympic race."

Her eyes flashed at him and every fiber of her being was crying out to let anger rule. But she couldn't. Not with Phil.

Slowly, the green in her eyes began to cool and, reaching out, she draped her arms wearily around his shoulders and leaned against him, whispering as a very sad child might, into his sweater, "But I'll never know now. I won't run the race and I'll never know."

He wrapped his arms around her and held her. He held her as he had always wanted to hold her and softly he spoke into the freshness of her hair. "No. You won't know about that race. But you can still win the prize in the other race. . .in your Christian race. All Christians can win that prize." He pushed her head away from his shoulder and motioned to the ancient athletic site around them. "All those men who ran their races here. Do you know of any of them now? You are a runner and yet, you don't even know any of their names. They won their prizes, prizes that made them and their families heroes and financially solvent in their home cities for generations, yet now, we have practically no idea who they were."

She let her eyes wander the site and watched as a dust devil picked up the dirt and swirled it around the broken stones. She let her soul listen to Phil's very wise words. What had been so magnificent, a sports center of marble and stone and statuary unlike anything the twentieth century had been able to produce, was no more. But even more important was that its contestants were no more either. They ran their race and for what? A crown made of withered celery, and glory in their hometowns. Did she want to win the Olympics for personal glory? She'd never thought so before, but now she wondered.

She shook her head. That thought was too much for her. She was suddenly exhausted and wanted to leave. She looked up at Phil. She wanted him to know that she wasn't angry with him. She had asked him to be her spiritual coach, after all. "You're a good coach." She placed her hand wearily on his arm. "But I think I've had enough training for today. Please take me home."

He nodded and supported her as she leaned her head against his shoulder. They walked back up the way they came, through the museum, to the little car. Phil breathed a prayer of relief. Niki was a great runner. She had stamina and determination. And he was sure that her character applied both to her footraces and to her Christian race. He had no doubt that she would win a gold medal in her Christian race. He only prayed that she would still want him when it was all over.

Chapter 10

S pring blossomed in Corinth. Glorious days of warmth and sunshine marched one after the other over the green and golden land, while the sky above was an arch of blue, devoid of clouds. The earth became a riot of color with wildflowers and cultivated flowers covering the life-giving ground and filling the trees with blossoms like confetti that had been sprinkled over the land.

With the improved weather, Niki's exercise classes filled up with participants wanting to tone their bodies for spring clothes. Niki's reputation as an athlete, and good reports about her abilities as a trainer, drew people from around the Corinth area in addition to the hotel's patrons. Niki's uneasiness about directing the classes disappeared and she admitted that Mary had been right that the best way to help herself was to help others. When she was exercising with her enthusiastic classes, her pain and anger were forgotten.

The demand was so great that Niki had to increase from two to four classes per day. Before long, she was pleased to discover that she had gotten back into pretty good shape herself, without even really trying.

It had been arranged with her doctor in Athens, and with Kristen and Paul, that her pins would be removed shortly before Easter. In the meantime, swimming continued to take the place of running. She arose at dawn, before anyone else was up, and swam lap after lap across the small Bay of Cenchrea.

It was cold at that time of day but as soon as Niki slid her lithe body into the water and worked her muscles, she didn't feel the chill any longer. She relished the peace and quiet and she honestly didn't think that the Garden of Eden could have been any better. As she swam, she was able to think about what she and Phil had talked about at ancient Isthmia without anger, making her thoughts a jumble of twirling impulses. Sometimes, as she pushed her body across the bay, she succeeded in pushing the anger into a far corner of her mind. Maybe Phil was right about God and His protection of her. Maybe God did protect her, if not her dream, that dark November night, and maybe He did have a purpose for all her suffering.

Sometimes, as she considered Phil's words, her spirit felt as light and as free as her body as it cut through the water, unencumbered and graceful. Still, she never succeeded in expelling the anger completely from her mind. When she was least prepared, an unexpected thought—*What would I be doing right now if the accident hadn't happened?*—would slither into her mind, and it would torment her and anger would fill her and grow until it made her feel as though she were swimming with a cumbersome chain tied around her. At those times, seeing Phil was all that could relieve her of her inner battle.

But she knew that wasn't fair to him. She knew that no human being should ever place such expectations on another. She'd been a Christian since she was a little girl and she knew that she should be turning to God. But how could she turn to Him when He was the very One with whom she was angry? He was the One who had allowed her to miss the Games.

Then Phil's words would come echoing back: "Yes, the Olympic Games," and that little shrug, "but games nonetheless. . ." That was a bitter and extremely difficult pill for her to swallow. At the moment, its sour taste was slowly melting in her mouth, slowly seeping into her system, in spite of her stubborn attempts to reject it.

"Dear God. . . ," she breathed early one morning as her thoughts began to weigh her down, "have I been reading Your will for my life wrong all these years?"

When she realized that she had actually prayed her question to God, she shook her head in amazement. It had been months since she had talked to Him. She rested her head against the lifesaver's can that, for safety's sake, always accompanied her on her solitary swims, and she grinned happily up into the sun as it rose in the Hellenic sky. "The rosy fingertips of dawn" was how Homer had described the rising sun in *The Odyssey*. As its light swept over Homer's ancient land, Niki was amazed at how accurate his description was, practically every morning. It made her feel cozy and warm.

Letting the can bob out behind her, she breathed out and sank slowly into the cool waters of the bay, exchanging the dusty pink of the dawning sky for the light and bubbly water. Her hair fanned out behind her, feminine and free, and as she started to kick her legs and swing her arms in their steady swimmer's arc, she suddenly realized that the black mood of anger was gone.

She smiled under the water and blinked her green eyes as she realized that going to God with her thoughts had given her this peace. She could hardly wait to tell Phil.

But talking to Phil had to wait until much later in the day. He, too, had become very busy. His fame as an English teacher of excellence had spread like wildfire throughout the Corinth area and all the mothers of the area wanted him to teach their little darlings. Although Niki was happy for him, it meant that their time together was greatly reduced. She was glad that Mary had finally prevailed upon him to accept one of the hotel bungalows as his apartment; otherwise, Niki feared that they might never see one another.

Niki wondered who missed Phil more. She or Stavros? Stavros had become accustomed to coming home from school and having Phil as his companion for an hour or two or more. He had been doing fine, much to all of their delight, but when he returned home one afternoon and was told that Phil wasn't expected for at least another two hours, the disappointment on the little boy's face was keen.

"But what will I do until he comes home?" he asked of his mother, sounding to Niki every bit like her little brother used to when he had been bored or upset about something. Mary smoothed her son's full head of dark hair down as much as it would go and with a twinkle in her eyes suggested, "It's such a beautiful day and so warm. . . . How about. . .we have a pool party?"

Through his thick glasses Stavros's eyes flashed excitedly. "The first of the year!"

Mary nodded and explained to Niki, "We don't normally get much opportunity to swim once the season starts, so we've always promised Stavros that the first swim is one we all take together as a family. We've always made it into an impromptu barbecue party as well."

Stavros's countenance fell and Mary realized her mistake. She had spoken in the plural, inadvertently including her dead husband in her words. She placed her arms around Stavros's dejected shoulders and drew him close to her, wishing with all her mother's might that she could protect him from such pain. "Oh, Stavros. . .I know it's hard. . . ," she whispered. "I miss *Baba*, too."

He turned eyes filled with tears up toward his mother. "Why, Mamma? Why? Why did God allow my *baba* to die?"

Mary looked at Niki and the sorrow in her eyes brought tears to Niki's. She didn't know how she would have answered Stavros if he had been her son, but even more, in that split second, she realized that she needed Mary's answer too. Stavros had asked the age-old question, the same question Niki had asked a million times. Why? Why does God allow something bad to happen?

Mary turned back to her son and when she spoke, Niki heard the wisdom of mothers throughout the ages in her tone; a wisdom, an instinct, that seems to become a part of a woman when she nurtures and cares for a child. "Stavros, you must never forget that the ways of God are wonderful and that we must always trust Him. . ."

"But how could it be wonderful for Him to take my *baba*?" Stavros cried. The question had burned in his mind since the moment he learned of his father's death.

"I don't know," Mary answered truthfully, with all the longing for her husband she herself felt in her words. "I don't know. . . ," she repeated, but then continued with conviction, "but we must not forget that it is not always necessary to see everything with our own eyes. Sometimes. . ." She looked off toward the horizon, which was visible through the huge picture window, and whispered, "Sometimes, Stavros. . .we must see through the eyes of our belief in our Savior." She turned back to her son and gently touched his glasses. "His vision is much clearer than ours."

Stavros looked off toward the horizon for a moment, seeming to search for that which his mother saw.

"And too," Mary continued, "you must not forget that your father was not a young man. He was nearly seventy years old, and you, my son," she patted Stavros's shoulders with pride, "you were the joy of his life—the fruit of his old age—the son he never thought he would have. And in you, Stavros, your father lives on in this world just as he lives on in the next world with Jesus."

Stavros nodded his head and seemed to grow in maturity before their very eyes. He had asked his mother, he had listened to her answer, and he believed her. Niki knew that she had to accord God, her heavenly

Father, the same respect. The boy stood on his toes and kissed his mother's smooth cheek.

"Thank you, Mamma," he whispered. Then he smiled and declared, "Since *Baba* isn't here to light the barbecue, I will do it this year and from now on—until I have a son and he takes over for me."

Mary nodded, and her unshed tears were heard in the timbre of her voice. "Your father would like that, my son."

Stavros nodded and Niki thought she saw a new strength in the boy now, as if he suddenly realized that the baton in the race of life had been handed to him regardless of whether he wanted to take it or not. For the last few months, he had been unwilling to reach for the baton, thinking that it was too soon to grasp it, as if the previous runner's timing was off. But now, in that split second of time, he seemed to understand that it wasn't his father's timing, as directed by God, that had been off, but rather his own.

Niki knew, as she stood in the busy hotel lobby with this lovely mother and her son, that she was witnessing the miracle of a boy growing up, the miracle of a boy turning into a man. It wasn't Stavros's choice—he hadn't wanted to fill his father's shoes so soon—but he now seemed to accept it as God's choice for his life and Niki was sure that he would no longer give his mother cause for worry.

Stavros informed them that he was off to make all the preparations for the barbecue-swimming party. Mary turned, with a smile that needed no words to convey the joy in her mother's heart over her son's recovery, and returned her attention to the hotel business that was always close at hand.

As Niki wandered away from the lobby toward the gym, she knew that there was a lesson for her in all of this as well. She knew that she had to listen to Mary's words to Stavros. They were the universal answer to the universal question of 'Why, God?' Even more, Niki knew that she had to start listening to God as He answered her as well.

❧

The party was a huge success. The pool sparkled in the afternoon sun and Mary's son shone in his role as host. Stavros ran from guest to guest trying to get as many people as possible into the pool. For many, it was still a bit too cold, but when the traditional first big splash was finally made, at least twenty people could be counted in the pool, with Mary and Stavros leading the way.

Niki knew most of the people from her exercise classes, but it was unusual for all the guests to be together at the same time. It felt like a combination of a reunion and a Fourth of July celebration, especially when Stavros lit the barbecue pit and the smell of charcoal drifted over the grounds. There was a moment of respectful silence from the merrymakers when Stavros softly said, "I do this in remembrance of my father," as he lit the tiny flame that would grow to fill the entire pit.

Mary's pride in her son was evident. There was a new softness about her stance now, as if she could finally relax, finally let go, finally stop grieving for both her dead husband and her traumatized son. And Niki was happy for her, grateful for the relief that was in her heart.

Niki was happy for herself when Phil finally appeared. She spied him from her lookout post at the pool's edge as his eyes, like a magnet to shiny metal, immediately found hers. His gaze didn't falter and Niki felt the current that ran between them escalate from liking and caring to love.

He walked toward her slowly, as if he didn't want to break the connection, and squatted down next to the pool. Niki's skin tingled as he reached down and ran his fingertips over the drops of water that clung to her face.

"I've missed you," he said and smiled.

She returned his smile. "I've missed you, too."

"Do you want to take a walk?"

"To the lighthouse?" Niki asked hopefully. That was their spot, their own private place where she felt like anything was possible. And Niki thought that this was a day for the impossible to happen.

Today, Stavros had recovered.

Today, she wanted to recover as well. She wanted to forget all anger and to be with Phil forever.

He nodded. "To the lighthouse."

Phil finished his sentence in his mind. *To the lighthouse, where the light will either shine on our relationship, dim it, or go out entirely.*

He felt a deep need, a deep desire to love her forever, and he knew that God was leading him to tell her about his part in her accident today.

It had to be today.

It had to be today because he had to confess before he could ask her to marry him. He would ask for her forgiveness and then, if she would forgive him, he would ask for her hand in marriage.

Placing her hands on the edge of the pool Niki lifted her body out of the water and sat on the side, intending to let her skin drip-dry naturally in the warmth of the sun. Phil's intake of breath told her that was a mistake. He managed to keep his eyes trained to hers, but for the first time, he really didn't want to look into their pretty depths. He wanted to let his eyes run down the length of her body, and he wanted to let his hands follow his eyes, and he wanted. . .

Abruptly, he stood and, with his hands on his hips, he looked off toward the horizon. Niki quickly slid back into the water. Her suit was modest—a plain, no-nonsense, navy blue athletic suit—but Phil's befuddled reaction told her everything she needed to know, and she loved him too much to tempt him in this way.

He glanced back at her and saw that only her head now showed above the water. He smiled, a whimsical smile of thanks. "Meet me at the lighthouse in fifteen minutes," he softly intoned, and, turning on his heels, he walked away.

Niki crossed her arms on the edge of the pool and watched with a smile that was almost as big as the Aegean Sea as he strode across the grass toward his bungalow on the other side of the hotel. When he disappeared from view, she slowly sank into the pool and, with the water muffling the sound, she yelled out in delight, "Yippee!" She knew that things were happening between them. And she was glad. Very, very glad.

She wanted to tell him so much, all about her thoughts that morning and her prayer, but more than anything, she wanted to tell him. . .that she loved him. . .and that she had loved him since. . .the very beginning of time at least!

Chapter 11

P hil returned to his bungalow to pick up his New Testament before heading out to wait for Niki at the ancient lighthouse. Climbing up onto the old stones he leaned his back against one large sandstone block. It had baked all day in the strong Hellenic sun and, even though the orb's golden rays no longer touched it, it had retained the heat in its porous surface. Phil found it warm and comforting.

He looked off toward the colorfully painted fishing boats that bobbed, as much as their tethers would allow them, in the gently lapping sea. He couldn't help but think about the mosaic, the "Shore Vista," at the Isthmian museum. The fishing boat's song was a faint echo of the bustling past this shore had known. Once, all the mighty wealth of both the Roman and the Byzantine empires had passed through this harbor. The sounds then had been those of merchantmen and soldiers, hawkers and adventurers, mixing with the sounds of a city that was alive and prosperous, and households filled with husbands and wives and their children.

He looked down at the little Bible in his hands and flipped through its pages. He stopped at the sixteenth chapter of Romans and read out loud what Paul had written, most likely from this very city, to the church in Rome: " 'I commend to you our sister Phoebe, a servant of the church in Cenchrea.' " Phil looked toward the modern-day village and thought about Phoebe, a woman who had lived so long ago but had been such a helping force in the early church that St. Paul had mentioned her in his epistle.

The sound of cheerful conversation drifted over the stillness of the day from the party at Mary's hotel. He smiled as he thought he heard Stavros laugh and knew that the village of Cenchrea was still alive and well. It had changed with time but it was still home to men and women and their children; home to people like Phoebe—and Mary. When he had met Mary in the lobby of the hotel as he returned from teaching, he had

375

known immediately that something was different about her, something different in a good way. She had told him that the difference was that her heart was no longer heavy concerning Stavros and, with joy, she had briefly recounted what had transpired that day.

Phil smiled and with a gull singing its ancient tune far above him, he bent his head and prayed, a prayer of deep gratitude to his heavenly Father, "Dear Father, thank You for the healing of that precious boy. . . ." He sank to his knees and rested his hands on one of the ancient lighthouse's huge dressed stones. With his forehead resting on the back of his hands, he continued, with longing, with desire in his voice and in the very muscles of his body: "And please, Lord, please let Niki forgive me. Please give me the right words to speak. I know that this is the day, the moment You have chosen for me to tell her about my part in her accident. I trust You to guide the conversation, and I trust. . . ," his voice cracked as he whispered, "I trust. . .that You will guide her to forgive me. . . ."

He lifted his eyes to the huge rock citadel of Acrocorinth six miles across the plain of Corinth. The sun was now directly behind the citadel. Its golden rays silhouetted the fortress, turning the light brown stone into a muted pink against the blue glow of the western sky. Phil stood and smiled at the pink coloring. Pink was a happy color, a color that reminded him of joy and laughter, of spring and summer—but most of all, a color that reminded him of Niki.

He sighed, a sigh of hope and faith, before turning his eyes out over the bay. It was an evening of storybook proportions. Swallows swooped above his head, bees busily buzzed from one colorful flower to another, the sea was a mirror to the clear, but softly hued, pastel sky above. Most important of all. . .the beautiful woman he loved. . .was coming toward him.

Phil turned in the direction of lightly approaching footsteps and smiled. One look at Phil's face and any doubts that Niki might have harbored that her feelings for him weren't mutual fled as far away as winter now was from this warm and gentle shore. Her heart soared to the heights of the seagull that was playing far above Phil's head and she stepped lightly and as quickly as she could toward him. She wanted to run to him. She was certain that if her ankle would have allowed it, she could have easily broken her world record in reaching his waiting arms. As it was, she enjoyed the moment, a forever moment. When he reached down his hand to help her up onto the stone platform, and she stepped up close to him, she didn't consider her words, but freely gave voice to the look that was in both of their eyes. She said what was in her heart and had been from their very first meeting.

"I love you, Phil." Her voice was firm, her voice was soft, her voice was the voice of a woman very much in love. Phil had no doubt that it was true.

"Darling Niki. . . ." He looked at her with his sparkling blue eyes, eyes so blue and so alive with the look of love that Niki thought that her heart just might burst from the bubbling pressure of happiness that was building within her.

"Darling Niki," he repeated, and just before his lips claimed hers he whispered, "I love you too."

This kiss was different from the others. It was a pledge, it was a decree, it was a pact of love. It was a kiss of opening one's heart, one's life to another.

But it was a bittersweet kiss for Phil, because he didn't know whether she would still love him after he told her what he knew he must tell her. Now.

Gently, slowly, their lips separated, but Phil and Niki remained close and Niki could feel the groan as it grew from deep within Phil's being even before she heard it.

"Niki—there's something I must tell you. . ."

Niki was so certain that he was going to say that he couldn't love someone who didn't place God first in her life, that she quickly placed her fingertips against his lips to stop him. "Shhhh, darling. . .first let me tell you. . ."

With excitement barely contained by the reverent quality in her voice she said, "I. . .prayed. . .this morning."

"Niki. . ." Phil breathed out her name on a breath of joy and closed his eyes in thankful prayer. He understood how God was orchestrating everything so perfectly. Niki had prayed—a big step, a giant step in her healing. Communication with God was open again—and Phil marveled at God's timing. Now he knew why it was time to tell her about his part in the accident. She would have not only her human friends to rely on but, most important of all, she would have her heavenly Father to comfort her and guide her. And maybe, just maybe, Phil thought with longing and hope, their declared love for one another would be enough for her to forgive him. "Niki. . .I'm so glad."

She quickly continued, wanting to explain. "It wasn't a formal prayer or anything." She shrugged her shoulders. "Actually, I just kind of happened into it."

"Tell me."

She looked out over the water where she had been swimming that morning and hesitantly began, "I was out there," she nodded toward the bay, "and I was thinking about what we talked about in ancient Isthmia. . ." She turned to Phil and qualified what she meant, "About God protecting me and the Olympic Games being," she faltered over her words—the idea was still hard for her to swallow, and even harder for her to say—"just games," she finally admitted. "And next thing I knew, I was asking God if I had been misreading His will for my life all these years."

"And—?"

"He gave me peace," she said simply.

"Niki—" he drew her close to him. But when he felt her shoulders slump, he frowned and leaned back to look at her. The questioning lines that crisscrossed her face confused him. "What is it, darling?"

"I don't know. . .I felt peace then, but now. . . ," she rushed on, trying to get her jumbled thoughts out, "I've lived my life by these racing verses for so many years that it kind of leaves me empty to think that I was wrong to do so." Cocking her head to the side she smiled self-consciously. "Help me out, coach."

"I. . ." He wanted to tell her that he resigned from the job of coaching the moment that they declared their love for one another. But he knew that that kind of thinking was wrong. His desire to bare his soul to her would have to wait until God directed its truth to come out lovingly and with kindness. Right now, the only words that were coming to him were in answer to her plea. So, following God's lead, he found himself asking, "Is there a particular verse that makes you feel this way?"

She closed her eyes and nodded her head. There was a particular verse, the verse that had reverberated in her mind and had fed the anger for so many months. "Acts 20:24," she finally whispered, and Phil knew that she was climbing deep within her thoughts to admit to the angry feelings.

Quickly, he flipped through his Bible. He found the verse highlighted in pink just after she started reciting it from memory.

" 'However'. . ." She wanted to mask the hurt, the anger, the confusion, but she couldn't. Her voice was an honest reflection of everything inside of her. " 'I consider my life worth nothing to me, if only I may finish the race and complete the task the Lord Jesus has given me. . . .' " Her voice trailed off and Phil waited for her to finish the verse. Instead, she turned to look at him with eyes that were as sad as they had been happy a few minutes before. "That verse makes me feel like I'm a failure, Phil. . . ," she admitted.

"But why?"

"Don't you see. . . ," her voice was almost the pitch of a wail, "not only didn't I finish the race. . .I didn't even get to run it."

Phil looked from her eyes back down to the Bible. "But, Niki. . . ," he said, looking back at her, "you're forgetting the rest of the verse." He pointed to it in his Bible and read ". . .The task of testifying to the gospel of God's grace."

"I would have testified that gospel to the world if I had won in the Olympics!" she shot out, the venom in her voice startling Phil. "And so many people would have listened to an Olympic winner!" She spoke with a conviction that she still felt keenly.

"But, Niki," Phil spoke calmly, evenly, knowing that they both needed the peace of the Lord to calm their hearts, "how can you be sure that for you to be an Olympic winner was God's plan for your life and not your own?"

Phil's question inadvertently echoed Niki's thoughts from that morning, which caused Niki's anger to flare.

"What do you mean?" she asked through clenched teeth.

"I mean, maybe God wanted you to have the desire to run in the Olympics but, in the end, to use it in a different way from what you expected."

She turned away from him. She didn't want him to reconfirm the very thought that had terrified her, the thought that had changed the course of her life.

"Maybe," he pressed on softly, "God never intended for you to participate in the Olympic Games."

Her eyes flashed up to meet his. "But, Phil," she whispered, "why did God give me the dream, the desire, the ability even, to run in the Olympics if I was never going to be given the chance to do so?"

"Perhaps," he looked down at the little New Testament and tapped the page that was still opened to the Book of Acts, "for the exact reason written here. So that you would testify to the gospel of God's grace."

"I don't buy it," she groused, her shoulders almost heaving in anger. "I wasn't even able to participate in the Games. What grace is there in that?"

"How many people do, Niki?"

"What?" She swiveled back to him, eyes flashing like bright bits of burning coal.

"How many people do get to run their Olympic race?" he repeated, then sought to clarify himself. "Look—there are far more people in the world who are disappointed about their lives than there are Olympic winners, or winners at anything for that matter. People who can feel with you, people who can identify with you, people who can cry with you, Niki." He reached for her shoulders and gently, lovingly, squeezed them. Tilting his head to the side, he smiled. "You are known—you're America's little darling. Look, even Kristen and Paul remembered you—"

"So—?"

"So, people everywhere—people who have had disappointments, and who hasn't?—can feel with you and," he took a deep breath, "and they are all probably wondering how you are going to finish your race."

"How can I finish a race I can't even compete in?" she stubbornly asked, refusing to leave the literal track for the figurative one that Phil was talking about.

"You can finish your race, Niki," he encouraged adamantly, nodding his head. "You can finish it and complete the task the Lord Jesus has given you—"

"Which is. . . ?" she asked obstinately.

He tapped the page in the New Testament. "The task of testifying to the gospel of God's grace right here and now in the situation you now find yourself in."

She sighed. She felt defeated. But in defeat, she was amazed to realize that she also felt relief. Relief, because this defeat wasn't directed toward her, but rather, for the first time, toward the anger that had made her soul its battlefield.

Reaching for Phil, needing the comfort only his arms could bring, she rested her head upon his shoulder. It felt so good, so comforting. She knew that what he said was right and true. It all went back to the

Christian race they had talked about that day in ancient Isthmia. But there was still one thing she couldn't understand. Softly, stubbornly she asked, "But why, Phil? Why didn't God protect me last November? Just one second would have made all the difference, *one second.*"

Phil squeezed his eyes closed and drew her tighter against him as his old enemy—shame—came running in to attack him. He shuddered against the blow. What could he say? Because the beer-drinking fool that had been a passenger in the car that rammed into her had been bored with his rich-boy existence and had insisted on going out that night driving with his reluctant buddy?

He knew that wasn't the right thing to say. After months of prayer, Phil could see past the small picture to the big picture, and with all his faith in action he knew that God's answer, the answer he was expected to give, was different.

Using the precious name of Jesus, Phil pushed his old enemy away and whispered God's answer to the woman he loved. "Maybe because He had something better planned for your life than winning an Olympic gold medal. And maybe your trying for that Olympic gold is what makes His better plan work."

"What could be better?" She knew that she sounded like a little child whining, but she couldn't help it.

Phil placed his arm around her shoulder and they stepped over to their favorite stone perch and sat down.

"You know, it wasn't in St. Paul's plans to be in the place from where this verse was spoken."

"Really?" Niki's attention, as always, was caught by stories of that great apostle.

Phil nodded. "He had planned to sail from here directly to Syria." Phil looked out over the sleepy little fishing harbor of Cenchrea, seeing through time to the busy port it had been during St. Paul's times.

"I didn't know that," she admitted and looked out over the harbor, imagining the past as Phil's words led her.

"He hadn't planned to visit the churches in Asia Minor again," Phil continued as he flipped ahead in his Bible to the twentieth chapter of Acts. He pointed to it and said, "But because of a plot against his life, he had to change his plans and travel overland back through northern Hellas, that is the area of Greece known as Macedonia—Thessalonica,

Appolonia, Philippi—on his trip back to Judea. And believe me, Niki, it was a very hard road to walk in those days."

Niki looked out over the rocky terrain of the Greek countryside and murmured, "Literally a rough walk."

Phil nodded. "Exactly. But because St. Paul wasn't able to sail directly to Syria from here as he planned, he stopped off in Miletus, a town on the coast of Asia Minor. From there, he sent for the elders of the church in Ephesus to talk to them. This verse comes from that talk."

"Really. . ."

"So, don't you think that St. Paul knew about 'races' that turn out differently than planned, Niki?" Phil took her hand and gently, almost coaxingly smiled at her. "He didn't just miss the boat that he had planned to sail on from here." He glanced out over the still bay. "He had to escape from here before he was murdered."

"I didn't know that verse's history. . ." Niki murmured humbly.

"What was it that Paul and Kristen Andrakos said?" Phil asked.

Niki knew what Phil referred to. She hadn't wanted to admit it back then, but now, knowing how St. Paul's path had been so different from the one he had thought to follow—and from this very spot—made her wonder. Finally she whispered, "The path of life. . ."

" 'You have made known to me the path of life. . . .' " Phil quoted the verse from Psalm sixteen. "St. Paul traveled a different path, the path God led him on, and the words he spoke while on that path have helped so many people throughout time." He squeezed her hand. "Maybe your disappointment is to help others too," he prompted.

"I–I don't understand how," she murmured, but at the same time, for the first time, she realized that she really wanted to know how.

"Maybe," he continued softly, "through your disappointment you will help many more people than if your dream had become the reality you sought. And perhaps. . . ," he continued so quietly that Niki had to lean closer in order to hear his words, "that's why God gave you the dream. . . and then took it away."

She shook her head. "I still don't understand how that could help others," she questioned, but now neither anger nor antagonism was in her voice.

Phil answered carefully. "In order that you might help others like you —others who didn't succeed at their 'Olympic Dream,' whatever it might have been—through no fault of their own."

Niki breathed out deeply and looked out over the deep sea. "So much of what you say makes sense, Phil." She sighed, a deep releasing sigh as if she had been holding her breath for months. "But it's so hard."

"Harder than training for the Olympics?"

"A million times harder!"

"Maybe that's what makes it the race you are to finish in order to testify to the gospel of God's grace."

Something inside Niki seemed to click into place, as if a major part of a puzzle had just found its spot. She felt as though she had finally been given a satisfactory answer, as if there were some sense to be made out of all the confusion and pain she had gone through. To think that maybe God did have a different plan for her life, and that her dream had been necessary in order for her to fulfill it, gave her a sense of purpose, a reason for being the person she had become through all the events of her life.

She turned to Phil. More than anything, she was thankful for this man, this wonderful man, who helped her to see it all and she wondered what events had formed him into the man he was today. Lifting her hand to the chiseled and beloved planes of his face she softly, lovingly asked, "What has happened in your life, my love, to make you the wise and wonderful man you are?"

In spite of the warmth of her body pressed close to his, Phil felt his blood run cold. She had asked the exact question that could only be answered in one way.

The shadow that suddenly covered the brightness of Phil's face like haze on a summer day told Niki that his wisdom had been gained through pain.

She gently squeezed his shoulder. "Phil. . .I love you," she reminded him. "Please tell me."

Breathing out deeply, he prayed for strength. "I hurt someone very badly once—" his voice broke.

"Someone you loved?"

Slowly he answered. "Not at the time—but I do now." He paused and his eyes bored into hers as if they wanted something from her—understanding, forgiveness—Niki wasn't sure what. His intensity confused her and it was beginning to concern her.

"Because, you see, Niki—the one I hurt was you."

Chapter 12

Niki suddenly felt very cold. The sun had set below the western horizon and she felt as though it was setting on the world she had made for herself as well. With dread lacing her voice she asked, "What are you talking about? You've never hurt me."

Phil gathered her, confusion and all, into his arms and as he held her he prayed that it wouldn't be the for the last time.

Niki pulled back and looked at him. Her eyes were intense as they anxiously scanned his face. "Please, Phil. . .tell me what you're talking about."

With the tips of his fingers he pushed her strawberry-blond hair away from her face, then reached for her hand. Turning to gaze out at the darkening sea, he softly spoke the words he had been wanting to tell her, been dreading to tell her, since he discovered their truth that first afternoon in Olympia.

"I was a different man, Niki," he paused and turned to face her, "before last November the third."

Niki's eyebrows drew together in a straight line that cut her face in two. "November the third. . . ," she whispered, thinking back to the awful event of that day, to the accident that had changed her life. She shivered as the implications of his words slowly seeped into her consciousness. As she looked at him, she wished with all her being that what she was thinking wasn't true. But with a sense of betrayal that made her face feel first hot then cold, she knew that it was.

Pursing his lips together to keep from crying out his remorse, he nodded and confirmed her thought. "Yes, darling, the day of your accident. Because you see, Niki, the accident. . .that changed your life. . .also changed mine."

She stepped away from him, shaking her head in mute denial before she found her voice. "You. . .you were one of the beer-drinking—" her voice cracked.

"Fools," he supplied the word for her.

Emotion ran rampant across Niki's face. Hurt, anger, disbelief were all there. But mostly anger, anger that such a trick would be played on her by God, by Phil, by the two she loved most in the world.

Phil slowly nodded his head.

"And you never told me!" she cried out. It was an accusation.

He breathed out deeply and tried to explain. "I wanted to give our friendship—"

"Friendship!" she spat the word out in disbelief, violently shaking her head from side to side in denial. "Friends don't ram each other's cars, and friends definitely do not lie to one another."

"Niki. . ." He wanted to explain to her—he had to explain to her—and he prayed to God that she would understand. "I didn't lie to you. I just didn't tell you everything about my past—"

"Or how your past met my past to make me miss the Olympic Games!"

He ran his hand distractedly through his hair. Her response to the news was as bad as his worst fears had been. "I wanted to tell you, but God led me to believe that I shouldn't until now—until our friendship had a chance to grow without the accident coming between us—"

"What a cop-out!" she cut him off. "You're trying to blame straight cowardice on God!"

Phil ran his hand through his hair again. Even though he had considered many times that she would be angry when she learned that he had been involved in the accident, he hadn't truthfully expected such bitterness from her. But he now saw that he was going to have to run the hard race of patience with Niki. Her forgiveness would not come lightly or quickly.

"Niki, I'm not blaming God for anything. After I realized that you were the woman in the accident, I started praying about what I should do. Believe me—it would have been easier for me to blurt out my identity then and there, but God led me to believe—"

She cut him off with a breath of disbelieving exasperation that left little doubt about what she thought about that overused line. But even in the face of her blatant disbelief, Phil knew that he had indeed been following God's leading in not telling her sooner. If she didn't want to believe him, that was between her and God. He pressed on.

"*God,*" he repeated, putting emphasis on his Sovereign's name, "led me to believe that I would have been helping only myself if I had done that, and not you."

Niki snorted again, a groan that tore through her body. Part of her, the part that had spent months hating the nameless, faceless fools who had crashed into her, wanted to run away from Phil and never see him again; but the other part, the part that had grown to love the man Phil was, wanted to stay and hear him out—and be convinced that it was still okay to love him. The two parts warred bitterly and ferociously within her.

"Niki," Phil continued, "when I learned after the accident what my senseless action had caused you to suffer, I. . .well. . .it was the catalyst that led me to Christ. And after I asked Him to be my Lord and my Savior, I asked Him to let me somehow help the girl who I had hurt." Phil shrugged his shoulders. "Bringing us together here in Greece is an answer to that prayer. Not the answer I expected. . ." He reached out for her hand and she let him take it, which gave him hope. He continued quietly, "I never expected that I would fall in love with that girl."

Niki felt his hand on hers and wanted with all her being to squeeze it back and tell him everything was all right, but that old, hateful anger, the anger that had held her tightly in its grip for the past several months, just wouldn't allow her. It was too much a habit now to be angry, too much a part of her. She shrugged off his hand and with her back as rigid as a doorpost, she turned away from him.

"Niki. . .I'm so sorry about the accident. So, so sorry. . . ," he finally apologized to her, the thing that he had wanted to do since he had found out who she was in Olympia.

She looked at him measuringly. "Do you really think it's as simple as that?"

"I think the last few months have proven that I know forgiveness is not simple," he replied truthfully. "But I also think that these months together have proven to you what kind of man I now am as well. I'm no longer the beer-drinking fool I was."

She sighed and turned out toward the sea, wrapping her arms around herself as though she could bind up her heartache. After a moment she whispered, "It hurts, Phil. . .it hurts. . .and I feel so betrayed by you." With tears gathering in her eyes, she stammered, "The very one I had grown to trust the most in the world."

He reached out his arms for her, begging her to come to him, begging her to let him help to ease the ache he himself had unwittingly caused her. Niki stared at him with the blank, empty look one might give to a complete stranger. Finally, he let his arms drop back to his sides.

"I'm sorry, Niki," he whispered again. "There's nothing else I can say."

"I–I need time." She shook her head. "I trusted you and now. . ." She shook her head again. "I'm so confused."

Phil swallowed hard. That was her decision. He had to accept it. With patience and hope and love, and much prayer, he would accept it. "If you ever find it in your heart to forgive me. . .I'll be waiting for you. But, Niki. . ." He stepped up to her and gently brushed his fingers across her cheek. "Just remember, unforgiveness is as heavy a cloak to wear as guilt." He smiled sadly.

What does he know about guilt? she wondered bitterly. He certainly hadn't seemed like a guilty man during the last few months. But before she could ask him, and before she realized what he was doing, he lowered his hand, stepped down from the stone platform of the ancient lighthouse, and walked slowly into the dark night away from her.

Niki stood dumfounded. At the same time she knew that she shouldn't be surprised. Phil wasn't a man who would push himself on anyone. He had asked for her forgiveness. She had refused to give it. It would be up to her now to go to him.

She wanted to.

Her body was aching to go after him. But she couldn't.

She couldn't because she didn't forgive him.

Anger and bitterness still ruled.

❧

The night was as long and as confusing as Niki had feared it would be. The only issue she could resolve was that she had to get away.

In the morning, she called Kristen and asked if she could come to visit a few days early. Kristen was thrilled and insisted on sending her aunt's car and driver down to pick her up and bring her to Athens. Niki gladly accepted. She was too numb to deal with making other arrangements. When a luxurious Mercedes sedan pulled up in front of the lobby an hour and a half later, she was ready.

Mary was shocked when Niki entered the lobby carrying a suitcase.

"I didn't think you were due to go to Athens until next week."

"I wasn't, but—" Niki hadn't wanted to burden Mary with her problems but the look of concern on her friend's face brought the truth tumbling out. "Oh, Mary. Phil told me last night—he was one of the men who slammed into my car."

"What!"

"Your angel. . . ," Niki said, with a sour note in her voice.

Mary pursed her lips together before speaking. "Did something happen to him after the accident?" Mary was trying to reconcile her mental picture of the careless drunks in the accident with the fine gentleman that Phil was today.

"What do you mean?"

"I mean. . .I think he must have had a radical change since the accident. Has he?"

A streaking sense of betrayal flashed through Niki's mind. She had expected Mary to be as appalled as she had been by the information. Carefully she answered, "That's what he claims."

"Did he ask you to forgive him?"

"Yes."

Mary looked at her. "And did you?"

Niki slowly shook her head. "I don't know if I can forgive him," she spoke, finally verbalizing the thought that had haunted her throughout the long night. "That's why I have to get away. I. . .I can't face him right now." She handed Mary the note she'd written for Phil.

"Please make sure he gets this."

Mary fingered the white envelope. "Are you sure you don't want to wait and talk to him?"

"I'm sure." Niki was adamant about that. She didn't want to see Phil right now. She couldn't.

Mary licked her lips as if she were weighing her next words carefully. "You know—it's possible that the guilt he wears from knowing that he was the one who destroyed your dream could be even greater than the anger and bitterness you still wear."

Niki's brows drew together. Phil had said something like that the night before. "He doesn't act like a man weighed down by guilt," she pointed out caustically.

"Well. . .since he's a Christian. . .he shouldn't be weighed down by it. God has forgiven all of us our sins because of what Jesus did at Calvary. I think Phil has learned the secret of giving his guilt away to Christ." Mary paused. "Maybe you should learn how to give your anger away. I did."

"What were you angry about?" Niki thoughtlessly shot out.

"My husband dying," Mary replied softly.

Niki shut her eyes in embarrassment, embarrassed that her self-centeredness had cause her to speak so insensitively. "Oh, Mary. . . I'm sorry."

Mary shrugged off Niki's apology as being unnecessary and the two women smiled at one another, friends that pain had brought close together.

"Go to Athens," Mary finally urged. "Go and think a bit, Niki. But if Phil has asked you to forgive him, I think you should. The love of a man such as Phil is not a thing to throw away because of a past that neither one of you can change. God has a purpose for everything." Mary laughed lightly. "Even the canceling of gym classes a week early."

Niki's mouth opened wide. In thinking only about herself she had totally forgotten about her classes. "Oh, no. . .I forgot. . . ."

Mary smiled. "Don't worry. I'm sure everyone can manage on their own for a few extra days." Mary nodded toward the waiting car and held up the envelope in her hand. "Just. . .promise me that you will think very carefully about all this, Niki. Think carefully. . .and prayerfully."

Chapter 13

Judging by the car they had sent to drive her to Athens, Niki knew that Kristen and Paul Andrakos were fairly well-to-do. When the Mercedes pulled into a large, circular drive with the words *Villa Vasilias* emblazoned across the marble pillar at the entrance and Niki beheld the beautiful neoclassical mansion with its large and well-manicured gardens, she understood that they were actually quite wealthy. Like the White House, which Niki had visited as a member of the U.S. Olympic team, this house looked as if it had come from another era—a peaceful, calm era that wasn't as rushed or filled with tension as the world that Niki had grown up in.

It looked perfect to Niki, and she knew that there was nowhere else in the world she would rather be, especially when the car stopped and Kristen, dressed in blue jeans and a sweater, a regular all-American girl, came running down the marble steps toward her.

"I'm so glad you came early!" Kristen cried out and enveloped Niki in a big bear hug.

"You're sure you don't mind?" Niki was still afraid that she might be intruding. Paul and Kristen were newlyweds, after all.

"Mind? I'm thrilled. God's timing never ceases to amaze me. Paul had to leave unexpectedly on a business trip abroad this morning, so we have the entire week to do exactly what we please." Kristen laughed, effectively putting all Niki's fears to rest. "Not to say that Paul would have been in the way," she qualified with a special light in her eyes for the man she had married.

"I know what you mean," Niki reassured her.

Kristen's eyes twinkled back. "I think that you do, otherwise you would have come to Athens with your handsome friend, Phil." The light immediately dimmed in Niki's eyes.

Kristen gently pulled Niki to her side and said, "So that's the reason you've come early." Kristen's soft, southern accent made her words sound like a mother's gentle caress, warm and comforting and just what Niki needed. Squeezing her lips together, Niki nodded her head.

"Do you want to talk about it?" Kristen asked as she guided Niki up the marble stairs.

"Maybe later."

Kristen smiled. "Anytime. Come on," she pulled her into the foyer of the huge house. "I want you to meet the most wonderful woman in the world. My aunt Aphrodite."

※

When Niki met Kristen's aunt Aphrodite, whom she was immediately invited to call by the fond title of *Thea,* she quickly understood why Kristen thought so much of the older woman. She was a grand lady, a regal lady, a lady who wore her many years comfortably and with grace. The three women spent the days before Niki's operation chatting and laughing, talking about the past and the present, things they had done and things they were going to do.

The women stayed close to Villa Vasilias, except for when Kristen took Niki to visit the Acropolis and the hill across from it, called the Areopagus or Mars Hill. The Areopagus, the hill upon which the Apostle Paul most likely preached to the Athenians was very special to Kristen, because she had accepted Christ as her Savior there, and Paul had also proposed marriage to her there.

Niki called her parents to tell them where she was, and she was happy to learn that they were planning a trip to Greece in June. Hesitantly, she dialed Mary to find out how things were—to find out how Phil was. She was a little disconcerted to learn that, as far as Mary could tell, Phil seemed to be the same. He had organized a seaside Bible study, which met at dawn each morning. Surprisingly, Mary said, he had practically the entire hotel arising at that early hour to attend.

"Of course," Mary laughed into the receiver, "the hotel is as quiet as a nursery during siesta time now! Everyone takes a nap after getting up with the sun!"

Niki had laughed at the time, but when she replaced the receiver she was dismayed to realize that she wished with all her heart that she were in Cenchrea and could participate in the Bible study as well. To hear

Phil's deep voice as he read the words that meant so much to him, while the "rosy fingers" of Homer's dawn gently painted the Hellenic sky sounded like something out of a romantic tale.

Niki sighed as she reminded herself that a romantic tale was all it was—something fake, something that wasn't real. How could there be a romance when feelings of love were hidden in a heart that was so cold with anger and hurt that it was unable to melt the pain away?

In Athens, Niki could almost forget her anger. Almost, but not quite. All she had to do was walk into the library, across the room from where she now stood, and look at the Vasilias family's own private museum of the modern Olympics. She hadn't been in the library since the first day she'd arrived, when *Thea* Aphrodite had proudly shown its treasures to her. At the time, Niki had sent only a cursory glance around the room, having no more desire to see the Olympic display here than she had while in Olympia back in January. So, without quite understanding how it happened, she was surprised to find her feet carrying her into the room now.

The well-tended room was quiet, hushed, as befits a library, as if the very walls felt privileged to be a part of such minds that had learned and had recorded their wisdom on paper. Niki looked down into the glass display case that held memorabilia from the first modern Olympics and sighed, a melancholy sound, as she longingly ran her hand over the glass.

She didn't want to feel this sadness whenever she thought about the Olympics. Even though she couldn't participate, she still wanted to enjoy them and everything associated with them. She hated the envy that kept her from enjoying the Games.

Envy.

The word surprised her. She had never in her life thought she would feel envious of someone else's Olympic successes. She, of all people, knew how hard each athlete had to work to get there, and it depressed her to think that she had sunk so low as to resent their achievements.

"But why not add envy to the list of emotions. . . ?" Niki spoke dejectedly to herself. "Envy belongs with its friends Anger, Bitterness, and Hatred." Her facetious tone was in keeping with her mood and her mood was so black and so self-pitying that she nearly jumped a meter into the air when the soft touch of *Thea's* hand rested softly on her shoulder.

"I'm sorry I startled you, my dear," the older woman apologized, her sharp eyes kind and compassionate as she commented on what she had overheard, "but you don't have to add envy to that list. In fact, you don't even have to possess a list of such disreputable emotions." She spoke with an understanding forged only through years of living.

"*Thea*—" Niki breathed, embarrassed that the woman, who had been one of the most successful businesswomen of her generation, had witnessed her self-pitying murmurs.

Aphrodite waved aside Niki's embarrassment. "It's a choice to forgive another, you know. A choice that only we ourselves can make." Aphrodite smiled knowingly as she slowly lowered herself into the chair at the closest desk. "I hope you don't mind, but Kristen explained to me some of your history." She looked over toward the modern Olympics display. "I know something about dreams going awry too. . ." She looked out the window as if she were seeing a different place, a different time, before turning back to Niki with a glad smile. "But I also know something about God giving us new dreams, new directions. If we aren't stubborn. . .and if we listen to Him. . .so much pain may be avoided. He is, after all, in the business of working everything out, and working it out beautifully."

"*Thea*. . . ," Niki began, "I know that what you are saying is true. My friend, Phil. . . ," she whispered his name but couldn't go on, due to the lump that had formed in her throat.

"Phil. . .the man you are in love with?" Aphrodite prompted.

Niki nodded. That was the problem. She was still in love with Phil. "He. . .he tried to tell me the same thing. . .about dreams." She paused again and Aphrodite waited patiently, with wisdom, for her to continue. "But you see—there's something not even Kristen knows. . .something I just recently found out. . . ."

Aphrodite reached out and placed her hand on Niki's. Niki looked down at the capable hand that had done so much through so many years and, turning hers to meet it, squeezed it tightly. It was as if strength flowed from the older woman into her, just enough strength to go on.

"Phil was one of the men who ran into my car the night of the accident." She looked down at her leg. "The accident that broke my ankle."

Aphrodite smiled. "My. . .but you are blessed."

Aphrodite's words totally flabbergasted Niki.

"Blessed?" she questioned, as if she had misunderstood.

"My dear. . .don't you understand? You have been given the opportunity to forgive the man in person. . . ."

"I. . .I hadn't thought of that as a privilege," Niki replied honestly, her mouth twisting into a grimace.

"Well, it is. Especially if Phil has asked you to forgive him. Has he?"

"Yes," Niki admitted weakly, feeling smaller and smaller by the moment in the presence of this lady, whom she now recognized as a spiritual giant.

"Then, my dear, I think you should search your heart and understand that we are all human and we all make mistakes. And remember that the only One who was perfect is the very One who forgave the most." Aphrodite looked out the window at the land that was blooming forth with new life and all the brilliant colors of spring. "Easter is coming soon. Our Savior knew that He would be betrayed, yet He continued to serve mankind so lovingly. In fact, the first words He uttered as He hung on the cross—the most innocent of men enduring the most hideous form of execution ever devised by wicked man—were, 'Father, forgive them, for they do not know what they are doing.' "

Aphrodite paused and gently ran her fingers across Niki's arm. "If Jesus could ask God to forgive men for what they did to Him, then can't you forgive your—love," she paused over the word to let it sink in, "for an accident he never intended to happen?"

"When you put it like that. . .how can I not? It sounds so simple."

"Quite." Aphrodite's wise old eyes continued to study Niki. "But the question is. . .will you?"

Chapter 14

Will you? That was the question running endlessly through Niki's mind in the remaining days before her pins were removed.

Will you? was all she could think about on the day that the pins were removed.

Will you? The question reverberated throughout her brain. Like running shoes pounding against the ground, it drummed on and on, over and over in her head. Could she forgive Phil for being one of the men who had destroyed her dream?

She knew that she needed to, and she had finally reached the point of wanting to. It only remained for her to understand how.

Her flesh wound healed and she rejoiced when she was able to swim again. She missed her early morning swims in the Bay of Cenchrea. She was glad that Villa Vasilias had a large swimming pool, which, of course, she was welcome to use. Her orthopedic surgeon had been impressed by the fitness of her body and had told her that she could start running again soon. Niki was thrilled. It was like welcoming back an old friend.

Her stay at the villa was a pleasant, peaceful time. Kristen was the perfect hostess and the perfect friend, who never once pried into Niki's thoughts. As the days passed, both Niki's leg and her mind were able to recuperate.

Paul returned and Niki enjoyed watching him and Kristen together. They were adorably in love, with a love that rested upon their mutual faith in God. But although this cloud of love seemed to wrap around them like cotton candy on a stick, they were always open to others, never exclusive.

When Kristen and Paul invited her to stay and spend Easter with them, Niki accepted, even though her heart really wasn't in it. What she really wanted to do was spend Easter with Phil. But she knew that was an impossibility until she could give him what he had asked for.

Forgiveness.

And that wasn't yet hers to give.

Nevertheless, Niki was surprised to discover that the pain of being away from Phil was much greater, much sharper than that of not participating in the soon-to-be-held Olympic Games.

On Good Friday morning, at Kristen's urging, Niki went to visit Athens' 2,300-year-old stadium, the Panathenaikon, which had been reconstructed to host the first modern Olympics in 1896. While sitting high in the marble seats of that historic stadium, Niki realized that the Olympic Games had finally become just that to her—games. It was just as Phil had said. Niki knew that Phil, and their love for one another, was far more important than competing in the Games. With something close to awe, she realized that visiting this ancient stadium had accomplished for her the very thing she had hoped her visit to ancient Olympia would do. It enabled her to finally say farewell to her dream, her Olympic dream, the dream that God had given to her so long ago.

She looked out over the symmetry of the stadium where an athlete would soon run the Olympic flame in from ancient Olympia, and then she looked up at the little church of St. George that sits like a Christian banner on the highest point in Athens. And she gave her dream back to God.

She gave it all back. And she was released.

Bowing her head, she prayed to her heavenly Father. "Dear Lord, forgive me for my anger toward You. . .forgive me. . .and please show me how to forgive Phil."

And He did. The darkness that had been in her was overcome with light as she was released from the dark prison of anger and bitterness that had formed in her mind. She finally understood that God had other races for her to run, more magnificent, more eternal races than simple footraces. There in the ancient stadium with the tolling of Good Friday church bells mournfully crying out over the city, God reminded her of the prayer, the most famous prayer of all.

Bending her head low, Niki repeated the words that Jesus had taught his disciples to say, " 'Our Father in heaven, hallowed be your name, your kingdom come, your will be done on earth as it is in heaven. Give us today our daily bread. Forgive us our debts, as we also have forgiven our debtors'. . .forgiven our debtors. . . ," she repeated and fell silent. This was the question. Had she forgiven her debtors? Had she forgiven Phil for the accident?

The sad sound of the church bells reminded her of the crucifixion of the Lord on this day so long ago. Niki knew that she could forgive Phil. How could she not in light of the first words that were spoken by her Lord from the cross? "Father, forgive them, for they do not know what they are doing," she repeated to herself. Forgive them. . .for they do not know what they are doing. . . .

Phil didn't know what he was doing that night. He didn't know that he would hurt her. He didn't even know her.

And the accident had changed him. As a direct result he had become the wonderful Christ-centered man she loved today.

Suddenly Niki realized that her Olympic dream had been accomplished in Phil. Her dream had been to witness to people around the world through her Olympic race. It didn't matter that she hadn't won a gold medal. What mattered was that even one man should find Christ because of her Olympic efforts.

That man was Phil, the man who found God's grace through the accident that had busted up an athlete's leg. The man she loved. The man she forgave with all her heart, with all her being. Niki finally could see that she had run her race. . .Phil was worth a million—no, two million—footraces. And the greatest thing was. . .her Christian race had just begun!

Throwing her hands high up into the air she stood above the historic stadium and with happy tears coursing their way down her cheeks, she softly said, "Thank You, God. . .thank You. . . ."

Making her way down the marble steps to the track, she walked back to the waiting car. She still couldn't use her ankle to run, but her spirit was no longer crippled and it was running—running fast—running her Christian race, a race that she now intended to run with Phil. . .all the days of her life.

≈❧

When she returned to the villa, Niki was happy to see that Kristen and Paul had a surprise visit from Melissa and Luke Karalis and their baby boy. Melissa was Kristen's friend from the States, the "castle expert" who had encouraged Kristen to visit Acrocorinth, where she and Paul had met Phil and Stavros.

Melissa and Luke had decided to spend Easter in Athens, as they had the previous year. Kristen was thrilled and Niki was also glad because having the Karalises show up made her sudden departure from Villa Vasilias easier.

Kristen eyed her wonderingly. "Something tells me that your trip to the stadium took you further than you expected."

Niki nodded happily. "It took me to recovery, Kristen."

Kristen squealed and wrapped her arms around Niki in a great big bear hug that nearly toppled them both. "Oh, I'm so glad!"

"Please share the joy," said *Thea* Aphrodite as she walked up behind them.

Niki turned and took the older woman's hands in her own. "You were right, *Thea,*" she said, smiling, "I am blessed. . .to be able to forgive the man who was responsible for breaking my leg. But even more. . .I'm blessed that God forgives me for all the anger that I've held in my heart toward Him."

Aphrodite's face broke into a smile that seemed almost eternal to Niki. "Ah, my dear. . .I see that you have finally recovered from your stumble. Go run your race, dear. Go run it and win!"

❧

On an Easter wind full of hope and forgiveness, Niki returned to Cenchrea that evening. She was a different woman from the one who had traveled the same road a little more than two weeks before. She liked who she was again, a happy girl who believed that the Lord of the universe had His hands very wisely upon her life. She had matured and understood now that, although things might not go her way, they would always go God's way and that His way was ultimately her way. She prayed that she would never stumble so badly again and she shuddered to think how her hardened heart had almost caused her to miss the best plan God had for her life.

Phil.

As she stepped from the car at the hotel, the melancholy sound of the little chapel's bells filled her ears. She paused. It was a poignant reminder that she owed her happiness on this Good Friday to the work of the

Man, the Son of Man, for whom the bells now tolled. She sighed and wondered how people had ever lived before Christ came into the world to give each the honor of becoming God's child and the freedom to leave all their cares at His feet.

Smiling, she thanked *Thea* Aphrodite's chauffeur for driving her back to Cenchrea, and with a jaunty step that immediately attracted attention, she walked into the lobby.

Mary looked up from behind the reception desk and a knowing smile brightened her face. But before Mary could speak a word, Stavros came running to greet Niki.

"Niki!" he shouted and hugged her tightly. "I knew you'd come back today! I told my mother that you would! I just knew it!"

"You did?" Niki laughed and ruffled his hair before giving Mary a hug. "Then you knew better than I did."

"I'm so glad you've returned," Mary said, and her eyes spoke of sisterly love. "We missed you."

Stavros nodded his head. "Now if only Mr. Theophilus would come back everything would be perfect for Easter."

Niki turned quick and questioning eyes to Mary. "Phil's not here?"

Mary shook her head. "He left a few days ago."

"Why didn't you tell me?" It was almost an accusation.

"Would you have wanted to know a few days ago?"

After a moment's thought, Niki finally shook her head.

"I have to go." Stavros quickly spoke up, too preoccupied with the delight of Easter to notice the current flowing between Niki and his mother. "I'm going to help the priest with the service tonight. It's going to be at our chapel. Are you going to come?" he asked Niki.

"Definitely." Niki smiled. She was thrilled by how different Stavros was from the boy she had met when she first arrived at the hotel last January.

"Great!" He ran off and Niki and Mary watched him fondly.

"He's living proof of hope fulfilled," Mary said. The joy she felt was evident in her eyes.

The resounding chapel bell echoed Mary's sentiments and Niki nodded her head. "Hope fulfilled. . . ," Niki murmured.

"You seem different," said Mary after a moment.

Niki smiled, a bright smile of truth that was an honest indication of how she really felt. "Anger and bitterness no longer have a part of my heart, Mary."

"Niki. . ." Mary pulled her into a happy embrace. "It's just what I've been praying for. But what about Phil?"

"Oh, Mary. . .I love him so much."

"Yes. . .I know that. . .but. . .do you forgive him?"

Niki breathed out. "Mary. . .I'm the one who has to beg for his forgiveness. . .for not forgiving him when he asked."

"Then call him and tell him," Mary urged, her womanly matchmaking instincts now coming to the forefront.

"Do you know where he is?"

Mary nodded. "At his uncle's."

Niki nodded thoughtfully. "Of course he is." Then she groaned. "But his uncle doesn't have a phone."

"That's not uncommon for private homes in some of the remote mountain villages," Mary commented. "But the village store would definitely have one."

Niki's face brightened, but then she sighed. "But I don't even know the name of the village."

"Ah. . .but I do." Mary smiled an "I know something you don't know" sort of smile and waved her hand in the direction of the switchboard.

"Come with me."

Chapter 15

Mary was able to locate the village store's number, but she was unable to get through. She called the telephone company and was informed that high winds had disrupted phone service in many areas of Greece. They hoped to have the lines restored some time during the night, but nothing was certain. Mary assured Niki that the hotel operator would keep trying the number late into the night.

Although Niki was disappointed, her faith was now such that she was able to trust God to work everything out according to His plan and she prayerfully left the situation in His capable hands.

As evening fell, she crossed the lawn to the hotel's little chapel. Darkness had erased the last trace of color from the horizon when the solemn reenactment of Christ's funeral began. The service bridged the sadness and the hope of this most historic of days in a way that touched Niki's soul. Carrying candles of pure, brown wax, the congregation followed the beautifully decorated *Epitaphios*, the symbolic tomb in which Christ was laid, around the neighborhood of the hotel, accompanied by the lamentation of the priests and the choir. The congregation was hushed, and even the littlest of children seemed to understand the gravity of the procession.

Christ's funeral was something Niki had never really considered before. She had, of course, read about Joseph of Arimathea offering his tomb to the crucified Lord and of Christ's body being laid in the grave. But as she followed the symbolic tomb, with only the light from the handheld candles lighting the way and the bells of the little chapel tolling the death knell, the pain of Christ's atoning death was more real to Niki than ever before. She felt tears gather in her eyes for the God who loved His people so much that He had been willing to suffer the worst sort of death in order to save all who believed in what He said and in what He did.

As she looked around at the quiet congregation, Niki saw that she

401

wasn't alone in shedding tears. All were feeling the sadness of God's pain. But along with the tears, something else was shining in each eye.

There was the hope of Easter morning.

Unlike that Friday nearly two thousand years ago, his followers today knew the rest of the Easter story. In the wavering flicker of individual candles, that hope, that wonder, shone in each and every face.

Niki looked into the flame of her own little candle and thought about Phil. Physically, he was far from her this night, but because of what God had done on this day so long ago, she felt as though Phil were closer to her now than when they had actually been together. Because their spirits meshed totally now, they spoke the same language, the language of ones who believe wholeheartedly and not halfheartedly as she had before.

After the service, when all made their way quietly, reverently, to their beds, and Mary sadly informed Niki that there was still no change in the phone situation, Niki didn't despair. She went to bed with a quiet and thoughtful heart, a trusting heart.

❧

The winds that had brought down phone lines in many parts of Greece the previous day hit Cenchrea during the deep of the night. Niki awoke early Saturday to a wind that seemed determined to shake every lemon and orange from their green branches and hurl every plastic patio chair over the railings of the hotel's balconies.

Blustery and quick, the wind was nonetheless warm, so Niki dressed in shorts and a T-shirt with her swimsuit on underneath. Clutching her lifeguard's rescue can under her arm, she dug out her Bible from its lonely and forgotten resting place in the bottom drawer of her dresser, and walked to her favorite spot.

Sitting on the historic stones at the lighthouse, she felt as though she were the only person in the world. But she wasn't alone—her God was with her.

She gazed up at Acrocorinth, spotlighted in the clear, windswept light of the new day. She laughed and, squeezing her Bible against her heart, she practically squealed out her delight. "Oh, dear Lord. . .thank You. . . for sustaining me and never leaving me. . .even when I deserved so much less." She breathed out deeply and let her senses fill with the wonder of the moment. Niki was celebrating—celebrating life, celebrating her first morning of freedom from anger since her accident. She felt delicious.

Looking down at her Bible, she opened it unhesitatingly to the sixth chapter of Matthew. The sheets flapped in the strong wind but she held open the pages and read the Lord's Prayer. She knew that it would always hold more meaning to her after the life-changing hurt that her own lack of forgiveness had inflicted on her soul during the previous months. Her eyes continued past the prayer to the following two verses. Jesus had explained, "For if you forgive men when they sin against you, your heavenly Father will also forgive you. But if you do not forgive men their sins, your Father will not forgive your sins."

Niki's eyes widened. She now understood that the peace she had felt at the Panathenaikon the previous morning had come not so much from her forgiving Phil but rather from God forgiving her.

"Oh, dear Lord," she closed her eyes and prayed, the strong wind taking her words and sending them like a herald across the churning bay. "Please use my life as You have planned to use it since the beginning of time. I will never fight You again. I understand that as long as I am in Your will, You will work everything out perfectly according to Your plan. . .which is a far greater plan than any I might devise."

With her eyes still tightly shut, she thought about how Phil had become the man he was today because of the accident. Then, going a step further, Niki realized that she had become the woman she was today because of the accident too. She had to admit that even though she had been a Christian since childhood, she had been holding God to the unspoken condition that everything work out her way. For years it had just so happened that her way and God's way coincided—until the accident. The accident made her grow in a way she never would have grown if it hadn't occurred.

"And dear Lord, if it is your will for me to run and win footraces, I will do that, but if You have other plans for my life, then there I will go. Use me, Lord, according to Your will. . .Amen."

She leaned back against the stone behind her and rested. The warm wind played with her hair just as the cold wind had in ancient Olympia a few months before. It teased her lashes, enticing her to open her eyes.

But Niki didn't want to open them yet. She just wanted to savor the moment—to feel the wind as it pushed sea spray against her skin and to feel the sun as it rose in the sky, gently teasing her closed lids with a kaleidoscope of colors and shapes. To hear the song of the blowing trees mixed with the churning of the sea, a stereo of sound that not even a laser disc could hope to capture.

Niki was celebrating. She was celebrating being in exactly the spot where God wanted her. She was celebrating being in God's will.

Finally, she opened her eyes and looked out over the bay. Because the sun had been shining on her closed eyelids, everything looked a purplish-pink and fuzzy. But that was fine with Niki. Everything was fine with her at that moment.

Smiling, she stood and stretched before bending to remove her shorts and shoes. She was about to take off her T-shirt when a sound—one that didn't belong to the harmony of the new day—caught her ears.

She frowned and tilted her head, trying to hear better.

There it was again.

With horror slicing through her, she realized that a child was crying out for help. She quickly scanned the pounding surf but her vision was still too fuzzy to see anything in the whiteness of the moving water.

"Dear God...," she whispered, "if someone needs my help, please help me find him...." No sooner had she finished praying than she saw a small rubber raft riding the top of the white water. With a sinking feeling, she saw two small figures frantically waving their arms.

In an instant she realized what had happened. The children had been in the raft along the beach but in the strong wind they had been swept away from the shore and were now in danger of being carried out into the wide Saronic Gulf.

Without thought, Niki scrambled out of her shirt, threw the rope of the lifeguard's rescue can over her shoulder and dove into the ocean. The water was cold but she didn't feel it. She was thankful that she had swum the bay so often that she knew it like the back of her hand.

But that knowledge was bittersweet. She knew that if the raft passed the headlands upon which the lighthouse sat, the children would be swept out to sea and away from her help. She couldn't let that happen.

Measuring her strokes, she swam toward the point where she calculated she would be able to intercept the raft. The water was churning but, for the moment, the current was on her side. She didn't know how she would be able to pull the raft back to land with the current pushing them out to sea, but that was a problem for later; her only concern now was to reach the raft before it was too late.

If she panicked she knew they would all drown, so as she swam, she reminded herself of her coach's repeated advice: "Rhythm, Niki, rhythm. That's the key to finding the ballet to match your stride." She knew it would work for swimming as well as for running and she settled into a stroke that was swift and sure and able to slice through the angry waters of the deep sea on course with the floundering raft.

Niki didn't break her rhythm to look for the raft. To do so would cause her to miss it completely. Instead, she concentrated on breathing, stroking, kicking her legs, and she let God handle the rest. She knew that God was leading her on, that He was guiding her, and she never doubted for a moment that she would reach the children in time.

Her life-can trailed behind her, its marvelous, aerodynamic shape not hindering her at all. She thanked God for her lifeguard training and the good advice that she always have the can with her when she swam in secluded areas alone. It was a comfort to feel the slight tugging of the rope around her shoulder.

Before long, she heard the shouts of the children and she knew that she was nearing the rendezvous point. She maintained her pace. Onward she swam, like a dolphin following a ship.

At last, the yellow color of the raft loomed above her, and only then did she stop her strokes. She looked up into the frightened but relieved faces of two young boys. She reached for the cord that ran around the boat and shouted out above the wind, "I've got you."

Just as her fingers tightened around the cord, a gust of wind seemed to catch the boat from underneath. It rose up out of the water like a giant fish and capsized, throwing the screaming boys out into the sea like shiny pennies into a fountain.

"No!" Niki screamed.

She watched in horror as the raft was yanked from her fingers and taken out to sea like a soccer ball skipping across a field. For a shocked moment, she watched the receding raft, then quickly cast her eyes around for the boys.

The first one was close to her. She caught him by his neck and gave him the can to hold onto while she dove under the water to look for the second boy.

She couldn't see him.

She came up for air and frantically scanned the swelling waves, waves that continued to grow in the gathering gale.

She dove again and prayed with all her might for God to help her find the boy. She still couldn't find him.

Rising to the surface, she checked on the boy who was holding the can. He motioned to her that he was fine. Niki nodded and scanned the waves again. In every direction all she could see was foam.

"Dear God, help me find him," she breathed another prayer. When a seagull soared about ten feet in front of her, she knew that she had been given her answer. Grabbing onto the can and throwing her arm around the first boy, she pointed through the swells. Together they kicked with all their strength and moved in the direction of the seagull. Unfortunately, it was also toward the opening of the bay and the expanse of the Gulf.

Rising on a swell, Niki spied the missing boy. His blond head was the most beautiful sight she had ever seen. Treading water like a dog, he was about three feet in front of them. Niki let go of the can and lunged forward for the boy. She grabbed him by the neck just as a wave threatened to send him under.

"I've got you!" Niki shouted and pushed his arms across the float. "Thank God, we've got you." She breathed a sigh of relief and allowed herself a moment to look at their grateful faces. Then, slowly, she began to push toward the lighthouse.

"Thank you, Miss," the first boy spoke, "we would—drowned except you save us." Relief colored his heavily accented words, vaguely reminding Niki of somebody she knew.

The other boy grimaced, and for the first time, Niki realized that he was hurt.

"What is it?" she shouted above the wind.

He grimaced again. "My leg—" He was breathing as if in great pain. "It got caught in the raft's rope."

His leg. . . .

Niki almost wanted to laugh as she realized that if her leg hadn't been injured last November, she wouldn't have been here this day to follow God's plan and hear these boys cry for help. How minuscule an Olympic medal seemed in comparison. . . .

"But do not worry. . .I'm fine," the boy said bravely. "We go to shore now. Yes?"

Niki nodded. "Yes," she whispered, but looking at their rate of progress and comparing it to the distance they had to travel before being swept out to sea, she knew that their combined kicking wouldn't get them to shore in time. The current was much too strong. Bowing her head, she prayed, "Dear Lord, please let someone see us and come to our rescue."

God is faithful. No sooner had Niki finished praying than the sound of a motorboat could be heard coming toward them. Straining her neck above the waves, Niki could see that it was one of the hotel's yellow boats.

"Yes!" she shouted, giddy with relief, as she and the two boys started yelling and waving their arms at the boat.

The boat lights flickered, telling them they had been spotted. The first boy shouted out, "It's like—Hollywood picture!"

Niki couldn't agree more. The morning was like an inspirational Hollywood script and she half expected to see Phil in the boat to give the show the perfect ending.

He wasn't. But Stavros was. Moments later, after they were pulled aboard the swaying boat, Stavros explained that they had been having their Bible study out by the pier when they had seen the raft throw the boys into the sea.

"But we never would have made it in time to get them. You saved their lives, Niki! You saved their lives!"

Niki knew Who had saved all their lives and she breathed out a prayer of thanks. She smiled as the seagull circled the boat, the tips of his wings glowing golden in the light of the sun.

Chapter 16

To say that Niki was a hero would be putting it mildly. Several people had been gathered for the morning Bible study, the same one Phil had organized during Niki's absence, but because of the headland blocking their view they had not noticed the boys until the raft capsized. With solemnly shaking heads they all knew that they never would have arrived in time to save the boys—especially Alexis, whose lower leg bone had been snapped by the rope.

Even though it was *Megali Savato,* the Holy Saturday before Easter, a day that normally was hushed in anticipation of the morrow, this Saturday was filled with the happy sounds of joy for the boys' safety.

Alexis was rushed to the hospital in Corinth, where his leg was set before he returned to the hotel to spend Easter with his family. Meanwhile, Niki learned why the other boy, Petros, had seemed familiar to her: His father was the cabby who had driven her to Olympia the previous January.

There were tears in the dear man's eyes when he thanked her. "God bless you. You save my boy," he said and squeezed Niki's hand tightly in his own. "I know—I like you in Olympia," he looked over at his son and pulled the grateful boy close to him, "but I never realize. . .you. . .you would save my boy." His accent thickened with emotion.

"Thank you, Miss," Petros repeated his gratitude.

Niki hugged the boy. "It was God who was looking out for you," she said. She smiled as Mary walked up to them and handed Niki her Bible and clothes, which Stavros had fetched from the lighthouse. Niki held the Bible up. "God made sure I was in the right place at the right time."

"Yes," the cab driver agreed solemnly. "Of all the people in Cenchrea, only you could swim in that rough water today. Because you train. I see you—swimming in sea—from my house in village."

"That's right," Mary agreed and smiled at Niki warmly. "Without all your years of training, you would never have had the stamina or ability to fight that sea." She paused for emphasis before saying, "I guess we could say that you won a gold medal this morning."

"Mary, I won something much, much greater than an Olympic medal." Niki patted Petros quickly on his shoulder. No medal in the world could come close to giving her the joy or satisfaction that saving these boys had. No, not even an Olympic medal. She wondered if this was how God felt whenever someone accepted His life-saving hand and trusted Him and believed Him.

She thought about Phil and the joy that God must have experienced when this wayward son had turned to Him. She walked over to the operator to ask if there had been any change in the telephone connections. The operator shook her head sadly. With the spreading winds and with many people wanting to call their loved ones for the holiday, if anything the lines were even worse.

Niki thanked her and asked her to keep trying. She walked back out to the lobby toward Mary, who was deep in conversation with the cabby. Just then, Alexis Rallis limped in, with his shiny new crutches and a big cast covering his left leg, accompanied by his stylish mother and father. Niki went to greet them.

Tears were in Alexis's mother's eyes as she reached for Niki's hand and kissed it. "Thank you. . .you gave our son back to us today."

"Please," Niki felt uncomfortable with such praise. "I only did what anyone would have done."

Alexis's father reached out to shake Niki's hand. "Not anyone could or," he paused to clear the emotion from his throat, "would have risked their own life to do what you did. We thank you." He spoke English with a polish not unlike Mary's. Niki tilted her head in acknowledgment and looked over at Alexis. She was surprised to see that he wasn't as young as Petros and was actually taller than she was.

She pointed to his cast and smiled. "Don't worry. I wore one of those just a few months ago and look at my leg today." She shook her foot out in front of her. "Almost as good as new."

"I understand from Mary that you set a new world record at the world championships last summer," Mr. Rallis commented.

Niki tilted her head downward and smiled. She was thrilled that it didn't hurt her anymore to remember what she had done. What she was now had become so much more important. "I did pretty well last summer," she finally admitted.

"Are you going to be competing again?"

Am I? Niki wondered. "Well, as of Monday morning, the orthopedic surgeon has given me permission to start running again. I don't know whether this leg of mine will ever be able to compete on a world level, but, you know," she was speaking more to herself than to the three people attentively listening to her, "it really doesn't matter." As she continued, she knew that it was true. It really didn't matter. "I love running. It's been a part of my life for so long that I'm just grateful now that I will be able to run for the fun of it again."

"You were going to be competing in the Olympics this year though, weren't you?" Mr. Rallis asked.

Niki nodded and waited for the old, familiar knot to form in the pit of her stomach. But there was no pain left within her and she grinned broadly. "If I had made the team I would have, but this year's Olympics are too soon for my leg to be able to take the strain that competing would put on it."

"Oh, how sad," Alexis's mother murmured.

Niki shook her head. "No. . .not at all sad. I'm trusting that God has something else just as wonderful planned for me." *A life with Phil maybe,* Niki thought.

Alexis's father nodded soberly, but from the gleam in his eye, his wife was sure that he had just thought of a way to reward Niki for saving their son's life. "Uhmmm. . . ," he intoned thoughtfully, confirming his wife's suspicions. "I'm sure He does, my dear. I'm sure He does."

❧

The morning passed and, for once, Niki succumbed to the Greek habit of an afternoon siesta. Easter service, the celebration of the resurrection of the Lord on the third day, is held during the first hours of Easter Sunday in Hellas, and Niki knew that if she wanted to be able to stay awake later, she would need to get some sleep now. The excitement of the morning had exhausted her, and when her head hit the soft pillow, she slept immediately.

She was surprised to see that it was dark when she awoke. Deep and dark and special somehow. Rising from her bed, she rubbed her eyes and padded over to the window. She reflectively gazed out at the softness of the night. The sky was velvety by the light of the nearly full moon, which shone down on the sea like a gentle spotlight with the twinkling of brave little stars like dancing fireflies on either side. The wind had died down considerably. It no longer howled and whistled as it swept around branches and corners and across the top of the sea. Now it only gently swayed the royal palm outside Niki's window and tickled the sea with its soft breath, as if it too were waiting in hushed expectation for the celebration of the Lord's resurrection.

Niki opened the French doors that led onto her private verandah and walked out into the fresh breeze. The happy sound of boys far below drifted up to her. Looking down, she could make out Stavros and Petros, with Alexis stoically hobbling between them, making their way toward the chapel. They were glad to be helping the elderly priest ready the church for the joyous service which was to begin in little over an hour.

Niki sighed, a content, melodious sound that mixed perfectly with the soft wind that blew over and around her. She still could hardly believe the events of the day but the happy boys below her were living proof that everything had really happened.

"Thank You, God. . .for Alexis and Petros. . .and. . .for Stavros," she prayed as she watched the boys drift along the moonbeam toward the church. She looked up at the moon and sighed. "Now, Father, if You would only send Phil back to me. . . ," she whispered. Quietly, trustingly, she turned from the verandah and walked into her room to shower and dress. . .to make ready for one of the happiest of all Christian celebrations!

A little while later, Niki walked into the lobby dressed in a floral print jacket, a white silk blouse and a linen skirt of the softest pink. She carried a white clutch purse that matched her high-heeled shoes. Niki felt wonderful. It was the first time since her accident that she had worn high-heeled shoes and she loved the feminine way that the clicking of the heels against the polished marble made her feel.

Mary approached, with Stavros and Petros by her side. Niki's eyes opened wide at how beautiful Mary looked in a black dress of the finest silk. It was simple and yet elegant on Mary's comely shape. Her hair was set in a beautiful French twist and adorned with gold combs that Niki knew must be antique. She squeezed Mary's hand. "You look. . . stunning."

Mary smiled back. "You do, too."

Shyly, Petros lifted a long, narrow box that he had held by his side. He extended it to Niki and said, "My mother did this for you. She says that," he paused to get the words right, "the one who loves you would want you to have it."

Niki's brows came together in a happy frown. *The one who loves me?* As she opened the long skinny box, she thought about Phil. She removed the lid from the box and a gasp of pleasure escaped her as she beheld a beautiful candle of pristine white, elegantly decorated with antique lace and silk roses, nestled in layers of tissue paper. Picking it up carefully, her lips formed a perfect *O* in appreciation of the exquisite beauty.

"How lovely," she murmured. She wasn't sure what the candle was used for, but she was sure that it was intended for something happy, in total contrast to the sad, plain, brown wax candles that the congregation had carried at the reenactment of Christ's funeral. Joy seemed to be spelled in the intertwining of the lace and silk.

"It's called a *labada*," Petros shyly explained. "It is lit from—priest's candle."

At Niki's perplexed look, Mary explained. "At tonight's service, all the people hold white or pastel candles, candles of joy, that may be beautifully decorated as well. At midnight, those in the front of the church light their candles from the priest's and they in turn offer the light to those behind them, and so on. Soon, darkness is washed away as the entire church is ablaze with the flicker of hundreds of candles. This 'new light' symbolizes the new life brought into the world by the risen Christ."

"Amen," Niki whispered and, turning to Petros, asked, "Where are your parents? I would like to thank them."

"My mother is—at church—helping the priest. And my father—he's not back yet."

"Oh. . .he had to work tonight?" Niki felt bad for the boy who would have to miss spending this most special of Greek holidays with his father.

Petros looked up at Mary, and Niki thought that his chest seemed to expand with pride in the job his father had to do. "He had very important business. But—he will be back in time for church. He promise me."

Mary nodded at Petros. "I'm sure he will." She turned to Niki. "Come, let us go to church." Taking Niki's arm, she led the way.

❦

Everything was dark.

The torches that had been placed along the path to guide the congregation to the little chapel were now extinguished. Even the moon had gone behind a cloud.

The congregation was silent. Only the gentle lapping of the sea and the soft murmur of the priest's voice inside the little chapel could be heard. All but a few people stood outside the chapel on the gently sloping lawn above the sea. Mary and Niki stood near the back. In the strange light of a world that was almost totally dark, the people in front of them looked unreal, as if only the outline of their bodies existed.

Niki looked out across the sea. Normally, the lights from distant villages along the Epidaurus peninsula could be seen flickering in the night. But not tonight. Only the stars above glowed, like a heavenly choir waiting to sing their hallelujahs.

And then it happened.

The priest, dressed in happy robes of gold, walked through the chapel door and spoke words that Niki's soul translated for her, "Come ye, take light from the Unwaning Light and glorify Christ, who rose from the dead!"

The chapel bells pealed forth, a happy tune now, in harmony with church bells from near and far that simultaneously sang along. The light from the three candles that the priest brought to the congregation was passed from one person to another as the joy, the miracle of Jesus' resurrection, spread across faces now lit by the glory of Christ's light.

People were laughing. People were joyous. Fireworks were set off in Cenchrea and in villages across the sea as believers throughout the ancient land of Hellas celebrated together the resurrection of the Lord.

"*Christos Anesti!* Christ is risen!" people sang out.

"*Alithos Anesti!* Truly He is risen!" came the response as the Kiss of the Resurrection was exchanged among the people.

Niki watched it all with wonder in her eyes as the flame from the priest's candle was quickly spread outward toward where she stood in the back. It seemed to her as though the whole world was lit up. It was so different from just a moment before. So different, so wonderfully, life-savingly different and she prayed that God would always let her spread this light to people who were in darkness about the resurrection of the Lord. It was the most beautiful Easter service Niki had ever been a part of. It not only told about Christ's resurrection, but it came as close as humanly possible to showing it.

Niki watched as Stavros received the light. With a grin spreading across his face he turned to his mother. *"Christos Anesti*, Mamma!"

Mary leaned over and mother and son exchanged the Kiss of the Resurrection.

"Alithos Anesti, Stavros! Truly He is risen!"

With tears in their eyes they knew how important it was to them that Christ has risen; but even more, how important it was for the husband and father who was not with them this year, but who was with Christ in glory.

Stavros squeezed his mother to him and gave her the best Easter present of all. "It's okay, Mamma. I'm okay now," he nodded reassuringly to her. His nod was identical to the quick, assuring nod of his father, and Mary closed her eyes to savor the memory. Stavros turned and ran off to join the other boys, who were busy throwing fireworks out over the sea.

Mary smiled and turned with her lit candle to Niki. Niki extended her candle and smiled with anticipation. Her smile turned to a questioning look when she realized that Mary wasn't looking at her but at someone who had come up behind her. Niki started to turn but Mary stopped her and extended her candle to Niki's. They watched eagerly as the flame brought light to the beautifully decorated candle that Petros's mother had fashioned for her. It caught with a "pssit" and a burst of flame that made Niki laugh with joy. She couldn't remember ever being happier.

"Christ is risen, Niki!" Mary sang out the glad tidings.

"Truly, He is risen, Mary. . ." Niki threw back her head and sang, with all the truth of the words ringing in her heart, "Truly, Christ is risen!"

"Truly He is, Niki," a deep, familiar voice said quietly behind her.

In a heartbeat she spun around and threw herself into Phil's arms just as a new burst of fireworks blasted above their heads.

"You came!" she sang out, almost giddy with relief. "Oh, Phil. . .you came. . .but how?"

Phil nodded toward Petros, who was just extending his candle toward his father's. Over his shoulder, Petros smiled at her. "I told you—Father had important business," he said with a happy twinkle in his dark eyes.

Niki nodded her thanks to the cab driver and his family, who were all pleased that they had had a part in reuniting the two lovers.

She turned back to Phil. He took her hand and quickly guided her a short distance away from the merrymakers. Before Niki could say another word, Phil's lips captured hers and they shared a kiss of longing, a kiss of forgiveness, a kiss of need that left both of them standing on shaky legs.

Finally, not wanting to but knowing that she had to, Niki stood back from Phil. "Phil. . .I'm so sorry. . ."

He cut her off with a sharp shake of his head. "Do you forgive me?" He needed to hear the words.

"Phil, I'm the one who has to ask you for your forgiveness—" Anguish for the pain she had caused him was in her eyes.

He shook her protest away. "Niki, please—"

He couldn't wait another moment. He couldn't stand another moment of not hearing the words that he had longed to hear for so long. His need for her forgiveness came before everything else at that moment. He had to know. He had to hear her say the words. "Do you forgive me—do you truly forgive me—for all the pain—for all the grief—the accident—which I was responsible for?"

Niki smiled and waved her hand in the direction of the chapel. "In the face of all that Christ did for me, how could I not?"

"Niki. . .please!" he moaned, and at that moment Niki finally understood the price he had paid not to tell her everything about his involvement in her accident the moment he figured out who she was in Olympia. For the first time, Niki felt the guilt he had been fighting every bit as much as she had been fighting anger. Reaching up, she laid her fingers against his cheek. "Phil, I forgive you for the accident. I forgive you totally."

"Niki. . ." He expelled his breath and gathered her as close as he could against himself. "There are no more loving words in the world than those."

As Niki listened with her ear to the beating of her love's heart and with her soul to the beating of God's plan in their lives, she said, "I know three more." She tilted her head back to look fully into his candlelit face and boldly, without hesitation said, "I love you."

"Then. . .does that mean you'll marry me?"

"Does that mean—you're asking me?" she returned.

With fireworks lighting the sky, and surrounded by happy Christians celebrating the Lord's resurrection, Phil lowered his knee to the fragrant earth beneath him and asked, "Niki, would you do me the great honor of becoming my wife?"

Kneeling down beside him, she whispered, "That's a race I'm aching to run." They kissed. . .and they kissed. . .and they probably would have gone on kissing if Stavros hadn't jumped on Phil's back and demanded, "Hey. . .what's going on here?"

Knocking the boy good-naturedly to the ground, Phil said, "I've just asked this lady to marry me."

"And is she?" Stavros asked naively.

"Definitely."

Stavros beamed and jumped to his feet, shouting, "Hey, everybody! Niki and Theophilus are going to get married!" The people of Christ's Church on this early Easter morning showered them with applause and good cheer.

Niki looked at the stars as they twinkled above her head and she couldn't think of a better way to become engaged.

Chapter 17

Niki and Phil decided they would get married in the chapel on the hotel grounds on the opening Sunday of the Olympic Games. For Niki, it was symbolic of the race that God had in mind for her to run with Phil—the Christian race. Plans were made and invitations were sent.

In the meantime, along with these joyous plans, Niki had the thrill of being able to use her legs to run again. True to his word, Phil ran right along with her. When she became too fast for him to keep up, he rode his bike alongside.

Niki's desire to run well again was encouraged when the mayor of Isthmia came to the hotel one day and asked if she would be one of the Olympic torch relay runners. As always, the Olympic flame would be taken by a series of relay runners from ancient Olympia to the Panathenaikon in Athens. From Athens, it would be transferred to this year's host of the Games.

Because Niki had saved the two local boys' lives—which Alexis's father made sure everyone knew—and because she had trained to be an Olympian, the town honored her by asking her to carry the flame across the Corinth Canal.

Niki and Phil exchanged glances of wonder. In spite of everything, God had worked it out so that she would be a part of the Olympic Games after all, in a way none of them could ever have imagined. Niki told Phil about her visit to Athens' ancient stadium, the Panathenaikon, so he understood how symbolic it would be for her to carry the Olympic torch.

Knowing that she would be taking part in the Olympics added an extra flare to her running. With the poplar trees sending their spores down to earth thick as snow on some days, Niki ran throughout the month of May, strengthening her body and toning her muscles, with Phil cycling along beside her. When June came and Phil had to spend time helping

417

his pupils ready for English exams, Niki continued to run on her own. Her favorite route turned out to be the road between Cenchrea and ancient Isthmia—just as she had imagined. She ran it in the early morning and again late in the evening. Pink and white oleander blossoms, with their delicate fragrance, lined the road, adding to her enjoyment.

When the weather went from the coolness of spring to the hot, dry weather of an early summer, her runs started earlier and earlier each day. One quiet Sunday morning, as Homer's "rosy fingertips of dawn" were beginning to stretch their way over the land, she was heading up the hill toward the museum when she noticed something out of the ordinary.

Normally, the museum was deserted at this time of day, particularly on a Sunday. This morning, however, a closed truck was parked outside the door. Niki knew that something wasn't right when she saw some men walking along the flat roof, carrying things that looked like they had been hastily wrapped in blankets.

Hiding behind the trunk of a large tree, Niki paused and watched from a distance. Three men, all quite young and all dressed in black jeans and black T-shirts, were definitely moving things from the museum and handing them down to two more men who were standing at the base of a ladder putting things into the truck.

"It's being robbed," Niki whispered to herself, but it didn't seem real. TV had always made robberies out to be so dramatic, but here it was little more than a bunch of men walking into the museum and walking out with things, almost as if they were doing a legitimate job.

As Niki continued to watch, a blanket fell away and she recognized the door from ancient Cenchrea that she and Phil had seen the day they visited the museum. Now she knew that it was most definitely a robbery. Turning on her heels, she ran as fast as she could down the hill, past the main road, to the port police at the east entrance of the canal. It didn't take her more than two minutes to get there, but it took her a bit longer to make herself understood.

When at last she was able to make them understand, the police were at the museum within moments. The surprised thieves were caught in the act and the museum pieces were saved!

Niki watched as the thieves were brought into the station. She found it hard to believe that these young men were thieves. They looked so nice and so handsome—so typically Greek. When she saw TV cameras arrive, she quickly slipped out of the door and ran back to Cenchrea.

She didn't mention anything about it to anyone because, on top of all the events of the last few weeks, it seemed unreal to her that she should witness a robbery as well. That night, when the news showed her leaving the police station and jogging away, Mary, Stavros, and Phil were amazed.

"Niki—that's you!" Stavros yelled, pointing at the screen. Niki cringed as she realized that her departure had not been as discreet as she had hoped.

"Niki. . .?" Phil looked at her quizzically.

She smiled in embarrassment. "I didn't know they took that picture."

"Shhh. . .let's listen," said Mary.

"The world-champion distance runner who recently saved two boys from drowning in the Bay of Cenchrea has now saved the nation some of its finest artifacts. Her timely reporting enabled the police in Isthmia to capture a notorious gang of art thieves. During the past two years, these men have repeatedly eluded the police, while making off with some of the nation's most priceless treasures. Hellas has found a true heroine in American Niki Alexander."

Mary translated for Niki and Phil then asked, "Niki. . .why didn't you tell us?"

Embarrassed, Niki shrugged.

"Wow! A real hero!" Stavros yelled. He didn't mind a bit that she hadn't told them. "You nabbed the art thieves! I'll bet there's a reward!"

"I'm proud of you." Phil smiled, and the look in his eye was all the reward Niki needed.

About a week after the incident, Niki received a phone call from the president of Greece's Olympic committee. He informed her that the athlete who was supposed to run the Olympic flame into the Panathenaikon in Athens and light the Olympic bowl would be unable to do so. In his place, Niki had been chosen, out of thousands of others, for this honor.

With tears of joy shining in her eyes she replaced the phone and turned to Phil.

"Niki. . .what is it?"

"I've been asked to run the Olympic flame into the Panathenaikon next week," she whispered with awe in her voice.

Phil surprised her by throwing back his head and laughing, a boisterous laugh that she had heard one other time. This time, she smiled. She knew what he was thinking. "God's humor, right?"

He nodded. "Right," his eyes twinkled merrily as he pulled her close. "Tell me, soon-to-be Mrs. Taylor. What do you think about God's humor now?"

"God's humor," she whispered just before her lips were smothered by Phil's, "I think it is fantastic."

Phil couldn't agree more.

⚜

Niki's feet pounded on the pavement. The Acropolis of Athens was on her left, a shining tribute to a people who had set the tone for civilization in the modern world. The descendants of those people were now lining both sides of the road, cheering her on.

As Niki's feet pounded through the ancient city, down past the Theater of Dionysus, she realized that this was the allure of the Olympics. The sense of camaraderie that brought people from around the world together once every four years.

Enemies were no longer enemies during the Olympics. The ancient Greek Olympic truce still held. Good news was brought to the world by skaters, by swimmers, by volleyball players, by runners, by people racing their own Olympic race!

Niki realized, as she smiled at the people who waved to her by Hadrian's Arch and her feet carried her easily toward the Panathenaikon stadium, that it was indeed a small example of what it meant to run the Christian race, the race to spread the good news of Christ's gospel to the hurting, waiting, wondering world; a race that isn't run only every four years, but every day, every moment, every second of a good runner's life. And that, Niki knew only too well, was the run that fulfills everything.

It began that first Easter morning when two women who had brought spices to prepare Christ's body for burial ran to tell the others that the tomb was empty! There was no body to prepare because Jesus had risen from the dead!

Niki's eyes scanned the faces that surrounded her. Jesus had risen from the dead for her, for them, for everyone in the world. And as her eyes fell upon the graceful columns of the temple of Olympian Zeus, Niki knew that it was good news for all the people of the past as well as for those of the future.

The future. As she passed the beautiful Zapion, which was built to house the first modern Olympians during their stay in Athens in 1896, she thought about the running verse found in the third chapter of the epistle that St. Paul wrote to the Philippians, those Greeks who lived in Macedonia. "Forgetting what is behind," the months of angry agony and the years of wrongly making the Olympic Games the most important thing in her life, "and straining toward what is ahead. . ."

Niki turned the curve in the road and saw the ancient Panathenaikon gleaming in the light of the setting sun, as timeless a work of art as man could construct. Looking up at the torch in her hand, she proudly held it higher.

A few more feet and she would turn into the stadium. She, Niki Alexander, would run into the stadium from which all the modern Olympics started and place the Olympic flame in its bowl.

TV cameras zoomed in on her. She could hear the announcer in the stadium report that she was about to enter. There was an expectant hush and then, as her feet turned the final curve and stepped onto the red carpet that had been laid out for her historic run, all the world seemed to explode in a joyful chorus of brotherhood. Peace on earth, goodwill to men rang in the thousands of voices that filled the air around her. A heady sound, a marvelous sound, a sound that had such a heavenly quality to it that Niki was certain angels must be involved.

She ran through the gate and looked to where she knew Phil—her biggest fan—would be waiting. He was there, waving an American flag and cheering her on, with a smile that was about to split his face. Next to him was his old uncle Theophilus waving a Greek flag. Her parents were there, and her brother, her coach, and Mary and Stavros. Paul and Kristen Andrakos and *Thea* Aphrodite were there, along with her favorite cab driver and his son Petros. She smiled at all the people around Phil, her friends and family, before turning her head to look over her left shoulder at the little church of Saint George that sat on the highest point in Athens.

She felt God looking at her. And she knew that He was smiling. He worked out all the paths of her life to run into this one and Niki knew, as the crowd cheered around her, that she would never forget to trust His divine plan for her life again.

She looked toward Phil.

Not ever.

The Olympic bowl was straight ahead, shining brightly and waiting for the flame she held proudly in her hand. The Olympic flame, the flame that started in that magic place in ancient Olympia where she and Phil had met, was soon to cross a continent and an ocean to reach this year's Olympic Games.

Niki thought about another flame—the Easter flame—that was lit on Easter morning nearly two thousand years ago, which had transcended time and space to still burn brightly and spread its life-saving message to all the people of the world.

Niki stood at the base of the bowl. She stepped up to it. A hush fell over the stadium. Now was the moment that all had been waiting for— the moment when Niki would touch the torch to the bowl and all would watch the flame dance to life.

Niki paused. She stood tall and held the flame even higher.

With each moment that passed, the silence in the stadium grew. It grew into a gigantic hush of expectancy that sounded louder than all the cheers.

Finally, Niki stood on tiptoes, raising the torch still higher, looked toward heaven and with reverence in her voice but as loud as she could, said, "Thank You, God." That was all she said but it was all that needed to be said.

She touched the torch to the bowl and the flame ignited along with the cheers of the people.

Niki stepped back and laughed, a laugh of pure joy. She was a part of the Olympic Games after all—in a way she would never have thought possible. She wasn't a part of the Olympic team but, as her eyes met Phil's across the distance between them, she knew that she was a useful part of God's team.

And that was the greatest team of all!

❧

Phil smiled back at her. He hadn't taken his eyes off of her since she ran into the stadium, and he didn't take his eyes off of her now as his great-uncle Theophilus rasped into his ear, "Nikise! Our Niki won! She is victorious! She lived up to her name, Son! She lived up to her name!"

Phil nodded his head slowly and, like the woman he loved, he wondered at the God who had worked out all the events of their lives so beautifully. Ever since his hospital stay, he had never doubted that God would, but he still felt it marvelous to behold.

He gazed at the lovely young woman who stood beside the Olympic bowl, her torch still held high. In that torch, Phil could see the spiritual torch she carried and the glorious races she would run with it.

He reached for the gnarled hand of his great-uncle Theophilus, a one-time Olympian, and smiled. "Yes, Uncle. Our Niki. Nikise. Praise God, she is victorious."

With his other hand he reached up to wipe the tears of joy that had gathered at the corners of his eyes. He stopped his hand in midmotion. Tears of joy were much too rare and too precious to wipe away. Instead, Phil lifted his arms in the air and with the rest of the hundred thousand people who were gathered, he shouted out for Niki.

He shouted out for the Olympics.

But most of all. . .he shouted out for God!

CHRISTMAS
BABY

Chapter 1

It's Christmastime!" Christina Rallis sang out, just as she did every year when the Santa in the Macy's Thanksgiving Day parade passed by her parents' Central Park West apartment. This year, she thought, she would like to give her parents something really special for Christmas, to show them how much she appreciated them. She could never think what to give them, though; they always seemed to have everything they wanted. When Christmas Day arrived, she knew they would shower her with gifts, like always, and she would give her mother a blouse and her father a pen set or a tie, something they already had. If only this year, she could think of something they really needed.

Her dad chuckled, a good-natured sound that Santa might have made.

Smiling at him, Christina left her real-life view of the parade to join her father in front of the television to watch as it was telecast live from Harold Square. With his white hair, matching beard, and blue eyes, Christina thought her jolly father could have easily played Santa.

"It might be Christmastime," her mother said as she walked into the room, "but the most important thing of all is that our 'Christmas baby' will be celebrating her twenty-third birthday this Christmas Day." She placed a sterling tray, the same color as her shiny silver hair, on the coffee table, and glanced fondly at Christina.

Christina's father's eyes swung toward the baby grand piano where a group of framed pictures recorded most of those birthdays. He shook his head, "Twenty-three years. . .it's hard to believe. . . ." His voice trailed off and he looked at his wife with an intensity that sent a familiar unrest to Christina's soul.

She had seen that fleeting, almost haunted look pass between her parents again and again down through the years. Something about the way they looked at one another always sent pinpricks of uneasiness over

Christina's skin. But it was too brief a look, too dubious a sensation to even form into a question.

Wanting to defuse that vague feeling that hovered like an unwanted odor around them, Christina reached over to the table and picked up her mother's most recent women's magazine. "Well, I certainly feel twenty-three and after only two more finals I will have my Bachelor of Science degree! So I'm very glad to be turning twenty-three and not twenty-two." She shivered slightly. "I wouldn't want to repeat this last year of university." She laughed. "I like graduating—even though I'm not sure what I'm going to do with my chemistry degree!"

"Here! Here!" her dad cheered, his jolly self once again, and he held his steaming mug of coffee high in the air. "To our almost-graduate!"

Christina nodded her head pertly in appreciation and then held up the magazine toward her mother. "Does this have any interesting articles?"

"I don't know, dear." Her mother motioned for them to have some chips and dip. "I haven't had a chance to read it yet."

Christina nodded, understanding that her mother had been too busy putting together a new daytime drama to have had a chance to read a magazine. Her parents worked together; both were producers and writers of daytime TV, a very talented team, as the numerous Emmys on the mantel attested.

"How's the new drama coming along?" Christina asked, skimming through the glossy magazine.

Her mother expelled a breath of impatience. "The actress we want for the lead is playing the role of sensitive artist—"

"And she wants us to play the role of sensitive psychologists," her father finished with a grimace. "I think I'm getting too old for this."

Christina smiled as she continued to flip through the magazine, and her mom and dad went back to the parade on the TV. She had heard these complaints before and she wasn't worried. Practically every season one or both of her parents threatened to quit. But she knew that neither ever would. They loved their work. They loved dealing with people. They loved—

As if stung by a bee, Christina froze, her thoughts interrupted. Her eyes widened as she stared at a picture in the magazine.

It was a picture of a baby. But not just any baby. Dark brown happy eyes, silky brown hair to match, a perky little smiling mouth with a dimple on the left cheek. . . She didn't need to look at her baby picture that sat on the piano to know the picture in the magazine was a picture of herself!

She looked anyway. And then she looked back down at the baby in the magazine. No doubt about it. It was the same child. It was her.

Christina's blood ran cold. Her shock deepened as she read the caption next to the picture of the baby, the picture of herself. But as she read she finally understood that haunted look which she had seen cross between her parents so often through the years. She felt as though she had fallen into a nightmare.

With the happy sound of the TV heralding Santa's arrival in front of Macy's Department Store, a sound that mocked her dread, she read out loud, " 'Have you seen this child?' "

"What, dear?" her mother asked absentmindedly, not taking her eyes off Santa as he waved to the expectant children.

Christina licked her lips and repeated the caption. " 'Have you seen this child?' " Her throat felt dry and constricted as she read the history of the missing baby. " 'Christina was born on Christmas Day twenty-three years ago. . .this year. . . .' " Her voice faltered and she looked up at the people she had always thought were her parents. They had both turned to her. She had their attention now.

And they both wore that haunted look. But only for a moment. Quickly, the haunted look turned to one of horror. And Christina knew that she had stumbled upon their worst nightmare. Their faces had gone as white as paper, and she knew—there was absolutely no doubt in her mind—that she was the baby in the magazine. She was as certain that she was the smiling baby in the magazine as she was that she was the baby who smiled from the pictures on the baby grand piano. The two people before her were silent, as silent as the tears, the tears of guilt and love, that coursed down their suddenly old faces.

Christina shook her head slightly, as if by so doing she could erase the last two minutes, and then she forced herself to look back down at the magazine and continue to read, feeling as if she had stumbled into the set of one of her parents' drama productions. " 'Her mother hopes and prays. . . ,' " she read out loud.

Mother? Christina's brows came together, a hurt and confused line that slashed across her face. She had always thought that Barbara Rallis was her mother. She shook her head again, then licked her lips and continued to read, " '. . .that the woman her baby has grown into would please contact her if at all possible. . . .' " Christina shut her eyes for an instant, then continued, " 'She has never stopped loving her. . . .' " She looked up at the people she had always thought were her parents and whispered the last two words, " 'stolen daughter.' "

"No!" Barbara Rallis jumped to her feet, and for the first time Christina saw that she was no longer an elegant older woman but. . .an old lady. "We didn't steal you! We didn't!" She shook her silver head, denying the black letters written in her favorite magazine, looking both frightened and frail. "We didn't steal you," she repeated, as if denial could make it true. Her husband slowly stood and wrapped his arm around his trembling wife.

"Of course not. . . ," he soothed, "of course not." But Christina wondered if he were trying to convince his wife or himself.

"What. . .is going on?" Christina ground out between lips that refused to move.

Peter Rallis, the man Christina had always thought was her father, closed his eyes for a moment before answering. "If I were a praying man, Christina, I would pray right now. . .pray for you to understand—"

"Dad!" She cut him off. "Please!" Her life had changed irrevocably and he was talking about praying. For a moment, though, a part of Christina wished that she did know how to pray, that they all knew how to pray. It would be a comfort, she thought, if there were Someone beyond themselves, Someone they could turn to with this terrible thing she had discovered. But if awards were given for praying, like they were for TV shows, Christina knew that her family would never win any.

"Christina," Peter Rallis continued and his eyes were grave with misgiving, no longer jolly at all, "we adopted you when you were four months old. Perhaps we should have told you before. But we didn't steal you."

The thought boiled in Christina that they *most definitely* should have told her sooner, and feelings of betrayal, hurt, and anger rose between her shoulder blades. She clamped down on the stew of feelings with the force of a lid on a pressure cooker. The force of these alien feelings frightened her, and she knew she had to control them.

"Ho, ho, ho," mocked the jolly Santa on the TV. She swiveled her eyes between the two people she loved more than any others. "Tell me," she commanded.

Peter Rallis nodded, but before he spoke he helped his wife back into her chair. Christina noticed something she had never thought of before: Her parents were actually old enough to be her grandparents. They had always been so vivacious, so successful, so strong, so admired by so many people, that she had never really noticed how old they actually were. They had both passed seventy but until this moment, they had always made that age seem so young, so youthful.

"Your mother—" Peter Rallis motioned toward his wife, and the fact that he felt he had to clarify who her mother was felt like a knife slashing Christina's heart. She raised her hand to her mouth and pressed her knuckles against her lips to keep from crying. "Your mother," continued Peter, "was too old to have children when we married. We tried to adopt a child here in New York but. . .because of our age, we were told that it would be next to impossible to adopt a baby. We were becoming desperate—" His voice faltered, and his wife reached out and squeezed his hand. They exchanged a look, and Christina understood that her mother was silently assuring him that she was capable of continuing the story, the story which they had dreaded to tell for nearly twenty-three years.

"When we learned that it was quite easy for Americans of Greek ancestry to adopt children in Greece," the older woman said, her voice sounding as if she had just lost something very precious, "we traveled there in the hopes of finding a child." She paused and smiled into Christina's eyes, a small smile that hoped for forgiveness. Christina read the love mixed with the yearning, the same love Christina had never doubted once in her life. Not even now. "We found you."

"We—" Her father's voice broke again but he continued, "We loved you the moment we set eyes on you."

"You smiled at us," her mother continued and Christina could tell from the light in her blue eyes that she was looking back to that moment in time, "and your little fingers reached out for ours. . .almost, we thought, as if you were begging us to take you home with us."

Christina could only shake her head. So many questions, so many thoughts raced around her mind like balls in a pinball gallery. She glanced back down at the picture of herself in the magazine, then looked up once more at her parents. "But—" Her voice broke. She tried again. "Didn't you ask about my. . . ." The question trailed away.

Barbara Rallis picked it up and supplied, "Mother?" The only mother

Christina had ever known bit her lower lip. Grateful she had said it first, Christina nodded.

The older woman sighed, a heavy sigh Christina knew she had carried around inside her for nearly two and a half decades. "We did," she admitted. "We asked and we were told that she had violated her contract and had left you for longer than the agreed-upon four months at the orphanage."

"And since she hadn't come for you. . .well, everyone assumed that. . . she didn't want you. . . ." Peter Rallis spoke the words as softly as he could, but still, Christina flinched. *Why should I care?* she wondered. After all her natural mother was a total stranger to her. But somehow her father's words hurt her.

She looked down again at the magazine and reread the emotional appeal written there. Her natural mother had wanted her, Christina realized, otherwise she wouldn't have considered her daughter to have been stolen.

" 'Her mother hopes and prays,' " Christina softly reread as tears gathered in the corners of her eyes, " 'that the woman her baby has grown into . . .would contact her if at all possible. . . .' " Christina tried to catch the first tear with her finger, in order to dam up the rest. But it was useless. She gulped and sniffed. "I think this proves. . . ," she spoke as softly as the tears that ran down her cheek, "that she did want me after all. . . ."

The silver head of her mother nodded as she wiped at her own tears. "I think this means. . .that we should have investigated. . .further. . .especially when," she looked over at her husband and he nodded for her to continue, for her to tell the entire story, "the people at the orphanage asked for—" Her voice broke.

"For what?" Christina softly urged, but there was steel in her eyes and a maturity that hadn't been there before.

"A contribution." Her mother whispered the word as if it was a sentence of guilt.

Her father's head bobbed up and down and his lips moved a moment before any sound came out. "A rather large contribution," he amended. "As though we were paying them to keep a secret. We never wanted to admit that, though. . .not even to ourselves." His face creased. "We were just too scared of losing you, Christina."

Christina shook her head from side to side again. Suddenly, the whole scene seemed as unreal to her as a bad dream. The change in her parents made the nightmare sensation even stronger. Her parents, who had always been as tough and hard as Manhattan's granite, suddenly looked weak and old and vulnerable.

Christina's life flashed before her eyes. Her life with them had been wonderful, full of love and fun. They had never been too busy to spend time with her, never so busy that they missed anything important in her young life. She knew she had to meet her natural mother and maybe even her father—the need to see them was almost overwhelming—but she also knew that she wouldn't change the life she had lived for anything in the world. She loved these people, and in spite of their revelation she still loved them and felt honored to be their daughter. For the first time in her life, she realized that not only did she need them, but they needed her. For once she could give to them, truly give to them. It was a heady feeling, a grownup feeling. She was the only one in the world who could give them exactly what they needed.

As they had done for her a million times before, she held out her arms to them. They came to her, their faces wet with tears, and the three of them held each other and cried, a strong family that wouldn't be torn apart by the keeping of a secret that should never have been kept.

"Why didn't you tell me?" Christina whispered a few minutes later as she held their hands.

"We wanted to. . ." Her mother's eyes implored her to believe her.

"But we were too afraid," her father finished. Looking at these strong people, Christina knew that telling her this was probably the only thing they had ever been afraid of in their entire lives.

Christina sighed. And then she smiled, a smile that mirrored the forgiveness both her parents had given to her numerous times in her life. "Well, you don't have to be afraid. You have been my mom and dad for all but four months of my life and I love you both dearly. Nothing and no one could ever change that, but—" Her eyes landed on the picture of herself in the magazine. There was a need in her to meet the woman who had given her life, a need that was growing stronger and stronger by the second.

Her mother saw it, and cleared her throat, once again the woman of substance and action she had always been. "Call the phone number in the magazine, dear." She looked over at her husband, and at his encouraging nod, she continued. "We will do everything and anything we can to help you find—"

"Your real parents," her father finished.

Christina shook her head, and her parents regarded her in confusion. "You don't want to contact your real mother?" her mother asked, ironically disappointed to think that Christina would ignore her birth mother's appeal, an appeal that traveled through time to reach her daughter.

Christina smiled, a smile that brought out the deep dimple in her left cheek. "No. I do want to meet her but. . .you're wrong when you say my 'real' parents. Don't you know, Mom and Dad, that you two are the most real parents in the world to me? Nothing could ever change that."

"Find your birth mother, dear," her mother encouraged. "At this moment," she laughed shakily, "I don't know why I was ever afraid of telling you the truth. I should have known that there is enough love in you, daughter, to love two mothers."

"And two fathers." Her dad smiled that jolly smile Christina loved so much.

Tears of happiness filled her eyes, and she was glad now that she had clamped down on the stew of bad emotions that she had felt just moments earlier. Her parents' faces were lit up with the same wonder and joy that shone from the children on TV as they looked at Santa. Christina smiled. She had given her parents exactly what they needed this year: love.

❧

The following Monday, she called the number listed in the magazine, which in turn gave her a number to call in Athens, Greece. She learned from the agency there that her birth mother had put ads in newspapers, magazines, milk cartons, and bulletin boards around the world for two decades.

Christina took her last two final exams and with her parents' blessings flew to Athens. As she waited at the airport, she shivered with excitement, hardly able to believe how much her life had changed in just ten days.

Chapter 2

W hat a wonderful surprise!" exclaimed Christina's friend Kristen Andrakos as she opened the front door of her home. She spoke first in Greek, then switched easily to English and repeated herself.

Looking down at Kristen's very pregnant stomach, Christina gasped. "It looks like you're the one with the surprise!"

Kristen placed her hand lovingly against the child that was growing within her and tilted her head to the side. "A good surprise?"

"The best!" Christina and Kristen hugged. Their parents had been long distance friends for years, until Kristen's had died in a boating accident. But even though the two girls hadn't seen one another often, there had always been a bond of friendship between them, one which had easily extended into womanhood.

"I couldn't believe it when I heard your voice on the phone," Kristen said, as she ushered Christina into her home, "but when you said that you were coming to Athens—what a gift!"

From behind them, Paul Andrakos, Kristen's husband, chuckled as he placed Christina's luggage next to the wooden banister leading upstairs. "I thought my wife might have our baby then and there, what with all the jumping around she did."

Christina's eyes narrowed with concern. "If I had known about the baby—I wouldn't have accepted your invitation to stay with you. I can easily go to a hotel close by and come and see you every day—"

"Don't you even think of such a thing," Kristen warned, her soft southern accent making the words sound almost like a threat.

Paul chuckled, but understanding and appreciating the concern Christina felt, he turned to assure her, "Kristen has been very much looking forward to your arrival. We've just recently moved from my mother's home into our own so she wants a chance to play hostess. Plus, we have a big house, a wonderful and dear housekeeper who is pampering Kristen beautifully, and we would love your company."

For the first time Christina turned to look at the house. It was big. Big and absolutely beautiful in an old-world, almost Victorian sort of way. It was decorated for Christmas like something out of a magazine—except it was better than any magazine because love seemed to be wrapped around every post along with each twist of garland.

Christina sighed and feeling a bit like Anna in *The King and I*, she reached up and removed her traveling hat. Kristen clapped her hands. "Good. Now that that's settled." She looked up at her husband with a teasing gleam in her brilliant green eyes, then leaned close to Christina and in a stage whisper asked, "So, tell me, what do you think of my Paul?"

Christina laughed and with a conspiratorial whisper of her own responded, "I think any man who fights holiday traffic at an airport to pick up a person he has never met, must be a saint!"

"Ummm. . ." Kristen nodded her head and smiled up at Paul as if they carried a secret. "You're right there—he is a saint. . . ."

Christina felt something pass between the husband and wife, something special and wonderful. Whatever it was, it didn't make Christina feel uncomfortable and left out, as she sometimes did with married couples. Instead, their happiness seemed to cast itself like a blanket over her, sharing with her the warmth of their love. "Well. . .I thank you, Paul, for coming for me," she repeated. "So tell me, when is the blessed event?"

Kristen motioned Christina to a soft chair and then eased herself onto the sofa. She lovingly rubbed her belly and replied, "Christmas Day."

"Christmas!" It was on the tip of Christina's tongue to tell them that it was her birthday too, but something held her back. She wasn't sure whether it was because she didn't want to usurp their baby's day of birth in any way or whether it was tied up with the woman she had traveled to Greece to meet. Whatever the reason, she remained silent.

"The day of our Lord's birth," Kristen continued, and reached for her husband's hand as he sat on the sofa next to her. "I think only He could understand how much that means to us."

Christina brows drew together in question. "What do you mean?"

Paul and Kristen exchanged knowing glances. "We fell in love while we were both searching for Something More in life."

"And together we learned," Paul continued, his dark eyes showing the love he felt for his wife, "that that Something More was a personal relationship with Jesus Christ. What could be a better day for our baby's birth than the day we celebrate His birth?"

Christina's lips curved into a thoughtful smile. She found herself remembering her father's wish that he knew how to pray. She was certain Kristen and Paul knew how to pray. She had never given religion much thought before, but now she found herself thinking that prayer would be a very beautiful and intimate thing for a husband and wife to share. . . .

❧

Later that evening, after both women had napped—Kristen because of pregnancy and Christina because of jet lag—the three set in the living room, sipping homemade eggnog while gazing at the blue and silver ornamented Christmas tree. Christina's eyes moved to the *caique* that was set beside the Christmas tree. The *caique*, a traditional Greek Christmas decoration, was a model of a Greek fishing boat, colorfully painted and strung with lights. Christina liked it as much as the Christmas tree. She had a hard time differentiating, though, where the lights of the huge city shining in through the window ended and those of the tree and the boat began.

Paul and Kristen's house was located high on the last road before the cliffs of the Acropolis, that most historic of hills and home of one of the most photographed buildings in the world, the graceful Parthenon. Christina had found she had a view of the cliffs from her bedroom window and if she tilted her head, she could even see the walls of the Acropolis above.

But the living room looked out over the city of Athens with the three tall mountains to the east, west, and north of the city, fencing in the modern sprawl. The high and pointed hill of Lykavittos could be seen in the near distance, with a star made out of streaming lights topping it for the Christmas season.

Traditional carols filtered into the room from Paul's elaborate entertainment system, filling the air with Christmas cheer. The love and welcome she felt in the atmosphere, she knew, however, did not come as much from the music and decorations, as it did from Paul and Kirsten's air of joy and peace.

The thought occurred to Christina that the prayer going on inside this house might be what made this house so different from any place she'd been. She wasn't sure—but the sight of the well-worn Bible lying in a place of honor under the tree made her think so even more. Christmas —the true meaning of Christmas—was obviously celebrated in this home. For the first time in her life, she found herself thinking of Christ's birth as a real event that still had power to bring joy and peace to human hearts.

"So tell me," Kristen asked, after a few moments of companionable silence, "was there any particular reason why you chose to visit Athens so suddenly?"

Christina turned away from the twinkling lights of the city to face Kristen. She had been expecting the question. She knew that she could prevaricate and explain away her trip as a graduation gift from her parents, but in that split second before she answered, she also knew that she didn't want to do that. She didn't want to lessen the importance of her visit by giving a flippant answer. But neither did she want to explain everything; she needed to meet her birth mother before telling anyone else about her reason for coming to Athens.

Before she could think of an answer, the door chime interrupted her. As if he had been expecting someone, Paul quickly stood. "That must be Dino—a working associate of mine," he explained to Christina, as he walked toward the entrance hall. "A fantastic shipping lawyer, but also one of my very best friends."

As Paul disappeared into the hall, Kristen further explained. "Dino's been away on business for the past month and we've really missed him." She rolled out and up from the sofa. "He's a wonderful man, an even better Christian—" Kristen stopped, and her emerald eyes lit up as the two handsome men came into the room. "Dino!" She reached out her arms for the man who was even a bit taller than her own tall husband. "We missed you!"

Dino hugged Kristen. He seemed not to have noticed Christina yet, but when he spoke, something in Christina's heart jumped to sudden life. "It looks like that little baby has been doing some growing while I've been gone." His voice was deep and slightly gravelly, the English words accented with the inflection of Greek.

Kristen rolled her eyes and laughed. "A lot of growing!" she corrected, and turned to Christina.

The man named Dino turned with her and that thing within Christina's heart that had pulsed to life at the sound of his voice started pounding when his blue eyes looked at her. Christina didn't think that she had ever seen such beautiful eyes before. They shone with a light that seemed to reach out from his inner being to touch her, to touch a part of her that had never been touched.

"Dino Mathis, I would like for you to meet my very dear friend Christina Rallis—"

From her peripheral vision, Christina saw her hand reach out for his, to be taken by his. But from the periphery of her mind, she felt something she had never felt before. She wasn't sure what it was—magic, hope, love? All three—or something else entirely. She wasn't sure. The only thing she knew was that she felt alive in a way she had never felt alive before. As if . . .as if a part of her that had lain dormant slept no more. . . .

"How do you do?" she heard her voice respond, glad of the manners that came automatically to her rescue.

His eyes seemed to sparkle more as he smiled at her. "I do very well thank you." His words were softly accented. "Even better now than I did a few minutes ago," he admitted, still holding her hand, still smiling at her, still making her feel. . .magic.

Christina thought what she felt was magic—but Dino knew that what he was feeling for the woman with the doe eyes and the dimple on her left cheek was a feeling he had never before had. A feeling, in fact, that he had always teased his friends about. But the joke was on him now. The logic and precision of his profession had no place in his being now as strong, self-assured Dino Mathis knew that what he felt for the woman before him was the proverbial love at first sight. A love that he knew was God's answer to his prayer.

Dino had always thought the bachelor's life was for him. But watching Paul and Kristen together during the two years of their marriage had changed him. While he was away, he had finally admitted to himself that he wanted what Paul had, the gift of a lovely woman like Kristen to share his life with him. All the while he was gone, he had poured out his dreams and longing to God. And now he was quite sure that he was looking at her. . .a woman named Christina.

"What brings you to Athens, Christina?" he asked, but he was certain that he already knew. God had brought her to Athens so that they could meet, fall in love, marry, and live happily ever after.

"I. . ." She ran her tongue over her lower lip. "That was what I was just about to explain to Kristen and Paul when you rang the bell." *And changed my life*, she finished mentally. Although she didn't say the words out loud, in the moment before she turned to Kristen, Dino saw the message in her eyes. His heart sang.

"I came to Athens because I have to meet with a—" Christina paused as she scanned her mind for a vague word to describe meeting her mother. Her face brightened when she found it. "A relative, actually." That's what her birth mother was after all. A relative. "I don't really want to explain everything but—"

"Oh, Christina," Kristen interrupted her and motioned for them all to take a seat. "You don't have to explain a thing."

Paul nodded his head. "You are our friend and welcomed here for as long as you wish."

"Thank you," Christina whispered. "I need good friends right now," she admitted.

"You've got them," Kristen assured her and Paul nodded his agreement.

"I, too," Dino spoke from her side and Christina turned her brown eyes to meet his blue ones, "would like to be your—friend." The way he said the word made everyone in the room, probably even the baby in Kristen's tummy, know that what he really meant was that he wanted to be a whole lot more than friends.

Kristen and Paul glanced at one another, and that part of Christina's heart that had come alive when Dino had walked into the room nearly skipped a beat. Her lips wouldn't let her even try to deny the pleasure his declaration brought to her. Of their own accord, they curved upward.

"In fact," Dino continued, "I would be honored if you would let me show you around my city."

His city, Christina thought and her smiled deepened. Little did he know, did any of them know, that it was her city too. "I'd like that."

"Starting tomorrow?" he inquired. Dino sensed, with a lawyer's skill, that it was all right to push for something definite.

Christina wanted to agree. But until she met with the agency that was representing her birth mother she didn't feel she could plan anything. "I have a meeting to go to in the morning." She didn't have to say anything more, she realized, and she could see by their faces that they would wait until she was ready to tell them more. "After that, I'll be able to let you know."

"Good enough." He smiled.

She smiled back. Athens, she realized, had a lot more to offer her than just a mother. A lot more. . .

Chapter 3

While making her nervous way to the agency that morning, Christina hadn't noticed how gaily decorated for Christmas Athens was, but on her return trip to the Andrakos's, she noticed. Strung with lights and garlands, with either Christmas trees or the traditional boat, the *caique*, decorating every house and shop window and with manger scenes filling many of the squares, the city reflected her mood; happy, wondrous, almost carefree.

The woman at the agency had been kind and helpful, and after comparing her information with Christina's, she was certain that Christina was her client's long-lost daughter. The only reason Christina could not meet her birth mother immediately was the fact that her mother was out of the country and not due to return until Christmas Eve. That meant that Christina would have to wait until Christmas Day, her birthday, to meet her.

Christina had smiled. What better time to meet the woman who had given her life than on the anniversary of her birth? And surprisingly, Christina hadn't felt at all impatient that she would have to wait another week before meeting her; instead, she felt relieved, as if granted a reprieve. So much had happened during the last few weeks, that Christina discovered she was actually glad her birth mother was unavailable. It gave her a chance to gather all the changes in her life and to ponder them without having the pressure of having to do something about them. From the moment she had seen the picture in that magazine on Thanksgiving Day, she had been in motion, and now she found she was grateful to be able to sit back and let her thoughts settle.

She looked out the cab window as it passed by the huge Parliament of Greece and she smiled as she caught a glimpse of the tall evzones, the Greek soldiers, as they stood in ceremonial guard in front of the tomb of the Unknown Soldier. Her smile deepened as she sank back into the rich seat of the taxi.

She had never thought much about her birthplace, readily accepting her adoptive parents' explanation that they had been in Greece when her mother had gone into labor with her. But now, as she rode the taxi back to the Andrakos's home and she looked out at the vibrant city that pulsed around her, she knew that she wanted to get to know the city of her birth as well as she could in the week before she met her mother. She wanted, in fact, to be a carefree tourist and let the wonders of this city sink in, this city that had seen so much of recorded history. And. . .she knew that she wanted to see it on Dino's arm.

She had never before met a man whom she had felt as attracted to as she did Dino. With Dino, everything was different. She felt as though a magic button had been switched on in her, a button she hadn't even known she possessed.

When she walked through the door of the Andrakos's home a few minutes later, Dino was there waiting for her. His smile told her that he felt the same about her. Again, Christina rejoiced that she had a week free before meeting her mother, a week in which she could concentrate on getting to know Dino. She was even more glad when Dino told her he had the next week off as well.

Winking at Kristen, he said to Christina, "My boss," who Christina knew was Kristen's husband Paul, the owner of the shipping company, "knows how deserving I am of a holiday. So," he turned to face Christina, "I am at your beck and call, my lady." He bowed slightly with old-world charm. "How best may I serve you?"

Playing along, Christina tilted her head imperiously. "By showing me this beautiful city of yours, my lord," she replied, and happiness rose in her like water from a tap rises in a glass.

His blue eyes looked into hers and Christina felt her heart do a flip-flop. "That I will be honored to do," he finally responded, and Christina knew it was true. He wanted to be in her company every bit as much as she wanted to be in his.

Kristen clapped her hands together, and Christina and Dino turned to her. "Well," Kristen's eyes danced in merriment. She knew what was going on between her two friends, and it had been a subject of discussion between Paul and herself the night before, a subject that had delighted them both. "I don't think you could have chosen better weather for sight-seeing."

"I know!" Christina exclaimed, glancing past the sparkling Christmas tree and out the window to the sunny and bright day that lit up the city. "I can't believe it! It's so hot! When I left New York it was snowing and here—" She motioned to her double-breasted suit jacket. "I was too warm with this on."

Kristen laughed her agreement. "That's Athens weather for you. However," she felt the need to warn, "it's highly subject to change. One day it might be like late summer, and the next, wintry, with the mountains around the city so covered with snow that you'll think you're in Switzerland and not in Greece."

Looking out the window again at the bright Mediterranean sun, Christina was skeptical. But at Kristen's insistent nod that it was true, she quirked her lips and asked, "So you mean we might have a white Christmas?"

Dino laughed. "Anything is possible in Athens." The timbre of his voice and the way his eyes slanted toward her told Christina he was talking about a lot more than just the weather. Smiling boldly back at him, she was glad.

Christina liked it when possibilities were endless.

And as that day wore on, and then the next and the next, and they spent every moment together until late every night, Dino not only showed her the wonders of the ancient city but he also showed her that her first impressions of him were correct. Christina knew that he was a man she could easily spend the rest of her life with. There was something special about him, and Christina soon understood what it was. He was quite simply a man who believed in God, a praying man, a man who wasn't confused about who he was or where he was going in life like so many of the men Christina had met. He wasn't offensive in his beliefs but rather giving and tolerant, and he slowly whetted Christina's appetite for the knowledge he possessed; a knowledge he freely gave.

And while telling her about the God he loved, Dino showed her the city. He showed her the Acropolis, he showed her the ancient stadium where the first modern Olympics took place, and he showed her the old town of Athens, the Plaka.

They walked and talked, and they laughed and held hands as they traveled from one end of the Plaka to the other. From the oldest known theater in the world, the Theater of Dionysus, from which Aristophanes, Sophocles, and Euripides saw their plays performed, to the site of Plato's famous Academy they went, falling more deeply in love with every step they took.

The Acropolis shining overhead, little domed chapels popping up in every direction Christina looked, shops selling anything from leather goods to copies of Byzantine icons and Greek dolls, rose bushes still spilling out their fragrance even in December; all of it blended together to make Christina feel as though she had stepped into a totally different life from that of a month before. Not only had she discovered that she was adopted and that her birth mother lived in this amazing city, but she had discovered the love of a good man, a complete man.

As they walked they stopped off at all the little churches along the way and talked to the friendly caretakers who loved the American woman who was interested in their little chapels, and who was amazed by their history. Out of all of Athens' multitude of treasures, Christina discovered that it was the Byzantine churches she loved the most. They were so unassuming as they sat in the middle of busy streets several feet below the modern level, or with restaurants in their courtyards or even modern buildings built above their domes. Every one of the little Byzantine churches would have been considered a national treasure in any other capital of the world, but in this city, this city of such concentrated history, they were almost forgotten, like a king's forgotten gems. Most had been built at least five hundred years before Columbus sailed to America, but even more amazing was that many still held church services.

When Dino told Christina that the beautiful Parthenon had been converted into a Christian church in the fifth century, when the building was already nearly a thousand years old, she insisted that they trek back up to the Acropolis's windy height for her to look at it again. They stood on the ancient windswept hill with the blue of the sea shining in the one direction, the three tall mountains of the city surrounding them in the others, and Christina looked up into Dino's eyes, sharing her joy and exhilaration with him. He leaned close, and she thought for a moment he would kiss her. Her heart beat fast, but then he drew back, as though something had stopped him. She frowned, but the smile he gave her was as warm as ever.

The wind played a song around the golden columns above them and looking up into his eyes, eyes that were as deep and as blue as the sea that sparkled to the south of them, she had no doubt that he loved her, though he had not said the words. She sensed that the love she read in his eyes was rooted in something much greater than mere human love. The knowledge gave her a sense of security and joy that she had never felt with any other man. She smiled, showing the dimple on her left cheek. *I love you too,* her own eyes answered him. She knew that she did. With Dino she was alive in a way she had never been alive before.

He gathered her close to him and whispered, "I long for so much— but for the moment," his accent gently bathed his words with love, "this is enough, I think." She wasn't sure she understood, but she nodded her head against his shoulder.

Dino felt her breath like a feather against his skin. He closed his eyes and forced himself to draw back just a little. Even though Christina still hadn't told him the real reason behind her coming to Athens, he knew that it was something that she had to see to before they could make any plans for the future. More importantly, though, he knew they couldn't plan a life together until she came to the same personal relationship with God that he had. A marriage between them wouldn't work without it. They would be unequally tied together. . . . *Dear God, if Christina really is the woman You want me to marry, then please bring her to You. Soon.*

Christina shivered slightly inside the circle of his arms. "I think the weather is about to change," she murmured, blaming the weather for the feeling of dread that had suddenly swept through her.

Dino held up his hand to catch the direction of the wind. "Northerly winds," he commented. "They quickly bring the arctic chill with them this time of year."

Just a cold draft of air, she told herself, *that's why I shivered.* She smiled up at him. "So you mean we just might have that white Christmas after all?" She had to admit, she liked the idea.

He chuckled and leaned toward her. "Like I said before—anything is possible in Athens." She waited for his kiss on her lips, but it fell lightly on the tip of her nose instead. She smiled, hiding her disappointment. Anything was possible here. . .even the start of a lifetime of love.

❧

By the time they returned to the Andrakos's house, not two hours later, the air had cooled considerably and the blue sky had turned into a steely gray. Paul had left a message asking if Dino could help him out at the office that evening, so for the first time in days, Christina and Kristen were left alone.

The long look Christina and Dino had shared before he left didn't escape Kristen's happy notice. When Christina turned away from the door, Kristen didn't give her a chance to say a word before she sang out, "You're in love!"

Christina ran to Kristen's side and took her friend's hands in her own. She squeezed her eyes shut and admitted, "I never realized that it could happen so fast. . . ."

Kristen patted her tummy and remembered back to when she had first met Paul. "All it took for me was one afternoon to fall in love with Paul."

"One afternoon. . . ," Christina murmured. *It took me one moment*, she thought. "You've never told me how you and Paul met and fell in love. I always thought it sounded a bit like a fairy tale."

Kristen laughed as she remembered back to the joy of falling in love with Paul, but then a cloud crossed over her face as she remembered the times of agony too. Christina saw the shadow and she knew then that Kristen's romance had not been the easy one she had believed it to be. "Tell me," she gently encouraged. "If you want to," she amended. She didn't want to be pushy; it was just that, with her own love so new, she really did want to know.

Kristen told Christina how the thing that first drew her to Paul was that they both knew that there was Something More in life than the empty social scene and the endless climb to make money. They searched and learned together, while falling in love with one another, that that Something More was a personal relationship with God.

"That was an amazing time." She looked down at the baby that was hidden within her flesh. "And it all happened here in Athens. . . ."

Christina looked out the window at the ancient city that had grown so gracefully into a modern one. "Something about this city. . .it makes one consider. . .God," she admitted.

Kristen simply nodded her head but her heart rejoiced to hear her friend's words. "Well, it's little wonder that people think about God here in Athens. So many of the early Christians visited here, the New Testament was originally written in Greek, and—" She motioned out the window at the domes that dotted the skyline. "Christ has been worshipped in this city from when Dionysius and Damaris accepted the truth St. Paul brought to them in his famous speech to the Athenians."

"Amazing. . . ," Christina whispered, looking out over the city which was lighting up for the winter night. She turned back to Kristen. Although she wanted to ask Kristen more about her belief in God, she also wanted her to finish the story of her romance. "But," she thought back to Kristen's letters a few years ago, "didn't you leave Athens. . .and Paul. . .for a while?"

Kristen held her palm protectively over her unborn baby. She knew, if not by the grace of God, that this little human would never have been made. Taking a deep breath, she nodded. "We had some serious struggles. To make a long story very short, we spent three long months thinking that we would never be able to have a life together." She fingered the beautiful antique emerald ring on her left hand.

"Oh, Kristen. . .how horrible for you. . . ." With the intensity of her feelings for Dino, Christina could empathize with the pain her friend must have felt. "I don't know if I could stand something like that happening to Dino and me."

"Well," Kristen said thoughtfully, "I have to admit, my new faith was sorely tested then. But you know—I appreciate the love Paul and I have more because of that time."

"But still. . ." A shudder like a cloud passed through Christina, and she felt the same cold foreboding that she had felt earlier by the Acropolis. "How hard it must have been for you, for both of you."

Chapter 4

Christina awoke the next morning, Christmas Eve, to the sweet clear notes of children's voices drifting over the city in song. Stretching, she looked out the window and blinked as she saw groups of bundled-up children running from door to door, caroling to the accompaniment of little silver triangles they clutched in their mittened hands. Her lips curved into a happy smile.

When she glanced upward, she saw the reason the children were wearing heavy ski parkas and stocking hats, and she squealed in delight. Rolling clouds of cotton wool sheets, clouds that held the promise of snow, marched above the city like a Christmas fantasy.

Christina was glad that the weather had changed. She loved snow, but never more than at Christmas! Scrambling out of bed, she hurriedly dressed in woolen pants and a plush sweater of soft honey that brought out the golden highlights in her dark hair.

She dialed the agency to confirm her appointment with her birth mother and was told that her mother was anxious to meet her. Their appointment was all set for ten the next morning, Christmas morning. Christina declined the agency's offer to escort her, wanting instead to meet her mother in private. Jotting down the address, she hung up the phone and paused for a moment. Here she was going to meet her natural mother the following day and yet, amazingly, she couldn't muster up the least bit of excitement, nor for that matter, trepidation. Nothing.

She wanted to meet her natural mother, but her feelings toward the woman were just a great big blank, as blank as a chalkboard that didn't have anything written on it. She thought that maybe that was good, but she wasn't sure. Not wanting to dwell on it, she pushed all thoughts of her upcoming appointment out of her head and thought instead about Dino.

Dino. . . Thoughts about him made her smile. He had promised to take her somewhere special today and glancing out the window, she hoped that it would be somewhere outdoors—and that it would snow. To walk through the falling snow with the man she loved had to be one of the most romantic things. . . .

She descended the stairs just as Kristen swung the door wide to welcome a group of children. Pausing, Christina watched as with frosted breaths they politely asked Kristen if she wanted to hear them sing. When Kristen assured them that she did, they smiled and swirled the metal stick around their triangles. To its tinkling notes they merrily sang out one of the prettiest tunes Christina had ever heard. She translated the words in her head as they sang, glad for the millionth time since coming to Greece that her mom and dad had insisted she learn to speak Greek, as they did themselves.

> *"Good Morning m'Lords,*
> *and if it is your will,*
> *it's Jesus Christ's birthday.*
> *May I come into your fine home?*
> *Jesus is being born today in Bethlehem!*
> *The sky is happy,*
> *and nature is happy,*
> *for in a cave,*
> *He is born in a stable of horses,*
> *the King of the skies,*
> *and the Maker of everyone."*

When they finished, Kristen clapped her hands and after offered them each a *kourabiede*, a Greek Christmas cookie made with butter and piled high with confectionery sugar. Then she gave them a nice amount of money to share among themselves. They went on their way, smiling at the powdered sugar that had stuck to the tip of the youngest's nose.

"That was lovely!" Christina exclaimed, and Kristen turned to her with a thoughtful smile.

"I think that *kalanda*, the children's caroling," she commented as she half walked, half waddled into the living room, "is one of the nicest Christmas traditions in Greece."

Christina followed her. She warmed her hands before the gently burning fire in the fireplace and remarked softly, "The song has such meaning." The simple beauty of the lyrics had struck the same chords in Christina's soul that Dino's soft words about God had touched upon during the last week.

"Ummm," Kristen agreed as she sank carefully into her chair. "This is getting difficult!" she admitted ruefully, while lovingly patting her tummy. "The carol is beautiful, isn't it? A beautiful way to remind people that it's the birth of God's Son that we're celebrating tomorrow and not all the secular things people have made Christmas into."

Christina's eyes went to the porcelain manger scene that sat on the mantel. She looked at the Baby, the Christmas Baby, that had been lovingly tucked into His makeshift manger bed by His mother, and Christina knew that she had to agree with Kristen. The song did remind people about the true Christmas Baby, the Christ Child. It had reminded her that she hadn't thought about Him, really thought about Him at Christmastime. . .ever. . .until now.

❧

She and Kristen were sharing companionable cups of coffee and eating *kourabiedes*. The weather was blustery and the two friends sat in the living room watching the winter show from its window. As yet undetected by the women, Dino stood in the hall for a moment and watched them.

A fire in the fireplace gave forth a cozy heat, and the colorful lights from the Christmas tree and *caique* fell upon their faces like starlight from on high. Dino thought that seeing these two women he loved so dearly, one as a sister and the other as a man loves a woman, was one of the most beautiful scenes he had ever beheld. It was as though they were posed for a Christmas card. Two friends happy with their lives; happy with Christmas coming, happy with all the changes soon to take place.

Dino fingered the velvet box he carried in his pocket. He knew that all his hopes and dreams were contingent upon things that were out of his control; on Christina coming to know God, on her mysterious reason for coming to Athens, and last, but certainly not least, on whether she loved him enough to give up the life she had always known to make his home her home, his city her city, just as Kristen had for Paul. He shook his head slightly and reminded himself that God had already overcome physical geography and human emotions to bring them together. He would be obedient and trust God for the rest.

He fingered the soft box in his pocket again. That she was the women for him he was absolutely positive. He just had to be patient and let the Great Designer work everything out according to His plan. He smiled. God wouldn't mind him pushing the situation along a little bit by taking her to the place he had planned to go to today. A hushed place, it was a place where God's voice seemed easier to hear, a place where he himself had heard God speak many times, a place where he hoped Christina might hear Him too. And maybe, just maybe, she would ask God to be a part of her life. He rubbed his fingers against the box in his pocket; only then could he ask her to share her life with him. . . .

He cleared his throat as emotions threatened to clog it, and two pairs of bright shining eyes, one brown, one green—both beautiful— regarded him. "Dino!" the pregnant woman with the green eyes exclaimed. "I didn't hear you come in!"

"Neither did I!" The woman with the soft brown eyes and deepening dimple confirmed. She leapt to her feet. Dino loved the sureness in Christina's steps as she came to him, the way her hand automatically found his and the way their fingers intertwined together just as he hoped their lives one day would. But most of all, he loved the way she looked at him, as though he was the most important man in the world to her. He felt cherished, loved, and all he wanted at that moment was to lean toward her, to kiss her, to hold her close to him, to—

Kristen cleared her throat, breaking the spell and reminding Dino of where he was and who he was. A smile touched the corners of his mouth as he and Christina turned their faces to her. Kristen didn't think that she had ever seen either of her friends look happier. "I wish Paul could see the two of you now," she commented, and her green eyes sparkled with humor. "Is it possible though that you two are in need of. . .a chaperon today?" she teased.

Dino's eyes touched Christina's but he spoke to Kristen. "Don't worry." He picked up Christina's navy peacoat and ivory cashmere scarf and matching hat and placed the coat around her shoulders, letting his hands linger there a moment longer than necessary. "Your friend is safe with me, Kristen. Besides, where we're going God has been the chaperon since the fifth century."

Kristen laughed. "That could be practically anywhere in Greece, Dino!"

"True," he conceded to Kristen. "But we're only going a few miles away." Leaning close to Christina, he spoke for her ears only. "But it may as well be a thousand."

❧

A few minutes later, Christina thought that it was more like a million miles or maybe even an eon away, with time and distance seeming to merge. Athens sparkled in the wide valley below like a toy city in a glass ball.

Dino had driven her through the bustling avenues and up a road that was like a beltway around the eastern part of the city. When he had turned off the road toward Athens' east mountain, Hymettus, it was as if they had not only traveled back through time and gone a million miles away but had gone into a remote world of reaching cypress trees standing like the very guardians of time. Christina had never driven through a cypress forest before, but she decided that it was a forest unlike any she had ever seen. The narrow evergreen trees shot straight up, proud and sure, optimistic somehow, into the snow-ladened clouds that hovered just above their reaching tips.

She waved her hand toward the trees. "It's like they're sentinels standing at attention!"

"Then they would have to be Christian sentinels guarding that," Dino said, and pointed to several stone buttresses that extended down to the edge of the road.

"A fortress!" Christina exclaimed as she looked up at the stone walls the buttresses supported. "What is it?"

"It's called Kaisariani—and I guess you could say it's one of God's fortresses."

She tilted her head to him. "What do you mean?"

"It used to be a monastery."

"A monastery," she repeated in wonder. They got out of the Jeep and walked down a stone path, passing an ancient ram's head spring that still ran with water, before reaching a long wall that led to the monastery's entrance. The peace, the solitude, was a part of the very air around them, with the rock walls not an intrusion but rather, a welcoming part of the land. It seemed to have grown right out of the earth and was totally at peace with it.

The west enclosure wall held the kitchen and the refectory, the north wall, a tower and the monks' cells, while directly across from the entrance was a Roman bath. But what captured Christina's attention was the beautiful little church that was the focal point of the well-kept courtyard. She walked toward the little domed building of stone. Even though it was very similar to those she had seen in the old town of Athens, she felt there was something special about this church.

"It's enchanting," she whispered and Dino squeezed her hand. He had known she would like it. They were too much alike for her not to.

"Tell me about it," she softly commanded, knowing that he would know its history as he had many of the beautiful churches they had seen in the Plaka.

"It was built in the eleventh century," he began but stopped when he caught a wry twinkle in her eye.

She smiled, a smile that matched the look in her eyes. "It's new then. . . ?" She was beginning to understand how a hundred years in American history could be likened to a thousand in Greece.

Dino chuckled, a low sound that Christina loved. "Compared to the ruins of the original fifth-century basilica which I'll take you to see in a little while—yes," he rubbed his thumb against the soft wool that covered her hand, "I guess you could say that it's new."

They stepped through the narthex and into the hush of the sanctuary. The church was light and airy, though cold enough to frost their breath. But it was the beautiful paintings of Bible stories that caught Christina's attention.

Dino waved his arm toward the icons. "When people couldn't read, as the majority couldn't back in the middle ages, these told them the amazing stories of the Bible."

"They're beautiful." Christina walked into the main sanctuary and looked up at the dome and its painting of Christ the Pantocrator, the Almighty, holding a Gospel.

Pointing up at the Book, Dino commented, "But I think, in the literate world in which we live today, that God prefers for all who can read to read His Word rather than to rely only on paintings."

Christina nodded her head, and she felt something like conviction wash through her at Dino's words. "I hate to admit it, but. . .I practically never read the Bible." She walked from one painting to another along the walls of the little church. "But these. . . ," she held her hand out, "they make me wonder what I've been missing. They make me want to read the Bible. . .to know God. . .and His Son. . . ."

Dino smiled, and within his heart, he breathed a prayer of thanks. "Then I believe they are fulfilling their purpose," he responded after a moment and she could hear the emotion in his deep voice. She knew that Bible reading was a daily part of his life, and she loved him more because of it.

Turning to him, she shyly admitted, "I've always admired people like you and Kristen and Paul. . .people who have strong religious feelings toward God. . ."

Gently, lovingly, he corrected her. "What we have, Christina, is a personal relationship with Christ."

Kristen had said the same thing. Christina hadn't wanted to ask Kristen about it then, but today, in this building, built and adorned to honor God, she wanted to know more. "What do you mean?"

Dino was ready for the question, had been ready for it since the moment he'd met her. "We who have made a commitment to God," he explained, "have been born into His kingdom. We've been given the right to become His children."

"Born into God's kingdom. . ." She shook her head. She didn't understand. She might have if he had said adopted into God's kingdom. But born? She had been born of one woman, raised by another. . . but still, only one birth. "What do you mean? How can a person be born. . .more than once?"

Dino smiled and guided her over to the painting that depicted Jesus' birth. "There once was a man named Nicodemus, a very smart man, who asked Jesus that exact question."

"Really?"

Dino nodded and continued speaking while looking up at the painting that showed Jesus born in a cave. "He came to Jesus late one night to talk and when Jesus told him that no one can see the kingdom of God unless he is born again, Nicodemus asked, 'How can a man be born when he is old? Surely he cannot enter a second time into his mother's womb to be born!' "

Christina's quick intake of breath stopped Dino. Looking at her he saw that she had gone white, that the blood seemed to have left her face. "Christina—what is it?"

Her eyes swiveled around his face, a frenzy of movement. *What is it? What is it?* She wanted to scream back his own question, but she didn't. She knew what 'it' was. Tomorrow, the very next day, her birthday, she was to meet the woman from whose womb she had emerged. She was to meet the mother who had birthed her, and somehow, out of all the stories in the Bible—and looking at the painted walls surrounding her she knew there were many stories—they had to stumble onto the one that told about a man asking about birth and mothers' wombs.

She realized then that the actual reason why she hadn't told anyone her reason for being in Athens was because, in spite of what she had told her parents, in spite of what she had intellectually believed, she was hurt, deeply hurt, to learn that she was not the person she had always thought herself to be. The lid of that symbolic pressure cooker she had clamped onto her emotions blew off. It sprayed all the emotions that had been simmering there for the last month—hurt, betrayal, anger—over her heart.

Her personal history, her genetic history was not what she had always believed it to be. It bothered her—it bothered her profoundly that her parents hadn't been honest with her from the beginning. And she couldn't understand how her birth mother could have lost her baby. People, responsible people, just don't lose their babies.

"Christina?" Dino repeated.

Wanting to get away from him and the question she heard in his voice, she turned and ran out the door of the church. But once outside she stopped and blinked. She pulled the gloves off her hands so that her sense of touch could confirm what her sense of sight was telling her, and her face relaxed.

She smiled. Then she laughed. Her delight cooled the heat of her thoughts, as snow, glorious, refreshing snow floated from the sky all around her. "Oh, Dino!" She held out her hand to him as he joined her. "Look!"

Dino smiled at the snow and silently thanked God for this perfect gift. He knew that this snow was a healing snow for Christina. He had known through the days of their being together that Christina's reason for being in Athens dealt with something traumatic. The knowledge wasn't anything he had been able to put his finger on, just a vague feeling of unrest, of denial even, which he had sensed in her. If he had needed confirmation, though, she had just given it to him in the church.

He didn't realize how intense his eyes were as he regarded her, but Christina knew that it was only because he loved her that they had turned black with questions. And she knew too, that she owed him an explanation. Her smile froze on her face, a smile that couldn't hide the hurt within her soul, as she reached up to rub her hand across the roughness of his cheek. "Oh, Dino. . ."

He grabbed her hand and pulled her close. "Tell me, Christina," he demanded, wanting to protect the woman he loved.

"I can't," she whispered into his shoulder.

"I want to help you," he urged, and his breath melted the snowflakes that had fallen on her hair.

"I know."

"Won't you let me?"

"Oh, Dino. . .until right now, I didn't even know I needed help."

"But I have known it," he said, surprising her.

Of course he would know, she realized. He cared enough about her to notice all the nonverbal, unconscious messages she herself had ignored.

The fog from his lips enveloping her, he said, "It has to do with your reason for coming to Greece." He didn't ask, he stated, and looking up at him she didn't even try to deny it.

"It has everything to do with it."

"And with your appointment tomorrow?" He had been surprised when she'd told him that they wouldn't be able to spend all of Christmas together. Surprised and suspicious. He watched as she again nodded her head. "I love you, Christina," he ground out, the gravelly tone of his voice mixed with his soft accent.

"I know, Dino. And I love you," she whispered.

He nodded his head. He knew that she did. "Promise me. . .that if you need me. . .you will call me."

She bit her bottom lip and whispered, "I promise."

It was all he could ask of her. But it wasn't all he could ask of God. He would uphold her in prayer. "I'll pray for you," he stated, and the peace which she felt flood her at his words showed on her face.

"I'd like that. . .no one's ever prayed for me before."

"How do you know, darling?" His thumb rubbed the sensitive spot on her wrist. "Maybe someone you've never even met has been praying for you for your whole life."

His words made her think. Hadn't the magazine article said, "Her mother hopes and prays that the woman her baby grew into would please contact her"? Maybe her mother—her birth mother—had been praying for her all these years.

The thought brought a warm glow to her heart. She smiled and suddenly, as when she had first found out about being adopted, she was again looking forward to meeting her natural mother. "You know, you may be right, Dino. You just may be right."

Silently, he took her hand and wound his fingers around hers as they walked out of the monastery and through a winter wonderland toward the ruins of the fifth-century basilica he had promised to show her. The walk through the falling snow with the man she loved was even more romantic than Christina had thought it would be. It wasn't just a dream fantasy, but real life, the type of life she hoped she'd always have.

Chapter 5

C hristina found out the next morning, Christmas morning—a day that glowed with sunshine and snow-covered mountaintops —that Dino had been right. Someone had been praying for her all her life. Her mother, her birth mother, had been praying for her throughout all the years of their separation.

A little before ten o'clock Christina stood before her mother's home, surprised to discover that it was close to the Andrakos's home in the old town of Athens. With citrus trees naturally decorated for Christmas with their own yellow and orange fruit, the road was one of the most picturesque she had seen, and she wondered why Dino had never shown it to her.

The house was by far the biggest and most elegant home in the area. She stood for a full five minutes across the narrow street below a sweeping eucalyptus tree, just gazing at her mother's home. *Her mother's home.* . .the thought echoed inside her mind. The woman who had given her life was sheltered within.

The house was neoclassical, the same time period as she had learned the Andrakos's to be, but this one was even bigger, more like a mansion than a house. Tiny white Christmas lights outlined its edges, and a huge live Christmas tree decorated with glass balls and ribbons was on the balcony above the front door. But it was the warmth of the golden light that spilled out through the unshuttered windows that most filled Christina with Christmas cheer.

She glanced at her watch and discovered that the moment set for her to meet her mother had arrived. The radiant light that shone out like welcoming banners gave her a sureness of movement as she crossed the narrow street and reached out to press the doorbell.

The bell had hardly stopped ringing when the door swung open. A beautiful woman with blond hair, hair that softly brushed her shoulders, with eyes that were as giving as they were gray, stood before Christina. Christina knew she was looking at her mother, and an unexpected love flooded her.

The other woman knew the moment she looked up into the soft brown eyes of the young woman at her door that she was looking into the eyes of her little baby once again, her baby grown into splendid womanhood. With a mother's knowledge, she was certain of it; and with a mother's heart, she loved her daughter.

Silently, the two women reached for one another. They both knew that words would never convey this moment's depth of emotion and meaning, and so they remained quiet as they held each other close. For the first time in nearly twenty-three years the beating of their hearts merged together once again.

Christina felt as though some primitive part of her remembered her mother, remembered the way she smelled, the way she breathed, the way she felt, and that blank chalkboard of her mind started filling up, filling up with good emotions. This woman was familiar to her, known to her, and Christina didn't need papers nor certificates to prove that she had been born of her. From deep within her being she knew it to be true.

Christina's birth mother felt the same. Christina might be a grown woman now, taller even than herself, but to her aching arms Christina was her little baby once again. With fleeting wisps of thoughts, thoughts that only mothers can have, she noticed that her daughter's hair was the same silky chestnut brown, her skin the same pale olive, and that even the way the nape of her neck smelled like fresh toast was the same.

Standing back, with tears of joy swimming in her gray eyes, she looked at the woman her baby had grown into and her smile deepened. She shook her blond head, her professional training the only reason she was able to push her voice through the clog in her throat. "Welcome home. . . Christina. . .my Christmas baby. . ."

" 'Christmas baby'. . . ?" Christina murmured, her eyes traveling around her mother's beautiful face. Her mom and dad, her adoptive parents, had always called her that. Had her mother, her birth mother, thought of her in the same way as well?

Her mother nodded and explained, "That's how I've always referred to you. You were born this day. . .twenty-three years ago. I named you 'Christina' in honor of the One whose birthday you share." She squeezed her eyes together. "It was the happiest moment of my life. Happy birthday, my daughter."

Christina rubbed her mother's hands, hands that were as long and tapered as her own. "Thank you. . .Mother."

Her mother, a woman who looked young enough to be her sister, made a sound that was half laugh and half cry as she dabbed at the corners of her eyes. "I've waited longer than half my life to hear you call me 'Mother.' " She tucked Christina's hand beneath her arm as if she didn't ever want to let go of her again. "You know, you are the image of your father."

"I am?" It seemed unreal to Christina that they should be having this conversation, unreal but nice too. The Rallises had never talked much about looks. Christina now understood why.

Her mother nodded as she guided her into the house. "Come. . .I'll show you."

On a grand piano in the elegant, second-floor living room sat not only the picture of herself, the one Christina had seen in the magazine, but a picture of a man Christina knew could only be her father. The coloring was the same, the eyes and the hair, even the dimple was the same. Christina ran her fingertips over the face of the man who had fathered her, letting them rest upon the deep dimple on his left cheek. "I've always wondered where I got my dimple from. . . ."

"Your dimple, your forehead, your eye coloring, your smile. . . ." Her mother's eyes traveled over each of those areas on Christina's face. Taking the picture of Christina's father from the piano, she motioned Christina over to the sofa in front of the silver-and-gold clothed Christmas tree.

Sitting together and holding the picture before them, Christina knew from the way her mother looked at the picture of her natural father that she had loved him very much. Christina felt glad somehow, glad and warm all over.

"You are so much alike. I saw that even when you were a baby. . . ."

"Really?" Christina was surprised at how badly she wanted to know more about him. "Please tell me about him," she encouraged.

Her mother nodded. "He was my best friend. We were both orphaned at quite young ages and we were both raised by elderly godfathers who were next-door neighbors and best friends themselves. We grew up together, we were family to one another even before we

461

married and made it official."

"You were married to my father?" Christina interrupted. That had never occurred to her, but when her mother sighed, as if hurt, she wished that she could have kept the incredulous surprise out of her voice. Her mother softly, almost reverently, placed the picture of her husband on the coffee table and then turned to face Christina squarely. "You don't know anything about me, do you?"

Christina shook her head. "Nothing." She smiled wryly. "I don't even know your name. They wouldn't give it to me at the agency."

"That's probably my fault," she admitted. "I asked that my name not be given."

"But why?"

Her mother held her hands together in front of her as though in supplication before answering. "I think we had better start at the beginning." She smiled, a smile that lit her face with joy. "My name is Aliki Pappas. It's a rather well-known name in Greece, and I wanted to avoid publicity."

"Aliki. . . ," Christina repeated, as if to taste the name, and her eyes roamed hungrily around her mother's face, trying to make up for all the years of not seeing her. Her mother had exceptional good looks, like the movie sirens of the early Hollywood years, and somehow the name fit her perfectly.

Her mother nodded and continued. "Your father and I were very much in love and when he died—" She paused and looked into the warmth of the gently burning fire in the marble fireplace. Christina knew that she wasn't seeing the glow of the embers, but rather, she was seeing that difficult time. "I almost didn't want to go on," she admitted. Turning back to Christina, she took her hand and smiled. "But your father had left me with a part of himself. I was pregnant with you, my daughter, and it was because of you that I knew I had to go on so that in you, a part of him would live."

Her mother's love seemed to hover in the very air around her. "Did he. . .did my father. . .know about me?"

Aliki nodded, her fair hair brushing her shoulders. "He knew." Tears swam in her mother's eyes. "And he couldn't wait for you to be born. We had planned on having a houseful of children."

Christina squeezed her mother's hand. Learning that not only had she been wanted but that siblings of hers had been wanted as well, was like a gift, a most fantastic gift. It told more than a million volumes ever could about the love her natural parents had for one another.

Aliki ran her slender fingertips over the smoothness of her daughter's face. "He used to rub my tummy every night with lanolin and talk to you, telling you—" Her voice broke. She swallowed and continued, "Telling you about all the wonderful things the three of us were going to do together. . . ."

Christina looked at the handsome young man in the picture, a man who couldn't have been any older than she was now. "I'm sure that I would have liked—and loved—my father very much."

"He was. . .one of the best," Aliki said, and Christina's heart was gladdened with pride. Her mother shook her fair head and continued, "After you were born, reality stepped in. I had no one to help me and—no money."

"No money?" Christina couldn't help casting her eyes around the house that told an entirely different story.

Aliki smiled in understanding. "I've since changed that condition," she admitted. "I'm an actress."

Christina could easily believe it. Her mother was stunning. Suddenly Christina was certain that her mother was a very famous actress, at least in Greece.

"But back then, I was only nineteen and very poor," Aliki continued, "and I had to turn to social aid to help me. I was allowed to leave you in a home for children for six months before you would be given up for adoption."

"Six months?" Christina frowned. Her adoptive parents had said it was four months.

Her mother nodded her head. "Not the four they were telling people who adopted babies from there."

"So my—" She licked her lips and tried to continue, but she wasn't sure which words to use. "That is. . .the people who adopted me—"

"Your parents, Christina," her mother stated emphatically, startling Christina with the fire that was in her eyes. "Don't ever do them the injustice of taking that away from them. What happened wasn't their fault any more than it was mine and they are every bit as much your parents as Costas," she motioned to the picture of Christina's natural father, "and I are." She stopped speaking and smiled at the picture of Christina's father before she softly continued. "Besides, if you are anything like your father, I think that your heart must be big enough to have two sets of parents, isn't it?"

Slowly, Christina smiled and nodded her head. Her mom—Barbara Rallis—had said something similar. Looking at the picture of the handsome young man who was her natural father, she knew she could easily love both sets of parents. She already did.

"Anyway," her mother continued, and Christina understood that she wanted to tell her everything. "I visited you every week, sometimes two times a week. I didn't have money for the bus so I walked, during the winter, to and from my little one. A twenty-mile round-trip walk during the darkest days of winter." She looked out the window at the blue, cold sky and the gleaming snow-covered mountains in the distance. Her lips curved ruefully. "I don't remember any sunny days that winter. They were all rainy and cold." She shivered, and Christina understood that her mother had very little to smile about regarding that long-ago winter, regardless of the weather.

"But I didn't mind the walk." Aliki's lips curved into a smile of remembrance. "I saw my little Christina—and in you," her eyes searched Christina's brown ones, "I saw a bit of your father." She fell silent, and Christina squeezed her mother's hand, wanting to give her the courage to go on. Her mother took a deep breath and said, "Well, I finally found a job working in a movie theater as an usher and, most important of all, a grandmotherly woman who offered to look after you for money I could afford to pay. After only four months and three days of your being at the children's home, I went to bring you home."

Her voice changed. It became hard, formidable almost, and yet it quivered with the despair she had felt as that young widow. "I was informed. . .that you had been adopted by a loving, capable couple and that I was no longer legally your mother."

Christina felt as though she were the girl who had been told that her baby was lost to her forever. A girl who was four years younger than what she was this very day. But despite Christina's feeling of oneness with that girl, a question had been on her mind and she needed an answer to it, even though she might hurt her mother by asking. "But. . .didn't you try to get me back?"

Aliki looked at Christina with both anguish and fire in her eyes, and her voice shook as she went on. "I tried!" She implored Christina to believe her. "I asked a lawyer to help me find you and we tried for years. . . but nothing. That it was a scam was certain. That we couldn't prove it was equally certain." Her mother squared her shoulders. "But through the years, I have made sure that it never happened to another young mother. No woman should have to go through the agony that I went through. No one!" Christina was certain that her mother had spared many the heartbreak she herself had experienced.

They were silent for a moment as their mutual history settled around them. A medley of church bells rang out over the city, bringing another question to Christina's mind. "Mother. . ." She was surprised by how easy the word rolled from her lips, and she was glad that she had used it when she saw the light that jumped into her mother's eyes. It was something, one small something, that she could give to her birth mother.

"Yes?"

"Have you ever. . ." Christina paused and licked her lips, before softly continuing. "Have you ever blamed God for what happened?"

Her mother sighed deeply, a sigh that traveled back through the years. "Well. . .I didn't know Christ when all this happened." Christina gave her a look that was full of questions, and she quickly explained, "What I mean is, I was only a traditional Christian, someone who went to church occasionally and believed in God—but that was like possessing a lamp without knowing how to turn the switch. I had never accepted Christ as my Savior and Lord. So I suppose I did cry out to God. Remember, not only had I lost my baby, but I had just lost my husband a few months before that." She turned her eyes to the smiling youth in the photograph. "And I loved him very much."

"So—you did blame God?" Christina pressed. She wasn't sure why the thought of her mother blaming God made her feel as though shackles were being clamped upon her.

Aliki turned back to her. "No." She shook her head emphatically. "No, I didn't. How could I?" She raised her palms questioningly before her and Christina felt lighter as those symbolic shackles fell away from her. "If it wasn't for God, I would have gone insane worrying about you," she explained. "As it was, because I lost you, I knew that I had to depend on God to keep His eyes on you. I couldn't see you. . . ." She looked off into that time that was years away from her, before turning her gray eyes back to Christina. "But I knew that God could still see you. Not a day passed that I didn't ask Him how my little baby was. In fact, it was your loss that brought me to a deep personal relationship with Him. I couldn't have survived without my faith." She smiled. "Quite simply, *agapi mou*, my love, I learned how to switch on that lamp."

"You. . .learned to trust God?"

"Totally."

"Even though He had allowed your little baby to be taken from you?"

Her mother sighed. "I guess I should answer something like Joseph in the Old Testament did when he reassured his brothers that he didn't hold a grudge against them for selling him into slavery. What someone—the people at the home for children—meant for evil, God meant for good. And it was God who led me to put ads around the world in whatever form I could—newspapers, magazines, milk cartons. He led me to believe that when you were old enough, that you would find me. . .just as. . .you would find Him."

"Oh, Mother. . ." For the first time since Christina was a little baby, she fell into her mother's arms, and rested her head against the warm comfort of her mother's shoulder.

Chapter 6

"Have you, darling girl," her mother asked after a moment as she smoothed her daughter's hair, "have you found God?"

"I. . ." Christina sat back, and as she looked into the hopeful, gray eyes of the woman who had given her life, she knew that she wanted to have a relationship with the God who had led her to this remarkable woman. She nodded her head. "I want to." And she knew that she really did. "Can you show me how. . .to turn on that lamp?"

Emotion, happy, glad emotion played across Aliki's youthful face. "Darling—leading you to birth into Christ's kingdom will be even more wonderful than when I gave you earthly birth."

Christina's smile froze on her face. She felt confused. After finally meeting her birth mother and after witnessing the joy Paul and Kristen had over the soon-to-be birth of their child, she didn't think anything could be better than giving life to another human being. "How can that be?" she finally asked.

"It's simple really," her mother said as she reached for her Bible. "In physical birth you had no choice in being born. But in spiritual birth—the choice is entirely your own. It's not dependent on anyone else." Aliki's smile deepened. "Spiritual birth is based on the decision you, Christina Rallis, make and on that alone."

Like a light being switched on in her soul Christina suddenly understood perfectly what her mother was saying. The choice to be born into God's kingdom was hers, just as the choice had been her mother's, Kristen's, Paul's and. . .Dino's.

*Dear Dino. . .*Christina smiled as she thought about him and at how happy all this would make him. Turning a thousand-watt smile on her mother, sure of her decision, she asked, "What do I have to do?"

Bowing their heads, mother and daughter prayed a prayer of salvation. Twenty-three years after the birth of Aliki's Christmas baby, on yet another birthday of the true Christmas Baby, Christina accepted Jesus Christ as her Savior. From now on she would have three birthdays to celebrate on Christmas Day: the birth of Christ, her own physical birth, and now her spiritual birth.

After a moment of silence, a silence filled with the very spirit of God, Christina felt a need to share with her mother what Dino had told her the previous day at the monastery. "I have a friend," she smiled, a smile that told her wise mother that this friend was a special one, "who told me about a man named Nicodemus. My friend said Nicodemus asked Jesus how a person could be born more than once."

Obviously familiar with the story, Aliki quickly flipped to the passage found in the third chapter of John and read, " 'How can a man be born when he is old?' " Nicodemus asked. " 'Surely he cannot enter a second time into his mother's womb to be born!' "

"That's it!" A new excitement and thirst to know more about God filled Christina's soul. "Does it say how Jesus answered?"

Her mother nodded and read Jesus' answer. " 'I tell you the truth, no one can enter the kingdom of God unless he is born of water and the Spirit. Flesh gives birth to flesh, but the Spirit gives birth to spirit. You should not be surprised at my saying, "You must be born again." The wind blows wherever it pleases. You hear its sound, but you cannot tell where it comes from or where it is going. So it is with everyone born of the Spirit.' "

Christina's eyes were wide. "It's all so amazing—but I think that the most amazing thing of all is how I," she touched her fingers to her chest and gave an amazed little laugh, "I understand it now and—I believe it!" She shook her head. "I wish I had let my—friend tell it to me yesterday."

With a sparkle in her eyes and in her voice, Aliki commented, "I think I'm going to like this—friend."

Christina nodded thoughtfully. "You will." She was glad that she could share her love of Dino with her birth mother. "He's a Christian and a wonderful man. In fact. . .I think that I'm going to marry him!" They hadn't said anything to one another about marriage but somehow Christina knew it to be true. She was as sure of this as she had been about their love for one another.

She was rewarded with her mother's cry of joy. "Praise God! I've missed so much of your life—but at least I won't miss your wedding day!"

They hugged one another tight.

"I'm glad too," Christina murmured.

"Mamma!" The deep gravelly voice called out from the front door, and Christina frowned. She knew that voice. They heard the man shut the door and then his footsteps on the stairs to the living room. Christina shivered, overwhelmed with the sense that something was terribly wrong. Surely, that voice belonged to. . .

"Mamma, are you—"

"Dino!" Christina gasped his name and their eyes collided.

"Christina. . .?" Confusion played across Dino's face at seeing her there and his eyes bounced back and forth from one woman to the other. "What are you—" He froze when his eyes saw the framed picture of the man sitting on the coffee table behind Christina. And then he understood.

He understood why Christina had traveled to Greece. Understood why she couldn't spend Christmas morning with him. Understood even why his mother had asked for a couple hours alone this morning. The only thing he couldn't understand was how he had been so obtuse as to not realize who Christina was from the very beginning.

He turned to Aliki. "Mamma? Christina is your 'Christmas baby'?" He didn't need the confirmation of his mother's nod, but he wanted it anyway.

Christina swiveled to Aliki as realization dawned on her. "You're Dino's mother! Then—that means. . ." *No!* Her brain refused to consider the words that came next. *That means Dino and I are brother and sister.* She wouldn't let this nightmare be true. She wouldn't! "No!" she moaned out loud, knowing that no matter what she did, the nightmare was already real. She and Dino were brother and sister. "No!" Her moan was like a wounded animal's. She grabbed for her coat. She had to get out of the house before she broke down. Already she felt faint and her vision was fuzzy.

Dino grabbed her wrist and pulled her to him, knowing the agony she must be going through and knowing that he had to explain everything to her and quickly. "Christina. . .listen to me."

"No!" she wailed, shaking her head from side to side, her hair whipping against her cheeks. "I've got to go. I've got to. . ."

"Christina!"

The urgency in his voice made her pause, despite the tears that coursed their way down her cheeks. "Dino. . ." Despair filled her voice. "There's nothing you can say. . ."

"How about this? I am Aliki's adoptive son."

Her tears stopped flowing, her head stopped shaking, her very breath even seemed to still. "What?" It was more a sigh than a word.

"I am your mother's adoptive son."

"Adoptive?" Her voice squeaked up an octave as she spoke the word.

He nodded and smiled that wonderful smile she had fallen in love with. He repeated the most fantastic word in the world to her. "Adoptive."

"You mean. . ." She pointed her finger between the two of them. "We aren't related in any way?"

He shook his head. "I'm not related by blood to Aliki." He smiled. "And I'm not related to you either."

"Oh, Dino. . ." His name was a relieved wisp of air as she fell against him. "I thought. . ."

"Shh. . ." He rubbed her neck, trying to relieve the tension of the last few minutes. "I know what you thought."

Aliki had been caught unaware at first, but she hadn't needed more than a moment to understand that Dino was Christina's special friend. Putting one hand on each of her children's shoulders, she explained, "Christina, I adopted Dino when he was seven years old." She looked from her handsome son to her beautiful daughter and smiled. "That and giving birth to you were the best things I've ever done."

"Oh, definitely." Dino laughed and rolled his eyes. "If you're someone who happens to like mean, incorrigible, dirty street urchins."

Eyes twinkling, Aliki remembered back to that time. "I'm an actress—I recognized an act when I saw one. You were as lonely as I. You had lost your mother and father, and I," she squeezed Christina's shoulder, "had lost my husband and my baby."

Dino regarded Aliki, and Christina could see he loved her dearly. "She took me in and made me her son," he explained, and even after so many years Christina could hear the wonder of it all in his voice. She was coming to admire her mother more and more with each passing moment.

Turning to her, she commented, "So that's why you understand the position my adoptive parents are in?"

Aliki nodded. "I understand and empathize. And I would like to ask them to come and visit. I'd like to get to know them."

"I'd like that too." Christina was certain that her mom and dad would want to meet Aliki as well.

Aliki nodded but then, after a thoughtful pause, she commented, "You know, Christina. . .in a way, a spiritual way, you are related to Dino —you are both members of God's family, so—" Dino's indrawn breath interrupted Aliki, and she smiled. She knew that everything would work out just as God had ordained it now.

Turning sharply to Christina, Dino scanned her eyes with his own. Seeing the joy there, he whispered, "Alleluia." He knew now that all his hopes and dreams of a life with her could come true. The happily-ever-after could be theirs.

"Alleluia," Christina whispered back in confirmation, just before his warm lips finally came to meet hers in the kiss they had been wanting to share from the first moment they had met. For them to kiss was the most natural thing in the world. For them to love was a gift from God, the perfect gift, a gift they would cherish forever.

After a moment, Dino reached into his jacket pocket for the velvet box he had been carrying around, patiently waiting for just this moment. With their foreheads touching, he said, his voice even more gravelly than usual, "So. . .it's your birthday today. . ."

"Ummm. . .I was born of the flesh twenty-three years ago today—and of the spirit, only a few moments before you walked in."

"So much to celebrate," he murmured and stepped back from her, pulling the little box out of his pocket. "It's a good thing that I have a birthday present for you."

"A birthday present?" She didn't understand. How could he have a birthday present for her? He hadn't known that it was her birthday.

He tilted his head to the side and glanced over at his mother, who was watching the exchange with the concentration she might use at a dress rehearsal. She nodded her head and smiled encouragingly. She knew what was on her son's mind and nothing in the world could have made her happier.

"Well. . ." He turned back to Christina and held out the box to her. "Maybe it's more of an engagement present."

"Engagement. . .?" Christina lifted the lid and gasped at the diamond solitaire. Sunlight caught the angles of the gem and it flashed up at her.

Taking the ring from the box, Dino held it before her. "Christina—

will you do me the honor of becoming my wife?"

She smiled, and Dino saw reflected within her soft eyes the inner light that had been turned on in her when she had accepted Christ as her Savior. That light was the best Christmas gift he could have, because it meant the woman he loved was safe for eternity.

"Dino. . .the honor will be mine," she murmured.

"No, mine," he refuted as his mouth lowered to hers.

"No, mine," she argued.

But just before their lips touched they whispered together, "Ours," and their kiss told their love to each other, a giving-love based on the very love of God, the love that had become incarnate on this day two thousand years earlier when the Christmas Baby had been born.

Chapter 7

One week later, Christina stood on the balcony of her mother's home, gazing out over the city of her birth. After a week of cold weather, the air had again turned warm, melting all the snow on the mountains and making the first day of January feel more like Easter than New Year's. The diamond on her left hand flashed in the strong Grecian sun, and she smiled, still amazed at how God had taken all the events of her life and worked them out so perfectly.

Behind her in the living room, she could hear the happy sounds of the people she loved—her adoptive parents, her birth mother, and Dino. Aliki had been genuine and eager in issuing an immediate invitation to the Rallises, asking them to join her for New Year's.

While watching the birds that frolicked over the rooftops of the city, Christina remembered back to those first few tension-filled moments when her adoptive parents had arrived at Aliki's home. Aliki had defused the tension immediately in the gracious way Christina was coming to learn was an innate part of her mother. "I wish to thank you both for taking such good care of Christina and for being wonderful parents to her," Aliki had said.

"We. . ." Barbara Rallis had licked her lips and looked over at her husband for support. He nodded for her to go on. "We didn't know that she was taken from you falsely." She lowered her silver head before continuing, looking to Christina like a very old lady, a lady old enough to be Aliki's mother in fact, and Christina wanted to go to her and wrap her arms around her and tell her that everything was all right. But she didn't. She knew that had to come from Aliki this time.

"We should have checked into the adoption more thoroughly," Barbara admitted, before speaking the only words Aliki needed to hear. "We're very, very sorry." Peter Rallis nodded his head in grave agreement.

Aliki's lips trembled between crying and smiling as she arose from her chair and walked to where the two older people sat. She held out her arms in a welcoming and forgiving embrace, an embrace which Peter and Barbara Rallis gladly accepted. After a moment, while tears were shed by all, Aliki whispered, "I have to say to you the same thing I said to Christina the day that we were reunited, the wise words of Joseph in the Bible—'What someone meant for evil, God meant for good.' "

"I think," Peter Rallis nodded his head while swiping at the tears that had gathered in the corners of his eyes, "that I have to get to know some of those Bible sayings again. It's been a few years," he admitted. "Although," he looked at his wife and whispered words that were like gold to Christina's ears, "during the last few weeks Barbara and I have been praying again. . .praying that we wouldn't lose our little girl to her birth mother." His eyes pled with Aliki's, asking a question.

Aliki took a deep breath before walking over to Dino. She touched his face before turning to Peter Rallis again. "As you know, Dino is my adoptive son—so I know the position of an adoptive mother every bit as well as that of a biological mother."

Peter and Barbara hung onto her words as if they were a lifeline. In a way, Christina knew that they were.

"I'm sad of course that I missed my daughter's growing up years. But more than that sadness is a gladness, a joy, that she finally found me and that we will have many years ahead of us, years from which I will not exclude you. I won't try to diminish your role as her parents in any way whatsoever."

A cry escaped Barbara Rallis, a cry of relief and of joy, and Christina couldn't restrain herself any longer. She ran to the older woman and held her tightly in her arms. "See, Mom," she whispered into her ear, "where there is prayer, there is joy."

Barbara nodded her head against her daughter's chest. "I guess mothers can learn from their daughters," she whispered, smiling up at Christina through tears that had been turned from bitter to happy.

"And God did work everything out!" Aliki exclaimed as she held her son close to her. "I'm sure that our lives are just as they should be because of the events that have gone into their making. I probably wouldn't have adopted my son if I hadn't lost my 'Christmas baby'—and that would have been a tragedy." She jabbed Dino good-naturedly with her finger-nail. "Even if he doesn't tell his girlfriends about his mother," she said, and they laughed, knowing that Dino hadn't told Christina about his famous mother because too often, girls had wanted to date him just because of her.

The flutter of the birds around Christina's head as they darted back and forth across the ceramic roof of her mother's home brought Christina back to the present. She felt Dino's strong arms wrapping around her waist. "Here you are," he whispered into her ear. "I missed you," he admitted, just before he lowered his lips to nibble the sensitive spot on the side of her neck.

Christina smiled and brought her palm up to rest against his face. "I was just thinking."

"About what?"

"About how blessed we all are."

Dino squeezed his eyes together in thankfulness. For him the biggest blessing of them all was hearing Christina talk with the understanding of God's wisdom in her words.

"Ah. . ." Aliki joined them on the verandah. "So this is where you two lovebirds have escaped to." Her eyes twinkled. She was thrilled that her adoptive son and her biological daughter were going to marry.

"Is there a convention going on out here?" Peter Rallis's booming voice asked as he and Barbara joined them. Christina was happy to see he was once again the jovial man she had always known and loved.

"With this weather, who wants to stay inside?" Barbara commented and breathed in the warm air. "I love Athens' weather," she stated emphatically and they all laughed because she had made it very clear over the last few days just how much she loved the warm winter. Even Athens' cold days seemed warm to her.

"Then you are going to have to visit often," Aliki encouraged.

"And you," Peter Rallis spoke to Aliki, "are going to have to think seriously about acting in our new show."

Christina and Dino glanced at one another and smiled, the smile of a man and woman who can communicate without words. God had certainly worked everything out—even to Christina's three living parents having similar and complimentary careers.

At the sound of a car pulling up in front of the house, they all looked down. A new excitement buzzed between them when they saw who it was.

"It's Paul and Kristen!" Dino exclaimed.

"And the baby!" Christina caught a glimpse of a pink blanket through the windshield before they all hurried down to meet the newest member of the Andrakos family.

"We're on our way home from the hospital," the proud father said as he stepped out of the car. "But we just thought we'd stop by and wish you all a Happy New Year and. . ." Paul looked into the car where Kristen cradled their new little girl in her arms, "introduce you to Aphrodite."

"She's beautiful!"

"Look at all that hair!"

"And those gorgeous eyes!"

They all cooed and smiled over the alert infant. Kristen smiled the happy smile of a new mother, a Madonna-like smile. "She was born on Christmas Day." She softly kissed the infant's downy head. "She's our Christmas baby."

"Christmas baby. . . ," Aliki murmured, her eyes meeting Barbara's.

"Christmas baby. . . ," Barbara whispered back, and Christina's two mothers smiled at one another easily, sharing the love they both felt for their own Christmas baby.

Dino looked at the baby in Kristen's arms as she waved her little hands around. "To think that Christ was once so small and so dependent on earthly parents. . ." His voice was full of awe.

"And that He grew up to bring us Easter." Kristen instinctively tightened her hold on her precious little baby as she thought about the agony Christ's mother was to go through on that day thirty-three years down the road.

But Christina smiled. "Easter is the biggest miracle of them all." Her voice rang with confidence and joy. Resting her head against her soon-to-be husband's chest, she glanced up at him.

He smiled down at her, and Christina knew that the inner light radiating from his eyes was the light the Christ Child had brought to his heart. It was the same light Christ had brought to her too.

He had brought the light to the whole world. On Christmas Day nearly two thousand years ago, He had been sent to earth so that all humans everywhere, down through the ages, could have eternal life.

God gave His own Son for us all to cherish, adore, worship, believe . . .our Christmas Baby.

A Letter to Our Readers

Dear Readers:

In order that we might better contribute to your reading enjoyment, we would appreciate your taking a few minutes to respond to the following questions. When completed, please return to the following: Fiction Editor, Barbour Publishing, Inc., P.O. Box 719, Uhrichsville, OH 44683.

1. Did you enjoy reading *Greece*?
   ❏ Very much, I would like to see more books like this.
   ❏ Moderately—I would have enjoyed it more if _____
   _____
   _____

2. What influenced your decision to purchase this book?
   (Check those that apply.)
   ❏ Cover   ❏ Back cover copy   ❏ Title   ❏ Price
   ❏ Friends   ❏ Publicity   ❏ Other _____

3. Which story was your favorite?
   ❏ *Fortress of Love*   ❏ *Odyssey of Love*
   ❏ *Race of Love*   ❏ *Christmas Baby*

4. Please check your age range:
   ❏ Under 18   ❏ 18–24   ❏ 25–34
   ❏ 35–45   ❏ 46–55   ❏ Over 55 _____

5. How many hours per week do you read? _____

Name _____

Occupation _____

Address _____

City _____ State _____ Zip _____

$\mathcal{H}$EARTSONG ❤ PRESENTS

Love Stories
Are Rated G!

That's for godly, gratifying, and of course, great! If you love a thrilling love story, but don't appreciate the sordidness of some popular paperback romances, **Heartsong Presents** is for you. In fact, **Heartsong Presents** is the only inspirational romance book club, the only one featuring love stories where Christian faith is the primary ingredient in a marriage relationship.

Sign up today to receive your first set of four, never-before-published Christian romances. Send no money now; you will receive a bill with the first shipment. You may cancel at any time without obligation, and if you aren't completely satisfied with any selection, you may return the books for an immediate refund!

Imagine. . .four new romances every four weeks—two historical, two contemporary—with men and women like you who long to meet the one God has chosen as the love of their lives. . .all for the low price of $9.97 postpaid.

To join, simply complete the coupon below and mail to the address provided. **Heartsong Presents** romances are rated G for another reason: They'll arrive Godspeed!

YES!   Sign me up for Hearts❤ng!

NEW MEMBERSHIPS WILL BE SHIPPED IMMEDIATELY!
Send no money now. We'll bill you only $9.97 postpaid with your first shipment of four books. Or for faster action, call toll free 1-800-847-8270.

NAME _____

ADDRESS_____

CITY_____ STATE_____ ZIP_____

MAIL TO: HEARTSONG PRESENTS, P.O. Box 719, Uhrichsville, Ohio 44683
                                                                            YES1-99